PRAISE FOR
SHADOW KIN

"M. J. Scott's *Shadow Kin* is a steam-punky romantic fantasy with vampires that doesn't miss its mark."
   —#1 *New York Times* bestselling author Patricia Briggs

"*Shadow Kin* is an entertaining novel. Lily and Simon are sympathetic characters who feel the weight of past actions and secrets as they respond to their attraction for each other." —*New York Times* bestselling author Anne Bishop

"M. J. Scott weaves a fantastic tale of love, betrayal, hope, and sacrifice against a world broken by darkness and light, where the only chance for survival rests within the strength of a woman made of shadow and the faith of a man made of light."   —national bestselling author Devon Monk

GIVE AND TAKE

The pulse in his wrist drew my eye. The tiny shivers of skin vibrating a little with every slow heartbeat. Vampire hearts do beat. Not with the same rhythm of the human life they have left behind. But blood still pumps through their veins, and the muscles beat to drive it so.

Don't think about the blood. I swallowed softly. "Did you have need of me, my Lord?"

One side of his mouth curled slowly. My stomach clenched, willing him not to do what I thought he was about to. To punish me in such a way that only I would know it was a punishment, a sharp yank of the leash he held around my neck to remind me of where I was, who I was, and that my master was displeased.

"Oh no, my shadow," he said, beckoning me closer with one long finger. "Tonight I think you have need of me."

SHADOW
KIN

A NOVEL OF THE HALF-LIGHT CITY

M. J. SCOTT

A ROC BOOK

ROC
Published by New American Library, a division of
Penguin Group (USA) Inc., 375 Hudson Street,
New York, New York 10014, USA
Penguin Group (Canada), 90 Eglinton Avenue East, Suite 700, Toronto,
Ontario M4P 2Y3, Canada (a division of Pearson Penguin Canada Inc.)
Penguin Books Ltd., 80 Strand, London WC2R 0RL, England
Penguin Ireland, 25 St. Stephen's Green, Dublin 2,
Ireland (a division of Penguin Books Ltd.)
Penguin Group (Australia), 250 Camberwell Road, Camberwell, Victoria 3124,
Australia (a division of Pearson Australia Group Pty. Ltd.)
Penguin Books India Pvt. Ltd., 11 Community Centre, Panchsheel Park,
New Delhi - 110 017, India
Penguin Group (NZ), 67 Apollo Drive, Rosedale, Auckland 0632,
New Zealand (a division of Pearson New Zealand Ltd.)
Penguin Books (South Africa) (Pty.) Ltd., 24 Sturdee Avenue,
Rosebank, Johannesburg 2196, South Africa

Penguin Books Ltd., Registered Offices:
80 Strand, London WC2R 0RL, England

First published by Roc, an imprint of New American Library,
a division of Penguin Group (USA) Inc.

First Printing, September 2011
10 9 8 7 6 5 4 3 2 1

Cover art by Julia Rohwedder
Cover design by Eileen Carey

ROC REGISTERED TRADEMARK — MARCA REGISTRADA

Printed in the United States of America

This one's for Mum and Dad, who taught me to read,
fed me books, and gave me the world of words.

ACKNOWLEDGMENTS

There are a lot of people who've helped me on the path to getting this book in print.

Miriam Kriss, my fabulous agent, who stuck with me and believed in me for quite some time before we got here. And the equally fabulous Jessica Wade for wanting this story and helping me make it stronger.

The brilliant Lulus, Carolyn, Chris, Freya, Keri, and Robyn for critiquing, commiserating, celebrating, guaranteed laughter, and general awesomeness.

Three women who are wonderful people, wonderful writers, and wonderful teachers who have provided unfailing enlightenment and encouragement along the way: Anne Gracie, Barbara Samuel, and Valerie Parv.

And lastly, Jessie and Tabasco, who purred beside me through many, many years of writing but who never got to sniff this book.

They never hear me coming. Revenge is silent.
Shadows make no sound.
Nor do those whom I am tasked to visit. They only look
surprised, at the last.
No wonder. My kind is legend. A tale told in darkness to
chill the heart.
But all legends have a basis in truth and so it is with us.
Shadow Kin, they call me, those who know.
Wraith, they whisper as they look over their shoulders
and tighten their defenses.
Slave might be closer to the truth.

Chapter One

))

The wards sparked in front of me, faint violet against the dark wooden door with its heavy brass locks, proclaiming the house's protection. They wouldn't stop me. No one has yet made the lock or ward to keep me out. Magic cannot detect me, and brick and stone and metal are no barrier.

It's why I'm good at what I do.

A grandfather clock in the hall chimed two as I stepped into the shadow, entering the place only my kind can walk and passing through the door as though it wasn't there. Outside came the echoing toll of the cathedral bell, much louder here in Greenglass than in the Night World boroughs I usually frequent.

I'd been told that the one I was to visit lived alone. But I prefer not to believe everything I'm told. After all, I grew up among the Blood and the powers of the Night World, where taking things on faith is a quick way to die.

Besides, bystanders only make things complicated.

But tonight, I sensed I *was* alone as I moved carefully through the darkened rooms. The house had an elegant simplicity. The floors were polished wood, softened by fine wool rugs, and paintings hung on the unpapered walls. Plants flourished on any spare flat surface, tingeing the air with the scent of growth and life. I hoped someone would save them after my task here was completed. The Fae might deny me the Veiled World, but the part of me that comes from them shares their affinity for green growing things.

Apart from the damp greenness of the plants, there was only one other dominant scent in the air. Human. Male. Warm and spicy.

Alive. Live around the Blood for long enough and you become very aware of the differences between living and dead. No other fresh smell mingled with his. No cats or dogs. Just fading hints of an older female gone for several hours. Likely a cook or housekeeper who didn't live in.

I paused at the top of the staircase, counting doors carefully. Third on the left. A few more strides. I cocked my head, listening.

There.

Ever so faint, the thump of a human heartbeat. Slow. Even.

Asleep.

Good. Asleep is easier.

I drifted through the bedroom door and paused again. The room was large, walled on one side with floor-to-ceiling windows unblocked by any blind. Expensive, that much glass. Moonlight streamed through the panes, making it easy to see the man lying in the big bed.

I didn't know what he'd done. I never ask. The blade doesn't question the direction of the cut. Particularly when the blade belongs to Lucius. Lucius doesn't like questions.

I let go of the shadow somewhat. I was not yet truly solid, but enough that, if he were to wake, he would see my shape by the bed like the reflection of a dream. Or a nightmare.

The moonlight washed over his face, silvering skin and fading hair to shades of gray, making it hard to tell what he might look like in daylight. Tall, yes. Well formed if the arm and chest bared by the sheet he'd pushed away in sleep matched the rest of him.

Not that it mattered. He'd be beyond caring about his looks in a few minutes. Beyond caring about anything.

The moon made things easier even though, in the shadow, I see well in very little light. Under the silvered glow I saw the details of the room as clearly as if the gas lamps on the walls were alight.

The windows posed little risk. The town house stood separated from its neighbors by narrow strips of garden on each side and a much larger garden at the rear. There was a small chance someone in a neighboring house might see something, but I'd be long gone before they could raise an alarm.

His breath continued to flow, soft and steady, and I moved around the bed, seeking a better angle for the strike as I let myself grow more solid still, so I could grasp the dagger at my hip.

Legend says we kill by reaching into a man's chest and tearing out his heart. It's true, we can. I've even done it. Once.

At Lucius' demand and fearing death if I disobeyed.

It wasn't an act I ever cared to repeat. Sometimes, on the edge of sleep, I still shake thinking about the sensation of living flesh torn from its roots beneath my fingers.

So I use a dagger. Just as effective. Dead is dead, after all.

I counted his heartbeats as I silently slid my blade free. He was pretty, this one. A face of interesting angles that looked strong even in sleep. Strong and somehow happy. Generous lips curved up slightly as if he were enjoying a perfect dream.

Not a bad way to die, all things considered.

I unshadowed completely and lifted the dagger, fingers steady on the hilt as he took one last breath.

But even as the blade descended, the room blazed to light around me and a hand snaked out like a lightning bolt and clamped around my wrist.

"Not so fast," the man said in a calm tone.

I tried to shadow and my heart leaped to my throat as nothing happened.

"Just to clarify," he said. "Those lamps. Not gas. Sunlight."

"*Sunmage,*" I hissed, rearing back as my pulse went into overdrive. How had Lucius left out *that* little detail? Or maybe he hadn't. Maybe Ricco had left it out on purpose when he'd passed on my assignment. He hated me. I wouldn't put it past him to try to engineer my downfall.

Damn him to the seven bloody night-scalded depths of hell.

The man smiled at me, though there was no amusement in the expression. "Precisely."

I twisted, desperate to get free. His hand tightened, and pain shot through my wrist and up my arm.

"Drop the dagger."

I set my teeth and tightened my grip. Never give up your weapon.

"I said, *drop it.*" The command snapped as he surged out of the bed, pushing me backward and my arm above my head at a nasty angle.

The pain intensified, like heated wires slicing into my nerves. "Sunmages are supposed to be healers," I managed to gasp as I struggled and the sunlight—hells-damned *sunlight*—filled the room, caging me as effectively as iron bars might hold a human.

I swung at him with my free arm, but he blocked the blow, taking its force on his forearm without a wince. He fought far too well for a healer. Who was this man?

"Ever consider that being a healer means being exposed to hundreds of ways to hurt people? Don't make me hurt you. Put the knife down."

I swore and flung myself forward, swinging my free hand at his face again. But he moved too, fast and sure, and somehow—damn, he was good—I missed, my hand smacking into the wall. I twisted desperately as the impact sent a shock wave up my arm, but the light dazzled me as I looked directly into one of the lamps.

A split second is all it takes to make a fatal mistake.

Before I could blink, he had pulled me forward and round and I sailed through the air to land facedown on the feather mattress, wind half knocked out of me. My free hand was bent up behind my back, and my other—still holding my dagger—was pinned by his to the pillow.

My heart raced in anger and humiliation and fear as I tried to breathe.

Sunmage.

I was an idiot. *Stupid. Stupid. Stupid.*

Stupid and careless.

His knee pushed me deeper into the mattress, making it harder still to breathe.

"Normally I don't get this forward when I haven't been introduced," he said, voice warm and low, close to my ear. He still sounded far too calm. A sunmage healer shouldn't be so sanguine about finding an assassin in his house. Though perhaps he wasn't quite as calm as he seemed. His heart pounded. "But then again, normally, women I don't know don't try to stab me in my bed."

I snarled and he increased the pressure. There wasn't much I could do. I'm faster and stronger than a human woman, but there's a limit to what a female of five foot six can do against a man nearly a foot taller and quite a bit heavier. Particularly with my powers cut off by the light of the sun.

Damned hells-cursed sunlight.

"I'll take that." His knee shifted upward to pin both my arm and my back, and his free hand wrenched the dagger from my grasp.

Then, to my surprise, his weight vanished. It took a few seconds for me to register my freedom. By the time I rolled to face him, he stood at the end of the bed and my dagger quivered in the wall far across the room. To make matters worse, the sunlight now flickered off the ornately engraved barrel of the pistol in his right hand.

It was aimed squarely at the center of my forehead. His hand was perfectly steady, as though holding someone at gunpoint was nothing greatly out of the ordinary for him. For a man wearing nothing but linen drawers, he looked convincingly threatening.

I froze. Would he shoot? If our places were reversed, he'd already be dead.

"Wise decision," he said, eyes still cold. "Now. Why don't you tell me what this is about?"

"Do you think that's likely?"

One corner of his mouth lifted and a dimple cracked to life in his cheek. My assessment had been right. He was pretty. Pretty and dangerous, it seemed. The arm that held the gun was, like the rest of him, sleek with muscle. The sort that took concerted effort to obtain. Maybe he was one of the rare sun-mages who became warriors? But the house seemed far too luxurious for a Templar or a mercenary, and his hands and body were bare of Templar sigils.

Besides, I doubted Lucius would set me on a Templar. That would be madness.

So, who the hell was this man?

When I stayed silent, the pistol waved back and forth in a warning gesture. "I have this," he said. "Plus, I am, as you mentioned, a sunmage." As if to emphasize his point, the lamps flared a little brighter. "Start talking."

I considered him carefully. The sunlight revealed his skin as golden, his hair a gilded shade of light brown, and his eyes a bright, bright blue. A true creature of the day. No wonder Lucius wanted him dead. I currently felt a considerable desire for that outcome myself. I scanned the rest of the room, seeking a means to escape.

A many-drawered wooden chest, a table covered with papers with a leather-upholstered chair tucked neatly against it, and a large wardrobe all made simply in the same dark reddish wood offered no inspiration. Some sort of ferny plant in a stand stood in one corner, and paintings—landscapes and studies of more plants—hung over the bed and the table. Nothing smaller than the furniture, nothing I could use as a weapon, lay in view. Nor was there anything to provide a clue as to who he might be.

"I can hear you plotting all the way over here," he said with another little motion of the gun. "Not a good idea. In fact . . ." The next jerk of the pistol was a little more emphatic, motioning me toward the chair as he hooked it out from the table with his foot. "Take a seat. Don't bother trying anything stupid like attempting the window. The glass is warded. You'll just hurt yourself."

Trapped in solid form, I couldn't argue with that. The lamps shone with a bright unwavering light and his face showed no sign of strain. Even his heartbeat had slowed to a more steady rhythm now that we were no longer fighting. A sunmage calling sunlight at night. Strong. Dangerously strong.

Not to mention armed when I wasn't.

I climbed off the bed and stalked over to the chair.

He tied my arms and legs to their counterparts on the chair with neck cloths. Tight enough to be secure but carefully placed so as not to hurt. He had to be a healer. A mercenary wouldn't care if he hurt me. A mercenary probably would've killed me outright.

When he was done he picked up a pair of buckskin trousers and a rumpled linen shirt from the floor and dressed quickly. Then he took a seat on the end of the bed, picked up the gun once again, and aimed directly at me.

Blue eyes stared at me for a long minute, something unreadable swimming in their depths. Then he nodded.

"Shall we try this again? Why are you here?"

There wasn't any point lying about it. "I was sent to kill you."

"I understand that much. The reason is what escapes me."

I lifted a shoulder. Let him make what he would of the gesture. I had no idea why Lucius had sent me after a sunmage.

"You didn't ask?"

"Why would I?" I said, surprised by the question.

He frowned. "You just kill whoever you're told to? It doesn't matter why?"

"I do as I'm ordered." Disobedience would only bring pain. Or worse.

His head tilted, suddenly intent. His gaze was uncomfortable, and it was hard to shake the feeling he saw more than I wanted. "You should seek another line of work."

As if I had a choice. I looked away from him, suddenly angry. Who was he to judge me?

"Back to silence, is it? Very well, let's try another tack. This isn't, by chance, about that Rousselline pup I stitched up a few weeks ago?"

Pierre Rousselline was alpha of one of the Beast Kind packs. He and Lucius didn't always exist in harmony. But I doubted Lucius would kill over the healing of a young Beast. A sunmage, one this strong—if his claim of being able to maintain the light until dawn were true——was an inherently risky target, even for a Blood lord. Even for *the* Blood Lord.

So, what had this man—who was, indeed, a healer if he spoke the truth—done?

His brows lifted when I didn't respond. "You really don't know, do you? Well. Damn."

The "damn" came out as a half laugh. There was nothing amusing in the situation that I could see. Either he was going to kill me or turn me over to the human authorities or I was going to have to tell Lucius I had failed. Whichever option came to pass, nothing good awaited me. I stayed silent.

"Some other topic of conversation, then?" He regarded me with cool consideration. "I presume, given that my sunlight seems to be holding you, that I'm right in assuming that you are Lucius' shadow?"

I nodded. There was little point denying it with his light holding me prisoner. There were no others of my kind in the City. Only a wraith is caged by the light of the sun.

A smile spread over his face, revealing he had two dimples, not one. Not just pretty, I decided. He was . . . alluring wasn't the right word. The Blood and the Fae are alluring—an attraction born of icy beauty and danger. I am immune to that particular charm. No, he was . . . inviting somehow. A fire on a winter's night, promising warmth and life.

His eyes held genuine curiosity. "You're really a wraith?"

"Yes."

He laughed and the sound was sunlight, warm and golden, a smooth caress against the skin.

"Is that so amusing?"

"If the stories are to believed, you're supposed to be ten feet tall with fangs and claws."

I tilted my head. "I am not Blood or Beast Kind. No fangs. Or claws."

He looked over my shoulder, presumably at my dagger. "Just one perhaps? But really . . . no one ever said you were—" He stopped abruptly.

"What?" The question rose from my lips before I could stop myself.

This time his smile was crooked. "Beautiful."

I snorted. Beautiful? Me? No. I knew that well enough. The Fae are beautiful and even the Blood in their own way. I am only odd with gray eyes—a color no Fae or true demi-Fae ever had—and red hair that stands out like a beacon amongst the silvery hues of the Blood. "That's because I'm not."

He looked surprised. "I know the Blood don't use mirrors, but you must have seen yourself."

"Maybe the Night World has different standards."

"Then the Night World needs its eyesight examined," he said with another crooked smile. "Gods and suns."

Silence again. He studied me and I looked away, discomfited, wondering what angle he was trying to work by flattering me. Did he think I could sway Lucius into granting mercy? If so, then he was in for a severe disappointment.

"What happens now?" I asked when the silence started to strain my nerves.

"That may well depend on you."

"How so?"

His fingers drummed lightly on the barrel of the pistol. "There are several possibilities. Firstly, you might try something foolish like trying to get free. In that case, I'd probably have to shoot you. Gunshots attract attention, so I would expect to find the authorities on my doorstep. At which point you would become their problem if you were still alive."

I swallowed. Dead or captured. I didn't particularly like that option. "And if I'm not foolish?"

"Then, I imagine by the time the sun rises, I'll have decided whether or not to set you free to run home and tell your master that he picked the wrong man to trifle with this time."

I winced at the thought of returning to Lucius to tell him I'd failed. Lucius is unpleasantly inventive when displeased.

The sunmage frowned. "What?"

I shook my head, staying silent.

His frown deepened. "Will he hurt you?"

I shrugged. It was likely. In fact, almost certain. But not enough to permanently damage or kill me. Ignoring my current spectacular failure, I was uniquely valuable to Lucius. No other Blood lord had a wraith at his command. My kind are rare. The Fae are not prolific even when mated to their own kind. And wraiths are not born of Fae and Fae.

"You don't have to return." He sounded almost angry.

At this I laughed and there was nothing light or warm in the sound. "You really haven't spent much time in the Night World, have you?"

"I try not to," he said. The pistol flashed suddenly as he tossed it, flipping it with a showy twirl and catching it with surprising ease.

My gaze sharpened. There was one possible way of deflecting some of Lucius' displeasure. If I brought him information, if I could find a weakness in this man, that might be enough to buy me back some favor. "Who taught you to fight? You're a healer, aren't you? That's what sunmages do."

The gun glinted again as he twirled it a second time. "Most of them." Another twirl as he considered me. "Including me. But my brother's a Templar. He can be overprotective."

A Templar? Who in the name of the lords of hell was

this man? "A Templar taught you?" I tried to keep the impressed tone out of my voice but failed.

That earned me another smile. "Templars can be insistent."

I could imagine. Arguing with a divine warrior would be imbecilic by anyone's standards. Even Lucius tended toward leaving well enough alone when it came to the Templars. Which begged the question of exactly why I'd been sent to kill someone so closely connected to one.

The whole thing stank of intrigue. It made the back of my neck prickle and I twitched my bound hands, wanting to rub the sensation away.

The sunmage spun the pistol one last time, then laid it across his lap. Within easy reach, I noted.

"It's a long time until dawn. If we're going to sit here all night, I'd rather know who I'm talking to. Do I call you 'shadow' or do you have a name?"

My name. This time my eyes prickled rather than my neck. Lucius calls me "my shadow." The Fae call me "soulless" when they deign to acknowledge my presence. The Blood and the Beast Kind mostly don't use any name at all. No one had asked my name in a very long time.

I blinked and gnawed the inside of my cheek, seeking control. Distance. Cold detachment.

It was how I lived my life.

How I survived.

A blade can't afford to feel. This man, with his smiles and warmth, was dangerous.

"I'm Simon," he said quietly. "Really, Shadow, you may as well tell me."

Simon. It suited him. It sounded clean and strong. Like no one I should have anything to do with and no one that should want to have anything to do with me. But my mother, before the healer-wife had proclaimed me for what I was, had given me a name. One that was completely inappropriate, given the life I lead. For the first time in a long, long time, I wanted someone to know it was mine.

But I wasn't that foolish; this wasn't a story with a storybook happy ending. And names have power. "'Shadow' will do. It's what they call me," I said, lifting my chin.

"I didn't ask what 'they' call you," he said. "I asked your name."

I stayed quiet. He watched me for a long silent time, something sad in his eyes.

"Very well, Shadow," he said eventually. "Have it your way. For now."

After that we talked. Or rather he talked and I mostly listened. The topics seemed innocuous, but I got the feeling he was testing me. Though to what aim, I couldn't tell. He told me about his Templar brother, and also about his family, though I noticed he couched everything in careful generalities. No names. Besides the Templar, there were apparently two younger sisters.

I couldn't imagine growing up with other children. Lucius had taken me—bought me—when the Fae rejected me. But the Blood do not turn children, so I had no companions my own age. The lone child in a sea of adults, tended by the Trusted and skirted warily by the Blood. Treated more like a pet, or rather, perhaps a hound puppy—raised for a purpose. Valued but not indulged. Treated with a firm hand in case I turned vicious.

I'd never had a family. I had seen my mother amongst the Fae sometimes when they left the Veiled World, but she never spoke to me. Never even looked at me. As for my father, well, his identity was a mystery no one had ever seen fit to enlighten me about.

I found myself leaning forward as Simon spoke, drawn again against my will, like a moth seeking light.

I straightened whenever I noticed, reminding myself exactly what it was that happened to moths that flew into bright lights. Simon the sunmage could be nothing for me but trouble. And the reverse, even more so. Lucius already wanted him dead. His efforts would redouble if he thought I had developed some sort of fascination for the sunmage.

But, despite the cold hard facts, it was difficult to make myself pull back and not bask in the sheer novelty of someone speaking to me like I was a person.

Amidst his talk of his life, he kept throwing unexpected questions at me. About the Night World and my life there. I didn't answer. The truth of my life was nothing I wanted to share with this man. Nothing he would understand. Besides, I didn't want Lucius to have another transgression to lay at my feet.

Still, I got the feeling he was reading more than I wanted from my silences. But against my will, his warmth spread to me, easing a little of the icy ache I've carried inside all my life. It made me feel slightly dizzy and part of me wanted to escape to the clarity of the shadow. Which was never going to happen while the sun beat down on my skin in the few places it was bared by the black of my hunting outfit.

After a while, I started to feel more than dizzy. Hot and flushed. For a moment I feared it was the need calling to me, but then I dismissed the possibility. It was too soon, even if I'd been trying to push the limits of my tolerance lately, delaying the urge as long as possible. This felt different. The need feels hot, yes. But it's the dead scorching heat of the hottest part of a flame, the diamond note of a siren's song. Deadly. It demands as it burns, nothing warm or gentle in it.

This felt more like sitting too close to a fire for too long.

"Are you all right?" Simon asked as I tried to take a deep breath to ease the heat.

"I'm a little warm," I admitted reluctantly. Maybe it was the wrist-to-ankle black I wore. Leather and heavy cotton are not the coolest of choices in summer.

He scanned me, a different purpose behind that gaze now. I could almost feel the switch to healer again. Which maybe could prove useful. If he came closer I could . . . what exactly?

No plausible course of action sprang immediately to mind. I couldn't shadow in sunlight, and we had already established he was at least a match for me whilst I was without my powers. Unless I could somehow get him to leave the room, give me a chance to reach a window, wards or no, and try to reach the darkness.

I slumped a little in the chair, trying to look sicker than I felt.

He studied me awhile longer; then his palm hit the bed with a thump. "Sunburn," he pronounced, sounding disgusted with himself. "I imagine you don't go out much in daylight."

"No." The Night World isn't much for daylight activities and I live by their hours. My skin was Fae-fair anyway, not pure white—there was a slightly golden cast to it—and it had only grown fairer over the years I'd lived with Lucius. The Blood are pale, and those of the Night World other than the Beast Kind—the Trusted and the blood-locked and the Nightseekers—tend to emulate the look.

Still, Simon wasn't about to leave the room for a sunburn, so I had to try another plan. "Maybe you could turn it off?" I jerked my chin at the nearest lamp.

He grinned. "I don't think so. You'd just go 'poof' and then where would we be?"

Hell. Pretty and dangerous and not stupid. "I do not go 'poof,'" I said, trying to sound trustworthy.

That made him laugh and the warmth in my cheeks flared higher. Somehow I didn't think I could blame the sun for *that*.

"Maybe not, but you'd still vanish as soon as you could. You might even try to kill me again."

I shook my head. "You have my dagger." And even without that minor detail, I couldn't see myself trying again now that he knew about me—and now that I knew more about him. For one thing, there was the sobering image of a revenge-bound Templar knight rampaging through the Night World to separate my head from my body to contemplate. And for another . . . No. I wasn't going to think of any other reason.

"So I do," he said. He stood and came over to me, bending down to look more closely at my face. "Too late for a shield if you're already burned. I was careless. I apologize."

I stared at him. I'd tried to kill him and he was apologizing for sunburn? A more normal reaction would be to try to kill me. At least, that would be the case in the Night World. Violence for violence. A life for a life. Do worse unto others until they stop trying to defeat you.

But his world was different. So different it didn't seem real to me.

"Can't you . . ." I didn't exactly know what it was that sunmages did to heal.

He shook his head, nodded at the lamps. "Not while those are still burning."

So he did have limits. I filed the information away carefully with the other things he had revealed. Then tried to press the one small advantage I had. His healer instinct. It was a weakness that might make him careless. Part of me felt guilty for using it against him, turning his warmth into something darker, but I locked emotion down ruthlessly. I needed to survive this night. I would use whatever means necessary. "I just sit here and burn, then?"

He frowned for a moment; then his face cleared. "I have just the thing."

He vanished out of sight and I heard the wardrobe door open and close behind me.

When he reappeared, he was holding a battered straw hat—wide brimmed and high peaked—that looked as though it had been soundly trampled, then punched roughly back into shape. He held it out proudly. "Perfect."

He held it over my head, and the light cut off for a moment. Not enough to let me shadow—I couldn't do that as long as any sunlight touched my body—but enough to ease the heat in my face. Then he pulled the hat away.

"What?"

"It won't fit with your hair like that." He gestured at the twisted knot of braids at the back of my head.

I wriggled my fingers, which was about as much movement as I had in my hands with my arms tied. "I can hardly take it down."

"I'll do it."

Before I could protest, he started sliding pins free and unwinding my braids with ease. Each brush of his fingers against my skull made me want to simultaneously purr and run away.

No man had ever run his hands over my hair before. I rarely wore it down in public and never for the hunt. And no man came to visit me in private.

This man wouldn't be either.

I bit the inside of my lip, welcoming the pain to remind me of what was real and what was not as his hands moved.

At last he had my hair arranged to his satisfaction and slid the hat gently into place. It smelled of him. Warm spice scented the air around me, soaking into my skin with each breath I took.

Dawn felt a long, long time away.

In the end I fell silent again in self-defense, trying to draw my shields around me even as he tried to coax me into conversation. It felt oh so tempting to soften and bend and let him draw me out.

I couldn't afford soft. I couldn't afford to want something. Wanting can be used as a weapon against you.

Simon eventually stopped talking and instead sat silently, watching me. That was almost harder to take. But I couldn't quite make myself look away from those blue eyes.

The clock by his bed seemed to tick very loudly in the silence that bloomed between us.

"Dawn soon," he said after who knows how long.

I looked toward the window. Sure enough, the sky was lightening: not true dawn, not yet. Like the Blood, I'm sensitive to the rhythm of day and night. In daylight, my powers work if I am underground, but not without a greater effort. Dawn is the time to retreat to safety. To curl myself away in my room and sleep while the Blood slumber and the Trusted stand watch.

I could feel the dawn coming. And, as always, wanted to hold it off. Though this time I wasn't sure if it was the loss of my powers I dreaded or the fact that I would most likely never see Simon again.

Gradually the sky faded from indigo to purple, then grew pink and gold like a rose. Simon rose from the bed, pistol in hand. I watched as he pulled my dagger free from the wall.

"You don't need that or the pistol. The sun's up—you're stronger than me."

"So if I untie you, are you going to try to take this?" He held the dagger in his left hand, weighing it.

I shook my head. "No."

"I want to trust you, Shadow."

"Trusting me isn't a good idea." I didn't like the way his blue eyes darkened at my words. Didn't want to think I'd hurt him in any way. "But you're safe from me today."

"You'll come for me again?"

"I go where I'm sent."

He considered me. "Do you think Lucius will send you again?"

I shrugged, not wanting to think about what Lucius might do to either of us. "Maybe not. But trusting in Lucius' goodwill isn't terribly wise."

"Yet if I set you free, you'll go back to him," he said. A bitter edge made his words sting like acid.

"I have to."

He shook his head. "There are other choices."

"You don't understand." And if I had my way, he wasn't ever going to.

He tucked the gun into the waist of his trousers, but he still held the dagger. "I'm not giving this back to you. Not now."

My fingers curled. My dagger was part of me. It rode my hip whenever I was awake. Beautiful, like all Fae work. Beautiful and deadly. A reminder to the Night World of exactly what I was. "It's mine."

"I'll send it to you. I assume 'care of Lucius' would be the correct way to address such a package?"

"Yes," I said, grateful he hadn't pushed for any further details.

"Fine." He crossed to a dresser, tucked the dagger into a drawer, then locked it. The key went into the pocket of his trousers. Clever of him. I would hardly be attempting to retrieve it from there.

His face was serious when he returned.

"Have you decided?" I asked, trying to ignore the wary thread of fear rising in my stomach.

"Decided what?"

"What you're going to do with me?" I held my breath, knowing if he so chose, he could make a decision that would end my life. I hoped the side of him that healed would make such a decision hard on him. I knew what I'd do in his place.

Eliminate the threat.

But this man was very different from me. Very different from anyone else I'd ever met.

"If I turn you in, you'll try to escape. If you're successful, people will get hurt. If you fail, they might kill you."

I nodded, my mouth too dry to dispute any of this. It was all true anyway.

His mouth twisted. Then he braced his shoulders as if he'd made a decision that didn't entirely rest easy. He knelt and started to untie me.

I didn't try to fight or flee once I was free. The sun was

level with the window and added its paler light to the blaze of Simon's lamps.

"I'll take you downstairs. Send for an autocab."

"'Cabs don't like to go where I live." Hackneys even less so. The Beast Kind scents spook the horses.

"I know the driver. He'll go where I tell him."

In daylight his house was an oasis of light and peace. Windows and skylights filled the rooms with sunshine, each golden patch of light on the dark floorboards a reminder of my failure and the man who walked behind me.

We came to the front door. I reached for the handle.

His hand caught mine. "Don't go back there."

"I have to. Lucius will come looking for me." I looked at our hands, at his fingers curled around mine, and thought of the world I was returning to. No warmth or pools of sunlight there. No one who saw good where there was no good to be seen. No strong hand holding mine.

Only the familiar ruthless world I knew. But I had to go. Lucius would move heaven and earth to find me if I vanished. I doubted Simon would survive the search, Templar brother or no. "Don't try to save me, Simon. It's not worth it."

His smile went crooked again. "Saving people is what I do."

"I'm not hurt. I don't need a healer."

The smile vanished. "Are you certain about that?"

I tugged my hand free, wanting to ask what he meant. A dangerous impulse. I needed to go. "You should leave being a white knight to your brother."

"He taught me everything I know."

"Then you should have paid more attention. I'm sure he taught you not to tangle with the Blood over foolishness. Let me go."

"You think this is foolishness?" His finger brushed my cheek, and the sting of the sunburn faded under his touch. Another warmth altogether flared in its place.

I stepped back. "I know it is. This is the real world. White knights belong in stories." I was used to lies and deception, but my tongue stumbled over that one. To cover my confusion I pulled the hat from my head and held it out as the clatter and hiss of metal and steam in the distance heralded the arrival of the 'cab.

His hand fell to his side as if by refusing the hat, he could keep me here. "How about golden ones?"

I tossed the hat, relying on Templar-trained reflexes to make him catch it. "I don't need saving," I repeated, and stepped out into the daylight and away from him.

Chapter Two

"Stop here. I'll walk the rest of the way." I looked out the window of the autocab as Higgins pulled over to the side of the road. Midafternoon and Saint Pierre seemed quiet, but I wasn't taking any chances after last night, after my unexpected visitor with the deadly intentions. Hence the convoluted 'cab ride through the human boroughs before we'd reached our destination.

I leaned forward and paid. "Are you off now?"

Higgins nodded. "Another half an hour and I'm done." He took my money and didn't offer change. I didn't expect any. I'd already called in a favor this morning when I'd had him take Shadow back to the Night World. He'd told me he'd dropped her off at Lucius' Sorrow's Hill mansion. That information alone was worth the expensive fare.

"Heading back to the guild?"

"Aye. Gotta drop this beauty off before I head home." He patted the steering gear of the 'cab fondly. The Guild of Mechanisers produced the autocabs in limited quantities, and the drivers shared them to afford the guild's license fees.

Personally I preferred horses, but the 'cabs, noisy and smelly as they were, were faster and more secure than hackneys and carriages. If the guild ever solved the problem of how to make certain key parts of the engine with something other than prized steel, or managed to win a greater share of the iron ration, they'd probably take over the City.

Or maybe not. The Fae refused to use them, after all.

The 'cab shuddered to a start again as I got my bearings then set off through the streets. Saint Pierre was a merchant borough, full of shops and warehouses and the largest market in the human boroughs. All of which brought many, many people to its streets. Easy to be anonymous here and it was far from any of my usual haunts.

The other thing Saint Pierre was famous—or infamous—for was the number of taverns tucked amongst its streets. Full of cheap beer and cheaper food to fuel the shoppers and workers.

I checked over my shoulder a few times as I walked, but no one was following me. Which made me feel almost cheerful as I ducked down one of the twisted lanes and found the door to the Drunken Crow.

Another handful of coins secured me use of the private room upstairs and I headed up to wait for my companion to join me. It didn't take long—I'd barely opened the bottle of whiskey I'd acquired downstairs before the door opened with a bang and my brother, Guy, stalked in.

"What's so important?" he growled as he crossed the room.

"Maybe I wanted to buy my brother a drink?" I held up the bottle of whiskey.

"You don't usually wake me up to buy me drinks." He ran a hand over his close-cropped hair and yawned.

Damn. I'd forgotten he was on night patrol at the moment. I pushed a chair away from the table. "Sorry. Sit."

Guy sat, looking half asleep and cranky about it. He scrubbed a hand over the pale stubble at his chin. "Well?"

I poured him a drink and told him what had happened. When I reached the end of my tale, his glass was still untouched.

"Drink the whiskey," I said to Guy, watching him grind his teeth. There's no good way to tell a brother someone tried to kill you. Particularly if the brother is also a Templar knight. Templars tend to overreact.

Though so far, this particular Templar was holding himself in check. Just.

"Why," he asked slowly, "am I only hearing about this now?"

I'd been expecting that question. Truth was, I wasn't entirely sure. I'd needed time to think and I'd wanted to give her—Shadow—a chance to get back to the Night World. Even though the thought of her doing just that made me equal parts angry and sickened. "It was only eight hours ago. Drink. You'll feel better."

To encourage him, I swigged from my own whiskey. Mistake. It tasted like a rat had drowned in the cask. It probably had. The Drunken Crow wasn't the sort of tavern that worried overmuch about cleanliness. People came here to drink and ignore the world outside. Nobody would ask questions about anyone else who chose to drink here. My stomach burned as the whiskey settled.

"Judging by your expression, drinking this rat's piss isn't going to improve my mood," Guy drawled.

The drawl was a concern. Guy had spent a year or two of his training in the Voodoo Territories and had come home with a fondness for chicory coffee and a drawl that showed up when he was about to unleash his temper.

I sent an extra thread of power to the shields set around the room. As the sounds of the drinkers below grew slightly more muffled, I watched Guy carefully. He leaned back in his chair, hardened leather vest creaking in protest as he folded his arms and scowled.

I scowled back. "These days nothing improves your mood."

"Which begs the question why you're adding to my problems, little brother."

I ignored the "little brother" gibe. Truth was, we were the same height. Guy was heavier, his bulk coming from wearing mail and carrying a sword every day, but not taller. I might have that same bulk if not for choices made long ago. "The City isn't just your problem."

"No, but you are," Guy said.

His frown deepened and I felt mine do the same. "I'm not your problem," I said flatly.

The Templars helped police the streets and I helped patch up those who came to grief in them. Lately there had been far too much business for both of us. The City's mood was savage and boded no good for anyone. Half-light, some called the City. These days it was starting to feel more like near dark, like we were sliding inexorably toward the Night World. My visitor last night had only proved that. But I, for one, intended to stand against the fall.

"As I recall," Guy said, his drawl thickening, "we're still brothers, no? I might not have any other authority over you these days, but family is family. And apparently someone wants you dead. Sounds like a problem to me." Leather creaked again as Guy uncrossed his arms, one hand drifting to the pommel of his sword. "Or was there some other reason you dragged me out of bed?"

I met his stare without flinching. "I need a favor."

"Go on."

"Templars do, on occasion, make use of spies?"

Guy's brows drew together. "We have informants, if that's what you mean." He raised the glass, then stopped, peering over the rim at me. "Why do you need a spy, little brother?"

"I want to find out more about her."

The glass slammed back to the table. "About the wraith? About Lucius' fucking chief assassin? What more do you need to know?"

I took another swig of the god-awful whiskey. "I don't think it's that simple."

"Hell's balls, Simon. She tried to kill you. Tell me you aren't mooning over her."

I ignored the memory of red, red hair sliding over my hands. "I'm not an idiot."

"Then why do you need to know anything more about her?"

I frowned, trying to figure out how to explain it. "There was something there, Guy."

"Something? Fuck, you *are* mooning."

"No. I'm not. But I—" Light curse it. Guy didn't understand. It wasn't her face or body that intrigued me. It was what she didn't want me to see. The wounded woman behind the big gray eyes. Sitting there, tied to my chair, she'd sat quietly, awaiting her fate. No pleas or protests. Just mute acceptance. As if there were nothing she could do to change things. As if she had no right to expect mercy.

I knew that look—I saw it sometimes in the women who came to St. Giles when the men in their lives were too quick with their fists or boots.

She'd said she didn't need healing, but she was wrong. Every instinct I had told me that. Guy couldn't understand. He hadn't seen those haunted gray eyes.

"What, you think you're going to find her deep dark secret and somehow bring her over to our side? The woman's probably killed more people than I have. She works for Lucius. She's not a damsel in distress."

I reached for the whiskey. Maybe it would improve with another taste. "I know that. But she wasn't what I expected. I think—"

"With her history, the only way she could redeem herself would be if she testified against Lucius and helped us bring him down," Guy said disgustedly.

I froze. Testify? It was brilliant. "I didn't think of that," I admitted. But I was now. If we could bring a case against Lucius to the Fae queen—bring *evidence* that he had broken the treaty to her— then that might be the only thing that could tip the balance of power in the City back in our favor.

Guy regarded me with brotherly disgust. "Too late now, you let her go."

I grabbed the bottle and leaned across the table to refill Guy's glass, trying to hide the lingering stiffness riding me despite the hours I'd spent in the sun already. By the time the Shadow had left, I'd felt the ache in my muscles, tiny tremors of pain caused by the effort of holding the sunlamps alight for so long. But it didn't seem as though she'd noticed. She hadn't tried anything at the end. Just as well. I hadn't been in any condition to fight.

I wasn't even sure she'd really noticed *me* at all. Once or twice there'd been a flicker of something in those eyes or color staining her face that may have been more than the sunburn.

Gods and suns. The sunburn. I gulped whiskey to hide my instinctive wince.

Harm to none. Aid to all.

That was the oath I'd sworn. One that bound me as surely as Guy's bound him to his God. It was who I was. Aid to all. Everyone in the City would be better off if Lucius no longer ruled the Blood.

"You're right," I said.

Guy raised an eyebrow—the one bisected by the scar he'd gotten in a dispute with a Blood lord many years ago. It wasn't his only scar. Get mixed up with the Night World—or stand in their way rather—and scars are inevitable. "About what?"

"We need her to testify."

"Forget it, little brother. There's no way that's ever going to happen." His expression turned stern. "What we need is to know why Lucius wants you dead." He raised his glass with studied movements that only slightly camouflaged the well-trained killer hidden beneath the seemingly calm surface. The red crosses emblazoned on the backs of his hands seemed to glow like fresh blood despite the dimness of the room. "What did you do?"

"Who says I did anything?" I snarled. "Lucius is a loose cannon, you know that." Indeed, if anyone had to take a guess as to who was behind the escalating troubles in the City, they'd be likely to name Lucius. Proving it was another matter.

"Unpredictable, yes. But he's not stupid. Why would he risk violating the treaty to kill you?"

"He probably thought he'd get away with it clean. I doubt she leaves traces." I tried to rein in my temper. I needed a clear head to avoid telling Guy too much. But I only managed in pushing it back a little. The hard knot of anger that had ridden my stomach since last night was still there.

"You must have done something."

"Who knows why Lucius does anything? There have been a few more Beasts at the hospital than usual. Maybe I stitched up someone from the wrong pack." It wasn't entirely the truth. There was one other reason that Lucius might wish me dead. But no one who would betray me knew that particular secret. Suns, not even Guy knew it. My fingers tightened around my glass.

"He knows that violating the treaty like this would screw him when the negotiations come round. Didn't you ask the wraith?"

"Strangely, she didn't seem to want to tell me."

Guy's mouth twisted. "And knowing you, you didn't try too hard to persuade her."

My own mouth went flat. "I don't torture women, Guy. I don't torture anyone. My oaths are just as important as yours."

Guy's chair clattered backward as he stood. He leaned toward me, hands flat on the table. "So you just let her go. You could've handed her over to us."

He wasn't quite yelling. But he was close to the edge. I was glad of the shields as I stood too and took three steps around the table. If he wanted to go a few rounds over this, then so be it. Maybe he'd listen to reason once he'd worked off his temper. I stepped closer, crowding him. "And what would you have done with her? How would you have even held her once it was dark?"

His jaw clenched. "You're not the only sunmage in the City, Simon."

"True. But none of your Templar mages can call sunlight at night for more than a few minutes, can they?" I held his gaze. The conversation was skirting old and treacherous territory. Treading that path wouldn't help resolve anything. "Even if they could, turning her over to you for questioning would still violate my oaths."

"Thanks to your oaths, we have no proof that Lucius tried anything at all," Guy said, speaking through gritted teeth.

"And if it had been you and *your* oaths, then she'd probably be dead and we'd be no better off," I shot back.

"Hell, Simon, you—"

"Either punch me or shut up and listen."

His eyebrows shot up and I braced myself for a fist to the face, standing my ground. But then he backed off a step or two. For a moment he stood still, head bowed, breathing heavily. No doubt trying to rein in his own temper with a few pleas for his God to spare him from the plague of family.

Finally he raised his head and looked at me levelly for a few seconds. Then he bent, picked up his chair, and set it carefully back on its feet. "Say something worth listening to, little brother." The drawl was back but he seemed somewhat calmer.

I eased back, giving us both space. Calmer wasn't calm. One of us might yet end up with a blackened eye or two. "Even if you questioned her, what good would it have done? The Fae won't take testimony given under duress, you know that. Do you think she would've cooperated if I'd turned her over? I don't."

"No," Guy snapped. "I don't."

I could almost see the frustration rising from him. I understood it. I felt the same. Anyone who saw the damage inflicted by the Night World daily had to. But torture wasn't the answer. I settled myself back into the chair, waited for Guy to do the same. "What if I could talk her into helping us?"

Guy gave one burst of incredulous laughter, then choked it off. "Did you melt your brain with one of your sunbeams?"

I ignored his laughter. "No."

Pale eyebrows drew together like a lightning bolt of disapproval. "Fuck. You want to save her, don't you? This is another one of your crusades."

I didn't react. Didn't want him to see he was right, or partially so. The Templars were pretty damn pragmatic, and chivalry was hardly the priority in their code of honor these days. Guy cut down female Blood with no hesitation if they broke the law. Shadow wasn't Blood but she was hardly on the side of the angels.

"No, it's not. You're the one who brought up the idea of her testifying."

"I didn't think you'd take me seriously. She's Night World."

"And that means she's beyond hope?"

"Hell's balls, you never learn. Same old story."

"At least I try," I shot back, anger and regret rapidly loosening my grip on my temper.

"At what cost?" Guy's voice was rising again.

I sucked in a breath, held up a hand, palm out. "We are not having this argument again." I couldn't change the past and neither could Guy. Fifteen years of arguing had taught me that much. Opening old wounds wouldn't help anything right now.

Guy held up his hands too, his face grim. "Fine. But you can't save everyone, little brother."

"That's ironic coming from a man who has dedicated his own life to saving people." Ever since I'd become a healer, people had been telling me I couldn't save everyone, but no one ever lectured Guy.

"I'm sworn to defend, not save. There's a difference."

"Which is?"

"When you defend, the idea is to keep the greatest number safe. You know you'll lose some of them. You know that some of them will always choose the other side. And you know how to choose your battles."

"I am choosing my battles. Think about it, Guy. Think about what it would mean if she did cooperate. If we could present sworn testimony that Lucius tried to assassinate a human healer from his very own assassin? Putting aside the fact that you think I'm insane right now."

He had to see it. It was his idea, after all. The treaty negotiations were a little over three months away. They only came around once every five years. And for the last five years, Lucius had been growing stronger. He wanted more. If we couldn't push his power back during these negotiations, who knew if the City would still be standing by then?

Lucius had been steadily extending his power base, pushing into the border boroughs. Increasing the number of Blood and blood-locked. But thus far, he hadn't broken any tenets of the treaty. None that could be proven anyway. Without proof, we humans had little chance of getting the Fae to agree to move against the Blood during the negotiations.

Guy's gaze locked with mine. "I'm well aware of the politics. I'm the one out there keeping the peace."

"And I'm the one patching up the casualties. I see just as much as you." I leaned in closer. The wooden chair dug into the backs of my thighs, unyielding as Guy himself. "You always said there were things worth fighting for."

He looked at me for a long moment. "I thought you'd given up fighting."

"Just because I don't swing a sword doesn't mean I'm not fighting."

"Some things you should walk away from," Guy said quietly. There was sorrow in his eyes. Old pain. I imagined the same showed in mine.

"That's my decision to make."

Guy sighed, then shook his head. "You're serious about this? You think you can convince her? Why?"

Instinct. That was why. My gut told me there was someone behind the ice of those gray eyes. Someone who wanted out. "Call it faith, if you would."

That earned me a look of exasperation. But Guy at least stayed put. "What exactly are you suggesting? How would you even get near her?"

"From what I hear, Lucius keeps her on a short leash. Where he goes, she goes. So we find out where he's going to be—one of the Assemblies would be best. That's where your informants come in. They find out where she's going to be. I go in and find her and talk to her."

"And how do you get out again? Even if she does agree?"

"She's a wraith. She can walk out unseen." And as long as there was no trouble, there was no reason I couldn't get in and out of an Assembly unmolested if I disguised myself somewhat. "I'll leave the way I came."

"You're assuming there'll be no trouble. What if she objects to your proposal?"

"If I can't defeat her, you only have yourself to blame, don't you?"

"I taught you just fine. If you get beaten by a girl, then it's nothing to do with me." For a moment his eyes lightened, but then they turned grim again. "This is risky."

"I'll have you as backup," I pointed out.

He shook his head. "As plans go, it's kind of thin. You're putting a lot of faith in a woman who tried to kill you. And if you fail to convince her, Lucius will have an even better reason to come after you."

"Isn't it worth the risk?"

Guy looked down at the table for a moment—I wondered if he was praying for the strength not to flatten me—then his eyes rose. "It is if you succeed. If you don't, we might be worse off. Tell you what, little brother. Let's make a deal. You try it your way. If she won't come, then we do things my way."

My stomach tensed, the whiskey taste in my mouth suddenly sour. "Your way?"

"We take her anyway."

Kidnap her? I ignored my instinctive protest, forced myself to consider the offer. Even if she didn't come voluntarily, she would be away from Lucius and we had a chance of getting her to help us.

And I might be able to help her. But I had to make sure I wouldn't be trading her from one hell to another. I met Guy's gaze, mouth set. "No torture. You can hold her but not hurt her. I'll even help you hold her. But only if you swear. Lock her up, keep her where she can't do any more harm, but any information she gives us, she does so freely." Time enough to worry about what might happen if she wouldn't cooperate if it came to that. If Guy gave his word, he would stand by it. She wouldn't be hurt.

Guy started to shake his head. "I—"

I cut him off. "Your oath. Right here. Or we forget the whole thing. Besides, if she testifies and the Fae suspect she's under duress, they won't accept it, you know that."

"The Fae aren't the only ones who could benefit from what she might know."

"Your oath or nothing."

"You'd throw away this chance because of your precious healer morals?"

"If we throw away our morals to win, then we're no better than Lucius," I said steadily. "You know that as well as I do. For once in your life, trust me, Guy. You owe me that much. Swear that she won't be hurt."

"Hell's balls, little brother, you'll be the death of both of us." But he reached under the neck of his tunic and pulled out the heavy silver cross he wore. "All right. I swear in the name of God not to hurt the girl or let anyone else do so. Does that satisfy you?"

I nodded curtly, relief and guilt mixing uneasily in my stomach. "Yes."

)

I woke when Ricco threw open the door to my room with enough force to make it crack against the wall. I bolted upright, hand flying to my hip automatically. Where my dagger wasn't. Ice water flowed down my spine as the events of the previous night flooded back.

"Had an interesting night, did you?" Ricco said with a nasty smirk.

Hells. Ricco being smug meant the conniving bastard thought he had the upper hand. Which probably meant that somehow he—and Lucius—knew I hadn't killed Simon.

"You didn't tell me he was a sunmage." I rolled to my feet. I'd slept in my hunting clothes. They were rumpled and sweaty but far preferable to facing Ricco in a nightgown. I'd known I'd be summoned sooner rather than later.

Another smirk. "I didn't know."

Either he was lying or Lucius was playing games and Ricco was confident that the play was in his favor. Hells upon hells.

Of all the Blood who formed Lucius' inner circle, Ricco was the worst. Even by Blood standards he was vicious.

We existed in a state of perpetual mutual loathing. It was safest never to let him see any fear. Thankfully, his lack of restraint when it came to his temper meant that he would likely never rise as high in the Court as he aspired. Lucius never minded viciousness in his lieutenants, but he expected it to be accompanied by intelligence and control.

Still, Ricco was dangerous, like a half-trained attack dog. I smiled coolly at him. "I guess we'll see what Lucius has to say about that."

His smug expression didn't change. "I guess we will. He wants you. Now."

Cool fear swept through me. Hells. I didn't want to face Lucius. Not yet. But now meant *now*. And if Ricco's pleasure was anything to go by, Lucius was unhappy with me. I glanced down at my clothes. I was in no way dressed for the hall. Lucius indulged my preference for trousers over the formal dresses of the Blood, but I was still expected to look presentable. So, did I choose informality over the risk of angering him with a further delay while I changed?

My gut said faster was safer. I ran a hand over my braids. Redone in haste during my 'cab ride back to the warrens—the last thing I needed was anyone wondering why my hair was loose—they were, at least, intact, if less elaborate than my usual style. It would have to be enough. "Let's go," I said to Ricco.

Despite my efforts to appear calm, my knees shook as Ricco half pulled me through the corridors of the warrens, my feet skidding on the worn flagstones. When he headed upward toward the public levels of the Court's mansion, my stomach turned uneasily.

At least he let go of me as we left the lower warrens. Protocol dictated that I walk alone in public, afforded the same courtesy as the Blood themselves. When he led the way to the hall, I cursed under my breath, wishing desperately to be elsewhere.

I'd hoped for Lucius' office, but I should have known better. When truly furious, Lucius rarely administered a punishment in private.

He preferred the added humiliation of an audience.

But the tremors in my legs weren't all fear. No. With every step I took closer to Lucius, the need was coming in too. Calling me with its hated song. Maybe I should have goaded Simon into killing me. It might have been easier.

An end to this life. And a way of ensuring that he would never see me as I really was rather than whatever idealized picture had fueled the warmth in his eyes as he'd told me not to go.

No man could would look at me that way if he ever saw me as I was soon to be.

The towering wooden doors that guarded the hall were shut. Usually they stood open, guarded by the Trusted. Tonight those at the door were Blood. Private session. Blood only. Not a good sign. My throat tightened as the urge to turn and flee bit into my stomach.

Show no fear, I reminded myself as the nearest of the two guards opened the doors. I straightened my shoulders as I passed under the carved threshold and stepped into the vast room, trying to pretend I was perfectly at ease.

The liquid murmur of the gathered Blood halted as we proceeded down the main aisle toward Lucius, the groups and pairs falling silent as I passed until the room became a still life in black and white, the silence swelling until the eerie lack of noise completely filled the space between the black marble beneath my feet and the highest points of the vaulted arches far above my head.

The Blood stood motionless, silver haired, pale skinned, dressed in their customary immaculate black. The identical expressions of studied detachment on their faces were spoiled a little by the fear I sensed running deep beneath the surface.

I wasn't the only one made uneasy by Lucius calling a private meeting of the Court, it seemed.

The only color came from their eyes—the eyes of the Blood do not fade after they turn, unlike their skin and hair—and the clothing of the vampire I walked toward.

Lucius always wore a touch of red amongst his stark black-and-white. A cravat. Ruby cuff links. A crimson enameled watch on a red-gold chain. Tonight it was more than a touch. Tonight his long velvet frock coat was the color of the blood he commanded me to spill. I wondered if he'd donned it to avoid any coming stains and had to suppress a slightly hysterical urge to laugh.

His eyes tracked me as I moved closer, the deep brown seemingly tinged the red of molten iron. There was nothing for me to read in those depths; he could be about to kill me or kiss me for all I could decipher.

"Good evening, my shadow," he said as I came to a halt in front of his chair.

"My Lord." I inclined my head the correct degree, wishing again I'd had more time to make myself presentable. But at least the mess of my braids might hide the hairs on the back of my neck standing on end. "Night keep you."

He didn't nod in response, or offer me the customary greeting in return. Just watched me with eyes like banked coals, as if regarding an insect crawling across the floor.

He knew. That much was obvious. Knew I'd failed to carry out my mission. Failed him for the first time.

Not many were given a second chance at failure.

I kept my gaze on his. Might as well see what was coming. Behind me, Ricco's breathing and the small rustles and creaks of the near-silent Court sounded like thunder in my ears, matching the pounding of my heart. Ricco's continued presence reminded me that any retribution Lucius might care to mete out could come from behind just as easily as in front. Sweat beaded on my back.

It was always hot in the hall. The light of hundreds of candles carefully shielded in glass lamps hanging from chains bolted to the ceilings warmed the air. The Blood preferred it warm even though, in truth, neither heat nor cold truly affected them. Maybe because heat gave them more excuse to keep the Trusted—the humans who served them—scantily clothed. The Beast Kind and the Fae share their love of warmth. Normally I appreciated it too, but tonight the air pressed in on me: suffocating and clinging, perfumed with too many expensive colognes.

I made myself breathe slowly, waited for Lucius to speak. He was pale as always, as unmoved by the heat as an iceberg would be by a lit match, a perfect statue carved in white and black and red.

The silence stretched until my pulse echoed in my ears.

"You look tired, my shadow. Are you well?" He shifted

in his seat, easing the right hand cuff of his jacket and the linen below it upward, exposing his wrist.

I didn't let myself move. I wanted to look down, look away, deny. But I knew he could read the need in me anyway, hear the hastened heartbeat, see the tremors that quickened my skin now that he was so close.

"I am well." I kept watching. He'd never made me do this in public. Let me keep my sordid little secret—and the knowledge of the chain he used to bind me—to myself. Let others think he controlled me through fear and strength and will. It added to his power. But I knew the truth.

The pulse in his wrist drew my eye. The tiny shivers of skin vibrating a little with every slow heartbeat. Vampire hearts do beat. Not with the same rhythm of the human life they have left behind. But blood still pumps through their veins, and the muscles beat to drive it so.

Don't think about the blood. I swallowed softly. "Did you have need of me, my Lord?"

One side of his mouth curled slowly. My stomach clenched, willing him not to do what I thought he was about to. To punish me in such a way that only I would know it was a punishment, a sharp yank of the leash he held around my neck to remind me of where I was, who I was, and that my master was displeased.

Given that he had not tasked me with the sunmage's— Simon's, I couldn't help adding silently—death in public, then he was not going to reprimand me for failure in public. Doing so might risk lessening the fear with which the Blood regarded him, and to some extent, as the weapon he wielded, me. And that would never do.

So tonight it was not going to be the easy way—a beating from which I could take a few days to recover and lick my wounds in private before he dispatched me to perform the next act of revenge or intimidation or simple malice.

Tonight he would do something much worse and disguise it as a reward.

"Oh no, my shadow," he said, beckoning me closer with one long finger. "Tonight I think you have need of me."

Someone behind me sucked in a breath, a shocked sound that rang like a siren in the closely held silence. Maybe my secret wasn't so open after all.

"Isn't that so?" Lucius continued, pinning me with his gaze.

I squared my shoulders, knowing that begging would do no good. He knew me too well. Knew that the sensation of anticipated humiliation now crawled under my skin like bugs with razored feet. Knew that I would hate what he was about to do.

It wouldn't be enjoyable for him if I didn't.

It would be even more enjoyable for him if I fought him.

Providing Lucius with an opportunity for enjoyment was something to be avoided.

So I didn't fight. "Yes, my Lord." The words were shards of glass shredding my throat, but even through my revulsion, the need blazed into life, too long denied, too fierce to bank. If I refused now, I would pay with steadily worsening agony until I begged him for relief. As much as I wanted to be stoic, my body betrayed me. It wanted what he offered.

"Kneel."

I knelt, fixing my gaze on his face as he leaned closer. If I watched his face, rather than the pulse in his wrist, I could control myself a little longer.

"Good girl." He slipped his dagger—so similar to the one I'd lost—from its sheath. The lamplight flickered along the blade in shades of orange and scarlet and there was an answering flash of red in his eyes. Anger. Fury. Fear caught me again, clearing the need a little.

Danger still hung over me. He could still plunge that dagger into my heart. He was old. Old enough to be fast enough to strike before I could shadow. Old enough for it to be foolish for me to try anything. I stayed still, frozen like a bird confronted by a snake, hoping his anger would not overrule logic, that he would still think I was more valuable to him alive.

After all, it wouldn't be easy to find another wraith. The Veiled World guarded its females fiercely since my mother had slipped. The Fae did not appreciate the strength Lucius had gained from me even though they were the ones who had given me away. I'm sure they regretted whatever merciful impulse had prevented them from simply snapping my neck when my true nature was discovered.

But part of what always made Lucius so dangerous was his utter conviction that the world would shape itself to please him. If he chose to discard a flawed blade, then another would present itself in time.

The gap between my heartbeats seemed endless as I waited to see what he would do. Then the dagger moved, not toward me but across his own wrist, a thin line of bright red blood welling to mark its path.

I almost jerked backward. So much blood. Normally he gave just a few drops from his finger. Just enough to seal the addiction without slaking the need completely. This . . . this would be ten or twenty times that amount.

The scent of it called to me. Warm, metallic with that slight edge of something indefinable that lashed the need into a frenzy. Human blood doesn't smell the same. But this . . . the blood of a vampire. A Blood Lord. Irresistible.

Irresistible and addictive. I knew what would happen once I tasted it. My body had already started to heat and ache in anticipation of what was to come. But still I hesitated, knowing that the Court were watching, part of me wishing I could die instead of let them see me this way.

"Drink, my shadow." Lucius held his wrist toward me, drops of blood spattering to the floor, the scent of them bursting up toward me, melting away resistance, melting away the part of me that could care, melting away rationality and logic until only the need was left.

I pressed my mouth to his wrist, the ice of his skin searing my lips as the blood filled my mouth. As I swallowed, for some reason Simon's face swam to mind, before the pleasure rushed through me and I convulsed with ecstasy and fell forward as the orgasm took me.

Chapter Three

))

It was early the following evening before hunger drove me from my room.

No one had brought me food. Another of Lucius' subtle punishments. He wouldn't want me hiding away. Not when being out and under the knowing eyes of the Blood would only serve to reinforce my humiliation.

But it was early enough that the corridors were still largely empty of Blood, and I made my way down to the smallest of the dining halls, where the newest of the Trusted ate, without encountering anyone I really didn't want to see.

Even better, the hall itself was half deserted and I picked a small table in a corner after I'd filled a bowl without particularly paying attention to what was on offer. The stone walls were cool at my back as I started to eat. Comfortingly solid. Nothing could come at me through them.

Around me, groups of Trusted sat in threes and fours, talking softly as they ate their meals. No Blood sat amongst them. The Blood can eat and some choose to, but they dine in their chambers or in the far grander dining hall near the main hall. There the china was gilt edged and translucent and the crystal gleamed and the Trusted waited on every Blood whim.

Down here, we ate from earthenware and drank from solid mugs made from the same thick pottery. I didn't care what my food was served on as long as it was served away from the Blood. I ate mechanically, doing my best not to catch anyone's eye. I wanted to eat and get back to my room as fast as possible.

Easing the hunger in my stomach distracted me from the aftermath of what Lucius had done, but only a little. My body still burned. Which was wrong. Feeding should ease the need. But it hadn't.

And I didn't know why. Until I figured it out, I needed to be alone.

None of the Trusted approached me. I didn't expect them to. The newer ones were scared of me and the more experienced took their lead from the Blood they served and disdained me, fulfilling any duties they performed for me without acknowledging my existence.

I didn't blame them for it. I was not one of them, any more than I was one of the Blood. I was alone as always.

It was better that way. There had been times in the past when a Trusted had been kind to me. The last had been Louisa, sole Trusted of one of the younger Blood. She'd brought me food several times when I was being punished or slipped me packets of healing herbs when I'd been injured. Small kindnesses but even the hint of an ally was something to hold on to. I didn't know for sure if she—or any of the others who had helped me—had acted on her own or at the instigation of their Blood masters and mistresses.

I never would. Louisa and her master, Atherton, had disappeared from Court nearly two years ago and no one had made any overtures since. Perhaps I was now seen as too great a risk. Too firmly in Lucius' control to win anyone any advantage.

Not that anybody who showed any interest in me— whether Trusted or the Blood who commanded them— tended to survive very long. I'd never worked out whether those who did were the kind who naturally drew Lucius' wrath by being weak, or whether he deliberately cut down anyone who might be a threat to his hold over me.

Even though it meant I was more isolated than ever, deep down I was relieved to be ignored. I had enough death on my hands without adding those who just meant well to the tally.

I swallowed the last of the food—some sort of stew—

without tasting it. Thinking of those who wished me well had summoned the memory of Simon. The warmth in his eyes. The same warmth in his touch. What would it be like to live with that warmth? To live in the light?

I could find out who he was, of course. No doubt the library held a register of healers. Lucius' archivist—one of the oldest of the Blood—was meticulous. I could learn Simon's full name and probably his entire ancestry. I might even be able to do it without anyone realizing what I was looking for.

My fingers tightened around my fork. Foolishness. What good would knowing do? My life was down here in the dark, twisted intrigues of the Night World. That wasn't going to change. I needed to forget the sunmage. Remembering would only make things worse, and right now what I was facing was bad enough.

I left my bowl and fork on the table, gulped down two cups of coffee in rapid succession, and grabbed a roll of bread. That much would hold me. If I could make it back to my room, I might be able to hide away for another day or so.

But it seemed my luck had about run out for the night. When I got back to my room, Ricco was leaning against the door. Even worse, he wasn't alone. Ignatius Grey stood besides him. I halted abruptly. Ignatius wasn't one of the innermost circle, but he wanted to be. The fact that he could be described as Ricco with a brain meant he might someday achieve that goal. If he survived the politics of the Court.

The identical looks they slid over me made me want to kill them. Their smiles were worse. The knowledge that they'd watched me come, over and over, soured the back of my throat, burning. My fingers curled at my hip but closed on nothing. The missing weight of my dagger burned too. The long black stilettos I'd strapped to each thigh didn't give me the same degree of comfort. "What?" I spat.

Ricco straightened, his smile nastily victorious. "Lucius wants to see you again."

The hallway tilted. I swallowed as the sour taste threatened to become something worse. Not again.

Not so soon.

No matter how angry he was with me, surely Lucius

couldn't put me through that again? It was too great a risk. Even for me. The lore said I couldn't be locked or turned, but no Blood lord had ever truly tested the limits of a wraith either.

Who knew what would happen if Lucius poured his blood down my throat in large quantities? Feeding the addiction more often or in larger amounts might inflame the hunger beyond the point of no return.

The blood craving was deadly for humans. They returned to seek the blood again and again, wanting the unique pleasure only vampire blood could bring. Eventually they became blood-locked—mindless servants for the Blood, willing to do anything for the ones who provided what they needed, unless they were fortunate enough to find a vampire willing to turn them before they reached that point. Not many did. In the end, the craving became all-consuming, making them forget to eat or sleep.

Eventually they stilled and died.

In theory, that wouldn't happen to me, but I was still subject to the need and the hated heated longing and the vicious agonies of withdrawal. Those wouldn't kill me either, merely leave me in torment.

My only hope was that perhaps, just maybe, after what Lucius had done to me last night, I wouldn't have to worry about withdrawal for quite some time. Maybe the need would be sated rather than stimulated. But it was a slender thread, that hope. Some would even call it a lost one. Twenty-four hours had passed and the fires Lucius had lit in my blood still burned strong.

I'd spent a night and a day fighting a driving hunger to either go to him and beg for another release or find the nearest warm—or cold—body and let them take that which I'd always guarded until now.

The food had helped a little, but here, standing close to two males, my stomach tightened and pleasure ran through me again like a sparking flame. And if I was suddenly finding Ricco and Ignatius Grey attractive, then I was in serious trouble. Ricco wanted me; I knew that. It was part of the reason he hated me. But even in the worst depths of the need, I'd never been tempted by any of the Blood before this.

I didn't want them now. I sucked in a breath, seeking

control. It's difficult to function effectively when your mind is consumed by the need for an orgasm. Even worse, when you want blood rather than sex to provide that release.

Even beneath the horror that washed my stomach like acid at the idea of Lucius making me drink again so soon, there was part of me that wanted to do exactly that. The need prowled beneath my skin, barely tamed, snarling and not wanting to be so quickly denied after such a feast.

I dug my nails into my palms as Ricco leaned in close. Pain. That was what I had to call to mind. Pain. All that could come of giving in to the need would be pain. I had to fight it. Had to hope that Lucius wanted me for something else entirely and hadn't decided to see how far he could push me.

"You have time to change. Make yourself presentable," Ricco said nastily. "It's strange. Most females look better once they've come a time or three." His tone gave a whole new meaning to hell-dwelling scum.

I curled my lip and let myself shadow a little; that always made him nervous. He snarled but retreated a step. I faded back. "I'm surprised you'd know."

"You'd have to get in line, slave."

"Oh yes, I've noticed there have been more blood-locked around recently. I guess *they* might be witless enough to want to bed you." I let disgust tinge my tone.

His face darkened. "Keep that up and you might get to join them. Lucius looked mighty entertained by your little display last night. Perhaps he'd like to see you on your back, getting what you deserve."

I ignored the shiver that crept down my spine at the image and fixed him with a flat stare. "Lucius has never appreciated others putting their hands on things that belong to him."

"Lucius has never appreciated being kept waiting either," Ignatius said, finally joining the conversation. "I wouldn't recommend testing his patience tonight, shadow."

I swallowed, my bravado dampened by the warning in his tone. Which could either be Ignatius pretending to know more than he really did or an actual warning that Lucius was still dangerously angry. I wasn't in any position to gamble on which might be true. "Where does he want to see me?"

"We're going to Halcyon."

I hesitated outside the door to Lucius' private suite at Halcyon. From below, the sounds of those gathered to indulge themselves drifted upward. Music and laughter and conversation. Halcyon was the largest of the Blood Assemblies, places where the Blood came to mingle with the Nightseekers and the Beasts—even those Fae who chose to come—and entertain themselves. Dancing and sex and blood were all on the menu, and lust and fear scented the air beneath the smells of gas lamps and silk and perfume.

It was the last place in the world I wanted to be. During the journey here, closed in the carriage with Ricco and Ignatius, the need had continued to stalk me. I fought it as always, determined that there would be one part of me I would not give over to Lucius' control. But walking through the crowded floor of the Assembly, I was near dizzy with the stink of sweat and incense and desire swirling around me.

I did not need to smell the vampire whose blood tormented me and risk becoming even more unhinged.

Ignatius had joined his cronies downstairs once we'd arrived, but Ricco was still by my side. And apparently he didn't share my apprehension. He rapped briskly on the door. "The wraith, my Lord," he said, stepping aside to let me through.

I moved warily, not knowing what to expect. The door closed behind me with a soft snick. It seemed I was to be granted a private audience tonight.

Lucius leaned against the edge of his huge ebony desk. Deceptively casual. I paused. Casual, with Lucius, generally meant danger.

It was unwise to be fooled by him. His suite was designed to do just that. Apart from the desk, it was furnished like a parlor, with chairs and sofas grouped informally as if he might wish to take tea with those he invited here. But I'd been here often enough not to be taken in. The scent of fear was deeply embedded in the dark brocades of the furnishings. It probably tainted the very stones that lay beneath the veneer of civilization he'd laid over the room.

The only way to dispel it would be to burn the place to the ground.

I hated this room.

He beckoned me closer. I moved cautiously, hoping to appear obedient whilst trying to keep as much distance between us as I could without further angering him. Not far enough away for my liking. With every inch nearer, the need bit deeper, blood roaring in my ears, muscles going liquid with want.

I shouldn't need it again so soon. Fear undercut the want swirling through me. What had he done to me?

I schooled my face to calm. Lucius could hear my pulse moving too quickly and maybe scent the need upon me, but I wouldn't give him the satisfaction of letting him see any outward sign that his closeness affected me.

He studied me, eyes once again lit scarlet with a thread of anger. "The sunmage still lives."

Ice shivered over my back. Anger limned his voice, cold, not hot. I knew this mood. My punishment was not over after all. I squared my shoulders against whatever might come. "He called the sun, my Lord."

His mouth twisted, showing fangs. "You were too slow."

He wanted repentance, abasement, fear. The urge to comply surged, but somehow I found the strength to stand my ground. "I wasn't provided with all the necessary facts."

"Are you making excuses?"

No. No, that would simply be foolish. Anger him further. There were no acceptable excuses for not fulfilling Lucius' wishes. He wanted Simon dead and that hadn't happened. End of discussion.

Though I still hadn't figured out why he needed Simon dead. Simon was powerful, a sunmage and brother to a Templar. It seemed a ridiculously ambitious target, even for Lucius. Particularly this close to renegotiation. All the races should be keeping strictly to the laws. Any transgressions could reduce their votes and no one wanted that. The power in the City was delicately balanced. I'd heard no whispers of human plots against the Blood lately.

"No, my Lord." I kept my gaze locked to his, hoping he couldn't see the questions whirring through my head like angry wasps. Why did Lucius want Simon dead? Why risk it? Killing a human not blood-locked is against the treaty.

Blood-locking and the inevitable death that follows is not considered murder, but assassination is. What was he up to? Why risk war with the humans?

He blinked. Slowly. But the anger was there still when his lids rose again. "I do not permit failure."

Ice swept over me. "Yes, my Lord. I have never failed you before."

"And if I set you to this task a second time?" He crooked his finger and I inched reluctantly closer.

The scent of him filled my nose when I came to a halt at arm's length. The Blood smell of emptiness. Of ice and darkness. A smell not of the living. A smell, in fact, that makes the living recoil. The perfumes the vampires favor mostly hide the scent from humans, but I have keener senses. I always smell the scent of death and predators surrounding me.

As I smell the scent of the blood they drink. But I am used to the insidious odor and even though it is still unpleasant, I can control my reactions. Overlying the notes of death and fear, I smelled the heavy musk and wood cologne Lucius wore. It invoked a different sort of reaction. Lucius wears his perfumes dabbed on wrist and neck and misted over his clothing. They fill the air I breathe when I drink his blood, indelibly linked to memories of ecstasy.

My breath quickened and a slow pulse beat between my legs. Lust warred with rising horror. How long would the dose he'd fed me take to wear off? How long until I could regain control and school my body to ignore the need? Would this new fiercer hunger ever wane?

"Well?" Lucius asked. One hand smoothed the black velvet of his jacket, red glinting against the white skin. He wore his rings tonight. Heavy rubies set in iron. Iron that flaunted his power, a deliberate taunt to the Fae. The black metal had brutal edges, clasping the rubies with spiked tongues. His rings could carve flesh from bone with the force of a vampire's strength behind the blow.

My blood had fed those rubies more than once. Was that what he'd brought me here for? Remembered pain swam through me and I swallowed as the fear surged, trumping the lust.

I sucked a breath, braced my knees, focusing on staying upright. "My Lord, I believe he would be expecting another

attempt. I cannot imagine he will leave himself unde-
fended."

He adjusted one perfectly white cuff. "Are you telling
me to leave him alone? To call off my dogs?"

Yes. I almost flinched when the word sounded in my
head. I did not care about the sunmage. I *would* not care
about the sunmage. I needed to care about surviving the
next few minutes. "No, my Lord. But I do not think I am the
best weapon to serve you in this."

His fist clenched. "That is not your decision to make."

I wished he would just hit me and get it over with. I'd
survived beatings before and Lucius was always safer when
his rage had been bled off. "No, my Lord."

He moved then. Fast enough that I didn't have time to
react. His fingers closed around my jaw, forcing my head
back. "You do as I say," he said with deathly calm. "If I want
Simon DuCaine or any other man dead, then he dies. You
do not fail. You do not interfere. You obey. Always."

His nails bit into my skin, not quite hard enough to draw
blood but close. Tears stung my eyes even as Simon's name
rang in my ears. I stayed still. Lucius could snap my neck
from this position with one quick movement.

Just as I could sink a stiletto into his heart, I thought for
a wild moment. But I wouldn't. My stilettos wouldn't kill
him. And if he lived, I might escape if I shadowed, but he
wouldn't suffer me to survive for very long. I would be
hunted. Tortured. It wouldn't be an easy death. As much as
I sometimes longed to be free of Lucius, I was not ready to
give up my life to gain that freedom.

"Always," he repeated, shaking me.

"Y-yes, my Lord," I managed. "I am your shadow."

His grip eased slightly, not enough for me to get free or
move. "Yes. Mine. I think it's time to remind you of your
place, shadow." His breath washed over my face and I shivered, caught between fear and desire as his scent surrounded me again. I clenched my teeth, fought the whimper
rising in my throat.

He trailed a finger from his free hand across my throat.
"I could make you completely mine," he said softly. His
hand dropped, slid between my legs, pressed against me
and sent shards of hungers splintering through me.

"One drop of my blood and you'd be begging for it. Is

that what you want, shadow? Me between those pretty legs of yours?"

I should've said yes. My body wanted it. After all, would it really be so different from what I already submitted to? But I couldn't do it. Couldn't willingly give him the one part of myself still mine. I shook my head.

A slow smile spread across his face. "Good. Because I'm not interested in your pleasure today, shadow."

He pulled his hand away, then casually tossed me across the room.

I hit the wall with a crash and pain exploded down my spine. Lucius was on me before I could move or shadow or do anything at all to protect myself, lifting me effortlessly to plow a fist into my stomach, driving what little air was left from my lungs, leaving me clawing for breath as my insides cramped and throbbed.

He set to work, face calm as he struck again and again.

There's a trick to surviving a beating. You have to find the rhythm of it, so you can anticipate and send your mind away from the pain at the right time. But I couldn't do that. Lucius is a master at keeping you on edge and present for every second. That way, every hurt inflicted makes its intended point.

Instead of retreating I tried to use the pain, forcing my focus down to each shaky breath I took. Proof I was still alive. He didn't touch my face—he never did. But the rest of me was fair game. The pain grew with each blow and I had to fight the overwhelming urge to shadow. It would only be worse if I tried to escape.

Eventually there was a lull. I lay on the floor, tears wetting my cheeks as pain settled and dug its claws in the nooks and crannies of my body. Nothing shrieked with the burning red of a snapped bone. But there was a chorus of hurts clamoring for attention. I have strength beyond a human's, but I doubted there was an inch of me below my neck that wouldn't be purple-black with bruises tomorrow. I couldn't yet tell whether the damp patches I felt against my skin were fear sweat or blood where he'd split my flesh.

"Get on your feet."

I obeyed, unable to stop a moan as my body shrieked. Somehow I stood, knees locked against the adrenaline tremors.

Lucius smiled. He looked exactly the same as he had when I'd walked in the door. Cool. Removed. Icy. No sweat or wrinkled clothing to show he'd spent hells knew how long hurting me. I'd hoped violence would have provided an outlet for his rage, but pools of scarlet still rode the depths of his pupils.

If anything, they were brighter now. He wasn't as calm as he appeared. Would tonight be the night his control snapped? I doubted I'd survive if it did. Bile rose in my throat.

"Good. See, it is easier to obey, is it not? Easier to be mine?"

I nodded, not trusting myself to speak without sobbing. Shame and fear and hatred coiled deep in my stomach, spreading and burning far below the pain, settling into my bones. It had been a long time since he'd beaten me so badly. Part of my mind whimpered like a scared child but that part I ignored. Instead I focused on the hatred. Hate was a reason to live. Fear only made death seem appealing.

Lucius circled slowly. I wanted to turn, to track where he was, but I couldn't make my body obey. It hurt to move. He moved close behind me, one hand brushing my neck. "Yet you've never been truly mine, have you? Never served my needs in full."

The tremors flowered into shakes as his fingers settled against the place where my pulse beat below my jaw. Surely he wouldn't? None of the Blood had ever fed from me. Human blood sustained them. I wasn't human. Plus, Lucius wouldn't have stood for it. But he would hardly gainsay himself.

"Trembling," he whispered mockingly in my ear. "Anticipation, my shadow? Do you wish to serve me?"

I wished to kill him. The desire was a pure ache inside me. Clean. And simple. Fiercer than ever before. Yet, despite it, another want stalked me as well. I couldn't control my body's reaction to him being so near. Even battered and bruised and aching with the hurts he'd inflicted so mercilessly, there was the hated yearning. The whispers in my mind urging me closer, telling me to please him, to do anything for another taste of him.

I schooled myself to stillness, resisting the need. Movement was danger. Not only for the capitulation it demonstrated but for the simpler truth that it would trigger the predator within him.

But stillness did not save me. His fingers coiled into my hair, yanking my head sideways, baring my neck.

"Mine." The whisper came again and I winced. Lucius always rode a knife's edge of control, casually vicious in his rages when he chose to be, icy at other times. But now there was a thread of something . . . wanting in his tone. Maybe his control had snapped. Maybe, for him, insanity looked no different from reason.

The tone was something too close to what I'd heard in the voices of other Blood who'd become obsessed with a particular human. The object of a Blood's obsession rarely survived long. Arousing the true hunger of a Blood lord was a ticket to destruction.

So I needed to be unworthy of his attention. Be as any human. Submissive, willing, compliant. Boring. I tried to make myself relax against him a little as I tipped my head even farther. Wooded musk filled my nose and suddenly I was glad of the need that answered even through the pain. It could take me away as well, shield me from reality. "Drink, my Lord," I said softly.

His lips settled against my throat and his fangs scraped my skin. It wouldn't hurt, I told myself. Not like the beating. The venom in his fangs would numb the pain and his saliva would heal the wound once he was done. But still I shook as I stood there, shook like a rabbit cornered by a fox.

Then he bit. One tearing, stinging plunge through my skin. I gasped as his lips clamped down. The sensation of my blood being sucked out through the wound made my stomach roil. I bit my lip. Hard enough that I tasted blood. Harsh and coppery and salty. Not delicious like his.

It made my throat close and my body bucked against his. Lucius snarled, pulled me closer, his arm iron against my bruised body. His swallows were soft and wet in my ears and my stomach rolled as my knees sagged.

But despite that, I felt intimacy fall around us like a cloak. Felt rather than heard that his heartbeat matched mine. Felt that doubled pulse as if it were my own, a curious sensation as though I'd lost my place in the world. Like I no longer knew where the boundaries between us were.

His arm gentled around me, though the pressure of his

lip increased. I could feel his attention on me, somehow knew that nothing else existed for him at that moment. Our joined heartbeats skipped and then steadied. Grew louder in my ears. One beat. Two ... by the time I'd counted to ten, I was growing dizzy and my knees buckled.

Lucius gasped then and lifted his head, shoving me away with a snarl as he straightened. I half stumbled, reeling from the sudden sense of disconnection, but managed to keep my feet. "Go now," he said. His pupils no longer flared red, but something swam in the brown depths that I couldn't name. Something hungry.

Flee. It was all I could think, but some part of me remembered protocol and survival. I bent in a bow that hurt enough to make me want to vomit, straightened with teeth gritted and pinwheels of light starring the air before me as dizziness swept over me. I stepped back and he reached for me again, his movement almost seeming involuntary. He traced the curve of my cheek with one finger. The finger that he usually pricked to draw blood. It felt cold, almost soothing against the aches swimming under my skin. His touch moved down my cheek to my lips. It was as gentle as Simon's hands had been, but unlike Simon's, Lucius' touch brought only fear.

"Do not forget, shadow," he said softly as he stroked my mouth. "And do not disappoint me again."

"Stick to the plan," I muttered as I stared at the neatly clubbed black hair of the man in front of me. The throng of people crowded around the gates was moving slower than a dying carthorse, but that didn't stop the sense of anticipation from the Nightseeking fools surrounding me growing stronger with each step we took toward the doorway to Halcyon.

I tried not to breathe too deep of the oily smoke from the torches flaring around the gates. It was a long time since I'd been around so many Nightseekers. There'd been flames then also. Flames and worse.

The mild night air felt suddenly cold and I forced my mind away from the memories before they could rise, rolling my shoulders to ease the tension riding the top of my spine. I would never understand humans who sought the darkness of the Night World, turning their backs on their kind. Lesangre was one of the worst of the Night World boroughs, its streets and alleys often deadly to those outsiders who sought the dubious pleasures they promised. It was only natural to feel wary here. I could blame the uneasiness prickling the back of my neck on that rather than memory.

Or simply on the fact that I was waiting to enter a Blood Assembly to try to woo a wraith away from a Blood lord.

Or kidnap her out from under his nose.

Gods and suns, what had I been thinking?

Somewhere on a nearby roof, Guy lurked, ready to come roaring in, sword blazing, if things went badly and we had to resort to force to retrieve Shadow. Hopefully we wouldn't. I had no desire to endure endless retellings of "the night I pulled Simon-the-imbecile's arse out of Halcyon" at family gatherings.

He would delight in doing so this time, if he were proved right.

We never spoke of what had gone before. Of the night he hadn't been at my back.

My hands fisted and I uncurled them with an effort. The past was past, and tonight would be different. Our family was protected. Guy had taken precautions with Mother and Hannah, and Saskia was safe at the metalmages' Guild House.

Tonight would go smoothly. I didn't need the sort of trouble that would require Guy's intervention. Which did beg the question of why, exactly, I was so damned set on walking into a Blood Assembly owned by the vampire who'd tried to have me killed the night before. In order to see the girl who'd tried to kill me.

Mad.

Crazy.

Unholy fucking insane, to use Guy's exact phrase.

I didn't have any fitting comeback to that. There was no comeback. It *was* fucking insane. But we needed her. Needed her evidence. And beyond that, in the place I didn't want to think about, the part of me I was trying to bury deep, I knew I could help her.

Shadow.

Even if she didn't think she needed to be helped.

This one I could save.

Had to try to save.

Insane, indeed.

My fingers itched for a pistol, but guns weren't allowed in the Assemblies. Blow too big a hole in even a very old vampire with a silver bullet and he might not recover. So my only weapons were two daggers. The utilitarian one Guy had lent me and the more delicately wrought, though no less deadly, one I hoped to use as bait to coax its rightful owner into conversation.

Shadow.

Her dagger's haft bit into my skin as my hand curled around it. My fingers almost engulfed the handle. I imagined her hand there, resting against my hip. Then imagined it slightly lower.

Blood rushed to my groin. I set my teeth.

Brains, not balls, little brother. I could almost hear Guy's voice at my ear. A correct assessment of the situation. I was under no illusion that other wants besides the need to bring Lucius to heel and set someone free of the cesspool of the Night World were at play. But I could keep those other wants in check.

Had to keep them in check. I needed my wits about me to pull this off. I'd stained my hair black and dressed in uncomfortable foppish black velvet to blend in with the Nightseekers, but there was no guarantee of my safety.

After all, the creature who owned this place wanted me dead. Guy had tried to convince me to let him be the one to go inside. But his Templar crosses marked him as an outsider, if not an outright enemy, and there was no way he'd get anywhere near Shadow. If I was recognized, I would have to rely on the assumption that Lucius wouldn't kill me in plain sight in flagrant violation of the law. If he did, then Guy and the Templars could at least use that to nail his ass to the wall at the renegotiations.

I smiled grimly. Good to know my death would be good for something.

The crowd shuffled forward a little farther and I tried to curb my impatience. At least the stench of too many colognes and eager sweat somewhat lessened the oily reek of the burning torches and the darker stinks of the cobbled street. But the musky combination did nothing to ease me,

only reminded me I was surrounded by those drawn to the
Night World. Surrounded by danger.

I wanted to raise my head, scan the rooftops, see if I
could spot Guy. Tempting, yet I set my jaw and kept my
eyes forward. One, I didn't have a chance of seeing a Templar who wanted not to be seen and two, I shouldn't be
drawing attention to myself. All the Nightseekers were
staring toward the door of the Assembly as though it were
the gate to heaven.

Which it just might be if you had an extremely perverted
view of the perfect afterlife.

Personally I thought spending eternity—or close enough
to it—as a vampire sounded like hell. Cut off from the light
and the day and everything human. Thank you, but no. Not
a choice I would ever make. And the thought of *her* surrounded by all that darkness made me want to hurt something.

Guy was right. Unholy fucking insane.

Chapter Four

)

The smell of incense and human sweat swirled around me, clinging to my skin as I made my way downstairs from Lucius' office, fighting the need to wince with every step despite my cautious pace. I couldn't afford to let anyone see I was hurt. When surrounded by predators, never show weakness. Never be the slow, sick calf at the edge of the herd.

I resisted the urge to touch my neck, to see if the bite marks were still there, branding me. It would only draw the exact kind of attention I wished to avoid. The bites are supposed to heal almost instantly, but I had no way of determining if they had. I had pulled my collar high around my neck; it would have to suffice.

Slow deep breaths kept me focused as I navigated carefully through the room, trying to ensure that no one brushed against me. I longed for the cool gray of the shadow where, removed from the needs of flesh, I could think without pain clouding each breath. Where the brush of my clothes against my skin didn't hurt. But no doubt Lucius had his spies throughout the assembled throng. They would be watching. He might even be watching from his aerie of an office, high above the crowds.

I needed time to think. To plan. I'd never managed to fall this far from his favor before. Worse, I'd never aroused his blood hunger. Prey indeed.

I fought the urge to shiver as the memory of the look in

Lucius' eyes as I left returned. There was nothing good in that expression. He had always viewed me as a possession but a worthy one. What if I was now merely food?

No. I would not be. I would find a way to deter him.

Lucius had released me without giving me a target, so I assumed I was free. I wasn't going to leave—that would merely give him a reason to find fault if he changed his mind and I couldn't be summoned at a snap of his fingers.

So free but trapped here at Halcyon amongst the Nightseekers and the Blood. The masses amused themselves with the pseudocourtly intricacies of the Blood dances, but no one would ask me. No one ever asked me. It was no great loss. I didn't dance even though I enjoyed the music. Tonight, my set-apart status was a blessing. I doubted I'd be able to stand the length of a set even if Lucius himself ordered me to take the floor.

My gaze fell on the curtained alcoves lining the walls. Private little spaces for couples and small groups to steal away and have sex or feed or partake in any number of other activities.

A perfect lair to lie low in for a while and catch my breath. There I could shadow, gain some relief from the pain and shock riding my body, and gather my thoughts. I scanned the row, looking for any that didn't have a privacy lamp glowing red above the door. There. One almost on the end of the row was still dark

I sped up my efforts to get through the crowd, enduring the resulting small bumps and jostles with gritted teeth. As I reached the alcove, someone cannoned into me from behind. Pain flared and my temper along with it. I turned to see who was seeking an early death, only to find myself staring into an all-too-familiar pair of sky blue eyes.

"You!" My brain froze, then thawed, ratcheting into gear. I grabbed his arm and yanked him into the alcove, slapping the privacy lamp into life and triggering the spell for the aural shields a second after that. "What, in the name of hell, are you doing here?" He obviously had a death wish.

Simon—no, the *sunmage*; that was safer—looked slightly stunned. His hair was darkened by dye or magic to a shade near to black, but that only made his eyes a brighter blue against golden skin.

He smiled, his face filling with warmth in the dim light. "I came to return your dagger."

My hand dropped to the empty space I'd been all too aware of all night. "And what makes you think I won't just use it on you?"

"You didn't kill me yesterday."

He was so full of life and confidence part of me wanted to slap him. But another part wanted to let him show me how to feel like that. That part made me want to slap myself. Survival. That was the business I was in. The sunmage wasn't an option. "That was yesterday. Perhaps I've been made to see the error in my ways."

He frowned and stepped closer. "Did he hurt you?"

I moved out of reach. "No. But you should leave before he hurts you." I watched him as I lied. I didn't know a lot about human healers. Could he sense my pain? Smell the fear sweat still dampening my clothes? I didn't want his concern. Or his help. Or his death on my conscience.

He needed to leave.

I looked around. Some of the alcoves had discreet exits to the rear, doors hidden in the velvet drapery, to facilitate covert meetings and departures. This did not appear to be one of them. Simon would have to leave the same way he'd entered. I gestured to the door. "Go."

"Don't you want your knife, then?"

"Dagger," I corrected him, feeling its lack like I'd lost a hand rather than a mere weapon.

"Is there a difference?"

The idiot doesn't even know a knife from a dagger. He stood there, hands in the pockets of ridiculous black leather trousers, preposterous black hair rumpled, watching me with a casual air as though he wasn't standing in the middle of enemy territory. He even had a black metal disc—the latest fashion amongst the Nightseekers—hanging from a cord at his throat. He probably thought he blended in.

He shouldn't have been let out on his own, sunmage or no.

And I should not be feeling a distinct urge to move nearer to him. The alcove smelled like sex and blood, both vampire and human. Enough, it seemed, despite the beating, to set my hated hunger prowling again. Simon's scent cut a warm clean note through the musk.

It seemed to promise safety and ease and, yes, pleasure.

None of which was real. Anything I felt was due to Lucius' blood still riding me. Nothing more. An illusion that I would fight, as always.

Anger rose. It was safer than the desire and let me forget the pain. "Do you care?" I asked, not troubling to keep the edge from my voice.

"Do you?"

I hissed and ripped one of the stilettos from the sheath at my thigh. One quick move and its point lay against his throat, precisely at the place where his skin pulsed with the beat of his heart. "This is a stiletto," I said. "Thin. Sharp."

I increased the pressure. Hard enough to make him see I was serious but not enough to cut him. Not yet anyway. I didn't know if the blood of a sunmage would smell different from a normal human's—different enough to stand out in the stink of human blood that filled the Assembly and call attention to us—but I didn't want to risk it. "This has a point. My dagger has two edges. A knife typically has one."

"And you?" he said casually as though my blade wasn't testing his skin. "How many edges do you have?"

His eyes glinted at me. Humor and something else lurked in the blue. Something that called to me. The steady beat of his pulse vibrated up the blade. I wanted to feel that beat skin to skin.

Not real. I shook my head, trying to free myself of the illusion. It didn't exactly work. My hand trembled slightly against the stiletto. Though maybe that was just from the pain in my arm. "Believe me, Simon DuCaine, you do not want to find out."

"Oh, but I do," Simon said. Then his eyes narrowed. "You know my name."

"Yes. Not that it makes any difference to me." I tightened my grip, increased the pressure ever so slightly. If I were smart, I would do it. Plunge the blade into his neck. Spill his blood all over this room. Complete my mission and redeem myself.

Become the weapon again, not the prey.

My hand clenched tighter. *Do it. Do it* now*!*

The words shrieked in my brain. I felt like a chasm had opened beneath my feet, miles deep. If I took this step, if I killed this man whose name came so easily to my tongue, this man who had done nothing to me but offer kindness, offer choice, then I couldn't return. I would fall. I would be Lucius' creature completely. Nothing but darkness.

As soulless as the Fae termed me.

But I would be alive.

"If you're going to do it, make it fast," he said, voice still completely calm.

I snarled, not liking that he knew what I was thinking. "Tell me why I shouldn't?"

"Because you're not who you think you are. You're not who *they* think you are," he said. There was no lightness in his tone now. "You can be more."

I snarled again. But I knew I couldn't do it. I couldn't be the one who killed him. I had always offered Lucius my obedience for his protection, for survival. But something had shifted between us tonight, perhaps shifted in me as well. And right now the thought of doing his will was unbearable.

I stepped away and sheathed my stiletto, balling my fists. My hands still trembled and I knew I couldn't hide my hurts much longer. My vision was growing blurred at the edges and my head pounded. I had to get him out of Halcyon. Out of my head. "Do not think you know me, sunmage." I was careful not to use his name again.

"Does anyone, Shadow?"

I ignored the question. "If you want to survive another night, I suggest you give me my dagger and leave."

He shrugged, then bent and slid my dagger free of his boot. I wanted to reach for it but forced my hand to remain where it rested on my hip.

"I'm surprised the guards at the door didn't take it from me."

"They would sense no silver."

"And a knife with no silver can do no harm here?"

"At night, here in a Blood Assembly, you would need to be very, very lucky to harm a Blood or Beast Kind with a knife made of anything else." Not with just a human's strength anyway.

"My brother always said I was lucky."

"Did he mention stupid too?" I asked, watching the blade. I wanted it. But I did not want to have to take it from him. Hurt as I was, I wasn't at all sure I could.

He grinned, the smile lighting his face the way it always did. "Frequently."

I looked away. No letting myself be caught by the light and warmth in his face. "He must be a good judge of character."

"He likes to think so." He tilted the dagger in his hand, turning it to catch the light. "Not silver. Iron perhaps? Does he set you to hunt the Fae?"

"Most of the Fae have good sense enough not to anger Lucius."

"Most? Do you hunt your own kind, then?" The dagger glinted in the lamplight as he twisted it.

I watched the dagger. In truth it was neither silver nor iron despite its color. No, it was a Fae-wrought thing, gold and other metals shaped by their magics, stronger than any human alloy. Lucius had given it to me. Another way of taunting the Fae. "The Fae would say I am none of theirs."

"So you do hunt them?"

I met that clear blue gaze. "Why do you care?"

"I don't know," he said, truth ringing in the words.

"If I don't need a silver knife to hunt Blood or Beast Kind, what makes you think I would need iron for the Fae?"

I wanted to unsettle him, shake off some of that confidence. Maybe then he wouldn't pull at me so.

"From all I hear, the Fae are hard to kill."

I smiled, baring my teeth. "For a human perhaps." Let him think what he would of that. In truth, Lucius had never set me on one of the Veiled World. The few of them weak enough to need to fear him were not stupid enough to cross him. And in truth the relations between the Fae and the Blood were tied and cross-tied with history and a healthy respect for the power of the Veiled World.

Simon stayed silent. He didn't make any move to pass me the dagger. Perhaps I should take it from him after all. I could hear his heartbeat, not entirely at a normal pace for all his air of ease and bravado.

"A waltz," he said finally.

"Pardon?"

He cocked his head toward the door. "They're playing a waltz."

The aural shields kept our conversation private but the sounds of the Assembly were still audible. "Yes. Lucius prefers waltzes."

One corner of his mouth turned up. "Strange. So do I."

I didn't want to think about him dancing. Moving with someone, free and clear beneath a sunny sky. "Perhaps you should ask him to partner you. Since you seem intent on destruction."

"I've survived thus far."

"Then you shouldn't continue to tempt fate. Something tells me the Lady won't keep rolling in your favor."

His knuckles whitened against the dagger's haft. "Has he asked you to try again?"

"Why would I tell you if he had?" I tried to sound menacing. I wanted him to *go*. The longer we stood here, the more I struggled with the pain and the need. I wanted to either sink to the floor or fall into his arms. And would rather die before I let myself do either.

"Would you do it? Kill me?"

No, was the immediate protest that sprang to mind. But it would be completely foolish to let him see that. "I generally do as Lucius wishes."

"Why?"

"Because I am his."

His face darkened and I had to set my teeth against the urge to try to bring back the smile instead.

"People don't belong to anyone." Certainty and something close to anger deepened his voice.

"I'm not a person—"

"Not a human," he corrected.

And why, by the lords of hell, had I been unlucky enough to cross paths with one of the few humans who could make that distinction? "No," I agreed. "Regardless. I don't live in your world. Trust me, in the Night World the rules are different."

"Then you should leave it."

My mouth dropped open. "Did this brother who thinks you're so lucky drop you on your head when you were small perhaps? No one leaves Lucius."

His mouth quirked slightly. "There's always a first time."

"Unlike you, I have no desire to die. Now give me that, and go. Forget you ever came."

"And spend every night wondering if I'm going to wake up with your blade at my throat?"

"If you don't leave, you won't have to wonder. You'll be dead."

"Come with me." His face was now devoid of humor.

I could only stare at him as the words hung between us. Go with him? Did he truly live in a world where he thought there was any way under the sun or moon that such a thing could end well? "Then we'd both be dead. Go." I held out my hand.

Simon ignored my gesture. "I'm serious. You could leave this place."

"And what exactly is it that you think I would do in the human world? I doubt anyone would welcome Lucius' former assassin into their lives."

"Acceptance takes time. But it can be earned."

I couldn't decipher the expression on his face other than he seemed to be serious. I frowned. "It's hard to be accepted if you're dead. Lucius will not let me go. You need to leave."

He pressed his lips together, then sighed. For a moment he looked almost guilty, his hand toying with the disc at his neck, but then he straightened, face clearing, and passed me the dagger. As I took it, his other hand snaked out and circled my wrist. It hurt, but beyond that, it felt good. Warm human skin against mine. I wondered if I felt cold to him. I hoped so. Anything to make him stop making me want things that could never be and go away so my world would return to normality. To safety.

"Come with me," he repeated.

"Perhaps there was a whole tribe of brothers who damaged your brains repeatedly?" I pulled tentatively, braced for the inevitable jolt of pain, hoping he'd release me. His grip stayed fast. "You don't know me, sunmage. If you did, you wouldn't want me anywhere near you."

He shook his head. "You're wrong about that."

"What you think doesn't change anything. Go."

"No."

"Come with you and what, warm your bed? Is that what you want?" I didn't know what else he could seek to gain from me.

He looked away—just for an instant—and I knew I'd scored a hit. He wanted me. Foolish. He should learn to think with his head. If he knew the truth about me, knew my dirty little secret, he wouldn't want to touch me.

"I want to help you."

The words hurt. I was trying to be logical, but he kept slipping under my defenses. "You can't. So please go." We'd been talking too long now. Sooner or later Lucius would call for me. He loved to flaunt me, his tame wraith, his blade over his enemies—particularly when he knew I didn't want to be flaunted. It would be typical of him to call for me to-night when he knew I would struggle to hide what he'd done to me.

I twisted my wrist, trying to make Simon let go. Instead, I only managed to succeed in making my sleeve slide from beneath his hand, baring my forearm and the bruises start-ing to bloom against my skin.

Simon froze. Then his hold gentled. His other hand started to rise, then dropped back. His eyes blazed heated blue. "What did he do to you?"

"How do you know that isn't from you restraining me?"

He leaned closer, studying my wrist. "I was careful and I know fresh bruises when I see them." His voice had deep-ened again, rumbling with anger. "What. Did. He. Do?"

"You don't—"

From outside the chamber came a crash of breaking glass followed by an earth-shattering roar.

Simon's grip slackened, his hand lifting to tap the disc at his neck again. "What was that?"

I pulled my hand back, sheathing my dagger with the ease of long practice. Another roar shook the air. "It's probably Pierre Rousselline and his pack. Trouble. You re-ally should go now."

"I'm not going anywhere by myself," I said as the sounds of fighting grew louder. I knew exactly what had caused the disruption. When I'd triggered the charm at my neck, its twin, fastened round Guy's, would've let him know that we were moving to Plan B. He'd have set whatever diversion he'd planned in motion and be on his way to help me take Shadow out of here any way we could.

Though I had to admit, the gap between me triggering the charm and the fight seemed almost too quick. Perhaps

Shadow was right. Perhaps it was a Beast Kind riot, breaking out right now. Which would mean she was wrong about the Lady not rolling in my favor for much longer. Though just what interest the Veiled Lady of the Fae—goddess of luck and fate—might have in me, escaped me right now.

No matter. I figured I had only a few minutes before Guy arrived and I'd be forced to knock her out. Five minutes to try again to convince my reluctant shadow to come away with me. I couldn't tell her the truth of what we wanted from her. That would only ensure her resistance, and fighting our way out of Halcyon would hardly constitute a stealthy getaway.

No point letting Lucius know exactly who Shadow had left with. Because she would be leaving with me. I wasn't going to leave her here to be hurt again.

To be beaten again. Lucius' work, no doubt. Nausea rolled through my stomach. How had I missed the signs initially? Gods.

The rigid posture she'd maintained during our ... discussion wasn't rejection of me, or a warrior's alert wariness; it was the careful stance of someone who didn't want to move too far because it hurt. I knew that look. The same way I knew the too pale color of her face and the faint sheen of sweat on her brow.

Not heat from the lamps.

Pain.

And I'd kept her standing there arguing for how long now? Too busy admiring the sleek lines of her body in dark leather and black linen, the contrast of her fire-touched hair against pale skin, to notice what any first-year student healer would have discerned.

Was I really so distracted by her mere presence?

Idiot.

But I didn't mean to keep being one. She was leaving with me. Whether she wanted to or not.

I had a powder in my pocket that would almost certainly knock her out if I blew it into her face, but I didn't really want to render her unconscious. It would be easier if she came willingly, though I doubted she would. She stood a few feet away, looking as though she was regretting the fact that she hadn't killed me already.

I slid my hand down to my knife, readying myself. I had

no doubt she could kill. Despite her injuries, every sleek muscled inch of her had come to attention at the first roar. She held the dagger like an extension of her arm. A trained warrior, the way Guy was.

Guy, who'd be here any second.

Gods and suns. One last shot to convince her.

I thought fast. She hadn't killed me. She wanted me gone. So I could use that. Play on her sympathy. Let her think I needed her help to get out of here. Get her closer to an exit, then knock her out if I had to.

"Is there a back entrance?" I asked, trying to sound nervous. In truth, I was nervous. Just not about the fighting.

"No." She shook her head, strands of red falling across her face. One hand pushed them away impatiently. "You should go now. This will get violent."

There was another roar and something crashed nearby with a force that shook the walls of the alcove.

"Sounds like it's violent already. Can you help me get to the door? Without getting hurt?"

She rolled her eyes. "They can't hurt me, idiot."

"Because you've got your little dagger?" I snapped, reaching for my own knife, which was bigger and nastier than hers. Then I remembered I was meant to be acting more helpless than I was.

"No, because I can do this."

She faded from sight.

"Mother of—" I stopped myself midcurse. She'd disappeared.

Gods and fucking suns.

I'd known a wraith could do that, of course, but getting a half glimpse of her at night in my bedroom was different from seeing her suddenly vanish. Gooseflesh prickled my neck. "Are you still here?" As questions went, it felt foolish, but her sudden disappearance had me off balance.

"Yes." Her voice didn't sound any less exasperated for coming out of thin air. "Wait here, I'll see what's going on."

Walk through the bloody wall, that's what she meant. I tightened my grip on my dagger. I hadn't brought a focus for my sunlight; there'd been no way to get into the Assembly with something that reeked of magery. The charm around my neck was Fae work, unexceptional, low-level magic that wouldn't draw attention. Without a focus, there was no way for me to access the sun here. Which meant my knife and Shadow's were the only things improving our chances of getting out of here unscathed.

It seemed to take an endless time before she suddenly appeared again. I didn't jump a second time.

She looked pleased. "The fight's moving away, toward the ballroom."

"That's a good thing?"

"It means you've got a clear path to the door. I'm going to take down the privacy shield. Then when I say go, you go. I'll watch your back. If you keep your head down, you'll be fine."

"I'm not leaving you here." It was wrong. I knew it. She wasn't supposed to live with the monsters. To hell with what she could do for us, or what she had done. I didn't care. I wasn't going to leave her alone and hurt amidst a riot. I wasn't going to leave her to Lucius.

To destruction.

Harm to none.

I wasn't going to fail this time.

She scowled. "You don't have a choice. Now stop wasting time. On three, all right?"

Time. Guy. Right. I'd really hoped it wouldn't come to this. Once we went through that door and Guy found us, there was no turning back from our plan. "On three."

She counted slowly and I was ready when she reached three. The door opened and I ducked through, scanning quickly to get my bearings. The exit to the Assembly was to my right, an easy sprint, except for the panicked crowd surging around us.

Cover and camouflage, moron. Guy's voice in my head again. Indeed. Remember my lessons. Use the crowd.

For ten seconds or so, it went well. I found gaps in the crowd, shoving and punching when I had to and avoiding the small pockets of fighting. Better still, she was following. Maybe this would work after all.

I took another step; then something shoved me in the back with the force of a mule kick.

"Get down!" Shadow yelled as I sprawled forward.

Shock ran up my arm as I caught myself, but I ignored it and used the impetus to propel myself back to my feet. I twisted frantically and there she was, solid in black, dagger slashing almost too fast to follow as she confronted a Beast Kind in hybrid form.

I'd never seen one up close, but there was nothing else a six-foot–tall, furred, slavering man-thing could be.

It swiped at her and connected with her arm, making her cry out. But she didn't retreat.

"Go!" she yelled again as our eyes met.

The Beast moved forward with a howl and I didn't see how it was going to miss again. Somehow I knew she wouldn't shadow, not when it could get to me through her.

But as the hybrid raised its arm again, it suddenly froze, a puzzled expression on its face. Blood gushed from its mouth. Then it crumpled to the floor, revealing Guy standing there, shoving what had to be a silver dagger back into his belt.

Shadow was staring at Guy with an expression that was some strange mix of respect, wariness, and something else I couldn't quite identify.

At least Guy hadn't drawn his sword. Nothing like a Templar broadsword hacking people down to draw attention.

"Interesting tactics, little brother," Guy said calmly, as though we weren't standing in the middle of a brawl.

I tightened my grip on my dagger and stepped closer to Shadow. "We were doing fine."

Shadow looked from me to Guy as if she wasn't sure exactly what she was seeing.

Guy tapped the disc at his neck and raised an eyebrow. I nodded. Yes. Plan B. Guy jerked his head toward the door. "Let's go."

I reached for Shadow's arm, digging the other hand into my pocket for my knockout powder, determined to take her with us, but I hadn't quite gripped her before something big and wooden sailed through the air from behind, clipping her in the back of the head. The chair—at least that's what I thought it had been originally—changed direction slightly after it hit her and missed me by a hair-breadth.

I didn't waste time as I saw her start to fall, simply swooped forward, caught her, and hoisted her over my shoulder. Problem solved. We had her and we were taking her. I'd deal with the consequences when they came.

"You sure about this?" Guy growled as I adjusted Shadow's unconscious form on my shoulder.

"Completely."

Guy nodded once. "So be it."

We made like hell for the exit.

Chapter Five

)

Warmth on my back. That was the first thing that registered. The second, as I turned my head to figure out the source of the warmth, was a wave of pain from almost every muscle in my body. Lords of hell, what had happened? I cracked one eye open gingerly. The sunmage sat on an old wooden chair next to the bed. That got my attention. Then I remembered.

Lords of *hell*.

"Good morning," he said as I closed my eyes, hoping that I was dreaming.

Nothing changed. I still hurt. Like a whole pack of Beast Kind had trampled me. But no, if memory served it was mostly due to a single vampire. Lucius. My breath hissed as my anger flared at the memory of his beating. So much for dreaming.

I rolled cautiously onto my side, not ready to actually attempt sitting up yet. My right arm, in particular. Someone had apparently replaced my bones with red-hot pokers. I ignored the pain, my brain still assembling facts.

I was not safe in my room in the warrens, I was somewhere else.

In the human world.

With the sunmage.

Hells. Lucius would think I had run. I was a dead woman.

"What did you do?" I said, trying not to groan as I opened my eyes again.

Simon shrugged. "We could hardly leave you there unconscious."

I sat up very carefully, squinting against the unfamiliar light. He didn't waver and fade from view. This was definitely not a dream. More a living nightmare. "Yes. Yes, you could. In fact, any sane person *would*."

"There were rampaging Beast Kind everywhere." He sounded cheerful, but stubble shaded his chin and the shadows under his eyes dulled the blue. His hair was brown-blond once more, stripped of whatever had turned it black. It was an improvement but didn't make him look any less tired.

I wondered if he'd slept at all. Then cursed myself inside my head. What did it matter if he'd slept? It only mattered that I was here instead of where I should be and consequentially hell was going to rain down on all our heads. "I can handle Beasts."

"Unconscious? I'm impressed."

I ignored him. Ignoring insane people was only sensible. Though I did want to know where I was. That way I could work out the fastest way to get back to Sorrow's Hill. Maybe I could return to the warrens before Lucius even realized I was gone. I'd been willing to defy him last night by not killing Simon, but I hadn't wanted to give him a reason to kill me instead. "I assume you weren't foolish enough to take me to your house."

That would be one of the first places Lucius would look if he had noted my absence.

"No," he said. "Guy's."

Guy. For a moment I couldn't remember. Then it hit me. Simon's giant brother. The *Templar*. I had a sudden vision of Guy in the Assembly last night, dagger dripping blood, looking like the wrath of some ancient god—which, technically, he was.

He'd slaughtered a Beast with casual ease, using only a silver dagger. I'd recognized the expression on his face as he'd glanced at the body. He was a killer like me. Someone who met force with force. One who would dispatch his enemies with no remorse.

Enemies like me. Panic flared and I straightened with a jerk that made me hiss as my head threatened to come apart.

"The Brother House?" One Templar was bad enough ... but a whole building full of them? If Simon had brought me to the Templar Brother House, I'd kill him myself. If I had a chance to before the Templars decided to cut off my head.

"No. This is his apartment."

That didn't make me feel much better. Guy had no reason to trust me or extend me any courtesy. Even if he didn't know that I had tried to kill Simon—and at this point I had to assume he didn't or else why was I still breathing?—he might decide to cut off my head without the help of his brethren merely because of who I was. "Whose brilliant idea was that?"

"Mine. Even Lucius isn't crazy enough to attack a Templar directly."

After the previous two nights, I wasn't willing to gamble anything on what Lucius might or might not do. "I wouldn't be so sure about that. I should leave."

Simon shook his head, looking stern. "You don't have to go anywhere. In fact, you shouldn't go anywhere. You took a pretty hard blow to the head. And you weren't in very good shape before that."

This last was accusing, as though he was angry with me. Why? Because I'd lied to him about being hurt? Trying to work it out only made the pain in my head worse as I looked at his grim expression.

Guy was a warrior. Simon, though ... I was not at all sure what he was. He'd overpowered me at his house and he'd been more than adept at working his way through the brawl at Halcyon without even drawing a weapon. Not to be underestimated. Plus, he was a sunmage, commanding the very thing that robbed me of my powers. Yet he was a healer, dedicated to saving lives. A contradiction.

I rubbed my forehead with careful fingers, using my left hand. Even that small movement sent renewed awareness through me of how bruised and battered I was. I reached up and felt the crusted lump on my head with cautious fingers. "I heal fast."

"I beg to differ."

"Excuse me? What do you know about it?"

"I know that I've already spent several hours working on you during the night and you still can't move without groaning."

I set my teeth. "Yes, I can."

He folded his arms and leaned back on the chair, looking grim. "Is that so? Well, then, tell you what. You make it out of that bed and to the door without so much as a wince and I won't stand in your way."

I stared at him, frustration warring with the knowledge that my body wanted to simply lie still and not go anywhere, thank you kindly. Finally I looked away, over his head toward the window. From my position on the bed, I couldn't glimpse much more than a view of sky and a red-brick apartment building across the street. Nothing to reveal our location. Though if Guy lived near the Brother House, then St. Giles or Bellefleurs seemed likely.

"I thought as much," Simon said. "Are you going to be sensible about this?"

Did he really think I would be? I ignored his question and inspected the room instead. The walls were plain white and bare of decoration. Apart from the bed and Simon's chair, the only other furnishings were a rug in shades of gray and blue and a worn wooden chest, dark with age, pushed against one wall. It currently supported a simple white washbasin and a pile of dark leather. My trousers and vest.

The fact that Simon had undressed me almost bothered me more than the fact that he'd kidnapped me. I glared at the leathers, wanting to climb out of bed and drag them on to feel normal again, but that would mean not only moving but doing so clad only in a shirt and my drawers.

My fists clenched, but that only rekindled the fire in my arm. I released them with a muffled curse.

Simon cleared his throat and I turned my head to glare at him instead of my clothes.

"I can help with that. Now that it's light, I can do more." He stood and leaned over me. "May I?"

This I couldn't ignore. I wasn't foolish enough to refuse anything that would return me to full strength. In the light of day, without the shadow, I had to rely on my speed and strength for protection. "Yes."

He stretched his hands toward me, not touching, just hovering over my skin as he skimmed the lines of my body, a small frown of concentration creasing his forehead. His hands paused for a moment over my right arm but then moved up to my head.

The touch, when it came, was light, so light that for a moment I wasn't at all sure if he had actually touched me. Then his hands moved to cradle my head delicately. I squeezed my eyes closed, determined not to smell him, not to breathe him too deep.

Even hurt and exhausted, the need still coiled deep within me, barely contained. I didn't need the nearness of a man to set it off again. I was going back to Lucius before a war began. And before Simon learned the truth about exactly what I was. He wouldn't be so keen to heal me then.

Something akin to a cool breeze flowed over my skull, starting from his hands and radiating from there. The pain receded and I relaxed into the sudden reprieve. Simon's breath deepened and I heard the *thump, thump, thump* as his heartbeat started to race, but he didn't stop. Instead, his hands lifted and moved to clasp my right arm, his touch gentle as if he handled something incredibly fragile. Despite his care, it still hurt, shards of fire stabbing into me. I tensed.

"Relax," he said softly. "The Beast fractured your arm in several places. I worked on it some last night, so this should finish the job." He drew a deep breath, his eyelids lowering slowly. Another rasping breath, then another, and then once again, a cool sensation flowed through my skin, carrying the pain away in its wake. First my arm, then slowly outward across my chest and down my entire body. With each few inches farther, Simon's heart beat faster. Too fast.

The cool slid down to my knees as his heart pounded.

"Enough!" I pulled at my arm, breaking his grip.

Simon gasped, then staggered back a step, groping for the chair before sinking heavily into it.

I pushed myself up. This time the resulting pain was manageable, more the familiar aches and pains that rise after a good fight than the agony of earlier. "Are you all right?"

He summoned a tired-looking smile. Perhaps I was imagining things, but the shadows beneath his eyes were a deeper purple than they had been earlier.

"I'll be fine," he said. "I need to spend some time outside. Then I'll finish the job."

Outside? Oh. Of course, he needed the sun. The source of his power. The enemy of mine. "You shouldn't waste your power on me." His heart still raced, working too hard for a strong man sitting still.

"I'm a healer. It's what I do."

"No matter what your patient may have done?" Did he really help whoever needed it? It seemed unlikely to me. The Blood do little out of altruism. Their world is a careful dance of debt and counterdebt, of favor and deals and self-interest.

He nodded. "No matter what."

Maybe he— No. I wasn't going to think it. He might say no matter what, but I doubted he truly meant it. It was better this way. Better I be nothing more than one more hurt to mend. Still, there was a strange twist of something deep inside to think that maybe his interest in me was merely based on his desire to mend something he saw as broken.

And what would he do once he knew I was beyond fixing? No one had ever broken the grip of the blood. It was why the humans abandoned their blood-locked. Seemed to hate them, almost. Like they would hate me.

I straightened my shoulders. "As I said before, I heal fast. You've helped with the worst of it."

That earned me a sudden scowl. "I said I'll finish the job." His knuckles turned white against the wooden frame of the chair and his heart sped yet again.

He was angry. And he didn't need the strain. Really, his life could only be bettered by letting me go. Which he wasn't going to do in his current mood.

"Where does the pain go?" I asked, trying to divert his attention. Even as I asked, a nasty thought occurred to me.

His expression relaxed fractionally. "Pardon?"

"When you heal? Where does the pain go?" Please let him say that he didn't take it into himself. Insane or not, he didn't deserve to be hurt because of the likes of me.

"Our lore says we give it to the sun."

Thank the night. "It doesn't hurt, then?"

"No. It's merely tiring at times."

"You should go. You need to be outside."

"You won't disappear?" He twisted in the chair, turned his face to the sunlight streaming through the window, and breathed deep. The thump of his pulse slowed, approaching a normal beat.

"I can't. Not in daylight."

His gaze came back to me, eyes serious. "I meant leave."

"I doubt I can waltz out of a Templar's house undetected."

He smiled crookedly. "Perhaps not. You should eat something. The kitchen is down the hall. Guy will feed you."

A breakfast of cold steel, most likely. But I was starving now that I no longer felt the need to vomit with every movement. Might as well die with a full stomach.

Simon left me alone to dress. I wrinkled my nose at the state of my clothing as I climbed out of bed. It stank of pain and fear. But so did I, and sweat besides, so I wouldn't make anything worse by dressing. Still, I sluiced myself down with water from the washbasin, examining myself in the process of drying off.

I had gathered an impressive collection of bruises, but they were faded to yellow and green rather than glowing purple fresh. Painful, but not unbearable. My trousers and vest would sit uncomfortably against them. But leather and my dagger were the closest things I had to armor right now. Once I had them all in place, I made myself leave the bedroom.

I was still stiff and sore, but my head felt clear and my right arm was functional, at least. With some food, my own healing ability might be enough to get me to full strength quickly.

Like the bedroom, the rest of the apartment was sparsely decorated. Utilitarian, almost, and in sharp contrast to Simon's house. No plants. No pictures on the walls. No smells of wax and polish to speak of regular care. I walked down a faded hall runner toward the smell of toasted bread wondering if Guy spent much time here at all.

What did Templars do in their leisure time?

He might well ask the same question of me.

We were both fighters. We both knew death.

The main difference was that he believed in the reasons behind his killings.

I . . . well, right now, in this place, I wasn't sure what I believed.

True to Simon's word, Guy was in the kitchen, sitting at a battered wooden table, oiling his sword. A solid-looking pistol—the twin of Simon's if I wasn't mistaken—lay next to the rags and cleaning paraphernalia. Taking no chances apparently. Besides the weapons, looking slightly out of place, was a plate with crumbs and a crust or two, suggesting a pile of toast had been demolished recently.

My stomach rumbled at the thought of food, but I stayed put, eyeing the long blade. I could use a sword. Even though, in my line of work, the dagger was usually all I needed, I made sure I was well versed in the use of all weapons. But I doubted I'd even be able to lift this one. You could roast a pig on it. It would skewer me before I got anywhere near the gun. I swallowed hard, then finally spoke. "Good morning."

Guy studied me for a long moment. You could tell he and Simon were brothers, despite the fact that Guy was built on heavier lines. He had the same golden coloring, though in him, the tones transmuted somewhat. His hair was lighter than Simon's and his eyes a paler blue. A wintry sky, not a summer one. No warmth here. Perhaps only cold, righteous fire.

Wariness pricked the back of my neck as he regarded me. Finally he spoke. "Good morning. You seem recovered." His voice was lower than Simon's and his accent was tinged with something I didn't recognize that loosened his vowels and made them twang. He'd spent quite some time out of the City, I'd wager, to lose the more cultured tones of his brother. Despite the accent, his voice was cool.

"Simon healed me," I said, folding my arms.

"I expected as much. Where is he?" His voice warmed a little. Perhaps he wasn't completely cold. Not if he cared for his brother.

"He said something about going outside."

Guy shook his head. "Damn sunmages. They're all half cat."

I cocked my head. Some of the Blood kept cats. Lithe, dark, slinking things, whose eyes reflected mirrored gleams from the dimmest corners of the warrens. I couldn't think of anything with less resemblance to Simon.

Guy must have read my confusion. "Haven't you ever seen a cat basking in a sunbeam?"

I shook my head. "There aren't many sunbeams where I live."

He arched a scarred eyebrow at me. "Guess not. Well,

that's where he'll be, outside in the sunniest spot he can find. Good thing your boss' boys don't get around much in daylight."

"Yes."

Guy shoved the chair opposite him out from the table with his foot. "Sit." It was a command, his voice cooling again.

I obeyed, focusing on the long, steady strokes of his whetstone over the steel. The smell of metal and oil and gunpowder tickled my nose. Dangerous. My hunger died somewhat. "Are you going to kill me?"

The stone paused and I looked up to meet that cool blue assessing gaze.

"My brother seems to think there's good in you."

I said nothing.

"For now, I'll take silence as assent to that assessment."

"I—"

He raised a hand, cutting me off before I could say anything foolish. "Don't make me regret that decision. Or Simon. This was his idea."

He didn't look happy about it. Wrestling with family versus faith? He'd supported Simon at the Assembly last night, but that didn't necessarily mean he would continue to do so. I was a creature of the Night World. One who worked for someone who was a prime example of the dangers of that world.

The very dangers Templars swore to defend humanity from. Guy obviously valued his family, but I doubted he would let that regard turn him oath breaker if I gave him a reason to believe I was a threat.

He would roll over me like a blizzard and feel as little regret as ice.

"But you helped him. Why?"

"Let's just say I'm willing to suspend judgment for the moment."

I let go of the breath I'd been unaware I was holding.

"Mind you," Guy added, resuming his cleaning with another slide of the stone, "my brother's instincts only earn you a temporary reprieve. Permanent mercy has to be earned." His eyes were suddenly intent.

"Earned?" I tensed, making myself watch him, not the movement of his hands. Each pass of the stone felt as though my nerves, rather than the blade under his fingers, were being ground. What did he mean earned?

He nodded. "If you betray him, hurt him, play him for a fool . . . well, I'll come down on you—"

"With the wrath of your God?"

"Exactly."

I relaxed a little. He was worried about Simon. About what I might do. He was warning me to behave. That much I understood. "Your brother was the one who dragged me here unconscious," I said. "I didn't ask him to."

He put down the stone, tapped his fingers on the hilt of the sword in a movement a little too close to grip-and-swing for my comfort. "You'd rather be with Lucius?"

Did I *want* to be with Lucius? No. Not after last night. I only just stopped myself from rubbing my neck where he'd fed, forcing my hand to my shoulder instead as a chill went through me. Lucius had fed from me. I'd seen that strange hunger in his eyes.

I could take being beaten, could even take the humiliation of the need, but this was different.

I doubted I would survive it in the long run.

So, no, I didn't *want* to go back. But Guy had asked would I rather and that implied a choice.

A choice I didn't have.

I had to return to Lucius. The hunger would drive me to it. I'd never heard of anyone curing the need. It would be better for Simon if I left now, before he found out the truth. And better for me to return as fast as possible before Lucius' anger grew too great. But still I hesitated.

"Is silence yes or no in this case?" Guy asked.

"It's not that simple."

His right hand curled around the sword hilt. "Didn't think it was. The way I hear it, you belong to Lucius. Never known him to show reason about anything much. Or let anything he wanted go easily."

I watched his hand, seeking any sign that he might be getting ready to use the sword rather than just hold it. "No."

"Then again, neither have I known myself to want to make things easier for him. Without you, he's weakened. That's good for us."

Ah. So I was a strategic advantage. It wasn't just his brother he acted for. I didn't know if that was better or worse. It did mean I needed to be even more careful around Guy. He would play to his own agenda. For some reason, that made me feel slightly more at ease. I was used to agendas.

"You don't want a territorial war between the Blood." Which is what would happen if Lucius fell. Those with ambition, those who waited, would seize the chance for power. In the early years, when I'd first come to Lucius, he'd been challenged once or twice. And he'd laid waste to those challengers, pursuing those who'd rebelled with a near obsessional focus. I'd been too young then for him to use me in his war, but I remembered Blood with horrible injuries that took even them time to heal. Remembered Blood and Trusted who disappeared altogether. Remembered what Lucius had done to the ringleaders of those who opposed him. You could have painted every wall in the warrens red with the blood he spilled. The fight to replace him would be equally bloody.

Guy smiled and flattened his other hand on the table, giving me a clear view of the crimson cross tattooed there. His smile wasn't a pleasant expression. In fact, it was downright feral. "Says who?"

"I thought Templars were meant to keep the peace." I looked at the cross, wondering how much it hurt to have that done. Wondered exactly what rank Guy held in the Templars. Did he have other tattoos besides his hands? Crosses to seal heart and body to the service of his God? "This is a treaty year."

In fact, we were only three months or so before the official negotiation period, where the terms of the treaties—trade and territory and allowances of silver and iron for the humans amongst other things—would be set for the next three years. "I can't imagine your government or the Fae want the Blood to be . . . unsettled . . . for that."

The delicate balance of the City was maintained by the treaties, allowing all four races to live in something like harmony. Proven transgressions by any of the races were punished with cuts to their privileges. The humans could lose their precious iron and silver rations—key to so much of their industry and their protections against the rest of us. Similarly, Fae or Blood or Beast offenses might result in the humans winning concessions or territories being reduced. The negotiations were too important to risk.

His smile didn't change, but somehow it suddenly felt colder, more dangerous. "Political policy isn't something that I'm going to discuss with you. Though it would be wise to remember that political policy is not the only thing that Templars care about."

Meaning that they would do what they thought served the Church and humanity first? I had no idea where that left me. Other than having to fend for myself as always. My dagger suddenly felt heavy against my hip. If I were wise I would simply get up from the table and leave. I would have done it if I weren't fairly sure Guy would try to stop me. And that, in daylight, he'd likely succeed. "I see Simon's not the only reckless one in the family. It would be safer for everyone if I went."

One shoulder hitched and he looked down at the sword, working the cloth over a small spot near the pommel. "Maybe. Then again, I get the feeling that it wouldn't be so safe for you. Plus, I'd probably wind up having to drag Simon's sorry arse out of an Assembly again. He doesn't give up easily."

That much I had gathered. I shook my head at Guy. "Can't you talk sense to him?"

That brought those ice blue eyes back to mine, the oily cloth crumpling in his fist. "Is his faith in you misplaced?"

"I don't know much about faith. But you know what I am. What I do."

He nodded. "Yes. You kill. So do I."

"You kill for your God." Gods were one thing I'd never bothered to believe in. None of them had ever lifted a finger to help me.

"I kill to protect people."

"I kill because I'm told to."

"You follow orders."

"Orders from a Blood Lord. Not from your God."

"Not mine. Everyone's," Guy said. "You have a choice in the matter? Other than dying?"

"Not really. And your God wouldn't want anything to do with me."

He smiled and suddenly the resemblance to Simon was very strong. There was warmth and light and peace in that smile.

"My God believes in redemption. What matters is what people do when they are given a chance to change for the better. What they do with their choices. You're being given a choice here."

"If I stay here, there'll be consequences. People might die. That's not a good choice."

"No one ever said redemption was easy. People will die if you return to Lucius, won't they?"

But maybe not me. And that was exactly the kind of thought that made me a less than perfect candidate for redemption of any kind.

Guy started rubbing the sword with the cloth, long, easy strokes, watching what he was doing carefully as if giving me some privacy to think. I remembered what he'd said about having to earn permanent mercy. If I said I was going back to Lucius, then I knew the next time Lucius set me on a human that it was likely that the Templars would come after me.

Didn't mean that they'd catch me, but it would make life difficult.

Just as having Lucius after me if I stayed here would make life difficult.

So, which should I choose? The known or the unknown? The sunmage and his unfounded faith in me? Or the familiar and unstable Blood Lord?

There was something about Simon that pulled at me, I could admit that much. Lucius' blood might be complicating and amplifying matters now, but I'd been drawn to Simon the night we'd met and I couldn't blame the need for that; I'd still had it controlled at that point. Simon had made it clear that he wanted me to stay.

But he didn't know me. He was acting on whatever pretty fantasy he'd spun in his head about me. The damsel in distress and the valiant knight who saves her. What would he think if he knew the truth about me? Knew what I'd done? Knew about the blood? Both that which I'd spilled and that which kept me bound to Lucius.

Humans weren't kind to the blood-locked. There was no cure for the addiction, and most who walked that path were given up as dead by their families. Which was a reasonable response. Better to sever the ties, to grieve and move on, than know your son or daughter or sister or brother was destined to be cattle. An easy source of food. The Blood preferred to create more Blood from humans who weren't addicted, which is why they fed from the Trusted but did not feed them in return until it came time to turn them. Less chance of creating something insane.

There had never been love between the Blood and the humans, and the losses the humans suffered from the Blood's seduction of the Nightseekers and the blood-locked only fed the enmity. There had been wars between the species in the past. The peace of the last fifty years or so was largely maintained by the convoluted rules set out by the treaties.

The Blood obeyed most of the time. The humans tried to make their people conform through social pressures, but the numbers of Nightseekers remained fairly constant. There would always be those willing to risk—or abandon—their daylight human lives for the lure of the Night World. Some, a much smaller number, even chose the enchantments of the Veiled World. Humans were at the biggest disadvantage of the races. If not for their numbers and their mages, they would've been subjugated long before. But they had survived.

So, where did I belong?

"Did he feed you?"

I jumped at the voice. Was I so distracted that someone could sneak up on me? Careless. Very careless. Such a slip could be fatal. I turned.

Apparently the sunlight had worked its magic. Simon lounged against the doorframe looking bright and golden once more in neat gray trousers and a comfortably worn blue jacket over his white shirt. No stinking leathers for him.

I wished I could simply soak up some sun and have everything feel better. "We were . . . talking," I said.

I heard a soft click behind me as though Guy had put down his sword. Then wood creaked. My spine prickled. Was he easing back in his chair or standing? Armed Templar at my rear. Not a thought conducive to comfort, but I stayed facing Simon. Surely he wouldn't let Guy do anything? Simon smiled at me, positively radiating energy.

"She won't want to stay if you starve her and wave your sword at her." Simon frowned over my head at his brother.

Guy snorted. "I don't think she scares easily."

He sounded amused. I relaxed a little.

"Maybe. But I'll bet she eats." Simon focused back on me, frown deepening. "You do, don't you?"

"Yes. I eat." I could go for longer than a human without doing so thanks to my Fae blood. A trait that had stood me in good stead from time to time on long hunts, but eventually I needed food.

But it was a long time since my lone bowl of stew, and healing took sustenance. I was starving. I sat down in the chair with a nod. "Yes," I repeated. "I definitely eat."

"Excellent." He smiled. "How do you feel about eggs?"

Promising breakfast might have been too hasty, I thought, surveying the contents of Guy's pantry. Three brown eggs sat next to half a loaf of bread that had seen better days. No herbs, no jam. Plenty of tea and the vile chicory coffee Guy favored. Maybe there would be milk, butter, and cheese in the cool box.

I stared at the bare shelves, not yet ready to turn around. Not until I was sure the relief I'd felt on seeing Shadow sitting there at Guy's table wasn't written all over my face.

I'd thought she might well run. Yet she was still here. Of course, she didn't yet know what we wanted from her.

I hadn't yet determined how best to tell her that particular piece of information. Guy had agreed to give me a few days to convince her, but that hardly seemed long enough.

But she was still here. Every minute she was still here was a chance to convince her to stay for the minute after that.

Unfortunately, it wasn't going to be a bountiful breakfast doing the convincing.

Still, I didn't care if I was being recklessly optimistic. Regardless of whether she helped us, taking Shadow—gods and suns, I needed to find out her damned name—had been the right thing to do. I turned to shake my head at Guy. "Remind me to talk to Mother about hiring you a servant. One who might provide food occasionally—"

Pounding on the door interrupted me.

Shadow was out of the chair, hand on her dagger, before I could blink. Guy wasn't much slower. Sword in one hand, pistol in the other, every inch the warrior, even though he wore nothing more than a loose shirt and ancient trousers.

Beside him, Shadow looked small, though no less ready. Or deadly.

My own pistol was under the sofa I'd slept on. Out of reach. Suns. At least I still had the dagger from last night.

Shadow looked at Guy. "Are you expecting someone?"

"No." Guy glanced at her, then nodded once and tossed me the gun. "Take her out through the garden."

The pounding started again. "Guy, we know you're in there. Open up."

Guy's shoulders relaxed a fraction. "Templars," he said softly, and Shadow turned pale, looking poised to flee.

Thank God she couldn't use her powers right now or she'd be gone and I'd lose my chance.

But pale as she was, she stood her ground as she focused toward the door. "I smell Beast Kind." Her voice was even softer than Guy's.

"Templars don't work with the Beasts," Guy said.

"Then maybe those aren't your Templars. Or the Beast might be glamoured and unseen."

I tightened my grip on the gun. Guy's apartment was well warded, but that only helped prevent anything from entering, not from surrounding them. "Why would a Beast be here?"

Both Shadow and Guy looked at me as if I were lacking my wits. I shook my head at them. "Yes, obviously they're after her, but what I meant was, how would they know where we were?"

"Guy isn't exactly inconspicuous. Someone must have seen you at Halcyon. They could be here for him just as easily as me," Shadow said.

"Then why wait until now to make a move? If they waited for daylight, it would seem more likely it's you they're after."

She shrugged. "It may have taken them some time to find out where Guy lived."

"Or those are just Templars out there," Guy said, looking skeptical.

Shadow hitched one shoulder. "Maybe. But I smell Beast."

"Do the Templars know about her?" I ground the words through gritted teeth. I'd hoped Guy would keep his mouth shut about Shadow, but I'd known he would follow his own code of honor. He had given his oath not to hurt her, but that didn't mean he wouldn't report our plan to the Abbott General. And he'd left the apartment for a time earlier.

A shrug. Then Guy's eyes moved to Shadow. "Time to choose. If those are Templars out there, then I can talk them round if you're staying. If it's a Beast, I can buy you some time. Are you in or out?"

"What are you talking about?" I snarled. "Either way, we're not handing her over."

Guy lifted his eyebrows at this, but Shadow shook her head at both of us. "I'm in."

Guy gave a curt nod. "Right. So get going, little brother. Just remember what we talked about. Take her somewhere safe."

Easier said than done. If Shadow was right and Lucius already knew where she was and was willing to come up against a Templar to get her back, then not many places in the city would meet that definition.

Still, I could worry about that once we were safely gone from here. I grabbed her arm and ran.

Chapter Six

)

Simon dragged me helter-skelter through the apartment, out a back door—I should've known a Templar wouldn't have a home with only one exit—and down several flights of stairs to another heavy wooden door.

"Wait," I said as he reached for the handle.

"What?"

"Let me check first." I gestured for him to move back.

He stood his ground. "How? You can't do your disappearing act in daylight."

I ducked around him. "No, but my ears and nose are a lot more sensitive than yours." I moved closer to the door, sniffed the faint drift of air traveling from outside. It smelled clean. Like sun-warmed brick and grass and flowers. None of the musky earth smell of a Beast. Maybe they didn't know about the back entrance.

Or maybe Lucius had sent Trusted with the Beasts. Not that I could detect any fresh human scents either. Just Simon behind me, a smell I did my best to ignore before the need could latch on to it.

It didn't really matter what waited for us. We were safer on the run than trapped in a stairway. Still, I wished I had more weapons than just my dagger and the stilettos. I hoped Simon knew how to do more than twirl a pistol. Templar training should mean he was competent, and he'd fought well at Halcyon, but still ... the thought of going out into the daylight with only my daggers and Simon's gun made my skin crawl. Unpleasant choices seemed to be my fate right now.

I unsheathed my dagger. "All right. Let's go."

I threw open the door and we bolted out into the tangled garden. Simon grabbed for my hand and led the way. No Beasts appeared from between the neat rows of trees that lined the fence either side of the long lot. We didn't stop until we'd boosted ourselves over the fence and put several blocks between us and Guy's building.

With every step I wondered what, in the names of the lords of hell, I had done.

Agreed to stay here.

Signed my own death warrant with Lucius probably.

Signed my own death warrant with the Templars if I turned around and changed my mind.

Doomed myself either way.

Not a situation I was reconciled to.

I needed a plan.

First things first, survive the next few hours and days. Stay. Temporarily. Until Lucius got bored and Simon and Guy lowered their guard. Then I could run. Would run. Need be damned.

There were other cities. Other places my skills could be valuable.

Places I'd be alone. I slapped the thought away. I'd always been alone at the heart of it.

Ahead of me, Simon slowed. I looked around, trying to get my bearings. Back in the direction we'd come, the Cathedral spire poked up above the surrounding buildings. Guy's place obviously wasn't too far from the Brother House after all.

In the distance, hills rose behind the city. That way was Summerdale. West. Entrance to the Veiled World. Which meant we were heading into one of the rougher border boroughs, Lower Watt or Mickleskin, depending on our exact location. Boroughs where the edges of Night World and human territories blurred.

Good. Residents of the border boroughs kept their heads down and didn't ask questions. The weapons we were carrying wouldn't particularly make us stand out. On the other hand, there could be Trusted out and about. Or more Beast Kind. Likely would be, if my nose was right and there was a Beast at Guy's.

If it hadn't already gotten past him. My spine crawled and I tried to shake off the sensation of being followed. Guy was a Templar. He would hold.

I hurried my stride, caught up to Simon. "It isn't safe here. We could be seen."

"I know."

He didn't look glowing and happy anymore. In fact, he looked as close to furious as I'd seen him. "We need a 'cab or a hackney."

I wasn't going to argue with that. The problem might be finding one in this part of the City. Still, in full day, there might be some enterprising—or foolhardy—drivers out and about.

If they were around, they'd stick to the busier areas. "We might have a better chance near a station or hostel. Where's the nearest underground?"

Simon paused, doing the same rapid scan of our immediate surroundings as I had. Then he pointed. "Melchior's a few streets west."

Melchior. The station was nearly the center of the City, and the tracks that spat out of its tunnels heading north and south along the Great Northern Line almost precisely defined the boundary of day and night. Neutral territory but guaranteed to have both humans and Night Worlders crowding its platforms. Not my first choice but we didn't have many alternatives.

"Can you do anything to change our appearance?" I said, trying to think.

"No." Simon shook his head. "My talents never ran much to glamours."

Hell. There was nothing for it, then. We would walk until we found transport.

We set off, Simon leading. I didn't mind. At this point any attack seemed more likely to come from someone trailing us from Guy's than a frontal assault. Apparently the Lady liked Simon after all, because we'd only been walking a minute or so when a 'cab appeared on the horizon and actually stopped when Simon hailed it.

The driver looked relieved when Simon directed him to

St. Giles Hospital, tilting his grimy bowler hat with a muttered "Have you there in no time."

As soon as Simon shut the door, the 'cab shuddered from the curb and rapidly gained speed, engine hissing in protest, as we headed back toward the human boroughs.

"Is that a good idea?" I asked. "Won't we just draw the Beast Kind to the hospital?"

"St. Giles is a Haven," Simon said confidently.

I didn't share his certainty. If I'd been right and there was a Beast at Guy's, such a rapid attack didn't speak to Lucius being sane and rational and worried about minor details like respecting the treaties and honoring Haven laws. But I stayed silent. Simon was the one who knew the human world and its defenses. I'd put myself in his hands now.

I stared out the window, searching for any sight of the Trusted or Beasts I knew. Out of the sunlight, I felt marginally safer but knew it was an illusion. The windows still let in enough light that I couldn't shadow.

Silence, well, what passed for silence in a 'cab with the thumps and hisses of its steam engine, settled between us. Simon had taken the side nearest the driver and I'd made sure there was as much space as possible between us. I didn't want the need to flare here and now, distracting and weakening me even further.

Despite the gap and the odors of steam and coal, the smell of warm male, that peculiarly clean spice I was starting to automatically class as Simon, drifted toward me. Deep inside, the need stirred, softening my defenses, making me want to move closer, breathe deeper.

I set my jaw against it. Wanting wasn't on the agenda. Particularly not with this man.

"You're staying, then," Simon said after a minute or so. "What were you and Guy talking about?"

I shifted my gaze to him, considering. The words sounded in my head perfectly clearly. *Permanent mercy has to be earned.* A warning to choose the right side. Only in my world the sides weren't right and wrong. They were my side and everybody else's.

I'd be choosing me.

So I ignored the first part of Simon's question. I didn't have the Fae disgust for lying, but I didn't want to add to the list of sins he could lay at my feet after I left. "He explained his God's concepts of mercy and redemption."

Simon's expression turned fierce. "He won't hurt you. Nobody will."

"I think I have more pressing problems than your brother." Like how I could outrun the need or how I was going to get the hell out of the City. Like how I could stay alive.

"I'll keep you safe."

He sounded so certain. I knew he was wrong. He'd pay a price for this.

I most likely couldn't prevent that from happening, but I could do my best to keep the price as low as possible. "At this point, safe is a relative concept."

"It's always relative. Trust me, it's not easy to get through Guy."

Which presumed, of course, that Guy wouldn't be the one pursuing me in the end. I didn't reply, instead returned to watching out the window, searching the faces for any danger. Sunlight at least made that easier.

"Speaking of trust . . ."

I turned.

"I can't keep calling you Shadow," he said, giving me one of his crooked smiles. "Don't you think it's time I knew your name?"

Tempting. Oh so tempting. Easy to relax a little and lean into the light of his world. Pretend I was human. Pretend I was wanted. But I wasn't and I wouldn't be, no matter what he and his brother did.

Still, he was going to be hurt because of me. He might be killed. I couldn't stop it or make it any easier. I didn't really have anything to offer him. So a name seemed a small thing to give.

If only so he had something to curse when the bill for taking me away from Lucius came due.

"Lily," I said finally. "My name is Lily."

Lily? I hadn't expected that. The Fae often named their female children for flowers or plants. I was surprised her mother had gifted her with anything of Fae heritage if she'd known she was going to give Lily up.

Still, it seemed to fit her. Lilies were pale and slender but also tough. Beautiful and, sometimes, deadly. Maybe her mother had known something after all.

Assuming Lily had told me the truth, of course. She was wary enough to lie.

Which I couldn't exactly blame her for. Not when I was lying to her too.

She sat beside me and stared out the window as we wound through the streets toward St. Giles, looking calm and composed as the midmorning light made her hair gleam as red as sunset.

You'd never know that a few hours ago she'd been unconscious. That a few minutes ago she'd been running from people who quite possibly wanted to separate her head from her body.

She kept it all inside.

My hand curled around the pistol, the metal warm beneath my hand as anger bit. All that control, all that wariness and hiding had been learned. The Blood had shaped her into something cold, so carefully guarded there was no room for light or openness. She was ice. Determined to freeze me out, presenting only a cool slick surface that couldn't be penetrated. When she should be glowing and warm like her hair.

In her place, on the run, shut off from my powers, I'd be, well, agitated at least.

Yet she just sat there, looking carefully serene. As if this were perfectly usual and part of her routine.

Guilt coiled through me. Would she look so serene if she knew what I really wanted from her? Or would she see me as no different than Lucius: someone who wanted to use her?

I looked away for a moment, staring out my own window at the treelined street and the people just starting to go about their business. Men in suits or working clothes, the women in brightly colored dresses.

Lily wore black. A severe high-necked black linen shirt covered by a sleek leather vest. Trousers made of the same midnight leather. All of it proclaimed her as something out its element. That would change. I intended to see that the human world became accustomed to her, and she to it.

I turned back to her. One hand lay on her thigh, touch-

ing the strap to the sheath that held one of her stilettos. But
that was probably automatic for her rather than a sign of
nerves. Her other hand wrapped around the grab bar,
braced against the bouncing jolts of the 'cab's journey.

"Are you always this talkative?" I said, more to get her
to face me again than anything.

She turned her head, raised her eyebrows, glancing from
me to the driver and back again. "Silence is smarter where
I come from."

"Ah. Yes. I suppose stealth is useful in your occupation."
If not absolutely vital to survival. Silent as the grave, in fact.
Another wound to her to lay at Lucius' feet.

She looked back to the driver.

"He can't hear us," I said.

"Why not?"

"Because I'm shielding." Could she not feel the shield?
Most of the Fae I'd met could sense a working. Lily, though,
was only half Fae. And the thinly woven stories and legends
and whispers about wraiths were never truly clear about
what the other half might be. I needed to know more about
her powers.

"Why?"

"I thought it safer for the driver not to know who we
are."

Her eyebrows rose again. "If he'd recognized me, I
doubt he'd be taking us where you told him to." She glanced
toward the window. "We are headed in the right direction,
aren't we?"

"So far."

"Well, then," she said, her shoulders relaxing fractionally, "all should be well."

"He could still tell someone after he left us. If he was so
inclined," I countered. "It's better to be safe."

Amusement lit her eyes again. "Safe? Who's shielding
you?"

"Excuse me?"

Her head tilted slightly, face questioning. "What if this is
all an elaborate plot to catch you with your guard down?"
A chin jerk toward the driver. "He wouldn't hear you
scream."

She was trying to scare me, to make me cut and run. She
might have agreed to stay, but I didn't believe she'd meant

it. If she could make her escape by driving me away, that would probably be all the better for her.

Well, she was going to have to try much harder than this. I made my smile deliberately slow. "Who says I'd scream? It's daylight. The last time you tried to kill me in sunlight didn't go well for you."

The side of her mouth lifted. Close to a smile. It made my heart beat a little faster. Which made me, in turn, wish to beat my head against the window of the 'cab. I needed to guard myself. She was going to leave and she wouldn't care if she had to walk over my bleeding body to do so. Especially once she learned what I wanted her to do.

I'd wanted to set her free. And that must, by sheer logic if nothing else, include allowing her to be free of me, should she so choose. Though likely Guy wouldn't see it that way.

"Maybe that was all part of my elaborate plan," Lily said.

Was that a joke? I allowed myself a small slice of hope. Humor. A sign that, maybe, something survived under all the ice despite Lucius' best efforts. That I wasn't being ruled by my body and there might well be truth to my instincts about her. If I could make her smile, then I might be able to find a chink in her armor and get through to the real Lily below. "I didn't think Lucius was the elaborate plan type."

Her face grew still. "Don't underestimate Lucius," she said. "He always gets what he wants."

Not this time. At least not while I had anything to say about it. "We'll take care of you," I repeated.

"You have no idea what you're dealing with."

"Lily, I'm a healer in this city. My brother is a Templar. I'm not, by any definition of the word, naive about what goes on in the Night World. And I'm not helpless."

"I didn't say you were."

"Good. Remember that." I braced myself as the 'cab hit a particularly bad pothole. I appreciated the extra speed a 'cab offered but was yet to be convinced that the clattering, steam-belching machines were superior in any other way to carriages.

Lily slid a little on the seat but caught herself. She pushed herself back toward the door with a frown. "Regardless, the shields are pointless."

"Why?"

"You're taking me to St. Giles. Don't you have Fae working there?"

"Yes. And?"

"Any Fae who sees me will know what I am. They'll know who I am. Once the Veiled Court knows where I am, it won't take long for word to spread."

Sun's blazing balls. I'd forgotten that part. Fae who could sense human magic in the next room could probably feel a wraith at a thousand paces. But if Lily claimed Haven, then everyone in St. Giles was bound to render her assistance. Which included keeping their mouths shut about her whereabouts. It wouldn't last forever. Leaks were bound to happen—after all, someone had told Lucius something to make him want me dead—but it might buy us enough time. There were plenty of places in the hospital where we could keep her relatively isolated.

"The hospital staff will respect Haven laws." I'd just have to keep her away from the patients and visitors.

That earned me a headshake. "The humans will not thank you for bringing me there, the Fae even less so. Even if Lucius respects the rules, what happens next? I can't spend my life in a Haven." Her eyes narrowed. "I'm going to ask Guy whether he did drop you on your head after all."

"My head is just fine."

"Then what is your explanation, sunstroke?"

"Trust me, there has never, in the history of the world, been a sunmage who got sunstroke." That much was truth. The sun couldn't hurt me. Not my skin. Not my head. But if sunlight couldn't hurt me, it was becoming more apparent with every passing second that, if I weren't careful, Lily likely would.

Something about her tugged at me. Which was more than crazy. I needed to be careful. Not let my instincts run away with me. Right now she sat beside me under sufferance.

Part of me knew she'd run if given the chance.

The question was how to make her feel like she didn't need to. It would take caution and finesse. Like trying to coax a wild thing close, I needed her to trust me before I let her know what I wanted from her. And before I could think of there being . . . anything more.

I shifted on the seat as the 'cab hit another pothole, sliding toward Lily a little. She shrank away.

Proof positive that she didn't trust me at all. My jaw tightened. "Why is it so hard to believe that I want to help you?"

"Because people don't just help others for no reason. They're all playing their angles. The sane ones anyway."

Guilt tugged again. Those gray eyes saw too clearly. "Is that what you're doing? Playing the angles?"

A shrug. "At this point I'm mostly trying to just keep breathing."

"That's what I want too. I'm on your side."

She cocked her head, considering. "You're playing your own angle too."

"Who says I have one?" I hoped she wouldn't see the lie in my face or the guilt. I wasn't ready to show my hand just yet.

"Like I said, there's always an angle. How does this story go in your head, Simon? You rescue the poor trapped creature and in gratitude she falls into your bed?"

Maybe part of it went something like that. But I wasn't lack-witted enough to say *that* out loud at least. "No."

"You're lying."

Suns. Could she actually tell? She was half Fae, after all. Or was she bluffing? I chose to believe the latter. "I've never had any trouble filling my bed, sugar." I let my accent stretch into a parody of Guy's Territory-tinged drawl. "I don't need to chase the unwilling. You need to trust me."

Her face suggested she wasn't fooled. "Why?"

"Well, so far I haven't killed you or even tried to kill you," I offered. "Nor has my brother tried to kill you. I will point out that you, in fact, have tried to kill me. I also saved you at Halcyon. I think I've earned a little trust."

"I—"

Her words cut off as the 'cab screeched to a halt. I threw an arm forward to brace against the seat, and the impact jolted through me like a thump from one of Guy's wooden training blades. I let the shields fall. "What the hell was that?"

The driver looked pale. "There was someone—something—in the road."

Gods and fucking suns. This day was only hours old and

it was nothing but one disaster after another. "Did you hit them?"

"Don't know. I can't see anybody."

I leaned forward trying to see out the windshield. Unfortunately, the 'cab was a Mercury, long nosed and bulky, and it was impossible to see if anyone lay on the road near the front tires. I reached for the door handle.

Lily's hand clamped round my arm. "Don't go out there."

"Someone could be hurt."

"It could be set up."

She was right, of course. But still. I couldn't take the risk. "I'm a healer," I said shortly. "This is what I'm sworn to do."

"What? Get killed?" Lily snarled. I ignored her and pushed the door open.

$$\Large)\!)$$

I reached Simon just as he started to bend toward the motionless man lying in the road in front of the cab and grabbed his jacket, wrenching him back. "No."

"He's hurt."

There was blood on the man's face, true. Trouble was, to me, that blood smelled of Beast Kind. Earthy and musky and wild. Dangerous.

My spine crawled again. Watchers. Just the bystanders rapidly gathering or were there other Beasts nearby?

"Let the driver dealer with it. We should go." I looked around. A small crowd was forming around us and 'cabs, carriages, and other traffic halting behind our 'cab. All humans as far as I could tell, not the too-tall figures of Beasts in human form. Still, too many people. Too exposed.

We'd stopped opposite a row of crowded brick terraces, the paintwork on the windows and doors peeling and stained. Definitely still a border borough, though I wasn't sure which one. "We should go," I repeated.

Simon shook me off. "I can't leave someone lying hurt in the road."

"He'll be fine," I said. I kept one eye on the body and another on the crowd. Farther down the road the terraces changed to what looked like shops and maybe a livery. Faces were peering out the windows, and the crowd around us was thickening.

"What, you're a healer now?"

"He's breathing. There are plenty of people here to help. He'll be fine." I lowered my voice. "He's *Beast Kind*."

Simon raised his chin, determination clear on his face. "I don't leave when people need help."

His voice was disapproving. I had a sudden flash of him asking me whether I had come to kill him because of him stitching up a Rousselline pup. Idiot man. He truly didn't care that the man lying there might be a Beast. He only cared that he could help. "This is a trap," I hissed, drawing my dagger.

Simon ignored me and moved closer to the prone body. The man's chest rose and fell slowly. Apart from the blood on his face, I couldn't see any wounds. The stink of Beast filled my nose. If the man wasn't Beast Kind, then he'd doused himself in Beast Kind blood.

I drew my dagger, watching carefully for any sign of movement. Simon had shoved the pistol into his belt. My hand itched, wanting the extra weapon badly.

Simon squatted beside the man, then reached down toward his wrist. I moved before I knew what I was moving for, but I was still too slow. The Beast sat up with a roar, his hand starting to twist and change as he swung for Simon. I threw myself forward, trying to push Simon out of the way as I reached for the gun.

Too slow.

The Beast hit Simon in the chest, knocking him backward. I half-fell, what I'd been reaching for suddenly not there. Lucky for me, as my crouched position meant the Beast's backhand missed me, whistling over my head.

I had time to register the fact that his hand was now sprouting a nasty set of claws before I pushed myself up and forward to where Simon was rolling to a stop.

I didn't know if he was hurt. I couldn't see blood, so I guessed it was lucky that the Beast hadn't fully changed his hand before he'd hit Simon. Simon started to rise, diving for the gun, which had fallen free at some point.

This time I was faster. I had to be. Simon was unlikely to survive a direct hit from those claws to any vulnerable part of his body. I at least was wearing leather and had the advantage of speed and strength and faster healing.

My hand closed around the gun and I spun as I straightened, bringing it up to shoulder level.

The Beast was close, too close. He screamed at me, making a sound a human throat shouldn't be able to voice as he swung again with those claws. I dodged but not quite fast enough. His paw connected, claws slicing through my vest and tearing the skin beneath.

He got my torso, not my arm, knocking me off balance, but I kept my feet and my grip on the gun. As the Beast screamed again, I raised the pistol and put a bullet straight through the middle of his forehead.

Chapter Seven

)

The Beast dropped where it stood, its face frozen mid-change. The scream choked into a gurgle that died by the time the sodden thump of the body hitting the cobbles sounded. Apparently Guy used silver bullets. Suddenly I felt quite friendly toward the Templars. But I wasn't taking any chances. I kept the gun aimed at the Beast, debating the need for a second shot.

The size of the hole in the Beast's head suggested not, as did the rapidly spreading pool of blood around the body. A very old vampire might be able to heal such a wound, but I doubted a Beast could.

Still, it couldn't hurt to make sure. I prodded the corpse with my foot. Nothing.

"What are you doing?" Simon said as I bent toward the Beast, gun still at the ready. His voice sounded very loud. I realized the crowd had gone quiet. Several of the horses were snorting uneasily, their hooves beating a nervous tattoo on the cobbles, but the people were silent.

Shocked silent or "let's form an angry mob and attack the killer with the gun" silent?

"Making sure I finished the job," I said, loud enough for it to carry clearly to those watching. If they were feeling intimidated, I needed them to stay that way. If they weren't, well, I'd best make sure that changed.

Before Simon could protest, I drew the dagger with my free hand and laid it across the Beast's throat. The Fae do good work. My dagger slid, as usual, through skin and cartilage and bone like butter, separating the head from the body. The head, frozen midchange in a hideous mix of wolf and man, toppled sideways with another dull thump.

The noise made my stomach swoop. Generally, I kill with a single stroke to the heart. Noiseless. Fast. Blood flowed from the stump, joining the pool gathered under the body, horribly bright in the sunlight. I set my teeth, willing myself not to react as the smell hit me. Simon sucked in a sudden breath, stepping backward. Apparently I wasn't the only one disturbed by my actions.

The blood reeked of Beast. Behind me, hoofbeats clattered as one of the horses squealed; then someone cursed viciously, presumably trying to calm the animal.

Wrinkling my nose, I flipped the corpse's coat open with my dagger, looking for weapons. Praise the Lady, there was a pistol shoved in his waistband. I looked up at Simon and held out his gun. He stared at it for a moment, then took it.

I yanked the Beast's gun free, checked that it was loaded—normal bullets, which was unfortunate but better than nothing—then wiped my dagger clean on the coat. I half straightened and turned my attention from the dead Beast to the crowd, trying to read their mood. They were, thus far, giving us plenty of space. Good. There wasn't much point attempting to move the body. Not with this many witnesses. Even if we did, the blood would tell its own story.

Trouble was, Lucius would most likely take it to read something along the lines of "try to kill them harder next time."

I stood up fully and had to hide a wincing gasp. Now that my initial rush of adrenaline was wearing off, the wound on my side throbbed like seven hells and I realized I was bleeding.

Not good.

It was one thing for the Beast's blood to be found. It was another entirely for mine to be found with it. Still, there was nothing I could do about it right now.

"We should leave," I said to Simon, keeping my free hand pressed to my side. I held the pistol at the ready in the other. "Likely his pack mates will be on their way. They will have felt the death."

Simon stared down at the body, looking pale. "Shouldn't we . . ."

"No. There's nothing you can do here." I didn't care how good a healer he was; he couldn't reattach somebody's head. Nor did I want him to. "Let's go."

We didn't have time for niceties. He needed to understand the reality of the situation we were in. Maybe then he'd finally agree it would be best if I didn't stay.

Behind me steam hissed as the 'cab chugged into life. I twisted and bit down a curse. Apparently our driver agreed with my desire for a strategic retreat. He seemed equally determined that we wouldn't be going with him as he reversed the 'cab away speedily, eyes wild as he stared at me through the windshield.

So much for that method of getaway.

Maybe it wasn't such a bad thing. He'd gotten a pretty good look at our faces.

As had the rest of the crowd, though right now they were mostly focused on the body, various expressions of shock, distaste, and avid curiosity on their faces. Judging by the well-worn and grubby clothes most of them wore, they weren't necessarily the sort who'd be too keen to talk to the authorities if they turned up. And hopefully, as residents of the border boroughs, sensible enough to avoid getting caught up in Night World battles.

I pulled at Simon's arm. "We need to leave."

"You're hurt," he said.

"Let's worry about that later." The wound burned and oozed, but it wasn't bleeding heavily. Hopefully I wouldn't leave a blood trail.

The Beasts might track us anyway, but why make it easier for them? I started walking away from the crowd, then forced myself to break into a run. We needed distance between us and the body.

"We need to get St. Giles," Simon said, keeping pace with me. If he was hurt, he wasn't showing it. Yet the Beast had hit him solidly. If he was unharmed he was very, very lucky.

If he wasn't, then any number of things could be happening internally, but I couldn't do anything about any of them. I couldn't smell human blood and there didn't seem to be any spreading stains on the dark blue cloth of his jacket. In fact, apart from the dust on his back where he'd fallen, he looked almost as neat as when we'd left Guy's.

Whereas I had added torn and bleeding to stinking and rumpled.

Hells.

"No. They could predict we might head there. We need somewhere not connected to you. Somewhere unexpected. Preferably warded."

Not an easy thing to produce in this part of town. I quickened my pace and almost immediately regretted it as I slipped in some horse dung on the cobbles and stumbled, arms flailing to keep my balance. The movement felt as though someone had driven a red-hot iron spike into my side, and for a moment, my vision darkened.

Simon caught my elbow, then pulled us into the shadow of a narrow alley, leading me straight into another pile of dung in the process. The grassy stench rose around us, combining with the smell of rotten garbage and rat piss in the alley, not helping my attempts to breathe deeply and drive away the pain. But the stink was probably a good thing. It might hide our scent. At this time of year, the summer heat kept the streets mostly dry, no rain to turn the rubbish and worse littering them to muddy slush or to wash away our trail.

"Let me see that," he said, reaching toward my hand where it pressed against my side.

I stepped back. "It's fine."

"It's not. You look as though you're going to faint."

"I don't faint." Though right now I wasn't entirely certain that it wasn't a possibility. The wound hurt much more and the fabric of my shirt seemed wetter beneath my hand. Had I torn something when I'd slipped?

"We're going to St. Giles," he said. "It's the safest option."

"Safest for who?"

He ignored me. "I know this area."

"You do?" This wasn't the sort of neighborhood I expected Simon to be familiar with. He belonged in the well-manicured, safe human boroughs. Close to the spires of Our Lady of the Perpetual Rose and the Brother House. Places where light and order prevailed and the alleys didn't smell like three-week-dead fish.

"Yes. If we cut through this alley, we'll be closer to Melchior. We can get a hackney or another 'cab."

I hoped like hell he was right. So far the Lady seemed to like him. Perhaps she'd favor him a little longer.

One thing was certain, trying to make our way to St. Giles on foot would be foolhardy. I wasn't going to be much use if we ran into more Beasts. I drew in a breath, trying to forget the pain in my side. "All right. It's a plan."

"You should let me look at that," Simon said, frowning. He looked down to my hand. Blood coated the underside of my palm. Some dribbled between my fingers, down toward my wrist.

"It can wait. I'm not bleeding to death. He didn't catch me full strength. If we stop for you to heal me, then we might not be so lucky next time." The bleeding had slowed, but the torn flesh still throbbed with every movement, a deep burning pain that radiated up and down from the place my hand covered.

"You have a strange view of lucky." He held out his hand. I ignored it.

I wasn't going to touch him. It had been bad enough in the 'cab. I didn't need his skin on mine distracting me while we were trying to get to safety.

"Standing and breathing is lucky enough. Now let's go."

His face tightened in frustration but he nodded.

Our luck held as we made our way down the alley and out into the streets beyond. No Beasts waited to pounce on us. And we hadn't gone very far when a hackney rumbled into view. Simon stepped in front of it, holding out his hand, and the driver eased to a halt.

"St. Giles," Simon said curtly. His tone left no room for arguments. The driver merely nodded and Simon pulled the door open and stepped back so I could climb in. I'd barely taken my place on the patched leather seat when he climbed in after me and slammed the door shut, yelling for the driver to drive on. He dropped onto the seat beside me rather than opposite.

The hackney swayed as the horses set off. I braced myself with my good hand, resisting the urge to lean back and relax. There was still a way to go to St. Giles. I needed to be alert.

Simon made a half-muffled noise of protest as the hackney hit a bump in the road. Hells, was he hurt too? "Are you all right?"

"Standing and breathing," he said shortly. "Well, sitting

and breathing. Move your hand and I'll do what I can for that."

"Can't it wait until we get to the hospital?"

"If I do something now, we have a better chance of getting to the hospital in one piece if we do run into more trouble. Undo your vest and pull your shirt back."

I froze. I hadn't thought about him putting his hands on me to heal me. On my bare skin. "Can't you just . . ." I paused and nodded toward his hands. " . . . heal it?"

"I need to see it first, to know what I'm dealing with."

"But you healed me through my shirt this morning."

A grin flashed on his face. "Who do you think undressed you? I had plenty of time to see the damage." The grin vanished as suddenly as it had appeared. "I assume that was Lucius' handiwork?"

I didn't see the point in denying it. "Yes." Beneath the fresh pain of the claw marks, the remnants of pain from Lucius' beating still laid a solid layer of ache beneath my skin. Simon hadn't finished the job, I remembered. He'd needed to recharge. Well, maybe he could give me some sort of two-for-one deal now. It would be nice not to hurt. Would be nice to eat as well, I realized as I identified part of the ache in my stomach as hunger pangs.

I'd never actually gotten the promised breakfast this morning, and last night's bowl of stew seemed a very long time ago. Add in a beating, a couple of fights, and a run through the city streets and I was starting to push the limits of my endurance.

But it wasn't as though we could stop for a picnic lunch, so I'd just have to put up with it.

"Go on," Simon said.

I moved my hand gingerly and started unlacing my vest. Peeling the leather away from the wounds hurt like hell. I hissed through my teeth.

Simon made a sympathetic noise. "Sorry." He looked down at the wound. The linen of my shirt was shredded where the claws had connected. "That looks nasty."

I shot him a sideways glance. "You don't say."

"It should be cleaned first."

"We don't have anything to clean it with," I pointed out.

"I know," he said. "I was just thinking out loud. I can work around it."

He reached out and laid his hand over the wounds, twisting to do so. Another pained noise broke through his teeth, but he didn't change position.

"You *are* hurt," I said.

"Quiet, I'm concentrating."

I bit down on my protests. He should be healing himself, not me. As it had this morning, a cool feeling starting flowing across my stomach from his hand. I wondered vaguely why it was cool, not warm. Surely the power of the sun should be warm?

His hand was warm enough, though, and heat radiated from his body bent close to mine. I bit my lip, closing my eyes, trying to ignore the fact that there was a man so close to me. This man.

I am in control.

I didn't believe my own lie. A different sort of hunger stalked me now. The need was sparking, rousing to heat my blood. Damn Lucius to the lowest level of hell. I refused to be a slave to my body, subject to its artificially induced whims. I hated the blood, hated myself for wanting it. I'd be damned before I let the need it conjured control me.

The need surged again. Hells. I was damned already, had been since I was born. But I still wouldn't give in.

It wasn't Simon who made me feel this way, it was the need. So I wasn't going to make the mistake of getting confused. No matter whether the feeling wasn't entirely familiar, not all burning fire but something warmer and gentler threading beneath the insistent shrill of the need.

I bit down harder still on my lip, then winced at the pain.

"Sorry," Simon repeated.

"You're not hurting me." Another lie but one that was easier to live with.

"You wouldn't be hurt if I'd listened to you."

"Perhaps. Or maybe we'd have been ambushed. You did what you were oath-bound to do."

Harm to none. That was how the healer oath went. I had no doubt he would fight to defend himself—I had seen him do so—but I wondered if he had ever killed. Not by losing a patient but deliberately ending a life. And if not, what would it take to make him do so?

"Still, I apologize. There. That's all I can do for now.

Any more without cleaning it and there'll just be problems later on."

He took his hand away and I wanted to tell him to put it back. I didn't, though. The regret and conviction in his voice made me want to touch him, to tell him it was all right. But no. I would offer him no comfort. It wouldn't be fair. I turned my head away and stared out the window, need and confusion coiling through me like a snake unsure whether or not it should strike or flee, hoping the journey wouldn't take much longer.

When the hackney finally turned into the long, wide private road that ran the length of the hospital's northern side, I didn't know whether I was relieved or worried about what was coming next. We'd made it to St. Giles without incident, but that didn't mean I was safe. Lucius would try again at some point. And then again and again, until he got what he wanted.

And, in the meantime, I was about to walk into a place full of Fae and human mages.

All of whom had no reason to like or help me.

The hackney drew to a halt, the driver's low tones as he clucked to the horses rumbling into the carriage. The horses were blowing and snorting, their harnesses creaking and jingling. *Nervous.* Why?

Simon had noticed too. He twitched the tattered fabric shielding the window aside, giving me a clear view. "See anyone you recognize?" he asked.

I leaned forward. We'd arrived at the main entrance where the impressive white dome of St. Giles rose above the stepped marbled forecourt. A massive statue of the unfortunate saint himself kept watch over the marbled tiles, his arms stretched forward, open hands angling down as if to draw attention to the immaculate stretch of green grass that separated the forecourt from the road. The marble thorns curling around his legs looked liked they hurt. I sympathized.

The driver had pulled up on the far side of the road as instructed. The near side, according to Simon, was reserved for those with emergencies. I'd argued that we had an emergency but he disagreed.

I looked at the white steps. Less than thirty-odd feet to safety. Walk across the road, pass under the branches of the huge sentinel-like oaks ringing the hospital at fifty-foot intervals, and cross the grass. Set a foot on that marble and the Haven laws protected you no matter what species you might be. Though, in truth, each species tended to favor the Havens run by their own kind. Which didn't help me. My kind were few. I'd never met another like me.

I'd have to take my safety as it came.

Right now that was St. Giles. And right now the path to St. Giles was blocked.

A group of seven men stood on the grass, several strategic feet still between them and the edge of the marble. To a man they were taller than average, broad shouldered and dressed in dark colors that blended well in the dappled shadows beneath the oaks. Long hair in shades as various as their skin tones—which ranged from paler than mine to near black—flowed loose down to their shoulders, and their faces wore identical intent expressions.

The expressions of hunters sighting their prey. Beasts, all of them. I could smell them on the breeze blowing toward us. No wonder the horses were displeased. I had a distinct urge to bolt myself.

"The one in the middle is René Rousselline," I said softly. "The others are Favreaus, I think. Maybe a Krueger as well." All packs with ties to Lucius' court, even if the relationships were not as cordial as they could be at times. None of them were terribly old. They looked to be twenty or so. Juniors sent to scout me out.

But young didn't mean harmless.

Simon let the fabric fall back. "Should we drive on?"

"Where would we go?"

"To the Brother House."

Not an option I wanted to consider at this moment. Yes, it was likely that Lucius wouldn't set watchers on the Templars, not if he wanted those watchers to survive. But the thought of being surrounded by a regiment of Templars was far scarier than seven Beast Kind.

One of the horses squealed suddenly and the driver thumped on the roof. "You lot coming out? I've places to be."

"We should go," I said. Seven-to-two wasn't good odds even with the guns. Not when Simon was injured.

The horse made another annoyed-frightened sound. It would draw the attention of the Beasts if we waited much longer— if it hadn't already. The scent of them had grown fainter. The wind had shifted.

Blowing our scent toward them.

I banged on the carriage wall. "Drive—"

The door flew open. A large dark head appeared. Rene Rousselline. His too-pointed teeth gleamed whitely against his olive skin as he grinned nastily as me. "Well, well. What do we—"

He stopped short when he spotted my pistol pointing squarely at his head. "There's seven of us," he said slowly.

"Right here there's two pistols and one of you," Simon said. "Back away."

"We have no fight with you," Rene said. "Give us *her*"—he jerked his head toward me—"and we'll go."

His voice, like all of the Beasts', had a faint lilt, an artifact of the secret tongue they speak amongst themselves. It sounded pretty but those pretty tones didn't change the fact that he was lying. I had no doubt Lucius had issued orders for Simon to be killed or taken as well should the opportunity present itself.

"I'm not his to give," I said, tightening my finger on the trigger. "And you haven't thought this through, Rene."

He cocked his head slowly. "Oh?"

"If Lucius wanted me dead, you wouldn't be talking to me, you would've attacked already. If he wants me alive, then you can't hurt me too badly. I doubt he'll lock me up once I'm returned to him. Which means I'll be free to visit all of you one night."

His face turned unattractively sallow. "You wouldn't."

"Why not? I'm guessing they're all younger sons like you. No heirs. No one will miss you that much. Lucius certainly won't mind."

"He'll mind if we don't come back with you."

The scent of Beast grew stronger. They would be surrounding the hackney. But maybe not completely. Not yet. Perhaps they didn't want to draw too much attention to themselves this deep in human territory and this close to a Haven. Technically the law didn't protect you until you stood on actual Haven ground, but in practice, the surrounds of Havens were considered neutral territory.

Would they want to risk a full-out fight? Or could we escape if we acted quickly? If we could get away from them, we could get to St. Giles another way. Even leaping from the hackney from a closer position would be better than trying to fight through seven Beasts.

"Drive on," I yelled suddenly, kicking out at Rene, hoping to knock him out of the carriage. It half worked. He went backward, but one long arm snaked forward and his hand clamped around my left wrist, pulling me off balance. We tumbled out of the hackney and onto the cobbles with a bone-jarring thud. I was on top, though, and hadn't lost hold of my pistol.

I snapped my hand down, cracking the butt against Rene's head as he lay there, seemingly stunned.

Behind me I heard the driver curse and crack his whip and the clatter of hooves as the horses obediently leaped forward. I couldn't turn and watch, though, because Rene suddenly surged upward, dodging my instinctive punch and countering with one of his own. I launched myself up and back with an effort, hindered by the tugging pain in my side, trying to determine where the other six Beasts were and how far it was to the forecourt and to come up with a plan as I fought.

Rene was fast, and I was hamstrung by my half-mended side. His fist connected, right above the partially healed cuts. Stars bloomed in front of my eyes, bright as the pain.

I reeled back, blinking to clear my vision, then pointed the pistol in Rene's direction, still half blind, and fired. Over the roar and boom of the gun, I thought I heard horses squealing behind me. Hells. Bystanders.

Just what the situation needed.

As my vision cleared, I saw Rene had fallen back, holding his side. Silver was even more dangerous to Beasts than it was to the Blood. If I'd hit him, he would be in serious pain. Even a minor wound from silver could be fatal if left untended too long. The other Beasts were gathered in a loose semicircle behind him.

I started to back away, angling toward the forecourt. Normally I'd bet on myself being able to outrun a Beast, but I wasn't so sure right now.

One of the Favreaus, a brutish blond, started toward me,

mouth twisted in a snarl, hands starting to twist and sprout claws. My side throbbed in remembered pain.

"Lily!" Simon's voice startled me and I only just managed to stop myself from turning to see where he was. Or what in the name of darkness he was doing here when he should be safely disappearing in the distance in the hackney by now.

"Lily! Duck."

What the hell? I did turn at that, then dropped to the ground as a ball of flame whistled past me. It hit the ground with a loud *whoomp*. A line of fire sprang up between me and the Beasts. The Favreau boy stopped, looking as startled as I felt. None of the Beasts had a liking for fire. Besides silver, burns were the hardest injuries to heal, and this flame, whatever it was, burned a whitish shade of yellow that slapped hotly against my skin even from the ten or so feet between me and it.

Nothing natural about it, I was sure.

I hadn't known that a sunmage could throw a fireball. Apparently the Beasts hadn't either. But I wasn't going to waste the momentary advantage surprise was giving me.

I hauled myself upright, turned, and sprinted toward the forecourt. From the corner of my eye, I saw Simon, standing in the middle of the road, watching me run.

Next to him stood a Templar knight in full regalia, poised with a longbow, already drawn again, a wicked-looking arrow nocked and ready to fire. The shaft gleamed in the sunlight—silver—my mind thought wildly as I leaped over the ditch at the side of the road, sprinted under the oak shadows with a sudden sensation of passing through a boundary, and hit the grass. I was only a few feet from safety.

Three more strides.

Two.

There was another whistling *whoomping* noise behind me and I flung myself forward, thinking that one of the Beasts must have made a move if the Templar was firing again. I hit the marble at a dead run as someone roared in pain and it took me several more paces to pull myself up enough to turn and see what was happening.

My chest heaved as I took in the scene. One of the

Beasts—I couldn't tell which, other than not Rene, as *he* was staring directly at me, hand still clasping his side and a snarl of hatred distorting his face—was rolling on the ground, his clothing smoking and charred.

A distinct smell of singed flesh wafted toward me and I smiled in satisfaction. The other five Beasts stood very still. As well they might. Simon's Templar archer had brought some of his friends along. Guy, it seemed, had raised the alarm and sent the Templars to meet us. He must have guessed Simon would head for St. Giles.

I counted twelve mounted knights as they galloped from both ends of the road. There were probably others approaching on foot.

"Stand where you are," one of the mounted knights bellowed as he drew to a stop next to Simon and the archer. It sounded like Guy. When he raised his visor, his identity was confirmed. He looked over to me. "That means you too," he shouted.

I shrugged at him, quite happy to stay where I was. The marble beneath my feet was the nicest thing I'd felt all day.

Guy swung down from the horse, hitting the ground with a series of metallic clunks. I'd never actually seen a Templar in armor and mail before. It looked hot and uncomfortable. I couldn't imagine trying to fight weighed down by so much metal.

Guy nodded at the archer and suddenly both the fires went out. Not Simon, I thought. The archer was the one controlling the fire. Was he a sunmage too? Or a metalmage perhaps? They used fire in forming their compounds. Could they control it?

I didn't know enough about human magic. It was frustrating. And potentially dangerous, as I learned the night I'd tried to kill Simon.

"This is a Haven." Guy's voice carried across the silent forecourt and road, booming like a small thunderclap. "Why are you breaking the peace of the treaty?"

Rene straightened. "We have broken no law. We are clear of Haven grounds." His voice was steady with a rumbling undertone that told me his control was stretched thin.

Guy gave a small nod, his mouth set in a flat line that boded nothing good for the Beasts. "Technically, that is correct." Behind the Beasts, three of the knights dismounted, drawing their swords with a ringing slide of metal. "But my companions here have never been big on technicalities. I suggest you go back where you came from. There is nothing for you here."

His head didn't turn toward me, but I still felt a small glow at his words. Until I realized he might mean that I was the Templars' to deal with. But hopefully that was me being paranoid. Guy had said he would believe me and I had done nothing to play him false. Yet.

"We came for the girl. She belongs to Lucius."

Guy rested one gloved hand on his sword. "Belongs? She doesn't look blood-locked to me. And if she's a Trusted, then Lucius could call her to him. Anything else would have to be termed slavery." His fingers tapped the hilt, mailed glove clinking a soft staccato. "Slavery is, as far as I'm aware, outlawed under the treaties. If you're claiming her as a slave, then we would have to act to enforce the terms of those treaties. As we are sworn to do."

There were more clanks and the slicker hiss of metal sliding free of leather as the remaining Templars suddenly drew their swords.

The Beasts didn't move. If not for their coloration, you would have thought they were carved from the same marble as St. Giles himself. They might have liked the odds when it was two against seven, but apparently they weren't so keen on five against fourteen.

"Well?" Guy asked after a minute's strained silence during which I became aware that several people had gathered behind me. I kept my eyes on the action.

"Are you claiming her as a slave?" Guy continued.

Rene's face twisted, baring those inhuman teeth again. He was controlling himself with an effort. A Beast who has been fighting and is wounded will always have a strong urge to change. And the younger they are, the harder it is to resist. Rene, if I had the tangled lines of Pierre's sons by his various wives correct, was only twenty-two or so. Still very young in Beast terms.

Obviously he took after his papa and had an alpha's strength of will. I hoped for his sake, he had an alpha's courage and cunning to deal with Lucius when he returned empty-handed. Though Lucius' anger would have to be spread over all those he had sent to find me, so maybe

Rene would escape too much punishment. Then again, maybe not. I felt the renewed pain in my abdomen where he had hit me and couldn't bring myself to feel too sorry for him or any of his companions. Even the one still groaning as he lay in the road, smoking slightly.

"Well?" Guy repeated when Rene stayed silent. He held his sword loosely in front of him, double handed, blade lowered. I had no doubt he could bring it to a fighting stance and wreak some serious havoc in a matter of seconds.

Likely none of his brother knights were much slower.

Rene seemed to come to the same conclusion. "No. We will go." His voice was almost a snarl. Not a happy Beast pup at all. I smiled in satisfaction.

Guy gestured and the knights behind the Beasts fell back, opening a gap in their semicircle for Rene and his friends to retreat, which they did, after collecting their wounded comrade. We all watched as they left, the tension-filled silence broken only by the sounds of the knights' horses shifting on the cobbles and the wind moving through the oak trees that bordered the grass. As the Beasts disappeared around the corner at the end of the road, someone let out a soft sigh behind me.

This time I turned to look. Two women and a man stood on the marble just a few feet away, watching the scene curiously. The shorter woman and the man were both human from their scent. The other woman, however, was not. Dark haired, tall, and slender, she was Fae to the bone. Even if I couldn't smell the faint scent of wild places coming from her or sense the depth of her magic, the color of her eyes—a blue just a shade too rich and deep and bordering on purple like a night sky—would have given her away. No human had eyes that color.

Her green dress was simple as Fae clothing went, long and unadorned without any over robes, but she wore an intricately wrought chain about her neck that gleamed like a silvered rainbow. It could be nothing but Fae work. Likewise the elaborate Family ring on her left hand.

I waited for her to look through me or for her face to register disgust and turn away as the Fae normally did when they found themselves in the same place as me.

But she didn't, even though her face wasn't exactly welcoming. Instead, she met my gaze coolly. "Welcome to St. Giles," she said in a tone I couldn't read. Her gaze swept over me from head to foot. "It seems your day has not been entirely peaceful."

I wondered what the hell I might look like. My shirt was half shredded, and fighting with Rene couldn't have helped the state of the rest of my clothing any.

"I've had worse," I said, trying for the same air of cool control she projected. I couldn't quite contain a wince as I straightened my shoulders, but on the whole I thought I did rather well. One thing living in the Night World taught well was how to remain impassive in the face of pain or surprise.

"Indeed," she replied. "Well, let us hope that we can prevent the day from slipping any further down the scale of unpleasantness."

She looked over my shoulder. "Perhaps, Simon, we should continue this inside? Bring your . . . companions."

I swung around to find Simon, Guy, and the archer, a young man with hair and skin like ebony and eyes that were a startling green contrast, standing behind me.

"I think it would be wise to leave most of the men out here. Make sure those pups causing all this excitement have truly left the area," Guy said. "I want to take Simon and his . . . friend—" He looked at me with something close to approval, then continued. "To the Brother House."

I opened my mouth to protest this piece of news, then shut it again with an effort of will as the Fae woman shrugged. I had a sinking realization that I had no say in anything they wanted to do to me until darkness fell.

"Leave your men, certainly. But we will be going inside before you go anywhere, Guy DuCaine. She took a step toward Guy. Away from me. "Simon and this one have injuries that need tending. And the three of you, I believe, have a tale to tell."

This one. Perhaps she wasn't different from the rest of the Fae after all. Perhaps she just had more control. I lifted my chin and stared at her deliberately.

"I'm fine," Simon said. "Lily is the one who needs healing."

"You're not fine—"

The Fae woman cut me off. "We will go inside."

To my annoyance, neither Simon nor Guy made any fur-

ther argument. They simply nodded as if they knew protesting wouldn't be worth the effort. Guy turned and
shouted some orders at the other knights, who swung into
their saddles, splitting into three groups, two of which
headed in opposite directions down the road. The third sta-
tioned themselves along the grass lining the forecourt, silver statues in the sunlight reflecting off the marble.

They would be half boiled inside all that metal. I was
starting to feel overly warm in the direct glare of the sun
myself.

Once Guy had his men organized how he wished, he
turned to us. "After you, Lady Bryony," he said with another deeper nod that bordered on a half bow.

Hells. He'd called her Bryony. Not just any Fae, then.
The Fae in charge of St. Giles. Who didn't like me. This was
going to be every bit as unpleasant as I had imagined.

Chapter Eight

☽

As we approached the front doors of the hospital, Lady Bryony paused. "Simon, take her in the back way."

Her tone was sharper now, angry even. She avoided actually looking at me. Somebody wasn't happy to have me in her hospital. Guy and the archer didn't move. Simon's jaw clenched, but he took my arm without protest, leading me away from the others.

I was relieved to be granted even a temporary escape from Bryony's presence and didn't protest other than to remove my arm from Simon's grasp. He shot me a look but didn't try to take it again. We walked, following the building's wall, until we reached a small gap between one building and the next.

"This is better for security," Simon said to me as he turned into the tiny laneway formed by the gap.

"This is better for your Lady Bryony avoiding anyone seeing a wraith in her hospital."

He paused. "What do you mean by that?"

"The Fae don't like my kind."

"This is a Haven. We help everyone."

"Helping doesn't mean liking." Indeed. If Bryony's purplish eyes could've struck me from the earth where I stood, they would have. "Why else are we sneaking around to the back entrance? For all she knows, I'm hurt."

He frowned, then looked almost chagrined. "Are you hurt? Did you reopen the wound? Let me see."

I avoided his reaching hand. "You'll just hurt your ribs if you do that. I'm fine. You're the one who needs healing."

His fingers curled for a moment, not quite into fists but close enough before he relaxed them with an effort of will. "Let's just walk. Trust me, you'll be treated just like anybody else."

If he truly believed that, then he was in for a rude shock. But I didn't want to stand here and argue. The sooner we got inside, the better. They could take care of his ribs and my side. Hopefully they could find me a new shirt too.

We walked on. One lane led to another and another. The hospital, it seemed, was a veritable maze of marble-clad buildings, set narrowly apart like some giant's building blocks. Unlike in Brightown, the laneways were all very clean. Eventually Simon stopped by an innocuous-looking wooden door.

To my surprise, it opened onto a stairwell. One leading down rather than up.

I peered down the stairs. "Secret tunnels?"

"Not particularly secret," he replied, lifting an old-fashioned oil lamp from a rack lined with ten or so more. "Useful, though."

He lit the lamp with a match. The short spurt of flame reminded me about the fire that had stopped the Beasts.

"The fireballs—was that you or the archer?" I asked curiously as I followed him down the stairs and into, well, not really a tunnel. It had a floor tiled in marble and walls lined with wood paneling. Much more civilized than the tunnels I knew. But tunnel was close enough.

"That was Liam."

Liam. I filed the name away. He'd looked younger than Simon and Guy, but he was obviously another mage; someone else to be wary of. "Can *you* raise fire?" Better to know the enemy's weapons. Not that Simon was exactly an enemy.

He made a noncommittal noise. "I could set a vampire on fire by calling sunlight."

Not exactly an answer to my question. But for a moment I didn't really care, distracted by a sudden, pleasing vision of Lucius' face wreathed in flames. But then I dismissed the image with a shake of my head.

Foolish to wish for what one can't have. Even if I could

steal one of Simon's sunlamps, I could hardly activate it. No, better to put myself far out of Lucius' reach than to attempt to solve my problem any other way. Run and figure out how to deal with the need afterward.

The need . . . as if I'd conjured it by thinking of it—or maybe because the adrenaline from the fight had finally worn off enough to let it resurface—I felt a sudden rush of warmth to my face. I shivered and my side throbbed a protest, making me breathe deep to ease the pain.

The air in the tunnel smelled strangely dead somehow. Dry and faintly dusty but without much odor of humans or disease or blood or soap or any of the things I would expect to smell in a place of healing. In fact, the only strong scent was Simon's warm spice.

The need flared again, drawn to the fragrance, wanting me to move closer, breathe it deeper.

Easy, the ache low in my belly whispered. *Nobody around to see. Nobody to know. Just a few moments to ease the yearning.*

I found myself drifting ever so slightly in Simon's direction and pulled up short, wishing desperately for a gallon of cheap cologne to drench myself in. Maybe burning out my ability to smell would grant me some peace from this ridiculous attraction.

Simon turned, looking concerned, but I waved him on with a little gesture, then followed, careful to keep a few feet between us. Thank the lords of hell that Simon was human. I felt as though the need was a tangible thing marking my skin or warming the air around me, rushing to overwhelm me. Something anyone could sense.

Hopefully my impression was wrong. Simon was human with a human's senses, but we were headed toward Bryony. A Fae. With senses beyond even those of the Blood or the Beasts.

Damn Lucius and his insatiable desire for control. This was his doing. The fact that I was here in these corridors, the fact that I was fighting the urges that rose within with every step. All his fault.

Sometimes I longed for his death.

Distraction. That was what was needed if I was to get myself under control before we got to our destination. What had we been discussing again?

Flaming arrows. Right. Better to think of those than other things that burned right now.

"Not as useful as a flaming arrow in most situations, being able to set a vampire on fire, then, I mean." I carefully didn't look at Simon. "Is Liam a metalmage, then?"

"That's something you'll have to ask him."

A casual chat with a Templar knight about his powers. I couldn't see that happening anytime soon. If Simon didn't want to talk about the Templars, I needed another topic of conversation.

"Are there tunnels under all of the hospital?"

"Here and there."

He was playing his cards close to his chest. I couldn't fault him for that. In his position I wouldn't be telling me too much either.

"They seem deserted." We were yet to meet anyone else on our path.

"They're used more at night."

We reached an intersection in the tunnels. Ours ended with two branches, leading off right and left.

Simon jerked his head to the left. "This way. Not too much farther." He took the lead, holding the lantern up. I couldn't help glancing behind me, down the other branch. A faint draft wafted to me, scented with something heavy and metallic. Iron, I realized. A lot of iron. Something glimmered at the far end of the corridor, faint purple and gold, like the afterglow of a ward.

Wards and iron in a tunnel below a Haven? Lots of iron in a place where the Fae came regularly. There could only be one purpose to such a thing and that would be to keep the Fae out. My neck prickled as my instincts kicked in. The humans were keeping a secret.

"What's down there?" I asked, trying to sound innocent.

Simon glanced back at me. The light from the lantern reflected in his eyes, making him hard to read. "Nothing much, it leads to another building. Come on, Bryony will be sending a search party if we don't appear soon."

He was lying. I was sure of it. And, as I followed the light of his lamp away from the smell of iron and the glow of magic, I found myself wondering why.

Bryony hadn't sent a search party, but both she and Guy
looked somewhat impatient by the time I opened the door
to her office. My ribs had creaked in protest with every step
up the flights of stairs leading out of the tunnels and up to
the stone wing favored by the Fae. But I couldn't afford to
slow down. Not yet. Getting Lily here, to a Haven, was only
the beginning of things.

"Lose your way?" Guy asked with a frown. He stood in
by Bryony's desk, Liam on his right, both of them militarily
upright and ignoring the plethora of padded chairs Bryony
kept for visitors.

I frowned back. "We took the long way round." I didn't
mention the fact that I'd come as fast as my ribs would
allow. That wouldn't improve the mood of the room any. It
was already serious enough with the two Templars present.
Armor-clad and grim, they looked out of place. Bryony's
office was light and plant-filled, full of flowers and greenery. Not the place for soldiers.

Though if Lucius had his way, soldiers would be needed
everywhere.

Guy and Liam were apparently too disciplined to sit
down when the opportunity presented itself. I had no such
qualms. My ribs were on fire after the climb. I ushered Lily
toward one of the chairs, hiding a slight frown as she
twitched away from the touch of my hand on her back. I
lowered myself carefully into another and turned my attention to the other occupant of the office.

Bryony sat behind the desk, one hand resting on the
handle of one of her many silver teapots. Steam rose from
the spout, spilling the scent of something sharp and herbal
into the room. Damn. One of Bryony's tonics. They worked
but I could never quite shake the feeling I was drinking
something revolting glamoured to taste nice.

"Ribs, *m'hala*?" she said to me as she poured the tea.

Guy raised his eyebrows at Bryony's familiarity but
stayed silent.

I nodded. There was no point trying to hide my injuries
from her. "I'll live. Lily's hurt worse than me."

"I asked about you," Bryony said, placing the teapot on

the tray and rotating the cups before passing her hands over them in a blessing.

"I'm all right," Lily interrupted, not looking at me. She wasn't really looking at anyone, more staring into a neutral point in the distance.

"No, you're not," I countered. She still didn't look at me, leaving me once again contemplating the wisdom of applying my head to the nearest hard surface. I'd thought, back there in the 'cab and the hackney, that I'd made some progress. That she'd been starting to give me some small shred of trust. But now she had withdrawn again, back into her icy armor. She sat rigidly upright in the chair, tension drawn clearly in the vertical sheer of her spine.

"She got clawed by a Beast earlier," I continued. "I healed the worst of it, but it needs cleaning and more work."

Bryony tilted her head at me.

"I was drained," I said, proffering the same story I'd fed Lily for not finished the job myself. Hopefully Bryony would leave it there. Because my lack of power wasn't the entire reason I'd stopped.

No, the more prudent reason for not finishing the healing had been the sheer temptation of how good it felt to have my hands on her. Lunacy to be so drawn by casual contact. I was a healer, for sun's sake, a professional. Yet putting my hands on her skin had nearly set me on fire.

I'd felt an answering heat thrumming through her, as much as she was denying it. Because that much was also clear: she was denying it. Holding it at bay with a ruthless force of will that could probably move mountains should she set her mind to it. I'd almost been able to feel the battle in her nerves as I'd coaxed the vessels and fibers of her flesh to re-form. A confusion of pain and lust that flared and was tamped down and flared again with every beat of her heart.

Still, her rejection of what lay between us was clear enough. So I'd stopped touching her before my body over-ruled my sense of decency. I stared down at my hands, flexing them slightly where they lay against my thighs. Feeling her skin instead of the buckskin of my trousers. Gods and fucking suns.

"Simon?" Guy said.

Damn. I'd missed something. "Yes?"

"Bryony asked you a question."

Indeed, and when Bryony spoke, everyone jumped, even my brother. But today, I wasn't in the mood to pander to Bryony. Not unless she was about to sing a different tune when it came to Lily. Her sending us in the back way was hardly a good sign. "I was thinking."

"Never a good idea, little brother," Guy said.

"How would you know?" I shot back.

Bryony held out a teacup to me. "No squabbling."

Guy's mouth closed with a snap. I tried not to smirk at him as I accepted the cup. Pale green liquid steamed within. Mint and comfrey tickled my nostrils. No doubt there were other things in the brew. No self-respecting Fae would brew a tea with only two ingredients, and they delighted in being able to bamboozle their guests with complex blends a master herbalist would struggle to decode.

Lily also received a cup, though Bryony placed it on the desk in front of her instead of handing it over directly as politeness would dictate. Lily picked it up, held the china closer to her face, and sniffed but made no move to drink. Her gray eyes were suspicious as she watched Bryony. I wondered if she knew she was being as rude as Bryony by not drinking.

The air between them almost crackled with aversion.

"It's a tonic. Perfectly safe." I swigged mine to reassure her and ease the mood.

"Indeed. It will help the healing," Bryony said, looking from me to Lily. Still without meeting Lily's gaze. "Drink." Her expression was rigid, the way it was when she dealt with an uncooperative patient. My neck prickled. Suns. I hadn't wanted to believe Lily's warnings about her likely reception from the Fae, but it seemed she'd been right.

"I heal fast." Lily's voice was low and cool. Icily neutral.

"So I would expect. Faster still if you drink." Bryony's voice was, if anything, colder than Lily's. She tapped one finger on the teapot's handle, staring at Lily's untouched tea.

Lily made no move to raise her cup to her lips. "Simon should be attended."

Which almost made me spit tea all over Bryony's precious silk rugs.

"*Simon* is not the most pressing problem," Bryony said.

"No," Guy agreed. He rocked on his heels slightly. The clank and rattle of his mail sounded loud in the small room. "She is."

"Her name is Lily," I said, putting my cup down a little too forcefully on Bryony's desk. Thankfully the china didn't break. Fae work was tough. Like the Fae themselves, I was reminded as Bryony pressed her lips into a thin line of disapproval. I didn't react. St. Giles would take care of Lily. I'd given my word.

"Then Lily is the problem. What is it about you that Lucius wants you back so badly?" Guy said, looking at Lily.

"Well, it's not as if he has another of the shadow kin to hand," Bryony said tartly. "I imagine he misses his pet."

"Bryony," I snapped. "Lily has claimed Haven in this hospital. She is to be treated with respect."

Bryony didn't change her expression, but the rainbowed chain around her neck darkened a little. Angry. Which made two of us.

"What's more," I continued, "she is hurt and she needs treatment. That is our priority in any situation." I rose and crossed the room to yank the bellpull to summon somebody. Bryony could argue as much as she wanted, but Lily would still be seen to in the meantime.

Bryony's eyes snapped ice at me. "As you wish, Master Healer."

Suns. I really was in trouble if she was using my title rather than my name. But I'd been in trouble before, and seeing to it that the hospital treated Lily like any other patient was a key component of my plan. Treat her like dirt and why would she even think of helping us? Not to mention she didn't deserve anything less than any other person who crossed our threshold seeking help.

There was a soft knock on the door and Chrysanthe, one of Bryony's Fae aides, senior healer in her own right, appeared.

"Fetch Harriet," I told her before Bryony could speak. Harriet was human, which seemed a safer choice if all the Fae were going to react to Lily in the same way as Bryony. Chrysanthe, always quick on the uptake, nodded at me and disappeared.

"Lily is to be treated with courtesy," I warned as I turned back to Bryony. "By *everyone* in this hospital."

"The truth is always courteous," Bryony said with a sharp smile. "A belief, I would imagine, your friend here doesn't share."

Lily raised her chin. "Why should I? I'm not Fae. That has always been made perfectly clear to me. I owe nothing to your beliefs."

"Yet you wish to be protected by them."

"I thought Havens were treaty law, not Fae belief," Lily said.

"Enough!" I stood abruptly, regretting the movement as my ribs shot dull fire up and down my nerves. "I brought Lily here to be healed."

"Risking the Haven by doing so," Bryony said, standing herself.

Before she could say anything further, a soft knock sounded and the door swung open to reveal Harriet and Chrysanthe. Either Harriet had been working close by or Chrysanthe had run to fetch her. Chrysanthe's face was apprehensive and she twisted her Family ring—a small band of green and yellow stones—nervously. Harriet's brown eyes, in contrast, looked merely curious.

"Harry, this girl needs treatment. See to it." Bryony ordered. "Chrysanthe, Master Healer DuCaine requires your attention."

Lily's expression turned stubborn. "I'll wait for Simon."

I looked down. "It's all right," I said gently. She needed to learn to trust me, and now was as good a time as any to start proving to her that she could. "Harry is very talented. I won't be long." I beckoned Harriet over and briefly filled her in on Lily's wounds and my earlier treatment. Then told her to take Lily to my office rather than a ward. She would feel safer with fewer people around.

Lily looked like she wanted to protest, but she merely tightened her hold on the hilt of her dagger and rose to follow Harriet.

"It really is all right," I said as she passed me. She merely looked disbelieving.

"Veil's eyes, Simon," Bryony said as the door shut firmly behind Harry and Lily. "What were you thinking bringing *that* here?"

I looked pointedly at Chrysanthe, who hovered beside me trying to pretend she wasn't there. Smart girl. Still, I wasn't about to discuss the plan with her in the room. The less people who knew what Lily was—though Chrysanthe might already have sensed that much—let alone why she was here, the better. "I was thinking that this is a Haven and that *Lily*," I said, stressing the name—gods-damned Fae and their stiff-necked prejudices—"needed help."

Bracing a hand to my side, I stared at Bryony, waiting for her to respond.

After a moment or two she made an irritated clicking noise with her tongue, then came around the desk. "Chrysanthe, I'll look after Simon. I'm sure you have other duties to attend to."

Chrysanthe looked like she wanted to ask why she'd been summoned away from those duties in the first place but then obviously decided that discretion was the better part of valor or something similar and inclined her pale blond head a fraction before leaving the room, stalking like an annoyed cat. Guy and Liam both watched her go, expressions vaguely envious. Come to think of it, Liam didn't need to be here either. I turned to Guy. "I'm sure Liam has things to do as well."

Guy raised his eyebrows but nodded and sent Liam on his way.

"Are you shielding this room?" I asked Bryony as the door clicked softly closed for the second time.

"Of course." Bryony sounded even more annoyed. "Now take off your shirt and let me look at your ribs."

I lifted an arm to obey, then froze as fire shot across my side, a groan escaping despite my better efforts.

"Let me," Guy said, stepping between us.

"Don't you start," I warned.

Guy shrugged as he started to ease my jacket off my shoulders. He seemed to know how to do it so as not to hurt me. He'd probably had cracked or broken ribs a time or two himself.

"I've already said what I think. And that I'd help you."

"Both of you are *he'ti'al*," Bryony snapped.

"Nothing wrong with my sanity," Guy replied. "Though I'll admit, I do sometimes wonder about little brother here." He nodded at me as the jacket slid free. "Can you unbutton the shirt?"

I nodded and did so, then let Guy help me shrug it off.

Bryony jerked the top off a jar of salve, directing her annoyance at Guy with a jerk of her chin. "If you're not crazy, why are you helping him? Bringing a *wraith* here?"

"God believes in redemption," Guy said.

Bryony muttered something under her breath. It didn't sound complimentary. Guy's expression didn't change. I wished sometimes wished I shared my brother's deep, calm faith. But we mages had our own beliefs, which were somewhat more complicated.

As did the Fae.

Normally I could respect the differences, but in this matter, in their treatment of their half-breeds—the Fae were simply wrongheaded.

"I'm not asking you to approve of her," I said. "Just to treat her fairly."

"You're being led around by your cock," Bryony said as she picked up another jar, sniffed the contents, then banged it down on the desk.

Guy snorted, then controlled himself when I glared at him.

"My cock is none of your business," I said. "And I assure you, my head is in charge. We need her."

Bryony picked up another jar, then rejected it for another with a jerky movement. The chain round her neck was darkening rapidly, warning of her mood. "Need her? For what?"

My ribs ached as I sucked in a breath. "She can help us."

"Help us? She tried to kill you!"

Guy had a loose tongue, it seemed, if he'd told Bryony that much before Lily and I had arrived. "And today she saved my life. Any other objections?"

"She's an abomin—"

"She's seeking Haven." I cut her off before she could launch into another diatribe on abominations and soulless creatures. "The rest is politics. We treat Beasts here. We treat Fae and humans. We treat Blood."

"She is none of those things."

"She needs our help. That's all that matters." I took a deep breath. The air smelled like antiseptic and the various salves. Usually the smells of the hospital soothed me, but right now they were just irritating. "And we need hers. You're not looking at the situation from the right angle," I said.

"Oh? What other angle is there?"

"She's Lucius' shadow. Yes, she tried to kill me. And the important thing about that fact is that she is the only proof of it, other than my word. She can give evidence against him."

Bryony looked like she might choke. "You think she will turn against him? Why in the name of the Bright One would she do such thing? You truly are *he'ti'al*."

"She will. I can convince her."

"You're thinking with your cock again."

"I'm not. We can use what she knows to our advantage."

Bryony's arms folded, the amethysts and sapphires in her Family ring glinting in the sunlight. A reminder of everything she was and everything she believed. Everything she risked to serve as a healer here. "I disagree."

"As you're perfectly entitled to," I said, even though right now I longed for some way to shake some of that Fae-wrought superiority out of her. "But you're not entitled to let your prejudices prevent the hospital from sheltering her. Or you'll be breaking the laws."

"You'd treat Lucius himself if he came here," Bryony spat.

Guy coughed suddenly. I recognized a smothered laugh in the sound. At least someone was enjoying himself. "Yes, I would," I agreed. And then, as soon as Lucius stepped one inch off Haven grounds, I'd quite possibly do my damnedest to remove the vampire's head from his body, but that wasn't the point to make at this exact moment. "That's what abiding by the law requires."

"Some laws are foolish." Bryony motioned Guy aside and laid her hand along my side over the fractures.

I held still while she focused on the injuries. But I wasn't going to hold my tongue. "Yes. And I'd imagine most humans think the iron and silver restrictions that protect you and the Beasts and the Blood are amongst them. But we abide. The law prevents things from returning to how they were." A return to the wars between the races would be to no one's liking or benefit. Except, perhaps, whoever came out temporarily victorious.

"Perhaps you could look at it another way," Guy said. His low voice held a slight rumble of amusement, but it was scrupulously polite as it always was when he addressed Bryony.

Bryony looked livid as she turned her head to Guy. A sensible man might have retreated a step or two. But no one had ever called Guy sensible. It wasn't really high on the list of desirable qualities in a Templar. "Oh? And how would you suggest that I look at it?"

"Regardless of what Lily's intentions are," Guy said in that very polite tone, "isn't it better that she's here where we can watch her rather than loose in the Night World doing Lucius' bidding?"

I resisted the urge to grin. That was a subtle way to work around to our real agenda. Nobody was going to convince the Fae of Lily's worth overnight, but surely even they could see the benefit of depriving Lucius of one of his weapons? Then again, maybe not, I thought as the pressure on my ribs from Bryony's hand increased abruptly.

"How do you know she's not doing his bidding?" Bryony said as she hit me with a jolt of power that felt like a horse kick to my broken ribs.

Chapter Nine

"She has had several opportunities to kill me today," I replied when the pain from Bryony's burst of power subsided. Never annoy the person about to heal you. "I'm still alive. That fact counts strongly in her favor."

"Maybe she's just waiting for nightfall, when she's stronger," Bryony said, lifting her hand from my side.

"She's not exactly helpless in daylight," I said, remembering Lily fighting at Halcyon and shooting the Beast. I didn't think mentioning the Beast would help right now. "Perhaps you could consider giving her the benefit of the doubt?"

"Why? She's a killer. Lucius' assassin. She's probably killed hundreds of people." She passed me a jar of salve. Clearly I was to apply it myself.

"Are you so concerned about the deaths of Beast Kind and Blood? I've never heard that he's sent Lily against a human before." I stretched gingerly, testing my ribs. No pain. Bryony did good work; even anger couldn't change that. Unless the patient was Lily perhaps. I dug a gobbet of salve out and started to apply it. The bones were healed and the worst of the damage, but the herbs would help my body speed the rest of the process.

"Which brings us back to why he's come after you," Guy said, once again interposing himself into the conversation.

I carefully didn't look at Bryony. She was one of only two people who knew my secret. She'd sworn not to reveal it but Guy wasn't stupid. "I already told you, I don't know," I said, knowing Bryony would stay silent. The Fae do not lie. Which is not to say they cannot tell less than the complete truth.

Guy rubbed the spot between his eyebrows, armor creaking. He looked suddenly tired. "Which means he may try again."

"Without Lily, he's going to have to be very creative to get to me."

"You think he can't be creative?"

"Do you really think he'd break the peace, so close to the treaty negotiations?" I shot back.

"I think that Lucius has been growing steadily more uncontrolled for several years. And now he has a reason to focus his wrath on us rather than the Night World."

I paused. Guy was right, as I well knew. The number of patients passing through the doors of St. Giles and the other hospitals in the human boroughs had been steadily increasing over the last few years.

As much as a third of our time was spent stitching up or setting bones of those who learned the hard way that the glittering attractions of the Night World hid a dangerous underbelly. Another sizable chunk of it was spent dealing with the grieving families of the blood-locked, either delivering bad news or treating the grief and depression that loss brought. Grief I knew all too well.

The Night World had much to answer for, and Lucius was most likely the driving force behind the increasing violence. Not that we could prove it. Yet. But knowing things were growing worse, didn't mean I had to accept it. Not when I could still stand against it and try to pull some free of the quagmire.

Lily, for instance.

And then there were the—no, I wasn't going to think about that here. Think about it and I might be careless enough to talk about it, tired as I was. Besides, whether or not Lily chose to be helped was a question yet to be answered.

"He'd be insane to try something here." I sat down carefully. My ribs didn't protest. Hopefully Bryony would follow my example and the discussion could proceed in a more civilized manner.

"Insane is exactly what he is," Bryony said. She was packing away the jars and pots of salve with a little too much force. "Much as it was insane to bring *her* here."

"This is the safest place for her," I said. Apparently this argument had another round or two to go.

"And what about everyone else? She should be locked up. Let the human council deal with her."

"As far as I know, she's broken no human laws." Interesting that Bryony didn't propose that we hand Lily to the Fae. Which either meant she believed underneath it all that Lily had in fact not broken the law or she thought the Fae would be no help.

"She tried to kill you."

"She failed."

"I would think the attempt itself counts."

"No doubt it does. But if the human council locks her away, how do they keep her there? If they kill her—" I stopped abruptly, as angry denial surged through me at the mere thought. It wasn't going to happen if I had anything to say about it. I forced the anger away. Rage and bluster wouldn't convince Bryony. "If we lose her, we've lost all the things she could do for us."

Bryony continued shifting objects on her desk, toying with the teapot with restless fingers. "As far as I can see, all she can do for us is bring trouble. She already has. Beasts and Templars fighting on our doorstep. I will not risk everyone in this hospital over your foolishness, Simon."

"But—"

"No. You are Master Healer here but I run St. Giles. She can stay if she agrees to help. If she doesn't, then she must leave here by sundown."

"You would deny her Haven?"

"We can take her to the Brother House," Guy said. "She would be safe there. The Haven rules apply there too."

"You think that would convince her to help us? Locking her up in a place full of Templars?"

"If you're so sure of her, then it shouldn't matter, should it?" Bryony cut in. "If she isn't going to do as you think, then it is better that we know sooner than later."

"Why?"

Her eyes turned stormy. "So steps can be taken."

"She is not to be harmed," I bit out.

Bryony's mouth set in a stern line. I knew that look. It heralded nothing good.

"Well, then," she said flatly, "you'd better hope your faith in her is justified. You have until sundown."

))

The walk to Simon's office wasn't overly long. Up a floor and down a corridor or two. I got the feeling that Harriet was trying to take me a lesser-used way, but we still passed a number of other people, mostly wearing healer green.

Harriet greeted each of the healers and I tried to commit faces and names to memory. The first two, Alfred and Linette, were as human as she and I thought for a moment that we might make it without encountering any Fae.

But around the next corner, we encountered a trio of them, two women as golden blond as Chrysanthe and a man with even paler hair. Aster and Oleander and Barl, as Harriet greeted them, didn't hide their surprise at encountering a wraith in their midst very well. Their expressions darkened and they stepped aside, as though I might contaminate them.

I wondered how they might react if I told them that being a wraith wasn't contagious but held my tongue. Simon and Guy wouldn't thank me for starting a fight, and Bryony would only use it as an excuse to banish me from the hospital.

Besides, it was likely that they knew more about wraiths than I did. Not that any of them would tell me anything—other than to confirm my soulless state in their eyes. None of the Fae would tell a wraith how to bring about more wraiths. To their eyes, it would be better if no more wraiths were ever born. Their magic is tied to the earth and the land, to the bonds between all living things. The fact that a wraith can let go of those bonds and move unseen and that Fae magic does not touch us, that their wards cannot sense my kind is, to them, proof that we are abomination. Maybe they're right.

Given what I'd done for Lucius and the hold he had over me, what else could I be called?

None of them would lift a finger to help me unless forced to by their healer vows. Or by Simon, I assumed. I wondered if he knew the secret of the wraiths. Probably not. Lucius had always refused to tell me, sometimes dangling the promise to reveal the truth in front of me like a lure, but I doubted he ever would. He wouldn't want anyone else to make themselves a pet assassin to rival his, after all.

I'd learned to push away any thoughts of who my father might be a long time ago. My mother had rejected me. No doubt he had too.

I scowled at the thought, which prompted Harriet to ask if I was in pain. I shook my head and gestured for her to lead on.

Harriet left me alone after the healing. Wards shimmered over the walls and windows and doors, so it wasn't as though I could run. If I triggered the wards, no doubt somebody would come running.

The healing had been straightforward, though Harriet had been interrupted twice by other healers—a human woman called Victoria who looked plainly curious and two more Fae who made excuses but appeared to be wanting to confirm my existence with their eyes. Word was spreading, it seemed.

Which made me itch to leave. I didn't want to be the freak on show for all and sundry to stare at. Though, to her credit, Harriet had shooed the others away and apologized to me for the interruptions.

Not that there was much point in leaving while the sun still shone. I had no doubt the Beasts would've carried word back to Lucius by now. He knew where I was. There would be people watching for me.

Setting a foot outside the Haven boundaries would make me fair game. They would take me back. In sunlight there was nothing I could do to avoid that. And even though, logically, I knew that returning to Lucius was the sensible thing to do—even the necessary thing if I was to survive—part of me wanted to stay here in this world of light and warmth just a little while longer.

Surely I deserved that much? A small selfish portion of time to know something other than the warrens and the Blood and the dark of night?

Or maybe not. I remembered the Beast I'd killed earlier today. The bright red blood on the cobbles. I'd done it to save my life and Simon's, but that didn't mean the Beast was any less dead.

Another death on my hands.

Why did I deserve anything better than what I'd dealt to others?

Simon said I could be more but he didn't know the truth. Didn't know my secret, the hated hold Lucius had over me. What would he see if he learned I drank blood?

I rose from the chair and prowled around the office. It smelled like Simon and the dusty leather smell of the books on the many shelves lining one of the walls. Light and greenery and books. Much like his house. There weren't quite as many plants here as there had been in Bryony's office, but there were definitely more books.

I studied some of the titles. Medical texts, mostly. Herbals and anatomy studies. I pulled one of the latter out, curious. It fell open at a random page, a diagram of the muscles and organs of the chest, pink and red and white.

I slammed the book shut again. I was all too aware of the anatomy of that particular region of the body. How many times had I thrust my dagger through those layers of flesh and muscle to stop a heart?

So many that I could recall exactly how it felt with perfect clarity. The resistance and wet slide of a supposedly clean kill. Somehow here, in the bright daylit room, the memory made me want to retch, nausea swooping through me, an unexpected guest. I leaned my head against the nearest shelf, squeezing my eyes shut.

Don't think about it.

Easier said than done. I sucked in a breath, then another, trying to steady myself. Just the warmth of the room and the fact that I still hadn't eaten. That was all. I had no regrets. I couldn't afford regrets.

Behind me, the door snicked open and I turned, feeling the room spin slightly as I did so.

Simon stood in the doorway, his expression rapidly changing from pleasant to concerned. He crossed the room in three quick strides. "Are you all right? Didn't Harriet heal you yet? Where is Harriet?"

I held up a hand to ward off his string of questions. "I'm fine."

"You don't look fine. You're too pale."

I folded my arms, wishing I'd put my vest back on. Standing before him in just my half-shredded shirt made me feel curiously vulnerable. "I'll be fine once I've eaten something."

I moved my arm and pushed back the shredded shirt so that he could see the faint scars on my side, all that was left of my wounds. "See, perfectly healed. Harriet was very . . ." I hesitated, unsure of the correct word. Kind, was what I wanted to say, though I didn't know if it had been kindness or just ignorance that informed Harriet's warm manner. Perhaps she just didn't know who I was. After all, if she did, surely she wouldn't want to know me. Or was Simon not the only human who could surprise me?

"She was thorough," I finished as an afterthought.

"That's good." He leaned in, reaching out a hand as if he wanted to inspect the wounds. I stepped backward, letting the shirt fall again. No touching. Not if I was to keep the need at bay. He didn't press the issue.

"She didn't, however, feed me."

That raised a smile. "Food I can manage. Some new clothes would be in order too."

"I'm hardly in a position to go shopping."

"We have clothes here. People leave things behind. I'm sure we can find something. Something that will blend in."

"I'm not wearing a dress," I said defiantly. Skirts were hard to fight in, even if a dress was cooler than leather trousers at this time of year.

"A dress would blend in," Simon countered.

"It's not really a secret that I'm here, is it?" I said. "The Beasts will report back to Lucius."

"I wasn't thinking about the Beasts."

"Who, then?"

"Everybody else. The fewer people who know you're here, the safer you are."

"You mean, the fewer Fae who know who I am."

He didn't deny it. There was little point after Bryony's reaction. "I said before, no one w.'l harm you here. Everybody will do their job."

Inside these walls at least. But I knew that already. The Haven created an artificial environment. I would do well to remember that the human world wasn't the hospital. "You just have to let people get used to you," Simon said. "Give them a reason to—" He broke off, frowned suddenly. "But we're standing here talking when you need food and clothing. Let's go."

The abrupt change in topic made me wary all over again. What had he been about to say? Give them a chance to what? Like me? Know me? Neither of those things seemed terribly likely, after my earlier encounters with Oleander and the others.

But I couldn't summon the energy to confront him about it just now. Not when I was drained and tired and beginning to feel as though I were imagining the whole last twenty-four hours or so. Maybe soon my door would crash open and Ricco or Ignatius would be there to summon me to Lucius and this would all prove to be some sort of fever dream.

Unlikely. I was becoming as bad as Simon, thinking the world worked like a storybook. I needed to keep a firm grasp on the reality of my situation.

Simon led the way from his office, back down the stairs, and onto the first floor. No sneaking around the back way this time, I noted. Which was strange, given his earlier speech. But perhaps he believed in hiding things in plain sight.

As we walked, he talked and I listened. He gave me a potted history of St. Giles, some of which I knew already, talking about how it had been built by the same human families who had funded the cathedral over a hundred years ago. Rich patrons of the Church who believed in charity and succor for the needy.

I wondered if any of them had been named DuCaine.

Whoever they'd been, they had built the hospital to last. No expense had been spared. White marble gleamed in the sunshine flooding through the many windows, and where there wasn't marble, there was polished wood and intricately patterned tile.

The light seemed to fill the rooms and corridors, making them both unfamiliar and unnerving. So much sunlight. I hoped that perhaps Simon might head back down to the tunnels that had brought us into the hospital, but no such luck.

Our first port of call was a small room off one of the many branching corridors. It was lined with racks of clothing, smelling like soap and fresh air. These might be discarded garments, but someone had obviously laundered them.

"See what you can find," Simon said, pointing me toward one of the racks. He turned to the one against the opposite wall and started examining what hung there.

The rack he'd directed me to held shirts. Lots of shirts, both male and female styles. Mostly white. Not unexpected. Not many humans wore black linen like me. Only Nightseekers or those mourning the dead.

Most humans didn't need to blend into the darkness. At least, I thought as I regarded the choices, Simon hadn't directed me to the dresses hung on another of the racks. They ranged from gaudy to serviceable, and while one or two of them shimmered prettily, proclaiming silk or finer fabrics and colors like flowers, they were nothing I had any need for.

I wore black and white like any good member of the Blood Court. I never wore red. It was the one color I hated.

Behind me, Simon's small movements made the clothes rustle and the racks creak softly. The spice of his scent rose around me in the room, warming the air. Just like in the hackney. The room was too small, too intimate. He was too close.

The need raised itself from slumber, sending coils of heat through my limbs. My hands tightened into the fabric of the shirt I held. I would not reach out and touch this man.

I made myself loosen my grip. "Why did you need a healer?" I asked, casting around for a topic of conversation. Conversation and information, I told myself. Know thy enemy. But don't look at him. It was hard to think of him as the enemy when I looked at him.

"I can't heal myself." His reply came after a moment's delay, sounding surprised.

I blinked and turned, somewhat surprised myself. "Why not?"

"No one's entirely sure. No healer can. One theory is that it's because you're trying to use your own energy and put it back into yourself at the same time. Cancels itself out, so to speak."

"The Fae can heal themselves," I protested. So could the Blood. And the Beasts. Though they didn't work magic to do so.

"The Fae are near enough to immortal. Their bodies don't work in exactly the same way as ours, nor does their magic."

"Can you work other magic on yourself?"

"External things—shields or the odd bad glamour, yes. Otherwise, no."

So he'd gone into a Blood Assembly with really little more protection than his dagger? And approached a Beast today with the same lack of defense? He had the self-preservation instincts of a . . . well, a berserk Templar knight, I realized. Guy had taught him to fight. Obviously it had left an impression.

From what I knew, most Templars weren't mages. They didn't rely on anything other than their skill with weapons and combat techniques and their faith in their God and any protection they might be granted.

Crazy humans. Survival was what mattered. Which meant using every resource you had, and every weapon you could get your hands on.

"Do you treat Fae, then?"

He nodded. "Sometimes. They keep somewhat to themselves, even those who live outside Summerdale. They don't often need a healer, but we treat anyone who asks here."

"Your Lady Bryony would seem to disagree on that point."

His expression clouded, making me wonder what exactly had happened after I had left. Nothing that boded well for me if the sudden anger in his eyes was any indication.

My mouth felt suddenly dry as I waited for him to say something. But then he surprised me by shaking his head, anger gone from his face as quickly as a summer storm. He seemed perfectly at ease once again. Which only made me feel more wary.

This man wasn't as simple as he seemed. I needed to remember that.

"Ignore Bryony." He turned back to the rack and pulled out a pair of trousers made from heavy black cloth. They looked small enough to fit me even though they were obviously meant for a man. "Here, try these."

I looked around the small room. It offered no privacy and I wasn't about to climb out of my clothes in front of Simon. "Perhaps you could wait outside?"

His cheeks went faintly pink then. "Of course. I wasn't thinking." He moved past me to the door, angling his body to avoid mine.

But in the small space, he was still far too close and the need flared, making me ache. I pressed backward against the rack of clothes, hoping he wouldn't notice anything untoward.

When the door closed, I hurriedly scrambled out of my clothes, tugging at them roughly to distract myself from the hum of want in my veins. Peeling off leather trousers is never that easy a process, but I managed eventually and pulled on a shirt and the black trousers. Both were slightly too big but would do. I could move easily enough in them anyway.

I put my vest back on. The leather had three neat slits where the Beast had caught me, but lacking any proper undergarments, I wasn't going to walk around with just a shirt.

Unlike most females, I didn't wear corsets and frills beneath my clothes. You can't fight in a corset, nor are they designed to work with trousers. And, built as I am, along Fae lines and therefore not running much to curves, my close-fitted leather vests provided more than enough support along with their protection.

I felt better with it in place. I wrapped my belt around my waist, made sure my weapons were in place and secure; then, with all my flesh safely covered again, I opened the door to join Simon.

His expression was indecipherable but he merely nodded and said, "That looks better. Let's find you some food."

We resumed our progress through the hospital, Simon starting again on his "history of St. Giles." We had reached the wards, it seemed now, and he paused at each to look through the door and say a word or two to a patient or one of the healers. Inspecting his domain?

Most of the beds were full and most of the patients I saw were human. Which seemed slightly strange. I hadn't heard of any outbreaks of illness in the human boroughs, nothing to cause patient numbers to be unusually high. Normally one would expect those in the Night World to suffer more of the sorts of injuries that would require a healer than humans.

Curiosity got the better of me.

"Is it always this busy here?" I asked after Simon finished speaking to yet another of the healers. She was another Fae, with dark hair and silvery green eyes, who kept her expression scrupulously polite in Simon's presence. She didn't meet my eyes, though, and I added her name—Endine—to my list of Fae to avoid.

"Yes. The City is a dangerous place lately. We're close to the border boroughs, so we have plenty of custom."

There was an edge to his voice, the anger he'd swallowed earlier swimming up in his eyes again. "Of course," he continued, "there are always those beyond our help." His tone seemed suddenly almost disgusted.

Did he mean the dead or those lost to the Night World? The blood-locked? Did he despise them for their weakness? And if so, what might he think of me once he learned the truth?

Something deep inside me rebelled at the thought of hearing that same disgust aimed at me.

I looked away, back into the ward. How could he feel anything but disgust? Here they fought to heal. How many times had he tried to save someone only to lose someone who embraced their destruction by drinking vampire blood?

As I did. No matter how unwilling, I still did it. As I killed. Simon would never understand that either.

At least, I had never left someone maimed and mangled. I killed fast and clean. Mercy of a kind. The only kind I had to offer.

I looked back at Simon, who would no doubt find out just how costly I was in time. I needed to make him realize I was another of those lost causes if I wanted to spare him that. The thought made me lose my appetite, but I knew I needed food, so I forced the sick feeling away.

"I thought we were going to eat," I said.

Chapter Ten

"There's something you're not telling me," Lily said.

I looked up from my plate. She sat opposite me, across my desk. We'd returned to my office with our meals. I'd thought she would appreciate the privacy. If her appetite was any indication, she did. Several plates lay empty in front of her—she'd put away a surprising amount of food. So had I.

But between bites, I'd also tried to keep her talking. I wanted her to feel comfortable with me. I'd aimed the conversation toward safe waters but was aware of time ticking away. Bryony's deadline was looming as every hour passed and the sun grew lower in the sky.

"There are lots of things I'm not telling you," I said, stalling for time.

I had to ask Lily if she would help us, but I knew it was too soon. I needed time to let her grow to trust me. Time for her to see that she could make a difference to the City. I had taken her around the hospital, shown her the people hurt by the Night World's encroachments, but a few hours wasn't enough time to undo the effects of a lifetime lived with Lucius. I knew there was good in her, that she could change, but Bryony was asking too much.

"I imagine that's true but I meant something specific," she said. "You've been giving me chapter and verse on the history of St. Giles for several hours now. It's an interesting place but not that interesting. So, what aren't you saying?"

She sounded relaxed but her posture gave her away. She was on alert, ready to respond. Her right hand rested, as it often did, on the hilt of her dagger.

My pistol was in the top drawer of my desk. I refused to wear a weapon within hospital walls. It was against everything I'd chosen to become when I'd set my feet on the healer's path. My fingers itched, though, wishing I had it to hand. I didn't know how Lily would react. I thought I was fast enough to beat her if I had to, but the fact was she was armed and I wasn't.

"Bryony isn't happy about you being here." That much, I supposed, she had already realized.

"That's not exactly new information," she said.

"No. But she does have power over this hospital."

"I thought you were a Master Healer."

"I am. But Bryony runs St. Giles. Final decisions are hers."

"Are you saying I can't stay here?" Her hand flexed over the dagger.

"I'm saying there are conditions."

Her expression turned intent. "Such as?"

I hesitated. Too soon. Wrong timing, wrong place, wrong message. Lily was going to be furious as soon as I spoke, any fledgling bond between us shattering.

"There's—" My door banged open and Bryony came storming in, Guy close on her heels. Lily sprang to her feet and I rose as well.

"There are Beasts outside," Bryony snarled.

Gods and fucking suns, this was all I needed. More ammunition for Bryony to use against Lily. "On Haven grounds?"

"No. But I can feel them testing the wards."

"How do you know they're not just passing by?" I extended my own senses to the wards, hoping like hell that Bryony was overreacting. But she wasn't. There were too many Beasts registering around the hospital boundaries. This was human territory. The Beast packs didn't venture here often.

"They're after her," Bryony said, ignoring my question. She jerked her head in Lily's direction. "If they try something, we're putting everyone here at risk by allowing her to stay."

"Lucius isn't going to risk attacking a Haven. You said I had until sunset to ask."

"Ask me what?" Lily demanded.

"How about we talk about that part later?" Guy said. "We can solve this by taking Lily to the Brother House."

Lily took a step back. "I don't think so."

"Guy," I said warningly.

Guy, in true pigheaded, I-know-best, Templar fashion ignored me. "It's the safest place for you," he said to Lily.

"Easiest place for you to lock me up, you mean," Lily retorted.

"Don't be paranoid. How exactly are we supposed to keep you locked up?" Guy said.

"You would if you could," Lily snapped.

"Of course we would." Bryony joined the argument. Exactly what we didn't need.

Gods and suns. "No one's locking anyone up." I tried to look calm and sensible. Not that any of the three of them appeared to be in the mood to listen to calm and sensible.

Bryony looked like she was about to launch into one of her lectures. I held up a hand. "Lily, Guy's right. The Brother House might be the best option."

"So I should just let you lock me up there for the rest of my life? No, thank you."

"Just until Lucius loses interest," I said, trying to reason with her.

She shook her head. "What makes you think he's going to lose interest? It would be better for me to leave the City."

"No!" The denial came as an unbidden roar. I was not going to have this discussion yet again. I knew in my gut she wouldn't make it alone. Plus, there was this inconvenient longing I felt. If she left, I'd never get to do anything about it. Nor was I at all sure that it would go away if she did.

Everyone was staring at me. I cleared my throat. "I'd like to speak to Lily alone. Please." The "please" came as an afterthought. Guy looked at me for a long moment, as if he could see exactly what was going through my head, but then finally he nodded. Extending his arm to Bryony, he escorted her out of the room.

The door shut behind them and I wove a quick aural shield. Just in case Bryony was tempted to listen in. Once I was satisfied the doors were secure, I crossed to the window to check the wards there, then, planting myself on the windowsill so I could soak up some of the light to replace the power I'd just used, turned to Lily.

"This isn't exactly how I planned this." The sun soaked through my skin, trickling down to the part of me that fueled my powers. But for once, the flow of light didn't calm me.

"Planned what?"

"Helping you."

Anger flushed her face. "I don't understand."

"Before I tell you, I want you to remember something."

"What's that?"

"That I do want to help you."

Her lips pressed shut and she looked away. Damn. She was going to hide from me. Perhaps Bryony was right and I was crazy. Lily was a creature of the Night World. Shaped by Lucius into a weapon. I doubted she'd ever trusted anyone in her life. Did she even know how?

Could she learn? There was only one way to find out. "Would you look at me, please?" I asked.

"Why?

I was starting to think *why* was her favorite word. "I prefer to see who I'm talking to."

This made her frown slightly. "You know who you're talking to."

"Lily, I doubt anyone who speaks to you knows that."

That made her frown deepen. But she didn't reply, so I continued on. "Do you really want to run?" It seemed we were going to have the discussion again whether I liked it or not.

"I . . ." She hesitated, one hand straying to her thigh again. Seeking the comfort of her weapons. What did it say about her life if cold metal was what she turned to for reassurance? "I still think it would be better if I did."

"Better for who?"

"Everyone."

"Why?" I threw the word back at her.

"Because it's dangerous with me here."

"It's always dangerous."

"They don't want me here," she said accusingly.

They being Guy and Bryony. "I think you're underestimating Guy. His offer was genuine."

Bryony, I didn't bother defending. The Fae didn't generally acknowledge their half-breeds. And wraiths were the worst of them. "Try thinking about it from their viewpoint. They know about you. What it is that you do for Lucius. But they don't know *you*."

"Neither do you, apparently," she said bluntly.

The accusation stung. More than I liked. But that was the part of me that wanted her in my bed talking. I had to ignore that part and use my head. Try to break through to her. "I could. They could too."

"For a price," she said. "That's right, isn't it? You want something from me. You have an angle after all."

She sounded disappointed. My stomach twisted. "It's not that simple."

"Just tell me."

Time to be honest. Lance the boil, so to speak. One quick stroke to deal with the problem. "Lucius is dangerous. He's been pushing for more territory, more power over the last few years. He's succeeding. We need to stop him."

"'We' being the humans."

"Being anyone who wants a decent life without the Blood—without *Lucius*—running the City," I shot back.

She shook her head at me but didn't argue.

"We need to stop him," I repeated. "To do that we need to limit his power. Which requires the Fae to help us. They hold the balance of power at the treaty negotiations. They could check him. But they won't without proof that he's actively violating the treaties."

"Proof?"

"I want you to give evidence against him. Tell them that he sent you to kill me. Under oath."

The color drained from her face. "You want me to betray Lucius?"

I tried to make my voice gentler. "I want you to do the right thing."

She looked as though I'd slapped her. "You might as well just let Guy cut off my head. It would be a more merciful death."

"I'll protect you."

"No." Her hand sliced through the air as she shook her head again. "You wouldn't be able to. Not for long enough. I won't do it. It would be suicide."

"I can keep you safe, Lily," I said. How the hell could I convince her? "If you do this, I promise I'll keep you safe. You could have a life here."

Her face twisted. "You should let me go."

"Go where, back to him? Is that really a better option than trying to stop him?"

"You don't understand. I could . . . just leave the City."

"You really think you can outrun Lucius? If you think we can't protect you here, then what makes you think you'll survive on your own?" I moved from the window, not fast, not enough to scare her, but I needed to be closer. If I could just make her see . . .

"I can try."

"You'll fail." You'll die, was what I should have said. That would be the price for failure. But I couldn't say it. Didn't want to speak the words and maybe conjure them to life.

Her whole body twisted now as she half turned to the door, then back to me, the leather of her vest creaking ever so faintly against the brush of cotton from her clothing. Fighting her instincts again. The soft rustles sounded like leaves breaking under the hooves of a deer about to flee a hunter.

"So it's better instead to be locked up by the Templars? Trade one set of bars for another?" she asked.

She'd spent enough of her life chained to Lucius. I wasn't going to see her forced again. If she chose, she would do so willingly. "I wouldn't let them do that. We can help you. If you help us."

"Why? Why do you even care?" Her voice almost cracked.

I moved closer still. "Because it's the right thing to do."

She actually stepped back at that, chin snapping up defiantly. "I told you I didn't need to be saved. Find someone else to die heroically for."

Another half step forward. "It's not just you who needs saving. We're talking about the City itself. Anyway, who says I'm going to die?"

"Who says you won't?" She retreated. Much farther and she'd have to turn herself into a book and slot herself onto a bookshelf to escape me.

I paused. Free choice. I was no better than Lucius if I used intimidation. But gods and suns, I wanted to take hold of her and either shake some sense into her or— No. Not wise to think about alternative activities. "What does it matter if I die? Why do you care about that?"

She looked away. "I don't."

Liar. Certainty burned in my gut. She did care. I also knew she didn't want to, but that wasn't important. She did. I could work with that. Maybe I was going about this backward after all. Maybe I should try to use that tiny flame of emotion, that vulnerability which had to feel brand-new for her and make her feel even more.

Hook the heart—or suns, at this point, even the body would do—and perhaps the brain would follow. "There's another reason."

Her head turned. Slowly. Forever hung in the few heartbeats it took for her eyes to meet mine. "What?"

Just do it.

I stepped, reached, caught her hand with mine, tangling our fingers together and squeezing so my palm pressed to hers, flesh to flesh. Nothing in between. Nothing separating. Heat flared at the contact, tore through me. Made me want to do far more than hold her hand. But I kept watching. Waiting. And I saw what I was looking for.

Her pupils went wide and black, and she swayed toward me, just a little. A little was enough.

"That," I said roughly.

She tried to pull her hand free, but I held on, tightening my grip. "You feel it too. Don't bother denying it. I could feel it in you when I healed you."

Her hand jerked under mine. "That isn't worth dying for," she said in a voice not entirely steady.

"How do you know?" I couldn't look away from her mouth. Her lips were a deep, deep pink against that pale skin.

"I—"

No. I wasn't going to let her protest and deny. Not anymore. I was going to show her I was right.

Even if she stabbed me afterward. My other hand reached, found her, pulled her close. And my mouth came down on hers. Settled there. Tasted her. Salt and life and warmth.

At first she stiffened in my arms and I thought she was going to pull free. But then her mouth opened beneath me, and she sank into me, her free hand reaching up to grab my head and pull me closer.

It felt like swallowing the sun.

Pleasure so intense it seared rushed through me in a burning wave and turned everything else to ash. There was only Lily in my arms, only the taste of her and the smell of leather and cotton and female and the need to burn even hotter.

It felt as good as the first time my power had quickened to the sun. Or perhaps even better.

I groaned against her mouth, pulled her closer, wanting to climb inside her. Where? Desk? Floor? Suns. Who cared? Just more.

My fingers found the top button of her shirt without thought, flicked it open.

And suddenly she pushed me away with a gasp that sounded as though it tore her throat. The sudden lack of her made my head spin, and by the time my vision had cleared and some vestige of sanity returned, she was halfway across the room.

Glaring at me while her chest heaved.

Mine heaved too but right now that didn't matter.

What mattered was getting my hands on her again. Though I was willing to wait until she wasn't looking quite so murderous before I attempted it.

Gray eyes narrowed at me, looking like she wanted to kill me.

She looked beautiful.

Beautiful and deadly. I remembered suddenly that she was very well armed. And my gun was across the room locked in a drawer. Still, she could have stabbed me during the kiss and she hadn't.

"I hope you're not waiting for me to say sorry," I said. "Because I'm not."

"No. You're just crazy." She planted her hands on her hips, balled them into fists. Which at least was better than reaching for her stilettos.

"Not crazy, realistic. I told you there was another reason."

"You want to risk everything for simple lust?"

"Whatever that was, it wasn't simple, shadow," I shot back. "And I doubt it was entirely lust either."

"You *are* crazy," she said flatly.

"We could be crazy together." I risked a half smile.

Her glare intensified. "No. We will not be doing *that* again."

"Ah. Well, maybe I'll be able to change your mind about that."

"You want me to be *your* pet."

"No." I was serious now. "No, I want you to be yourself. I want you to see the woman I felt in my arms when you look in the mirror. Someone beautiful. Someone worthy. Someone free. Someone who belongs to herself. Someone who chooses for herself."

The anger faded from her eyes a little. And if I'd had to name the emotion that replaced it, I would have to choose fear. The same fear any caged thing might face when presented with a chance of freedom.

"How do you know what I see in the mirror?"

"Just a wild guess."

The anger returned. Not unexpected. She was returning to what she knew. To her walls and ice.

"You know nothing," she said.

"Then let me find out. Let me in, Lily. I can help you."

She actually took a step backward. "No."

"Would you rather stay in your cage, then?"

"No!"

I was pushing too hard. I could see it written on her face. She wanted to run. Her skin practically quivered with the need to flee. But I couldn't help it. I wanted her to see. "Then what do you want?"

She bit her lip, hard enough I wondered that she didn't draw blood. "I want to be left alone. I want to be free. Of everyone."

Including me and that oh so inconvenient lust she felt. That was perfectly clear from her tone.

I spread his hands wide. "Letting someone help you isn't an obligation. Nor is helping them."

She shook her head. "Everything is an obligation."

Time to withdraw. It seemed I was making things worse at this point. I let my hands fall, pretended to smooth my shirtsleeves. "I want you to think about it. What I asked. Regardless of anything that followed. If you help us, you can be free. You don't owe me anything."

"What?" she said scornfully. "You expect me to believe you don't want to bed me?"

I looked straight at her. No pretending. "Oh no, I want that. I think that's clear enough. But I don't expect you to. I won't force you to. I'll still be on your side if you don't."

"Why?"

And we'd come full circle. "I don't think you'd understand if I told you. But hopefully you will one day. Now I think I should let you be alone for a time. You have things to think about. You don't have to decide straightaway. I'll go talk to Bryony."

She didn't respond. Hopefully she was thinking about what I'd said. What I'd asked. What I'd done. Regardless, it was time to leave, as much as I wanted to stay and soothe her until she wasn't so afraid.

But she was the only one who could set herself free. She had to choose. I schooled my face to casual and crossed the room, paused by the door. "Oh, and, Lily?"

"Yes?" Her eyes met mine and the confusion in their depths was hard to see. Being cruel to be kind wasn't exactly my style. But I didn't know what else to do.

"One more thing I know," I said in my best know-it-all-just-like-a-Templar tone.

"What?"

"If you run, you'll never be truly free."

))

Empty, Simon's office was a calm oasis. The plants and sunshine looked peaceful. Were peaceful. Unlike me. I leaned my head against the bookshelf and sucked in the cool green scented air, willing it to calm the turmoil in my head and body.

But I'd only taken a few breaths before the door swung open again, startling me. Bryony appeared in the doorway. I wondered how she'd avoided Simon. Hidden herself with a glamour, I imagined.

She stalked toward me. The Fae generally glide, not stalk. I felt a petty surge of satisfaction. Here was someone perfectly suited to exercising my temper on. I would be happy to fight if she tried her grand Fae attitude on me again. Fighting was easier by far than thinking about everything that had just passed between Simon and me.

Better yet, if I made her angry enough she might leave me alone again.

"You're still here," she said without any preamble.

"Did you think I'd leave?"

"No," she said. "I thought you'd do whatever suited you, no matter the price to others."

"I don't see why it's any concern of yours what I do."

Bryony's blue eyes turned thunderous blue like the depths of a cloud brewing lightning. "You—"

"Yes, I know," I said impatiently. "I'm shadow kin." Her lips thinned at the interruption. Good. She was mad. I made myself smile at her and perched on the edge of the desk, letting my legs swing.

She already thought I was worse than garbage. I doubted there was anything I could do to change that despite Simon's urgings. So I might as well be myself. "*In'sai'hal a'tan*. Soulless. Abomination, whatever you wish to call me," I continued. "You despise me. I'm perfectly clear on that. The feeling is somewhat mutual. But I'm not leaving." Maybe everyone else here thought the sun shone out of her oh so perfect arse, but I'd grown up with a lot scarier things than a Fae healer.

"Every patient in this hospital is at risk while you're here."

She meant the Beasts. I chose to misunderstand her, in no mood to make anything easier for the Fae. The Fae who prided themselves on being so controlled and calm. So powerful. The Fae that Simon wanted me to convince to intervene for the better of the City.

As far as I could tell, the Fae should do it because it was the right thing to do. They could curb Lucius. The Veiled Queen could turn him to ash on the spot if she willed it. The fact that they chose to remain aloof—using the treaty as an excuse to avoid acting— only demonstrated how little they cared for anyone other than their own kind. "You think I'm going to hurt people? What exactly do you think I can do right now surrounded by sunlight?"

Sunlight. Simon. My feeling of having regained control slipped as suddenly as if the desk had collapsed beneath me. My mouth still burned where he'd kissed me. I could taste him. Feel him. Feel the fires he'd left behind, glowing and rich like liquid sunlight flowing through my veins.

As dangerous as sunlight to me.

And definitely something I didn't want Bryony knowing about. Simon had said he'd felt me wanting him when he'd healed me. I was taking no such risk that Bryony could somehow sense it too. She already seemed to hate me without knowing one of her precious healers wanted to—

Help me.

That's what he'd said. Yes, he'd also said he wanted to bed me, but that seemed the least of what he wanted. He wanted me to trust him. Trust him with my life.

Wanted me to help bring down Lucius.

Wanted to use me as a weapon, just as Lucius did.

He'd offered me Haven, told me he could change my life. And even though I've always known that everyone has their own agenda, finding out that Simon did too left a bitter taste in my mouth.

He asked too much.

More than I could give.

Bryony didn't answer my question.

"Well? What do you think will happen?" I repeated.

"I think Lucius will want you back. I think we'll pay the price of that desire."

Her tone cracked like the lightning in her eyes. Good. Her anger roused mine again. Giving me back my focus. "I didn't ask to be taken from my world. Simon and Guy did that. Don't blame me."

She pointed at the door. "Go, then. Go back where you belong."

"Like a good pet should? Return to my master? To the one your people sold me to like a dog?"

"You stayed with him before now. What's changed?"

That one hit home. I sank down into the chair. A plant brushed my cheek and I pushed it away gently. What had changed?

Nothing.

Everything.

Nothing I wanted to explain to Bryony, even if I could.

But it *was* different now. Lucius had crossed a line when he'd fed from me.

And Simon had just drawn another line. Asking me to choose a side. To take a stand.

Did I want to cross it? Did I dare? Both of them wanted

to use me. But for the first time I had a choice. I could choose a side. Or I could run. My head ached, thinking about it.

"*Tchah.*" Bryony's delicate nose wrinkled. "You can't even answer. Yet you bring danger to my hospital, to my people. Why should I trust you?"

"*Your* people?" I said. "I wasn't aware St. Giles was under Fae control. Is that what worries you about me? That I might upset *your* pets?"

She recoiled from me as I'd drawn a gun. The chain round her neck jangled, its rainbow sheen dulling. "My—"

"It makes sense," I said, taking far too much satisfaction in the discomfort in her face. I'd never had an actual conversation with a Fae before. Apparently I had some things to say. "That you see them that way, I mean. After all, that's how the Fae deal with things. Assume they're in charge. Sell their problems off to be dealt with by others. That takes a certain superior point of view."

"Would you rather have been strangled at birth?"

"I'd rather have been treated as a person. Then again, given that would have meant growing up amongst your kind, perhaps I got off lightly. At least I do not see myself as superior."

"You see nothing," Bryony said. "You kill people."

"Are you telling me the Fae have never killed anyone? What about all those wars?"

"You are not a soldier."

I shrugged at her. "That depends on how you define war, I suppose."

Her lips thinned and she shook her head. The sun made her dark hair gleam, crowning her with light. But she was Fae and they were creatures of illusions and darkness as much as beauty and light. She was no better than me.

She pointed at me with the hand that bore the heavy Family ring. It gleamed too, heavy with blue and purple gems. I didn't know which Family they represented and didn't particularly care.

"Then you're worse, a soldier who would switch sides. A traitor. Untrustworthy."

"You can't have it both ways. I can't be terrible for working for Lucius and terrible for not wanting to work for Lucius."

The accusing finger jabbed at the air again. "For all we know, you're still working for him. This could all be a ploy."

"A ploy to do what? What is that you all suspect Lucius is up to?"

She shook her head. "We don't know." She pursed her lips, considering me. "Perhaps you do. Perhaps I should find out?"

My hand strayed down toward my dagger. "Oh yes? How exactly? Your enchantments don't work on me. Were you planning to torture me?"

Her silence was telling.

I suddenly felt vaguely sickened. Simon kept making me believe that maybe the world was different from how I thought it was. Bryony was disproving his optimism quite neatly. I hadn't expected that such a thing would upset me. "You know, I suddenly find the idea of the Brother House quite attractive. Guy gave me his word. I think I can rely on the word of a Templar at least. Unlike the Fae."

"The Fae do not lie!"

"The Fae don't do a lot of things." I turned. "The humans are willing to give me a choice. For the first time ever. Which I think probably makes them better than either you or me." I closed my eyes, picturing Simon for a moment. Something clean in all this mess. "So don't worry. Once Simon returns I'll be gone from your precious hospital. Maybe the Templars might loan me a dictionary. It turns out, Haven doesn't exactly mean what I thought it did."

Chapter Eleven

))

A sunmage to one side of me and a Templar to the other. If you'd asked me a few days earlier what my worst nightmare might be, I would have described something exactly like this. Not to mention the fact that we were in a tunnel heading to the Brother House and a second armed-to-the-teeth Templar walked *behind* me.

Add in the fact that they wanted me to help them bring down Lucius and it should truly have felt like a nightmare.

Right now, though, despite the fact that I'd refused to betray him to Simon, my worst nightmare would have fangs, iron and ruby rings, and a precarious grip on reality. It was the fear Lucius invoked that had driven my refusal. I had told Simon the truth. Betraying Lucius would be suicide. He would get his revenge. There was no way they could protect me unless I agreed to spend the rest of my life in the Templar Brother House.

Which I wasn't about to do. Even now, when I'd chosen to come here, I was apprehensive about exactly what waited for me.

I wanted to trust Simon. The fact that he'd been honest about what he wanted from me, even if what he wanted was to use me, was both infuriating and oddly reassuring. I was still angry with him, but somehow, the presence of Simon and Guy at each side and Liam bringing up the rear, I found almost . . . comforting.

Which might just be the strangest thought I'd ever had.

Our route through the tunnels wasn't exactly the same as the one Simon and I had taken earlier, but we still passed by the tunnel branch that smelled of iron.

As we came closer I watched both Simon and Guy closely. Neither of them so much as turned their heads in the direction of the entrance to the tunnel. But it was Simon who ignored it so studiously he might as well have held up a "Don't look over there" sign.

I made sure I didn't look either. Instead I sniffed softly, tasting the air, wondering what was down there. I couldn't smell anything but iron and the same strange deadened air we were breathing. Which only spoke more strongly of there being something heavily warded at the other end.

"Do the tunnels go all the way to the Brother House?" I asked Guy. I wasn't talking to Simon. Talking might lead to something foolish like wanting to kiss him again. Or punch him.

One of the two.

The need prowled restlessly as he walked beside me and I was trying not to pay any more attention to him than was strictly necessary.

"Yes. It's useful for us to have a quick way to the hospital sometimes," Guy said. He didn't say any more, but I could only think of one reason for Templars to need access to St. Giles. To carry their wounded here for treatment. Treatment for injuries inflicted by the Night World. I hid my wince and Guy pretended not to notice. He moved as lightly as his brother, despite the half ton of chain mail he wore. I hoped I'd never have to fight him. Not in daylight anyway.

I was walking lightly myself. Nothing hurt, though I was beginning to feel as if I might fall down if I didn't sleep soon. I had eaten and, thanks to Harriet and Simon, the wounds inflicted by the Beasts and Lucius had gone. The visible ones at least.

The other wounds were beyond help. With each step, the need clawed at me, fired by Simon's kiss. It seemed any pleasure sparked its hunger for more. And I wasn't so sure I could fight it into submission again. My whole body wanted. There was a constant whisper of Lucius' name in my head. A treacherous voice telling me how easy it would be to leave in darkness. To go back. To get what I needed.

I was doing my best to shut it out, calling on years of practice. I was stronger than it. I had to be.

If I could last a few days until I could come up with a plan, then I ... didn't know what exactly. There was no cure for the need.

The humans wanted me to help them, to choose their side—a chance at something new—but that choice, even if I were willing to make it, didn't offer a solution to my problem.

Don't think about it. "Isn't it dangerous?"

Guy looked down at me. "The tunnels?"

"Yes. The Blood could move through them in daylight."

"The entrances are well guarded. And the tunnels themselves are not without defenses." His tone made it clear he wasn't going to explain what those might be.

I didn't blame him. Not giving away secrets is a good survival strategy. But it stymied my attempt at conversation. It wasn't as if the tunnels had any features of interest to remark on. Just yard after yard of marble tiles and walls that were either wood-paneled or painted in a bland pale green with very little to distinguish one branch from another. Here and there wards glimmered over the walls, but it wasn't as if wards were unexpected in such a place.

It would be very easy to get lost down here if you had a poor sense of direction. But I had no doubt I could retrace my steps if I needed to. Knowing which direction I traveled being able to orient myself to the earth, was a gift from my Fae mother.

It had come in handy over the years.

The tunnel took another right turn and we were suddenly faced with a massive metal gate. It didn't smell of iron. Probably bronze fortified by a metalmage, though it was painted black.

The Brother House lay behind those bleak black bars.

Ready to cage me.

The Brother House itself was much as I had expected. Sparsely decorated, its gray granite walls spoke of discipline and strength. The floors were stone too, worn smooth by the many feet that had walked the corridors over the centuries. The Templar Order was a very old one. The thought of exactly how many holy warriors had lived here—how many might live here now—gave me an uneasy feeling in the pit of my stomach.

The air no longer felt dead. Now it reeked of armor and leather. Of gunpowder and oil and a strange thread of woody incense. Mostly it smelled of men. Many, many men.

Which hardly helped my efforts to control the need.

As we passed by a door guarded by two knights, Guy showed Simon and me to two small chambers, side by side, in the guest quarters. Each held little more than a basic wooden bed and a small table and chair. The stone walls and floors were bare and the window coverings were thick white linen. More like a monk's cell than a bedroom.

After explaining how to get to the bathrooms and dining hall and admonishing Simon to keep an eye on me and not let me wander around, Guy made his excuses and left us alone.

Or alone as we could be with guards posted at either end of the corridor.

"How long will we be staying?" I asked when it became clear that Simon wasn't going to leave me to my own devices just yet. Keeping my eyes firmly away from the bed, I perched on the table, pressing my back into the stone wall beneath two slim glass windows. The sky outside was a darkening blue, though the sun still rode its depths, heating the late afternoon. It would stay there for quite some hours yet. The days were long this time of year. The light shining through the windows was sliced into patterns by the bars beyond the glass.

More bars.

I swallowed, ignoring the caged feeling tightening my neck. Then put my feet on the chair, so Simon couldn't choose to sit there.

He merely raised an eyebrow, then leaned against the wall near the door. "Until Guy thinks it's safe."

"Or until his brother knights decide to chop off my head?"

"That's not going to happen. I'll speak to the Abbott General in the morning." Simon seemed unworried by our change in accommodations. But his calm appearance hardly eased my fears.

"I don't see why he would agree for me to stay here. Not when I'm not going to do what you want," I said, not wanting Simon to see my concern. I didn't need comfort. Particularly not the sort of comfort he was likely to offer.

"Don't worry about that," Simon said. "I'll deal with it. You're safe. They'll be eating soon. Then there'll be the evening services. Then they'll be sleeping or patrolling."

"Perfect," I muttered. Holy warriors newly inspired by their observances. Just what I didn't need. "In that case, maybe you'd be so kind as to leave me alone and let me sleep?"

"I want to talk to you."

Lords of hell. More talking. I'd done more talking since meeting Simon than in the several months—if not years—prior to that. The Court not being a place full of people I wanted to talk to. Still, if he wasn't going to leave, talking was better than silence and that hells-damned bed looming at us. "What now?"

"At the hospital you said that you didn't know why Lucius wants you back so badly. Is that the truth?"

"Can't Her Mighty Faeness tell you whether or not I was lying?"

"I didn't ask Bryony. I'm asking you."

Which didn't answer my question, I realized. I scratched my side. I might have been healed faster than was natural, but apparently the newly healed flesh still itched like any other wound. "You should learn to use your available resources better."

"That's not an answer."

I sighed. "Apart from the obvious, that I'm a useful tool to him, then no, I don't know why he would risk breaking the treaty to get to me." It was partly true. Blood hunger didn't seem like a good reason to go to war to me. Not that I was going to mention the fact that Lucius had fed from me to Simon. I hadn't completely lost my wits.

I studied him for a moment. "And anyway, what makes you so sure all of this is for me? Maybe he's still trying to get to you." I shifted, trying to find a comfortable position. "Why is he trying to kill you? Were you telling me the truth when you said you didn't know?"

I watched him carefully, looking for any telltale sign he was lying.

His expression didn't change, not even a little. "Other than the obvious, that I'm a sunmage and have a little power in the day world? No."

If it hadn't been for the iron in the tunnels, I might have
believed him. But I didn't, no matter how skillfully he lied. If
there was a secret hidden down there, then Simon, by his
own admission, one of the most powerful sunmages and one
of the most powerful healers the humans had, knew about it.
Something hidden so carefully had to be something that the
Night World and the Fae wouldn't necessarily like.

Something perhaps worth a broken treaty and a war.

"It seems we're both mystified, then," I said.

"Do you think Lucius is up to something?"

"Lucius is always up to something."

His blue eyes darkened with annoyance. "Something
big, I mean."

"Something that could impact the treaties? Yes." I held
up a hand before he could ask. "But I don't know what it is.
I'm not privy to his political councils. And Lucius plays
deep. He may be the only one who knows."

If he was, he would wait, spring his ploy at the best—or
worst—possible time. Either during the formal negotiations or in the backroom deals that went with them. The
formal process dealt with grievances, proven offenses, and
petitions for increased privileges. Which was why Simon
wished me to testify against Lucius. But behind the scenes,
the races and the factions within them made deals to vote
together or to block others. And where alliances couldn't
be forged through goodwill or common interests, sometimes they were forged with good old-fashioned blackmail.
With threats of making unknown misdeeds known or
worse.

Not that such a tactic would work with Lucius. The Blood
and the humans did not historically cooperate, and he would
laugh off any attempt at blackmail and then most likely turn
around and obliterate those who threatened him.

Which only made me even more certain that Simon was
somehow doing just that. Proving a threat. I needed to
know how. And unlike Simon, I believed in having as many
resources available to me as possible, so if he wouldn't tell
me the truth, then I would seek it out myself.

I left a few hours after midnight. Simon had finally left me
to sleep after we'd eaten and I'd dropped off for a few
hours despite my good intentions. Then it had taken an-

other few hours of listening to figure out the timing of the
guards' patrols down the corridor. Not because I was worried about avoiding them. That part was easy. No, I needed
to know if they were going to check on me.

The door of my tiny room bolted from the inside, but it
had a small flap in it at eye level that opened from the *outside*. Made me wonder exactly what the Templars used these
rooms for. If they were for guesting knights, then why the spy
holes? And if they were cells, then why the inner bolts?

A puzzle for another time.

The guards had made three patrols down the corridor,
roughly an hour apart, but they'd made no move to open the
flap. Still, I stuffed my pillow under the blanket, hoping it would look real enough in the dark of the room.
With the linen curtains closed over the windows, there
was little light. It wouldn't work to fool anyone if they
held a lantern up to look or something, but otherwise it
should suffice.

I still wore the dark trousers and white shirt Simon had
given me at the hospital. When Simon had suggested I
might get cold during the night, Guy had given me a quilted
linen tunic in what I was coming to think of as Templar
gray. Probably what the brothers wore to practice in if the
faint hints of male sweat under the laundry smells of soap
and sunshine were anything to go by.

Gray and white weren't as good for sneaking around at
night as my black, but given that I intended to stay shadowed, it didn't much matter what I wore.

I'd caught my hair in a single braid, pinned in a coil around
my head. I'd undone it before sleeping, hoping it would help
ease the ache in my head, but I wouldn't go out with it loose.

I drifted through the walls, feeling relaxed for the first
time in days as the world grayed around me. I found my
way to the tunnels easily enough. It didn't take long to
reach the intersection with the iron stink.

I paused to listen but everything was silent. I hadn't
passed anyone at all in the tunnels, but, remembering Guy's
words about them being well defended, I'd stayed shadowed. Invisible to magic as well as any living beings.

I let the silence speak to me for another few breaths,
then started down the dark tunnel. I see perfectly well in
darkness but I still moved slowly, trying to sense ahead of

me. The iron smell grew stronger the farther I went. Harsh earthy metal. A large quantity of it.

After fifty or sixty feet, I found the source of the smell. A metal door barred the path. I couldn't tell if it was solid iron, or merely ironclad. The door spanned the width of the tunnel as well as its height. A lot of precious metal to use on a door. A heavy lock, made of some lighter metal, sparkled faintly in the darkness. Warded, then.

I considered my options: move through the warded door, which was usually perfectly safe, or go around it through the earth and brick surrounding the tunnel. I erred on the side of caution, even though I dislike moving through solid substances for extended periods of time.

Sliding through dirt or rock feels like something being dragged through your insides somehow. The weight presses on you until you feel you can't breathe. Which is ridiculous because as far as I've been able to determine, I don't actually need to breathe when I'm shadowed.

This wasn't too bad, though. I moved sideways a few feet, then forward, then sideways again once I'd cleared the door. I stepped into another short passage. Darkened again. There were lamps on the walls but they were unlit. I suspected they were oil rather than gas. Gas leaks underground could be deadly.

The passage ended in yet another locked and warded iron door. Secrets indeed. Secrets worth guarding at a very high price. So much iron was worth a small fortune. The amounts of iron and silver allowed to the humans under the treaties were highly regulated. Iron was ridiculously expensive and silver hardly cheaper.

As far as I knew, the humans reserved the vast majority of their allotted iron for weapons and mechanical things. Not doors and locks. Those were generally fashioned from lesser metals and fortified by a metalmage when needed. The humans didn't have the same range of magically altered metals as the Fae—who had, after all, more power and centuries-longer lives to perfect their arts—but they did well enough. But no one had yet invented alloys that performed as well as iron and silver for certain tasks. Including deterring Fae, Beasts, and Blood.

Like the first door, the lock of the second sparkled with wardlight. I repeated my trip through the wall and beyond it. The room beyond was not completely dark. A few thick candles burned in wall sconces, shedding a small amount of light.

Enough perhaps for a human to see a little.

Across the room a figure sat, bent over a desk situated a little way from yet another warded door. For a moment I thought he was an older human from the neat white tail of hair clubbed at his neck, but then the candles flickered as air moved and I caught his scent. A scent that made the need flare like the candles.

Vampire, I thought stupidly.

Surprise almost made me lose the shadow and I tightened my control as the figure turned in his chair.

What was one of the Blood doing—

His face came into the light and I bit back a gasp. Where his eyes should have been were knots of horribly scarred flesh.

Someone had put out his eyes.

I'd never seen such a thing. The Blood are hard to kill, quick to heal. To scar a Blood permanently took many applications of silver and fire and a twisted sense of revenge. Humans hadn't done this, I realized. Humans wouldn't waste time torturing one of the Blood; they'd just kill him.

No, this was the work of the Night World.

I swallowed. Hard.

The scars extended down his cheeks, twisting the lines of his face. The damage gave the illusion that he wore a half mask of thickened red and white leather, the darkness of the gaps where his eyes weren't mimicking the eyeholes of a mask eerily.

"Is someone here?" he said, his face turning from side to side as if to search the room.

This time I did gasp. I knew the voice. It belonged to someone I thought dead long ago.

I let go of the shadow, though I took firm hold of my dagger as I did so. "Atherton? Atherton Carstairs?" I said softly, staying where I was.

The vampire froze, then slowly his head moved again, stilling, with eerie precision, when he faced me. "Who is there?"

I didn't fool myself that he wasn't processing information about me. The Blood have supernatural senses. Hearing and smell far sharper than humans, or indeed, most of the Fae. Even blind, he could tell a lot about me.

"Do you know who I am?" I asked.

He moved fast then, too fast, in the way of the Blood. A sword materialized in his hand and I didn't doubt he could use it, blind or not. "Wraith," he said, voice rumbling with hate. "Has Lucius finally sent you to finish me off, then?"

I readied myself to shadow if necessary. "Put the sword down, Atherton."

The sword didn't move an inch. "And make it easier for you to do his dirty work? I think not. If you wish to kill me, then you'll have to work for it."

"If I wished to kill you, I could have done it already," I pointed out.

"He wouldn't want it to be that easy."

Probably true, knowing Lucius. But if I didn't want to be attacked by a furious blind vampire any minute now, I had to convince him I was friendly. "Lucius doesn't know I'm here." I said. "Lucius doesn't know where I am at all."

His face moved in what would be a frown if his skin could still move in normal ways. "Don't lie to me, shadow."

"Atherton," I said, trying not to let the loathing in his voice get to me. "It's me. You used to talk to me sometimes. I'm not here to kill you. I give you my word. Listen." I threw my stilettos, then the dagger onto the floor, the metal chiming against the tiled floor each time. "There, I'm unarmed." It wasn't that great a risk. I was fairly sure I could shadow before he could reach me with the sword.

"You could have other weapons."

"I could but if I did and I was here to kill you, then, as I said before, you'd already be dead. Lucius enjoys toying with his victims. I don't." I studied his ruined face, remembering how he used to look with a sense of growing horror. He'd been young when he'd been turned, and the slim lines of his face had suited the icy pallor of the Blood well. His eyes had been blue. Bright blue like Simon's.

I swallowed again, against a rising tide of nausea, that killed any lingering hints of the need. I wanted him to believe me. Yes, I could return to the shadow and move beyond him, but he would surely raise the alarm if I did so. I needed him to trust me. And I needed to know how he'd

come to be living down here in the depths of St. Giles.
"Atherton, what did he do to you?"

There was no doubt as to who "he" was. Only Lucius
would do something like this.

"I would think it clear enough?" Atherton gestured toward his face.

"But why?"

He made a short harsh sound that might have been a
laugh. "Isn't that obvious?"

Not really. Lucius liked to rule by fear and sometimes
there was no reason behind his rampages. But I couldn't
help wondering if Atherton's downfall had something to do
with me. Because of Louisa? Atherton had never approached me directly, though he hadn't ignored me like most
of the Court. He was young in Blood terms, not yet fifty.

When he'd vanished from Court, it had taken me awhile
to realize what had happened. The Blood move between
favored Court haunts and not all of them attended Lucius
at all times. Those who are still building their own power
bases, and must hunt for Trusted and food sources as well
as playing politics, move around frequently.

After several months had passed without seeing him or
Louisa, I had assumed they were dead.

I hadn't wanted to think too hard about how he might
have offended Lucius, and even if I had, there was no one I
could have asked. Either Atherton and his Trusted had
been quietly done away with or, more likely, horribly done
away with in one of those Blood-only sessions I was never
privy to.

The ones that left the Court smelling of fear for weeks.

"You crossed Lucius," I said slowly, nausea rising again.
Crossed Lucius as I was doing.

"I got played as a piece in Court politics," he said. "A
sacrificial pawn."

"But you lived." Blinded, scarred, but he was alive.

"Yes. If you call this living. But it's fitting in a way. I was
blind to what was really happening. Blind and arrogant."

What did he mean? Did he know something about what
Lucius was up to? Surely not? Wouldn't he have told the
humans—who obviously had given him shelter—by now?
Basic gratitude would seem to warrant such information.
"Someone helped you escape?"

"Yes." Again that twisting of features, his mouth turning in what I thought was pain. "My Trusted found where Lucius was keeping me and set me free. We were pursued and she . . . she died. I got away."

Regret flowed through his words. One of the Blood, sorry for the loss of a human. My world kept growing stranger. "How did you end up here?"

"I avoided my pursuers most of the night," he said slowly.

That could be done, if luck was on his side, I supposed. Vampires didn't shadow, but they could wrap themselves in darkness and become invisible for all intents and purposes, even to other vampires. I nodded, then realized he couldn't see. "And then?"

"I couldn't move fast. Not being able to see, it . . . it slowed me down."

That had to be an understatement. The Blood feel pain. So he'd made his way through the dark with his face half burned off, unable to see, having to rely on his other senses and hide himself at the same time. Terrifying. My spine chilled at the very idea.

"I wanted to seek Haven. And wanted to be out of the Night World boroughs. But by the time I got near to St. Giles, it was almost dawn and I was weak. I heard someone coming from the direction of the hospital, and I decided I could either risk asking for help or likely die from sunlight or Lucius' people finding me once dawn came. I asked for help. It was—"

"Simon," I breathed. I couldn't think of anyone else likely to help a wounded Blood reach a Haven rather than treat him only if he reached safety himself. "It was Simon DuCaine, wasn't it?"

"Yes, how did you know that?" His voice was puzzled.

In his place I would be confused too, but I ignored the question. "That explains how you got to the hospital. It doesn't explain how you came to be hidden away down here. Or what else is hidden down here with you." I looked past him to the final door. Something else lay behind that door. And if a blind vampire hidden away was only part of Simon's secret, then I had no idea what it might be.

"I'm not going to tell you that."

"Why not?"

"Because I don't know if I can trust you."

"I haven't tried to kill you yet."

I moved closer to him, my steps deliberately heavy, to ensure that he heard. It was hard. A lifetime's habit of not putting myself within arm's length of the Blood when I didn't have to is difficult to break.

"Three nights ago, Lucius sent me to kill Simon," I said slowly. "I didn't succeed. Last night, Simon took me from Halcyon during a Beast riot. I'm fairly sure Lucius now wants me dead. I have nothing to gain by going to him."

There was silence in the room. I could hear Atherton's heart beating, the slow, steady rhythm of the Blood that wouldn't be enough to sustain a human life. A familiar background sound to my life. One I'd really hoped not to hear again.

"I would like to believe you," he said finally.

"What's stopping you from doing just that?"

His nostrils flared a little. "I am blind but I am not otherwise disabled. I can smell you perfectly clearly. Which means, shadow, that I can also smell the taint of Lucius in you."

Chapter Twelve

))

I thought for a moment that I'd accidentally shadowed and sunk through the floor. The room pressed in on me, suddenly airless. Of all the things he could have said, I hadn't expected *that*. It took an effort to make my mouth work. "You can smell . . . what?"

"His scent is part of yours. You have . . . tasted," he said, anger licking through his voice. "You're locked to him."

"I am not blood-locked," I said, in automatic denial, as my thoughts reeled. Atherton knew. He knew my secret. "I'd hardly have left Lucius if I was." I prayed he would believe me.

His head tilted, considering. "True. But I can smell him in you. The blood of our kind is addictive." His hand shot out, grabbed my arm, long white fingers circling my wrist with inescapable strength. "I can feel it in you. Feel the need you feel. Like a fire beneath your skin. The wanting. You are locked to him." He drew in a breath, then pushed me away, hard enough to make me stumble back a few steps. "You should not come so close to me when you burn so."

I didn't know which of us he thought was at risk. Did I smell more tempting because Lucius had fed me or did Atherton think I would hunger for his own blood? The need felt no different standing close to him and presumably he would control himself, so I decided to ignore the issue. I was more interested in the part where he said he could tell I was addicted. Had the Blood always known? Or was this too a result of the amount of blood Lucius had fed me that last time? "I am not locked," I repeated.

"Maybe," he said shortly. "Maybe it is different for you than a human. But you feel the need, don't you?" He paused for a moment. "Why did I never sense it before?" he said almost to himself. "Why did none of us know? It makes sense for him to leash her so." He turned to me, head tilted. "How long has he been feeding you?"

"Why should I tell you that?"

"Answer me if you wish to have any hope of gaining my trust." His tone was heavy with anger.

I stared at him in frustration. I should just shadow, walk into the hell-cursed room beyond and find out what the secret was. But Atherton . . . Atherton knew secrets of his own. Blood secrets. He might know how to help me. How to free me from Lucius. Which was the only thing that could make a difference to me now. If he trusted me.

He needed to trust me if I had any hope of convincing him not to tell Simon my secret.

"I was fifteen when he first did it. The same year he started sending me out to kill." The worst year of my life. I'd been clumsy those first few times, ending up blood drenched and shaken more often than not. More than one of my targets had woken, babbling and pleading for mercy, my ears ringing with their voices for days afterward, haunting my sleep. And then, of course, there'd been the time Lucius had made me tear out a heart in front of the whole Court.

My fingers tightened at the memory. I'd learned to detach myself from the kills over time. Learned to be swift and unseen in the darkness. But I'd never learned to forget that particular kill.

"And now you are how old?" Atherton asked.

I had to stop and count. The Blood don't celebrate birthdays. "Thirty, or near enough." If I'd been pure Fae, they would still consider me a child. But I wasn't. I had matured faster than a Fae would, grown breasts and sprouted hair. I didn't bleed like a human, but I'd looked like an adult at fifteen.

Had felt adult when Lucius had sent me a red dress one night and commanded me to attend him. Until then, he'd never paid too much attention to me other than seeing to it that I was trained.

But I'd been young. Young and foolishly unsuspecting. The recollection dried my mouth, even now. The way he'd taken pleasure in hurting me, beating me. Then forced me to my knees before him. Before he'd tilted my head back oh so carefully and drawn a dagger. The way the terror flooded through me, making me shiver and sweat. I'd thought he'd been going to cut my throat. Instead he'd merely sliced his finger and, when the blood welled, placed it in my mouth, made me suck the blood.

Watched me as the pleasure took me.

When I'd come back to myself, lying on the floor, with ecstasy still running through me, he'd given me both the name of my first victim and the dagger he'd used. The one lying on the floor a few feet from me now. My fingers closed over the empty space at my hip and I shivered.

"So long," Atherton said after too long a silence. "Then he did not feed you often."

"No. Not often." Just often enough to keep me chained to him.

"Or very much, I would imagine. Or we would all have known. Which doesn't explain—" He closed the gap between us, reached for my wrist again. "So strong." His fingers tightened for a moment. Then he stepped back with a blown-out breath. "He fed you more recently. A lot more."

"Yes," I admitted. "After I failed to do something he asked. He wanted to humiliate me."

"He fed you in front of the Court," Atherton guessed. "How like him. Unfortunately for you, it means that he has only bound you more tightly."

My stomach tightened. "What do you mean?" Lords of hell, was it going to get worse? Would I turn mindless and useless like the blood-locked humans? Knowing nothing but the need, not caring about clothing or food or anything beyond the blood? Generally the Blood kill the locked before they get too far into that stage—they don't care for too much inconvenience—but some of them sometimes keep them. I'd seen them in the warrens, tangled hair, clothes in rags, huddled in corners, writhing with need, stinking of fear and longing.

Would that happen to me? No. I'd kill myself before—

"The larger the dose, the greater the need. The need grows and must be fed and—" He broke off. "You said you thought he wanted you dead. Why?"

"Since Simon took me, there have been several attempts to . . . retrieve me."

"That means only that he wants you returned to him, not necessarily dead," Atherton said reasonably.

"You know what he does to those who betray him." I said. "What do you think he'll do to me?"

"That rather depends," he said. "Has he ever drunk from you?"

I had to swallow several times before I could answer him. "Yes. Once. The night Simon took me."

"Ah."

His tone wasn't reassuring. I suddenly felt very naked without my weapons, but I made no move toward them. Atherton would only misinterpret my motives. "Is that important?"

"It may be. Do you know why the blood-locked tend to die?"

"They stop functioning," I said impatiently. "All they want is the blood."

"That is true. But a large number of them are killed by the ones who lock them. They drink too much."

"Why? Because the human will not stop them?" The Blood fed from the Trusted and other willing victims too, but there were rules and limits and safe words that donors who still had some semblance of rationality could employ. The blood-locked would not do anything to protect themselves. Hells, was that why they died before they got to the worst stages?

"No," Atherton said, shaking his head slowly. The candlelight flickered strangely over his scarred face, making the skin seem to shudder. "Or rather, not only that. When you drink the blood of one who is locked to you, it . . . it can be addictive too. Something changes in their blood and it can become irresistible if one is not careful."

"You mean the Blood become addicted to the locked?" I had never heard such a thing. Though, I had to admit, if it were true, it would be a secret the Blood guarded closely. "So that's why you become obsessed? And why you hide it, making it out to be fascination or desire," I said as the implications became clear. "It's an addiction for you too."

Atherton was moving now, pacing slowly. Four steps right, then a smooth gliding turn and four steps back to where he'd started. Keeping an even distance from me the entire time. Was I really a temptation to him?

His movement made the light waver even more, turning him into a shadowy thing in the darkened room. But I knew he was less of a monster than most of the Blood.

"It doesn't always happen and when it does it is a temporary thing. When the locked one dies, the hunger passes," he said eventually.

No wonder so many of them died, then. A frenzy for blood coupled with a desire for secrecy was a perfect reason to kill. I shivered. "So you think Lucius wants me back because he wants to feed from me again?"

His head tilted, considering. "It's possible. And you would be wise to avoid giving him such an opportunity. Lucius is careful to avoid any weakness. I never knew him to create even a single blood-locked when I was in the Court. If he did, he did so in secret. No one knew who they were. He would've killed them quickly. He would likely wish to kill you. After all, a weapon who rebels is hardly a weapon any longer. And if the Court knows now that you have fed from him . . . well, some would want to exploit a potential weakness."

The words hit home like dull blows. Lucius did not tolerate weakness. Atherton was right. If I had turned from useful to threat, even being a wraith would not spare me. "No one knows he fed from me. He did that in private."

"Are you trying to convince me now that he isn't trying to kill you?" His mouth turned up for a moment, then he resumed his pacing.

"No." I bit my lip. But was I? Having Atherton believe that I was under a death sentence was probably the fastest way of getting him on my side. But it might be myself I had to convince. Admitting that Lucius wanted me dead was harder than I thought. Fear crawled my spine and send icy shards through my stomach at the thought of him turning on me. I tried to push it away but it tightened my throat and sped my heart. Deep down, I wondered if there was part of me that wanted to go back to him, insane as that might be.

Disgust chased away the fear. Could I really want that? Maybe Bryony was right and I was just a trained dog after all, willing to lick the hand that hit me in the vague hope of some sliver of affection.

No.

No. I was more than that. I turned away from Atherton, trying to think. Was he right? Was I doomed to have an even stronger need for Lucius because he'd fed me so much blood? Certainly my body was reacting in a way that supported that theory, but would it continue to? There had to be a way—

Wait. I backtracked, remembering what he had said. "You said that the vampire is freed from the need if the one they locked dies. Is the reverse true?"

He stilled between one stride and the next, mouth open. "I do not know."

"No one has ever tried it?"

"Killing a vampire to set the blood-locked free? I've never heard any talk that such a thing has been attempted or that it works. Why, are you willing to try?" His voice dipped to a lower register, suddenly thrumming with that edge of temptation the Blood use when they want something. Or someone.

"Try to kill Lucius?" It seemed ridiculous even saying it. Lucius was a fact of life. As unchangeable as air or gravity. He'd ruled the Night World in the City for a very long time. Others had tried to kill him before. He always survived. They always died.

"Who better than his own weapon? You could get to him when no one else could."

My skin prickled as though a storm were brewing nearby. "And why should I take that risk?"

"For freedom?" His entire focus was on me now, in that intent way the Blood have. Like a cat watching a small furry thing. Poised to react to whatever came next. Poised to strike.

I resisted the urge to retreat, to retrieve my weapons. "You said yourself you don't know if it would work."

"With him dead, you would have to be more free regardless of your other problem."

I stared at him for a long moment, skin still pebbled and tingling. Fear? Excitement? I didn't know. "I would have to think about it."

He shrugged and the tension in the air dissipated. "That seems reasonable." He eased himself down into the chair where I'd first found him, finding it unerringly.

He was Blood, I reminded myself. If he was interested, there was a benefit to him. "What do you get out of it? If I kill Lucius?"

The scars on his face wrinkled faintly, perhaps as close as he could get to frowning. "Maybe like you, I want freedom. To be amongst my kind again. To live without fear."

"How badly?"

"What do you mean?"

"If I do this, you would owe me."

"I would consider an obligation," he said slowly. The Blood, like the Fae, take debts seriously. So here was a measure of how much Atherton liked the idea of Lucius dead.

"What I want is simple."

"Oh?" Skepticism crept into his tone.

"If I do this, and during the time I take to decide, you don't tell Simon about me. About the blood, I mean."

"And if you decide against killing Lucius?"

"If it gets to that point, I imagine he'll find out soon enough," I said with a shrug. "But until then, I'd rather he didn't."

"Why?"

"He wouldn't understand."

"And that matters to you?"

Yes. It did. Simon had spoken of wanting me. Of needing me. I doubt he'd still feel the same way if he knew I was just another addict, someone who got her pleasures from a vampire's blood. How could he? The humans abandoned their own kind when they succumbed to the blood. And I wasn't even human.

The truth would kill anything he might feel. I couldn't afford that. His wanting was buying me time. And, if I was honest, I wanted too. Not just wanting what his kiss had awakened but wanting his world. I wanted to spend some more time with someone who saw me so differently to everyone else in the world. To be a person rather than a weapon.

Which was foolish when he too wanted to use me. But just for a little while, I wanted to pretend that whatever he felt for me had a chance. But I didn't have to say that aloud yet. I doubted I could. "Do we have a deal?"

Behind me there was a sudden hum from the wards. "Someone's coming," I said. I turned and scooped up my daggers, ready to shadow if I needed to. I touched Atherton's sleeve. "Quickly, tell me, do we have an agreement?"

"An agreement about what?"

I turned slowly. Simon stood silhouetted in the door, holding a lamp in one hand. The light touched me—not sunlight; that would burn Atherton—so I could disappear if I wished. But it was too late. Simon had seen me. Even if I shadowed, there was no way to hide now.

I looked at Atherton, holding my breath. His move. He could tell Simon the truth about me and change everything.

"An agreement about what, Lily?" Simon said again, moving into the room. I didn't like the edge in his voice.

Atherton smiled slightly when Simon spoke my name. "Miss Lily wanted me to stay silent about the fact that she had been here."

"In return for what?"

"I do believe it was something along the lines of her not returning one night and slitting my throat." Atherton's voice was calm but I heard the thread of underlying amusement. He might not be intending to expose me, but he was going to have his fun at my expense. I wondered if Simon knew Atherton well enough to decipher it too.

"You threatened him?" Simon said.

"I wasn't going to actually kill him," I said, trying to conjure a defensive tone. Better Simon think me sadistic than know the truth.

"Is that supposed to be any better?" Simon's eyes were hard to see in the dimly lit room, but if I'd had to guess, they were likely as icy as Guy's right now.

"He took me by surprise. I hardly expected to find you had a tame vampire down here."

"What did you expect to find?" He put the lamp down on a table. His hand came to rest on the pistol at his hip. Apparently Simon wasn't taking chances with me right now.

I tried to look innocent. Hard to do when you've recently been discovered somewhere you're really not supposed to be. "I don't know."

He looked past me to Atherton, who had the air of someone watching a sparring match and enjoying it immensely. "Did she see inside?"

"No." Atherton and I spoke together.

"At least," Atherton added, after a pause in which we

both stayed silent, "she has said nothing about what is beyond the door. I don't know if she has been in there, of course. Wraiths being what they are, I cannot tell where she had been before she came upon me."

Simon frowned. "True. Lily?"

"I didn't go inside. I came from the tunnel." I wanted him to believe me. If he turned against me, then who knew what would happen? Perhaps I shouldn't have been so quick to come here. Too late to change that decision now.

"Why are you here at all?"

"How did you know I was here?" I countered.

"Atherton triggered an alarm."

A ward. Of course. "Yet you came alone?" I wondered if that choice was because he knew he could handle whatever he was likely to find here or because not many people knew the tunnel's secret.

"I looked in your room. You weren't there. I figured you'd either left or you'd caught wind of something in the tunnels." He shook his head a little. "Should've taken you the other way," he said more to himself than anything. "What was it? Can you sense the wards?"

"I smelled the iron. I got curious."

His eyes narrowed. "Of course. How foolish of me. Unsatisfied curiosity is not to be tolerated."

He was angry. Understandably. But he had to start to understand that I did things my way. "I need to know what I'm dealing with. You want me to pick your side, to trust you. To help you. But you're keeping secrets."

"And you're not?"

"Not the kind you hide underground behind iron and magic," I retorted. "You would do the same thing in my place. If I'm to choose your side, I need to know what I'm choosing."

Though if I could have disguised my secrets so easily, locked them away from him under iron and magic, I would have. "You've brought me into your world. You want me to stay here. I'm not going to wander around blinded by ignorance. Whatever is behind that door is important. Important enough to spend a lot of time and effort and money concealing it. Important enough to break the rules perhaps?"

"Yet you want me to trust you with the knowledge before you agree to help me."

"Help you do what?" Atherton interrupted. "What's going on?"

"Lucius has crossed a line." Simon said. "And Lily can provide proof of that. If she chooses."

"You want her to turn against Lucius?" Atherton's head twisted toward me. I could almost hear the thoughts spinning through his mind. Reworking the equations and potential of our earlier conversation. "You didn't mention this earlier," he said accusingly.

"I haven't agreed to do it yet," I said.

"So, why should I show you?" Simon said.

I crossed my arms. "At this point you can either show me or I can walk through the wall. You can't call sunlight here, not without hurting Atherton."

"Atherton's fast on his feet. I could light you and not him." Simon moved forward, putting himself between me and Atherton.

I folded my arms and lifted my chin. "I'm sure you can. Which would stop me for now, but do you have enough sunlamps to keep me trapped forever? What happened to trust?"

"I want to trust you," he said.

"Then show me what's behind the doors."

"No."

I blinked. "No?"

"No," he repeated. "Trust goes both ways, Lily. It has to be earned. In this, my duty is to my oaths. So, no."

"What if I look anyway?"

His face was calm. "If you do that, then there is no trust between us. And I would be forced to conclude that I have been wrong about you and the others were right."

Bryony, I assumed he meant. And whoever else had been telling him not to trust me. I bit my lip. I wanted to know what was in that room. Instincts screamed that it was important. But if Simon didn't trust me . . . if he gave up on me, then no one else in the human world would stand up for me. I might as well go back to Lucius.

Then again, if what lay beyond that door might change my choice, I owed it myself to find out. I needed to use my head, not my heart.

There was something between Simon and me, yes, but the decisions I had to make were life and death. I couldn't afford to let emotion sway me.

It seemed it was time for another of Guy's choices. "I won't look," I said. "But I want you to show me. Show me what you're protecting."

"So you can run back to Lucius and tell him?"

I met his gaze clearly. "You say you know me," I said. "That you want me to be more. You want me to help you. So do this. Change my mind. Trust me." I held my breath, nerves pricking, muscles tensed, waiting for his response.

His body blocked the light from the lamp, outlining him in gold. It made it hard to read his expression as he stayed silent. Finally, just when I thought my stomach might actually have tied itself in a knot, he blew out a breath. "You're right. Trust goes both ways. So I'm going to trust you. Don't make me regret this."

Atherton rose to his feet, looking, as far as his face was able, as startled as I felt. "Are you certain about this?" Atherton asked.

Simon walked over to the inner door. "No. But I'm doing it anyway." He looked back at me. "If I show you this, and you betray us, then there's nothing I'll be able to do to stop them hunting you down."

I nodded. "I can live with that." If I betrayed his trust, it would be because I was running or desperate or crazy enough to choose Lucius. I would expect them to come after me in those circumstances. I wouldn't blame them.

Simon watched. "All right, then. Atherton, close the outer door."

The vampire moved easily across the room. Here, in his own little world, he would know every inch of the rooms, every bump in the floor and every piece of furniture. I wondered how he would feel if he suddenly had to move outside the limits of these spaces again.

The door closed with a soft clanging thud that seemed to vibrate through my bones. Simon took a slow breath, then laid his hand on the inner door. The warded lock started to glow with a cool silvery sheen. The light flared, bright enough to make me throw up a hand to shield my eyes. Then it died to a soft sparkle, as though the metal were new formed from the night sky, spangled with tiny glimmering stars.

Atherton had come up beside me and he turned his head toward the door as if he could sense the magic at work.

My stomach grew tight. What were they hiding behind so many wards, so much iron? What was worth so much?

Would I be able to keep the secret?

Keep Simon's trust?

Keep Atherton's? He was a secret too. At the moment, he was the more important secret, particularly if he could provide me with knowledge about the need.

When the last sparking lights faded from the metal, Simon pulled his hand from the door, shook it quickly as if it pained him, then turned the handle.

The door swung inward, near silent like the other. All I could see beyond was light. Atherton moved after Simon and I followed them slowly across the threshold.

At first I didn't understand what I was seeing. It looked like any other hospital ward, neat rows of beds, full of people sleeping. More beds than seemed normal perhaps but nothing more unusual than that.

Above each bed, a lamp burned. The air was faintly hazy with lamp oil and smoke. The smoke mingled with the soap and chemical smell of the rest of the hospital. The lamps shone pools of light down onto each bed, highlighting the sleeping faces.

This was the big secret?

I didn't understand. Atherton and Simon began to move from bed to bed, touching wrists, bending to listen to breathing. The separate rhythms of forty or so hearts beating, like a band of distant, clumsy drummers who couldn't quite keep time, filled my ears. Likewise, the sounds of slow human breathing.

I stood and watched, trying to decipher the puzzle.

Other smells came to me as I watched. Human smells of sweat and bodies. And the faintest hint of blood. So faint I wasn't sure it was there at all. None of the patients had bandages or bruises to indicate injuries, so where did the blood smell come from?

I watched a little longer, studying the forms lying still beneath pale gray blankets. Too still, I realized. Only their chests rose and fell. And despite the stillness, they weren't all asleep. Some had their eyes open, staring blankly up at the ceiling. Staring straight up at the lamps above their beds without blinking or squinting.

I knew that particular stillness, in humans.

"Blood-locked," I breathed. "They're all blood-locked. But . . . alive? You're keeping them alive." I turned to Simon, disbelieving. "You idiot! This is why Lucius wanted to kill you."

"Lucius doesn't know," Simon said sharply.

"Then he bloody well suspects," I replied, shaking my head in disgust. "Why else would he risk killing you?" My mind whirled with it. Blood-locked. He was trying to cure them. Lords of hell. It would change everything. If a cure existed, then the humans wouldn't be willing to cede the locked to the Blood. They would want to cure them, reclaim them. Which would remove one of the vampires' primary food sources. The Blood wouldn't give that up without a fight. This could turn the treaties—and the City—upside down. No wonder Lucius wanted Simon dead.

And who knew how the other races might react? It could be seen as working against the treaties, and the Fae seldom took that well.

I walked to the nearest bed, stared down at its occupant. A woman with short dark hair that needed brushing and skin I thought would be olive rather than sallow had she seen daylight recently. Her eyes were, mercifully, closed. She looked young.

"How?" I asked, that being the simplest of the myriad questions bouncing around my brain. "How are you keeping them alive? And how long have you been doing this?"

"We've been trying to find a cure for the locking for a long time," Simon said slowly. "But as for this particular line of research, only since Atherton arrived."

"I'm keeping them alive," Atherton said. He straightened from where he had been bent over one of the beds.

I suddenly put two and two together. "You're feeding them your blood?"

"Yes," Atherton said. "But not very much. Just a few drops now and then. Once they've reached this stage, that seems to be enough to stop them getting any worse. That and the care Simon gives them."

"No worse but no better?" I said speculatively.

"There are flashes, we think," Simon said. "Glimmers of consciousness. But no, we haven't cured anyone. Yet."

I shuddered, looking down at the woman in front of me.

This wasn't a life, lying here, trapped in a body that knew nothing. "Where do they come from?"

Atherton had been right when he'd said that most of the blood-locked ended up dead at the hands of the Blood. Once the cravings grew too strong, they tended to descend fully into the Night World. And the humans gave them up for dead. Which tended to be a self-fulfilling prophecy of a kind.

Simon sighed. "Sometimes a family gets someone away. Keep them locked up or restrained. They nearly always end up bringing them here."

"And what do you tell them?" What would convince someone to give up their flesh and blood to this living death?

"That there isn't any hope," Simon said. "It would be cruel to let them hope. Cruel and far too risky."

"So you steal the bodies away down here in the dead of night?"

"No. We wait for a suitable moment and tell them that their loved one has succumbed."

I stared at him. "And that's not cruel?" Faked deaths and stealing bodies or no, not *bodies*, though I didn't know what else you called these unmoving people. It seemed ridiculous that Simon would be involved in such things.

My throat tightened. Had I been so wrong about Simon? But he was trying to help. . . .

"It's no different from what they would have to hear if they hadn't come to the hospital," Atherton interjected. "These people would be dead for sure then."

"Yes," Simon agreed. "Once someone is locked, the best the family can hope for is to know whether they're alive or dead. Sooner or later it will be dead. It would be better to stop people going down this path in the first place, but there will always be those who choose badly. Those who are too weak to resist." He sounded bitter. As if his words came from personal experience. "God knows why anyone would choose to drink a vampire's blood. Nothing good can come from such a thing. Look how they end their days."

The cold anger in his voice made me shiver. What would he do if he knew that I was not so far different from those lying in the beds around us? Any warmth he felt for me wouldn't survive that icy fury.

Which meant I needed to make sure he never found out. I moved toward another of the beds where an older man lay. The wrinkles in his face creased slackly in the still skin. "What about the bodies? How do you produce a dead body if no one has died?"

Simon's tone was matter-of-fact. "The bodies of the blood-locked are customarily burned."

Then usually the ashes scattered over water, to take no chance they might rise as Blood. Not that there was really a chance. Turning was a very different process from locking. "No one asks to see the body first?"

Simon looked away. "Bryony takes care of that."

Glamoured the families, he meant. Made them forget or believe they had had that last moment with the dead. And lords of hell, if the Fae were in on this also . . . the Blood would be outraged. This had to be why Lucius had wanted me to kill Simon. The question was, how had he found out?

"All this risk, so you can keep them alive down here?"

Atherton shook his head, the white tail of his hair snaking behind him. "So we can find a cure."

"Why would *you* be interested in finding a cure?" I said. "The Blood don't care about humans."

He shrugged fluidly. "Don't judge all of us by what you have seen."

"I've seen many Blood over the years. None of you seemed overly concerned about protecting the humans in the Courts." My voice was sharper than I intended. After all, on the face of it, I had no more reason than Atherton to care about the fate of humans foolish enough to become locked.

"It makes no sense to have a percentage of your food source die and become unavailable to you," Atherton said. "Or to put your race at risk by angering the other races."

I wasn't entirely sure of the correct response to this. It was all so . . . clinical. Both of them. Working away down here, gambling so much on the off chance there might be a cure. All hell poised to break loose if something went wrong.

I moved restlessly between the beds, looking down into one too-still face after another. The ones with open eyes were the worst. "What happens when the Blood who don't share your views find out you're trying to find a cure?"

"I'd imagine there might be some trouble," Simon said calmly.

A pale phrase for possible war between the races. The thought made me shiver. "You said Bryony knows about this?" Bryony, if her ring were anything to go by, came from one of the high Families in the Veiled Court. The Lady in her title was more than Guy being respectful, it was her true rank. So, did her participation mean that the Fae knew and approved of Simon's work? Or was she keeping secrets too?

I pressed the heel of my hand into my forehead. Too many secrets. I suddenly understood why they claimed curiosity killed the cat. I wished I'd stayed put in the Brother House.

Except then I wouldn't have found Atherton.

Simon continued his rounds of the beds, pausing by each one. I stayed where I was staring down at the girl in the bed before me, thinking hard. A cure for the blood-locked. Perhaps a cure for the *need*. For my need. No matter what I thought of their methods, their desired outcome was mine too.

When Atherton suddenly appeared by my side, I jumped, rattling the nearest bed frame as I stumbled. The fact that it provoked no reaction in the occupant only sharpened the discomfort.

"How does it work?" I asked, looking away from the bed. "How do you feed them?"

"The usual way. A few drops on their tongues. Usually every two weeks."

"But you're not the one who locked them."

"No. But it seems to be enough. Maybe because I'm from the same Court."

That was no surprise. Lucius presided over the only remaining Court in the city. I had killed more than a few Blood for Lucius and I wasn't his sole assassin. He didn't suffer rivals to live.

"All of us owe what we are to Lucius." There was an edge to Atherton's voice.

"And where did Lucius come from?"

"I do believe all the elders in his line are now dead," Atherton said softly. "He isn't the type to let anyone have power over him."

Fought his way to the top and killed to make sure he stayed there. Yes, that was the Lucius I knew.

"Which is why you should do as Simon asks," Atherton continued in that soft implacable tone. "Lucius needs to be curbed."

I waited for him to add "or killed," but perhaps he knew that was pushing things too far just now. He'd always been far too empathetic for a Blood.

"You of all people know what he does to those who betray him."

"Yes. Which is why I know that it's the right thing to do. Someone has to stand against him. The humans are trying, but the Fae won't help them if the treaty isn't broken."

"Why should it be me?"

A fluid shrug. "Why not? You know him as well as anybody might. You are well placed to judge him. Do you think he deserves to win? To rule the City? To have thousands and thousands at his mercy?"

No. I didn't. But when it came right down to it, faceless thousands sounded better than *me* being at his mercy.

I shivered again. "It's suicide."

"It might be redemption."

"You sound like Guy. You're Blood, not human."

"So I cannot believe in good because I am a vampire? Why then did I ever help you?"

Lords of hell, he was deadly with his aim. He had helped me. Simon had helped me too. For his own reasons, true, but he had gotten me away from Lucius. "I didn't mean that you were like the other, I just . . ."

"I think you should do it. Help the humans. Bring Lucius down," Atherton said again. "In fact, I might have to insist."

I stilled. "Insist?"

"You have a secret you want kept. I think my silence now has a different price."

Fuck. I should've seen that coming.

Curses flooded through my head, but I bit down on them as I bit down on the urge to draw my dagger and show him exactly what could happen to those who tried to force me to their will. But Atherton had me over a barrel and he knew it. Sure, I could return and kill him, but there was one person that Simon would lay the blame for that act on. I might as well put the noose around my neck myself.

Atherton knew that as well as I did.

I was beginning to see why Lucius might have wanted him out of the Court. He was smart and obviously, despite his good side, he could be ruthless when he wanted to be.

"You're blackmailing me?"

"No, merely presenting you with another choice."

Choices. I was beginning to hate that word. Perhaps it was just easier to stay in my cage. I could go back to Lucius and resume my life. For as long as it might last before Lucius killed me out of addiction or madness.

I could also choose to tell Simon the truth, but that carried just as high a cost. He would look at me like he looked at these bodies in the beds. I would no longer see that different world in his eyes.

Or I could do as Atherton wanted.

Three bad choices. But one of them meant that Simon would still look at me as he had back in his office. Like I was real and worthy.

"I want your word," I said. "Swear to me you won't tell him if I do what he wants. Blood oath."

"Fine," Atherton said. "My word. Now give me yours."

"Yes," I said. "I'll do it. But I will tell Simon in my own time. Agreed?"

"Agreed. As long as your own time isn't any longer than the next day."

"Bastard," I said softly.

Atherton smiled. "It's for the greater good."

"Fuck the greater good," I muttered. My heart was racing. How had my life tumbled so far into madness in a few short days?

I didn't want to think about it anymore. If I did I might scream. I stared at the still forms of the locked in the beds around me. I had to believe that Simon and Atherton could find a cure. One that might work for me. It would be the one thing that would make my gamble worthwhile.

To be free of the need and Lucius. Perhaps then I could be something more than a killer.

"Do they . . . when you give them the blood, do they react?"

"Do they feel the pleasure?" Atherton said, sounding slightly amused. "Perhaps they do. But they give no outward sign. Their bodies and minds are essentially disconnected at this point."

"Oh."

"You sound disappointed," he said very softly. Too soft for Simon to hear. "Did you want to try it for yourself?"

"No." I shivered slightly. No, I wasn't going to take another vampire's blood. Not unless there was no other alternative. Especially not if it meant that I would react in the usual way.

"Then what are you planning to do?"

"I don't know." My hand clamped down on my dagger, fingers digging into the hilt in frustration. "I don't suppose you have any helpful suggestions?"

"The blood brings pleasure," Atherton said, voice dropping even lower. "It is the pleasure the body craves. I would suggest giving it what it craves."

"What?" I stared up at him. True, the blood-locked were indiscriminate in their bedding of anything that moved, but I had always resisted that path. I had to surrender my body to its needs when I drank the blood. The rest of the time, I guarded it as the one thing I truly commanded. The one thing that was mine. "Are you suggesting that I . . . with who exactly?"

He nudged my arm, turning me in the direction of Simon. "He smells of desire. And of you. I would think the solution is simple."

"That's your idea of simple?" It was an effort to keep my voice low. The thought of taking Simon to bed was . . . unnerving. To give up that last defense. But also made a horrible sort of sense. After all, I knew he wanted me and I knew I was not averse to him.

If it could buy me time from the need. Time to free myself. To step toward the place where I didn't need to hold myself separate. But to do so in these circumstances? When both of us were intent on our own purposes? It felt horribly calculating to contemplate. But if he were willing . . . how could mutual pleasure hurt him?

The harder part would be keeping it simply to that and no more.

"It's my idea of a solution."

"Will it work?" I needed to believe it would. Otherwise, why would I even contemplate making the situation still more complicated? I wanted to be free, not entangled in whole new ways. I needed a clear head. One that would let me choose to leave without a blink if the situation came to that.

Could I take Simon to my bed and then let him go again?

"It should at least buy you time," Atherton said. Then his mouth curved in a wicked smile. "But you'll never know unless you try it."

Chapter Thirteen

I paused as I closed the last of the warded doors. "Are you going to"—I wriggled my fingers—"what do you call it?"

"Shadowing," Lily said, tilting her head. "No. Should I?"

The question was more, would she reappear if she did? I still wasn't sure exactly what she was going to do with the information I'd just given her. Would she run to Lucius? Or would she prove me right and decide to help us? I had the feeling that, with Lily, the road to trust was going to be a long one. With no certainty of arriving at the destination.

"I thought you might wish to return the way you came." I tightened my grip on the sunlamp I'd picked up on our way out of the wards. I didn't want to light it. Not if I didn't need to.

She looked down at the sunlamp, then up at me with an odd expression. "I'd rather walk with you. If that is acceptable?"

"Of course." Guy wouldn't be exactly thrilled if he found us wandering outside the Brother House, but if we were together at least no one could accuse Lily of spying or something equally unsavory.

No one apart from me. But I didn't have to accuse. I knew she'd been spying.

Discovering Atherton *was* spying of a sort—but I had to hope she was doing it on her own initiative, not for Lucius. I wanted to believe she had good intentions. I'd shared my secret with her. A secret not even Guy knew about. All to see if she would truly choose to help us. But even if she did keep faith with me, if she fell back into Lucius' grasp, then suns knew what might happen. I swung the lamp in my hand, suddenly weary. "Let's go."

We walked in silence. I didn't want to push my luck and press my case. She'd been pushed enough for one day. We reached the main tunnels and turned back toward the Brother House. Lily's expression was distant in the gaslight, not seeming to really notice her surroundings.

I resigned myself to waiting, but then she stopped in her tracks, turned to me. She started to speak, then stopped.

"Lily?" I asked, prompting gently.

"I've decided to do as you asked," she said.

I nearly dropped the lamp, relief rushing through me. I tightened my grip, a small tremor shivering down my arm. I was pushing too hard again. Not smart. Whatever else I did tomorrow, I needed to spend several hours outdoors. Even if that meant climbing hundreds of steps to the roof of St. Giles. "What changed your mind?"

Her head tilted at me, her eyes filled with an emotion I couldn't quite identify. "You convinced me," she said.

"How?"

"My reasons don't matter. I said I'd do it."

I wanted to hug her but doubted she'd take it that well. "Thank you," I said instead. "You're doing the right thing." I fought to keep a grin off my face. She was staying. And she would help us bring Lucius down. Help us bring lasting change and peace to the City. Exultation drove away the lingering fatigue dogging me.

She half smiled, then continued walking. She moved almost silently. In her wake floated a hint of Bryony's tonic and the fresh bread they'd eaten for dinner and the soap the hospital laundry used. It shouldn't have been an appealing combination, but as I walked beside her, I found myself breathing deliberately deep as if to inhale her essence and understand her that way. Catch her within and keep her there.

She'd said yes. As the first surge of excitement faded a little, I found myself torn once more. I hoped she wasn't lying. In her place, I would lie if I thought it would save my skin. She was an assassin, a killer. Trained to survive. I didn't know if I could trust her, much as I wanted to.

Despite all of that I still wanted her.

Wanted to taste her mouth again.

Wanted to burn.

I didn't understand how or why she'd gotten under my skin so fast, but she had.

We reached the Brother House and the corridor that housed our chambers. The guards were nowhere to be seen. Hopefully that meant they were at services or elsewhere on their circuit, not off raising the alarm because they'd discovered Lily was missing. But there were no noises to indicate a house roused to hunt down a vanished wraith.

I opened the door to her room, holding it politely. "Good night, Lily." I didn't know what else could possibly be said.

Ask me in?

Kiss me again?

Tell me if you're going to cut out my heart so I can go grab a bowl to catch the blood?

Unholy fucking insane.

I should run to the chapel and prostrate myself before Guy's God and ask to be healed of her. But I could no more ask to be healed of my powers or the color of my eyes.

Stupid, stupid, stupid.

Gray eyes studied me for a moment before she walked into the room. Just inside the door, she turned. "Come in for a moment."

My heart froze, then stuttered back to life.

Calm down, Simon.

She probably wanted to talk more about what she had just agreed to do. Or bash me over the head with a chair so she could run. I had no idea which was more likely.

I nodded, though, and followed her into the room, unable to resist her invitation.

The room felt smaller somehow. The small bed loomed large. She'd stuffed pillows or something under the blankets to resemble a body. An unconvincing facsimile.

"The next time you want to make it look like someone's in your bed, you should try a glamour."

"I don't do glamours," she said. She crossed to the bed, pulled the pillows free, and shoved them both under the table. Her haste left the bed temptingly rumpled. I turned my gaze away, leaning against the stone wall, wishing the chill at my back would run through my veins and calm my racing heart.

"Was there something you wanted to talk about?"

I kept my voice deliberately low. The Templars were celibate inside the walls of the Brother House. It was pushing their boundaries enough to have Lily here without flaunting the fact that I was alone in her bedchamber so late at night.

"It's getting late," I added when she stayed silent. "Or early rather." It had to be close to three. In a few more hours the Brothers would be stirring and Guy would, no doubt, come to fetch me to talk to the Abbott General. At least I would have something better than "she said no" to report, but I still wasn't looking forward to the conversation. Father Cho had a way of making me feel like a gawky fifteen-year-old again. "I'm tired."

Beyond tired.

I put the sunlamp down beside my feet. Lily had lit the short, thick candle on the table and in the flickering light, she was a creature of flame. But flames didn't bite their lips and look nervous.

What now? "Lily? Either spit it out or I'm going to bed." She swallowed. "Did you mean it before?"

"Which particular before are you referring to?" Today had lasted several lifetimes already.

"At the hospital." Her tongue flickered out briefly as if her lips were dry. "The . . . the kiss."

I was suddenly doubly grateful for the wall at my back. "Did I intend to kiss you?" I hoped I didn't sound as surprised to her ears as I did to my own.

A nod.

"Yes. I wanted to kiss you." I still wanted to. I folded my arms, mainly to stop myself from hauling her close. Blood roared in my ears as it drained out of my head and rushed south.

I needed to remember that Lily had her own agenda. It would be wise to understand what it was before I did anything stupid.

"And you liked it?" Her voice was rough as if more than her lips were dry. The resulting husk seemed to rasp along my skin, raising the hairs on my arms. I went hard, as though she'd planted her hand on my groin rather than just spoken.

I swore softly. "Yes. Couldn't you tell?"

She looked away.

What the hell did that mean? Was she flirting or playing some other game? I'd expect her to be direct about her wants. She wasn't exactly shy and retiring. You couldn't be Lucius' chief executioner and be shy and retiring. Confusion mixed with lust as I schooled myself to wait.

Her gaze rose to my face again, eyes large and luminous in the candlelight. "Would you like to do it again?"

I couldn't speak. Suddenly my mouth was as dry as the stones beneath my feet. "What sort of question is that?"

"A fairly normal one." She sounded defensive.

I snorted, beating back the roar of blood in my veins and the voice inside yelling at me not to ruin things with questions and just do it. "Lily, nothing about this situation is remotely normal."

$$\mathcal{D}$$

I dug my hands into the rough linen coverlet, hoping it would ease the damp feeling of my skin. Ease the blood warming my cheeks and the knowledge that I was doing this all wrong. Simon was right. Nothing about this was normal. I wasn't normal. This was a completely absurd idea.

Why would I listen to what one of the Blood told me to do? Atherton had said it himself, he was only blind, not damaged in other ways. He was just as capable of scheming and misdirecting as any other vampire. He had been quick enough to grasp an advantage over me. His advice might be just another way of gaining a still greater hold over me. For all I knew, having sex would just make the need worse.

I should send Simon away. Before the need and desire beating at me made me do something irrevocable. His eyes seemed very bright and I felt my cheeks grow hotter still. Cheeks and the rest of me. I should stop this. Now.

"Forget I asked," I said.

He laughed. It didn't sound terribly amused. More torn.

"That's just it," he said. "I can't."

He moved then, glowing and golden in the candlelight. Came to me and knelt on the floor before me so our faces were nearly level.

"The thing is," he said softly. "I don't think you can either. Can you?"

His eyes locked with mine. His were open, guileless. Full of questions, wariness, and yes, more than a hint of desire. But also open like the sky they resembled. You could trust what lay behind them.

I didn't think the same was true of what lay behind mine.

"Lily." His hand stretched out, touched my face.

I shivered and my hands clung harder to the linen. His fingers were warm and gentle. Familiar. He'd touched me before with gentleness. But gentleness wasn't what I needed right now.

If I was going to be brave enough to go through with this . . . and yes, part of me burned to do so as I breathed his scent deep into my lungs . . . then I needed not to think too hard. Needed to let go and let everything I'd worked so hard to lock away take over. I shivered again.

"Lily, I'll go if you want me to. But I'd rather stay."

A pulse beat strongly in his neck and I could hear the matching *thump, thump, thump* of his heart.

"S-stay," I said thickly, mouth dry as my tongue stumbled on the word.

A smile flamed to life across his face. "All right."

Now what? My throat tightened. I didn't know how this worked. Oh, the mechanics, certainly, I was aware of those. I had seen plenty of couplings in my time. You couldn't walk through walls without coming upon a few unwary lovers. And the Blood tend to mingle sex with feeding. As do those who seek them. Growing up in the warrens beneath Lucius' Court precluded being ignorant of sex.

So I knew how flesh moved on flesh. What I didn't know was how it felt or how one went about moving from this point to the next. Did he kiss me? Should I reach out and kiss him? I remembered the taste of him all of a sudden, and the need gripped harder, sending a pulsing ache through my stomach and lower.

Heat flared in my face, and my nipples went hard against my shirt. Unnerved and uneasy, I reached up and pulled pins from my hair, freeing it to fall forward, sheltering my face from his gaze. Then, embarrassed, I hid the reason for my movement by reaching for the top button of my shirt.

Simon's hand captured mine. "There's no rush."

"I—"

"Shh." He pressed his mouth to mine, solving at least

one part of my problem. I wasn't going to have to make the first move.

I let him lead for a while. His kisses started soft. Teasing, even. Barely brushing my lips until mine began to tingle and burn and I leaned toward him, wanting more. His hands drifted through my hair, easing the last few pins and unwinding the strands as delicately as his mouth moved on mine. I reached and fisted my hand in his shirt.

He moved in closer and I wrapped my arms around his neck, drawing him in tighter against me as the kisses deepened. Hotter. Wetter. His tongue flicked against mine and the taste of him flooded my mouth as other sensations flooded other parts of me.

This was what I wanted.

This. His mouth against mine.

This. I grasped one of his hands and brought it round to my breast, pressing against him.

This. For a moment his hand stayed still, merely rounded to my flesh, but then it tightened suddenly and fingers flicked across my nipple.

I gasped and Simon laughed. "I like that," he said.

"What?" I managed.

"That noise."

He liked the noise? Strange. But maybe that was normal for human men?

"Although," he continued, "we need to be quiet."

"Worried about what Guy might think?"

He stopped what he was doing. "Actually, I thought you might prefer it if we were discreet."

Discreet? For a moment I didn't know what he meant and then I remembered. Humans could be peculiar about sex. Many of them considered it taboo unless they were married. Though the brothels in the Night World and boroughs like Brightown seemed to do well enough, so perhaps it would be more correct to say that many of them did do it, they just didn't admit to it.

Sex was also one of the main attractions of the Assemblies. Or rather, satisfaction. Not all Blood slept with their food. Or gave their blood to be consumed for pleasure.

I shivered suddenly, remembering Lucius and blood pouring down his wrist.

"What's wrong?"

"Nothing." I reached up and flicked my tongue against Simon's lower lip. I didn't want to think anymore.

He gasped, then followed it up with: "Are you sure?"

"Yes. Kiss me again."

He did. I let his mouth carry me away again, driving the bad memories from my head, let his touch teach me new sensations.

But I couldn't relax completely. Maybe it was the light, reminding me of the hall and all the Blood watching.

"Blow out the candle."

"Why?"

I didn't know how to explain it, so instead I pulled his head down toward me and kissed him, hard. "Just do it."

His brows drew together. "I want to see you."

"There's the moonlight."

In the darkness, I would feel like I could wrap the shadows around us and make a space for just the two of us. No room for doubts and indecision and the nagging fear that kept swimming up from beneath the other much pleasanter sensations he invoked.

Simon shook his head. "That's not fair, you see better in the dark than I do."

I kissed him again. "Do you want to argue or keep doing what we were doing?"

"Good point. But how about a compromise?" He climbed off the bed and crossed to the window. The curtains rustled as he pushed them halfway open to let in more of the moonlight.

He hadn't yet blown out the candle and the flickering light played over his skin, outlining each muscle almost lovingly. I wanted to put my hands on his body. I wanted to run away screaming.

I settled for lying on the bed pretending my heart wasn't racing and extremely glad Simon had human hearing and couldn't hear the frantic beat.

He doused the candle as he came back to me. He paused at the end of the bed, slid his belt free of his trousers. He was just as pretty in the moonlight.

Just as terrifying.

I tried to smile as the mattress dipped.

"Hello again." He lowered himself next to me. There

wasn't much room on the narrow bed, but for now a few inches still separated his body and mine.

I pressed a little farther into the mattress as my mouth dried. He smelled delicious. Clean male desire. Not blood-lust.

He wanted me.

I wanted him.

So why was I so hells-damned terrified?

Really, my virginity was a mere technicality.

It wasn't as though I hadn't had orgasms before. I'd just never had one involving two people that hadn't included vampire blood and humiliation.

Which really was another reason to just get on with it and give my brain another memory to attach pleasure to.

Simon must have read something in my expression, as he made no move to close the gap between us. "If I was going to be clichéd right now, I'd say something about your skin and moonlight and pearls."

"Pearls?"

He nodded. "You gleam." Very gently his hand trailed over my bare arm. His skin did look darker against mine though the moon cooled it, hiding the golden warmth from sight. He felt plenty warm, though, and, as his fingers traced patterns over my skin, I began to warm up again as well.

He knew how to touch, this man. Like he had a precise map of all my nerve endings. Come to think of it, maybe he did. Healers would have to have a thorough knowledge of anatomy and physiology.

Pleasure bloomed across my skin under his touch. Across and beneath and between as he pulled me closer and set his hands roaming. Different from the need. Slower and more . . . more . . . I didn't know what the word I searched for was.

More human perhaps?

But that didn't make sense, because I wasn't human.

The silvered darkness wrapped around us and my shirt hit the floor about the same time as his.

Yet despite the delight I felt when he touched me, I could also feel myself holding him off somehow. It wasn't quite enough. I was still thinking.

Still scared, a little. Still held by years of denial and fear of letting someone so close.

And I didn't know how to overcome that apart from confronting it. Taking it higher and faster. Letting the need take over and take me under.

I rolled, slightly, carefully, given the limited space we had to maneuver, but I still gained the upper position pretty easily.

Simon grinned up at me, clearly not bothered by the change in perspective. His hands sought and found my breasts again, flickering fingers seemingly knowing exactly what spots to touch to make me writhe against him, taken for a moment by pure sensation.

That.

That was what I needed.

I bent my head and scraped teeth against his neck. Not biting but not exactly gentle either.

"Oh? It's like that, is it? Impatient, my lady?"

I growled briefly against his neck and he laughed again. Then he moved with lightning speed—faster than I'd thought he could—so that he was once again above me, my hands held above my head. For a brief moment the sense of being trapped, held down, panicked me, but then his hips pressed against mine, the hardness of him hitting me exactly where I needed the pressure, and I suddenly didn't care.

"I'm getting a tad impatient myself," he admitted, and set to work again.

I never thought I'd regret not wearing a skirt, but the delay caused by the need to get rid of my breeches seemed endless. With Simon's help I managed it. His breeches were a lot easier to deal with and this time when he pressed me down to the bed, we were flesh to flesh.

He was warm against me, burning hot almost in one particular spot where his cock lay against me, hard and insistent. I arched against him and it was Simon who groaned.

"Not yet or this is going to be all too fast."

"I don't care," I said, arching again and pulling his head down to me.

"But I do." His voice was rough. "I want to touch."

His hand slid down my thigh as he half rolled so we ended up lying on our side. Nerve endings ignited. And then flared hotter as his fingers returned on the inside of my thigh. Trailing up. Up. Up. Slowly. Too slowly.

I bit my lip as those clever fingers traced the crease of thigh and body and then started stroking across the hair that lay between. When they finally slipped against me, hitting that part of me that had been burning and throbbing for far too long, the part of me where the need burned most fiercely, I thought I'd lost the ability to breathe.

He toyed with me then. Fingers dancing an infuriating pattern. First against me, then lifting and flickering to stroke somewhere else and returning again.

Until finally they slid inside me and the sensation was so startlingly intense that I couldn't help it, I slipped into the shadow.

"What in the name of—" Simon jerked backward, voice shocked. "Gods and suns, Lily, where did you go?"

I froze where I was, embarrassment flowing over me in a fiery tide that burned everything else away. Sweet lords of hell, what had I done? I was fairly certain that vanishing during such a moment was just not done.

"Lily? Did I hurt you?" Now he sounded horrified rather than shocked.

"No," I whispered.

His head jerked. "You're still here."

"Yes."

His eyes closed for a moment as if he was trying to gain some control before he spoke again. Then he shook his head and propped himself up on one elbow. "I should've known this wouldn't be straightforward."

He didn't sound angry; that was a start. Lucius would have broken something by now. Me, in all likelihood.

"Lily? Would you . . . come back, please?"

"No."

"No?" His brows drew down. "Are you sure I didn't hurt you?"

"I'm sure."

"Then what's wrong?"

The tide of embarrassment washed higher. Even in the shadow I felt I must be glowing bright red. I was going to have to tell him. "You . . . surprised me."

"Surprised you?" He blinked, and then his face went peculiarly blank. "Gods and suns, you're a virgin."

It wasn't possible to disappear any more thoroughly than I already had done without actually leaving the room, but I wished I could. "Yes."

He laughed.

Now it was my turn to be surprised. "What's so funny?"

"It's just that—" He broke off into laughter again, the richness of the sound echoing around the small chamber, but eventually brought himself under control. "It's just that if you'd heard all the stories about you . . . and now, no fangs, no claws, and, despite growing up in the Night World, you're a virgin."

He was still smiling, the moonlight turning his dimples into dark slashes in his cheeks. I still didn't understand what was so humorous. "I have standards, that's all." I tried to keep the edge of anger out of my words. He had no idea . . .

His cheeks sucked in as if he was trying not to smile any wider. "Of course you do. And I'm very glad of them. But you could have told me."

"It didn't occur to me."

He blew out a breath. "Of course not." He looked skyward as though seeking guidance, or patience. "Lily, will you please come back? This is a very strange conversation to be having with thin air."

"I feel . . ."

"Silly? Embarrassed? Lily, sweet, everyone feels silly at some point during sex. It's the nature of the beast. Even more so the first time. It doesn't matter. Just come back."

It suddenly occurred to me that he could've used his sunlamp at any point up to now to force me out of the shadow. But he hadn't. And he wasn't angry. He was right. The only thing stopping me right now was my own embarrassment. Which wasn't going to solve any of my problems.

Nor could I feel his touch again as long as I stayed where I was. I took a deep breath and let myself fade into view so that we lay almost where we'd started, side by side on the bed, facing each other with mere inches separating us.

Simon's eyebrows drifted upward again. "That really is the damnedest thing. How do you do it?"

I stared at his chest, not wanting to meet his eyes. "I don't know." It wasn't a Fae power, what I did. Nor one of Beast or Blood or human mages. Whoever or whatever my unknown father had been, I'd never been able to work it out. "Nobody knows." Other than Lucius and the Fae. And they weren't talking. My eyes prickled suddenly. Would I ever know who I was? Know the truth instead of only knowing what everyone—including the man lying here with me—thought I was or should be? I blinked rapidly, drew in a shaky breath.

"Lily? We can stop right here."

I shook my head. I didn't want to stop. One day my truths might be revealed and who knew if Simon would want anything to do with me then? I would take this chance while I could.

"Then can you at least look at me?"

It took an effort of will to force myself to lift my head. But I did. And his eyes were full of that same warmth and desire and light that had drawn me to him since the first moment.

"That's better." He leaned in slowly, slowly enough to give me more than enough time to draw back if I chose. I stayed put and he kissed me.

Soft at first but then the heat between us flared and took over.

It was Simon who drew back. "Don't take this the wrong way," he said. "But I'm going to light the sunlamp now."

I blinked. "What?"

"I'll stop whenever you want. All you have to do is ask and I'll stop. But I'm not letting you vanish again."

"I wouldn't—" I broke off. How was I to know what I'd do? "All right."

The lamp glowed into life before I had a chance to say anything else.

His arms tightened around me, pressing me closer. I closed my eyes again and gave myself up to it. The feel of skin touching skin and the taste of him and the mingled scents of our bodies. Let all of it carry me away.

His hands started their dance with my nerves for a second time, and this time I wanted to touch too. My hand slid down and closed around his cock, feeling the warmth and strength of it against my palm with shocked pleasure.

Simon groaned. "If you do that, this is going to go a lot faster than you might like."

"What's wrong with fast?" I tightened my grip a little,

then released it and repeated the action as he sucked in a breath.

"Nothing," he managed. "But you'll enjoy it more if— gods!" His hand gripped mine and stopped what I was doing. "Just trust me on this. Let me show you this time. Let me show you how this should be." He added little nibbling kisses to his pleas, running his tongue along the curve where my neck met my shoulders and setting off tiny shivers like butterflies dancing over my skin.

He knew what he was doing. I rolled onto my back. "Have it your way, then."

"Oh no, it'll be our way," he said. "It's a dance. You do it together."

"Then let's dance," I said, tugging him down to me. "Show me."

He did. Relentlessly. He touched and tasted and sent the flames under my skin rising higher and higher until I couldn't catch my breath. Until the world narrowed down to just Simon and what he was doing.

What we were doing.

I didn't want to flee the second time his fingers slid into me. This time I wanted more. Wanted whatever it was that would ease the burning ache inside me.

Wanted him.

Fingers weren't enough though I writhed under their touch. But he wouldn't let me get away. Just teased and stroked until finally I shuddered fiercely and came against his hand with a cry.

It wasn't like the need. Not a pleasure so sharp it burned. No, this was pleasure that swelled sweetly and turned my nerves transparent with delight.

When I rode the other side of the wave down, I didn't collapse or pass out. No humiliation twisted my gut. No, instead I wanted it again. Not because the need drove me. But simply because I couldn't not want him.

And because I knew there was more.

I curled my arms around his neck and kissed him. "Show me the rest."

"You're sure?"

I hooked a leg over his hip, pressing myself against him. He felt harder than before, his skin hotter. His breath was coming fast, and tension rode his muscles. I knew he wanted what I was offering. The trick now was to get him to forget himself and take it.

"Please, Simon."

It seemed that was all he needed. That last assent. His mouth took mine again as he rolled me onto my back, pressing my thighs open with his. The kiss deepened, burned, flooded through me, driving all thoughts from my head. Then he was pressing against me and I knew exactly what to do. I arched and he slid slowly inside me, the sensation like velvet drawn across my nerves.

This.

He moved within me. Sure and strong and with a passion that took me over and set me free. Sent me climbing once more as the pleasure built. Caught me when I fell and then, in turn, as I shuddered against him, sure there could be no more to discover, showed me even more as he gave himself to me and followed me over the edge.

Chapter Fourteen

))

When I woke, sunlight streamed through the window and Simon was gone. I hadn't heard him leave. I imagined he was being discreet, returning to his room before the Brothers rose and started their day.

I stretched experimentally. A little sore but nothing that signified in any way. Nothing that even really registered as pain after everything else I'd been through in the last few days.

My body felt good. More than good, I realized.

I felt wonderful, energized as though I'd managed eight hours sleep. A glance at the window to determine the angle of the sun told me that it was, in reality, probably closer to only two or three.

Which meant, the only probable source of my renewal was the sex. I stretched again. No one had ever told me about this. About the sense of well-being that hummed through your veins after a night in bed with a man.

The need was different. When you fed its hunger, it simply died, wiping you blank—or it had until the last time Lucius had fed me—until it started to grow again. Leaving you feeling no better or worse than you felt before the blood and the orgasms.

Or rather, no better or worse from the need itself. I'd usually woken up miserable and ashamed and humiliated, so feeling even vaguely happy after an orgasm was an unknown quantity.

And the happiness I felt was more than vague. Here,

lying in the Brother House, surrounded by Templars and crazy sunmages and possibly marked for death by Lucius, I felt positively content.

Of course, once I realized that, I felt content and *confused* but content just the same.

The need. I suddenly remembered exactly why I'd thrown myself at Simon. Had it worked? I stilled on the bed, trying to listen to my body, to sort out the sensations running through it into familiar and unfamiliar. I couldn't feel the need calling me. There was a distinct urge to find out where Simon was and coax him back into bed, but it was distinctly different from the howling, nothing-else-matters drone of the need through my blood.

Had Atherton been right after all? Could I sate the need with other pleasures?

And if I could, could I be free of Lucius once and for all? Regardless of cures? Regardless of whether I did what I had promised Simon?

Freedom.

I hugged my knees, curling into a ball. There was no use letting myself run ahead of things. Only time would tell if Atherton had truly found a way for me to be free.

Until then, I couldn't afford a premature celebration. Couldn't afford to relax and let myself believe it might be true. But despite my caution, I wanted to talk to Atherton, see if he might be able to tell if it had worked.

Talk to him alone, without Simon.

I didn't know how I was going to arrange another meeting. Simon had asked me not to go back there without him knowing. I wanted to try, at least, to keep that promise to him. So I would have to come up with a reason for him to want me to be there.

I threw back the covers and pulled on my clothes. Before I did anything, I wanted to bathe. Back in the warrens, I had a private bathroom and retreating to a hot bath was one of the few sanctuaries I'd had.

The Brothers should be well about their days and I didn't think I needed to worry about running into any of them in the bathroom. So I tied my hair back, then picked up the soap and towel provided and opened the door, intent on scrubbing myself clean of all the scents of last night so I could start afresh.

Liam sat in the corridor opposite my door, reading a leather-bound book. He looked up at me, his green eyes assessing.

"Can I help you?" he asked. His voice was deep and smooth.

"I was going to, um, wash." I held up the soap and towel. "The bathroom is that way, correct?"

He nodded and rose to his feet gracefully, closing the book with care. He was slimmer than either Guy or Simon, not yet fully grown, despite the voice, if I was any judge of human males. But I'd seen him in armor and chain mail wielding a sword as large as Guy's yesterday, so he was no weakling. Today he wore a short-sleeved gray tunic over gray trousers, leaving his brown arms bare to the elements.

Unlike Guy's, I noted, his hands bore no crosses. As far as I knew, that meant he hadn't yet taken final vows.

Simon would know for sure. Lucius had seen to it I was educated in weapons and fighting and the basics of reading and writing and human culture, but I'd never been taught the finer points of exactly what the Templars believed and how they ran their organization. The rest of the Night World provided little information beyond than making them out to be hell-bent on killing Blood and Beast Kind in the name of their God.

Big bad monsters.

Guy fulfilled the big and bad criteria well enough and Liam did too. But I could hardly see them as monsters. Warriors, yes, but so far they seemed perfectly well controlled and lucid and not prone to hasty decisions or fanaticism.

Of course, my experience was hardly extensive. The Order could be discussing my imminent demise right this very moment.

"Do you know where Simon is?" I asked as we walked. Liam was obviously not inclined to let me move around the Brother House alone. I presumed he was acting under orders. In truth, having an escort was comforting. It would prevent any misunderstanding if I came across other Templars. The thought made me relax a little. As did the one chasing its heels, that here in the Brother House, there would be no Fae to look down their pale noses at me either—though it was possible of course that the Templars might hold the same dim view of my kind.

"Master Healer DuCaine was with his brother at breakfast," Liam said politely. "I haven't seen him since."

Hardly helpful. "And was it Healer DuCaine or his brother who set you to watch over me?" I asked.

"That was an order from the Abbott General, my—" He broke off. I wondered whether he'd been about to tell me something he shouldn't or whether, more likely, he had no idea what to call me.

I was hardly a lady, after all. No, to the Templars I was likely to be considered devil hell spawn.

Though so far, Liam had been nothing but courteous. "My name is Lily," I offered.

Liam nodded. "I know."

We walked on. The stone walls were broken here and there by the same narrow barred windows as my room. Shafts of sunlight fell through them. As we passed through one, Liam turned his face to the light, a faint smile curving his lips. The movement reminded me of Simon. I'd been wrong about Liam. He wasn't a metalmage.

"You're a sunmage," I blurted.

Liam's focus snapped back to me, eyes narrowed.

"Don't deny it. Simon already said it was you who was responsible for the fires yesterday."

His expression didn't ease. "He told you that?"

"Yes. You are, aren't you?"

"Yes." He didn't sound entirely happy that I knew.

I'd solved one mystery but there was another. I knew that the Templars had counted sunmages amongst their ranks from time to time, but most sunmages chose, like Simon, to become healers. "Yet you joined the Templars? Why?"

"I wanted to make a difference," he said, his voice dipping lower than before.

Indeed. It seemed my fate to be surrounded by men who believed in doing the right thing. Hells.

"You'd rather fight than heal? Doesn't that make you kind of the odd man out amongst your kind?" Being different was something I could relate to.

"Others have taken this path before," he said. "And some of us walk more than one path before finding the right one," he added.

It seemed a strange comment. "You mean you can

change your mind? Drop your sword and pick up bandages and herbs?"

Liam shrugged. "Some do. Rarely." He nodded at a door in the wall. "We're here."

Damn. Just when he'd caught my curiosity. But I doubted he'd tell me much more. "Thank you. Do you have to accompany me inside?" I asked with an arch of my brow.

He shook his head rapidly, accompanied by, I thought, the slightly flaring of red in his cheeks. Hard to judge on skin as dark as his.

"No. I'll wait outside." He turned his back to the door as though to underscore his point. Definitely young.

"Good." I put my hand on the door and then couldn't resist adding, "It's safe enough. I can't disappear in daylight, you know."

His shoulders twitched but he didn't turn back.

I wondered if he thought I would try to seduce him or something equally shocking or if he was just embarrassed.

I hid a smile as I walked into the bathroom. I wasn't interested in corrupting baby knights. No, if there was anyone in the building that I wanted to entice into sin, it was Simon.

If I could find him.

"I guess I don't need to ask how you spent the night," Guy said to me as we walked away from the dining hall.

I glanced around. We were alone in one of the Brother House's endless stone corridors. No one to hear. I bit back irritation. I wanted to climb to the roof and sit in the sun to try to make sense of the turmoil in my head, not have a not so cozy chat with my brother. But it would be easier in the long run to let Guy say his piece. "You've been waiting all morning to say that, haven't you?"

"Didn't think you'd appreciate me announcing it to the whole order."

"Announcing what exactly?" I folded my arms and stared him down.

Guy didn't flinch. "Don't bother denying it, little brother. I know well enough how you look after you've spent the night in some girl's bed." Sun poured from one of the windows, highlighting the grim expression on his face.

I set my teeth, trying not to rise to the bait. "She's not just some girl."

"No, she's a wraith," Guy said pointedly. "Lucius' assassin."

"She doesn't belong to him."

"She doesn't belong to you either. I hope you know what you're doing."

"I trust her." Not entirely true. I wanted to trust her. I wanted to believe that what I'd felt in her bed, what I'd seen in her eyes when I'd been inside her, was real, but gods and suns, she'd already vanished from me once. And uncovered my most guarded secret in the process. On the other hand, she'd agreed to help us. "You're the one who always told me to go with my instincts."

"As long as you're using your gut and not something farther south."

"I'm perfectly capable of controlling myself," I said sharply. Another half-truth. I was perfectly capable of controlling myself as long as Lily didn't crook her finger and ask me to take her to bed again. I frowned, rubbing my temples. Sunlight. I needed sunlight. Once my power was fed, my common sense would return.

"You spent the night having sex in the Brother House," Guy said. "Your definition of control is something different from mine."

"Are you done?" I set off again, not wanting to continue the conversation. Guy caught up to me in three or four steps. His hand closed on my shoulder, pulling me to a halt.

"Just don't lose your head. Because right now I can't promise you anything about Lily keeping hers."

I shook off his grip as ice speared through my stomach. My hand tightening involuntarily around the hilt of the sword he had lent me. "What do you mean?"

"I mean, not everyone is as reasonable as me when it comes to your girl's past."

For a moment rage tore through me, red and fierce. Lily roused something in me I didn't want to see let loose. "Anyone who wants to get to her will have to come through me first," I growled. "I thought we were meeting with Father Cho later."

"We are. But I can't guarantee he's going to go along with your plan."

I stepped closer, anger biting jagged chunks out of my resolve to stay calm. "You tell Father Cho that Lily is under my protection."

Guy held out a hand, palm upward. "Easy. He's going to talk to you. To us. Don't do anything stupid."

I tried to relax, but it was hard when all I wanted to do was go find Lily and take her to somewhere safer. But there was nowhere safer. Which didn't make reining my unexpected temper back any easier. "I won't," I said in the end. "Thank you," I added grudgingly

Guy grinned, then clapped me on the shoulder. "Go soak up some sunbeams, little brother. And have some faith. Everything is going to work out as it should."

I watched him walk away, heading toward the Abbott General's office, where he'd do his best to convince Father Cho that Lily should be protected because he'd given his word and he trusted my instincts. Because he loved me. Because he believed me.

Even though I hadn't told him the whole truth. In fact, I'd been lying to him for several years. My gut tightened. Somehow, I didn't think sunshine was going to be enough to wash me clean this time.

))

When I finally reached the eyrie where Simon had hidden himself, I was a little out of breath.

I didn't know how many stairs I'd climbed, but my protesting muscles suggested it had been a few too many. With every step upward my nerves grew and there was currently a stampeding herd of something far larger than butterflies churning my stomach to acid. What if he didn't want to see me?

Simon sat, cross-legged, face turned to the sun, eyes closed. It should have been a relaxed posture, but something about the tight square of his shoulders and the set of his head told me he was anything but relaxed.

"Am I interrupting?" I lowered myself onto one of the slates besides him.

He opened one eye, squinting against the sun, and waved a hand vaguely. "Sunshine." His eye closed again.

"I understand that part," I said, resisting the urge to poke him so he'd look at me. "Are you all right?"

"Yes." He sounded calm but I wasn't convinced. I sighed, unsure what to try next.

Simon opened his eyes and turned so he wasn't looking into the sun. "More important, how are you?"

"I'm quite well. Should I be otherwise?"

"It's normal to feel some . . . effects after the first time." He cleared his throat, his expression . . . diplomatic.

Apparently, sex came with many complications. Not least of which were the awkward conversations afterward. "Nothing to signify."

"Good." His face eased toward a smile.

"And you? Any . . ." I trailed off, not sure what I was even asking.

He blinked. "I wasn't a virgin. And I'm not female."

"I didn't mean physically."

"Ah." He took a deep breath, turned his face back to the sun.

Nothing more seemed to be forthcoming. The not-butterflies returned and a chill shivered through me. I clasped my arms around my knees and looked out at the view, giving him time. From our vantage point half the City seemed laid out at our feet like a toy village.

I oriented myself automatically, picking out landmarks I recognized. The blazing white dome of St. Giles only a few hundred feet away to the left of us and the tall black spire of the cathedral to our right. Working my way from those, I found the building I thought held Guy's home. Simon's house in Greenglass was farther southeast, the borough an indistinguishable mess of trees and houses from where we sat. In the other direction, toward the edges of the Night World, the buildings became more jumbled together, crooked rows and alleys of squat town houses, tenements, and shops broken by the odd slightly higher building of a theater hall or storehouse.

I turned my back on that part of the view, focusing instead on the neatly ordered rows of the human boroughs.

All those people. Living neat safe lives every day. Going about their business with nothing more to worry about than what to wear or what to have for their next meal.

An oversimplification of course, but I wanted to believe it.

How would it feel to live your life in the light, free and clear?

I hugged my knees more tightly. For me, such a life, lived in the daylight, would mean giving up most of my powers. Giving up the very thing I'd relied on for safety all my life.

Of course, if I had such a life, I wouldn't need to concern myself overly much with safety.

It was too hard a concept to grasp all at once. So I just kept staring down at the autocabs and carriages and carts moving through the streets and the humans moving casually amongst them.

In the far distance, toward the hills of Summerdale, a train spouted a plume of steam into the sky. That far out, the railway left the safety of the underground and traveled beneath the open sky.

Could I do the same?

"Stop thinking so hard," Simon muttered from beside me. "Lie back and enjoy the sunshine."

I straightened, stomach fluttering once more. He'd broken the silence at last. But changed the subject. Well, I could live with that for now.

"Don't you have anything you should be doing?" I asked curiously.

"Yes. This."

"Have you told them yet that I agreed to do as you wanted?"

He frowned at me for a moment, then sighed softly. He snaked out a hand and tugged at my arm. "Come, lie down with me, Lily." He shifted position, so he was nearer to the shade thrown by the nearest dome, where the door to the stairs stood open. "See, lie here and you won't get burned."

"You didn't answer my question."

"Just come here and be still for a while."

I hesitated. The closer I got to him, the more I wanted to know what was going to happen to me next, to ease the butterflies. But for now, it seemed, the wants of my body were going to overrule my need to find out what he was thinking.

Maybe he just wanted to be with me. Even if what lay between us was horribly complicated and there was a good chance Lucius would be hunting both of us soon, it was very tempting to pretend that there was nothing at all that should concern either of us for a small moment of time. I lay down, let him draw me into his arms.

Warm and safe. I moved a little closer.

"Now, that's just asking for trouble." He chuckled, half under his breath.

"What is?"

He pressed his hips into me.

"Oh. That." One mystery solved, at least. He still wanted me.

"Yes, that. Which we can't do anything about in broad daylight on the rooftop of the Brother House."

"Guy would disapprove?" I quipped.

"Not just Guy," he said, letting go of me abruptly. He sat up.

I did the same. So much for small moments of time. "If you're worried about the Fae, there's little point. They're unlikely to change their mind about me, Simon. You need to come to terms with that."

I looked up at him, sunlight turning his hair gold. His expression was distant, blue eyes staring out over the City. "Truly, Simon, you're not going to change their minds."

"I was thinking of the Templars."

Hells. I hadn't considered the knights. "Do you care what they think?"

"When they're currently standing between us and Lucius, I do."

"Oh." I sat up, suddenly chilled, despite the warmth of the sun.

"No, I didn't mean . . ." He stopped, scrubbed his hands through his hair. "Suns, I don't know what I mean. This isn't what I expected."

"Expected from what? Last night? Or life in general? Did you think you'd just bed me and move on?"

"No. I—" He smoothed his hair down but couldn't quite smooth the look of frustration from his face. "What did *you* expect?"

I stared at him, imagining my expression pretty much mirrored the frustration on his. "I didn't *expect* any of this. Five days ago my life was perfectly simple. And then you happened."

His brows drew down. "You'll have to pardon me for not rolling over and dying."

"You didn't have to roll over, you just had to lie still," I pointed out.

He snorted but his lips curved. "I'll remember that next time."

"There won't be a next time."

"You're not the only assassin Lucius employs," Simon said, humor vanishing. "Once you give your testimony, then I'd imagine he'll be after your head too. Which means there's a high chance I'm going to encounter more of them. Besides, Lucius isn't the only danger we face."

More chills ran through me. He was right. Lying in the sun with this man thinking I was safe was an illusion. The reality lay below in those treacherous streets of the Night World. Danger. Death. Or even, I realized, in the cool gray rooms beneath our feet. The Templars hadn't come to any sort of official decision about me. They didn't have to keep me here, regardless of what I agreed to do.

And by staying here, I was making things worse for Simon. I shouldn't have slept with him. It would've been easier to walk away before. Before I knew how easy it was to let him hold me.

"You should let me go," I said. Before he got too used to saying "we" when he should be thinking of his own safety. My pulse started to pound as I spoke.

"You've changed your mind?"

No. Though it was tempting at this point to just run and Lady take the consequences. "After I do what you want, it would be better if I left."

"Go where, exactly?"

"Away." Away from the City. Far and fast. Even though I didn't believe I could really outrun what I'd be leaving behind.

"Lily, what makes you think you'll be any safer anywhere else?"

I scowled at him. Idiot man. He needed to learn how to take the opportunity to retire safely from the field when it presented itself. "I might not be. But you will."

One of his dimples flickered. "You don't know that. Lucius was trying to kill me before you, after all."

"Because of what you're doing down there." I jerked my chin in the direction of St. Giles.

"Maybe."

"Definitely. What you're doing could change everything."

"If we ever find a cure," he said shortly.

"Why do it at all?" I asked. "Last night it seemed as though you think the blood-locked deserve the consequences of their decisions." Had I misjudged him?

"No one deserves that, no matter what they've done. And regardless, I took an oath to heal."

"No matter what?"

"Yes."

I really didn't think I would ever understand him. Why help those you despised? But even though it baffled me, it also gave me a tiny sliver of hope that maybe, just maybe, if he ever found out about me, he'd be able to see past my addiction. "So you'll keep working even though Lucius is threatening your life."

"Yes. Besides, we don't know why Lucius sent you."

"What other reason does he have to kill you? You're a sunmage and Guy's your brother. You're too well connected for him to try for you without a very good reason. The question is, who was it that told him what you were doing?" I said seriously. Someone had to have betrayed the secret. I didn't see any other way for Lucius to have found out.

"Very few people know. And I trust them all."

"One person can keep a secret," I said. "After that, it's almost impossible. You only need one person to be curious about what's in that tunnel, the same way I was."

"That tunnel has some pretty strong 'don't notice me' magics," Simon said.

"That wouldn't stop a Fae. Might just make them more curious, in fact."

"They'd have to be strong to get past the iron. Besides, the wards are only keyed to a few people. I'd know if anybody else had been down there." He frowned as he spoke. Perhaps not quite as confident as he sounded?

"They wouldn't necessarily need to breach the wards. They could just watch and listen. See who comes in and out of the tunnels. Put the pieces of the puzzle together that way."

"You think a Fae would betray us to the Blood? The Fae who work at St. Giles are not the kind to side with the Night World."

"If the informant is Fae, then you don't know what game they're playing." The Veiled World wasn't called that just because it kept itself hidden. Part of the name came because of the almost impenetrable web of politics and family alliance, of feud and counterfeud, of social climbing and maneuvering of alliance and patronage that wove together the Fae Families. With such long lives, they could afford to set plans in motion that would take decades or longer to come to fruition. Who knew what one of them might do?

Simon looked unconvinced. "What do the Fae have to gain from war between the humans and the Blood?"

"Some of the Families would like nothing better, I'm sure. Just because the queen currently supports and enforces the treaties, it doesn't mean everyone agrees with her will. No more than all humans do. Or all of the Night World."

"No one can be stupid enough to think things were better the way they were."

I didn't find it hard to imagine any number of people in the Night World being precisely that stupid. "Not everyone is good, Simon. I keep telling you that."

"You really believe someone is giving information to Lucius?"

I nodded.

"It seems ridiculous." He tugged at the collar of his shirt irritably. "But ignoring your instincts would be foolish. How would you go about trying to find out who?"

"If someone is lurking in shadows, I would start by doing some lurking of my own," I said. "After all, I'm the expert in that area."

"That would only work at night, wouldn't it?"

"Not so far underground. The lamps aren't sunlamps, after all." It occurred to me that whoever had sold Simon out could well be long gone. On the other hand, if I could convince Simon that it made sense for me to spend time in the tunnels, then I could probably arrange some time alone with Atherton.

"Of course," I said casually, "if you want me to do this, then you will have to convince Guy and the others to set me free for a while. They don't seem overly trusting. Do the Templars even know what you're doing down there?"

"No," Simon said.

I looked at him, surprised. "Not at all? Not even Guy?"

"No," he said shortly, looking away. "Saving the blood-locked is not one of their priorities. They're more focused on stopping the Night World luring more victims. Besides, they're not healers. They couldn't help."

"I see." Presumably that meant the fact of Atherton's existence was unknown as well. I studied Simon for a moment. I might not understand him but I needed to remember that he was more than he appeared.

"Master Healer DuCaine?" There was a discreet cough behind us. I recognized the voice. Liam.

Simon looked up, frowning. "Yes?"

"The Abbott General sent me to find you. He requests that you attend him, if you have finished what you need to do here."

With another deeper frown, Simon rose to his feet, then offered me a hand up. "Yes, yes. We're done."

I brushed dust from my trousers, trying to ignore the sudden knot of nerves in my stomach. Why were they summoning Simon? "I'll go back to my room."

Liam shook his head. "The request included you too."

Chapter Fifteen

))

The Abbott General's office was no more richly appointed than the rest of the Brother House. His furniture was the same simple style as the furniture in my small room. Only an elaborately carved cross and a tapestry of the order's coat of arms hung on the walls.

Guy was already there when Liam showed Simon and me in. He was alone.

"Morning," he rumbled. His hand scratched at a stubbly chin. I wondered if he'd been to bed at all. If he hadn't, had he and the Abbott General stayed up all night discussing me? My hand strayed to check my dagger.

"Good morning," Simon said. "Where's Father Cho?"

"He'll be along."

"Why are we here?" I asked. If Simon hadn't yet told the Templars that I was willing to give them the information they wanted, then I wasn't sure what other reason there could be. Which left me little option other than to follow Simon's lead and hope no one was about to try to kill me.

"I think I'll leave that to Father Cho to explain." Guy nodded at me, looking slightly amused. "Did you sleep well, Lily?"

"Perfectly well, thank you," I lied. Did Guy know about Simon and me? I decided to ignore that possibility. "Being locked up must agree with me."

"You weren't locked up," Simon said. "You can walk through walls." His tone was sharp.

Was he angry? With me? With Guy? Whatever was bothering him, I didn't have time to work it out. The large doors opened again and this time, Liam saluted as Father Cho came in.

I knew him by reputation, of course. The Abbott General of the Templars is somewhat of a feared figure in the Night World. I'd expected an older, battle-scarred version of Guy. But the man who walked through the door couldn't have been more different.

Slimly built and shorter than any of the men in the room by half a foot, he wore a simple white tunic with the red Templar cross splayed across it over breeches rather than armor. His hair was cropped close to his head in the same style as Guy's, true black frosted with silver, and he had the golden skin and angled eyes of someone born in the Silk Provinces. Far from home if that were the case. More likely, he was descended from those who'd made that long journey several generations back.

But for all his un-warrior-like appearance, he exuded command. When he took his place behind the desk and motioned us all to sit, it was hard not to obey instantly. But I waited to take my place until the others were seated.

Guy and Simon took chairs to either side of me, leaving me directly in front of Father Cho. His dark gaze fell on me, and I resisted the urge to look away. Luckily my practice in staying stoic under scrutiny was vast.

"So, you are Lily?" Father Cho said. His voice held no hint of the Silk Provinces.

"Yes, Father."

"And what Brother Guy has told me is correct? You were formerly a member of Lucius' Court?"

Nerves dried my mouth and I swallowed once before answered. "Yes, Lucius *owned* me."

"I'm also assured that you have had a . . . change of heart?"

"A change of heart?"

"You've seen the error of your ways?"

"Oh. I see." I looked at Simon for some clue as to whether I was meant to tell them that I'd agreed to testify. His face remained blank. "You mean, now that Simon and

Guy stole me from Lucius and he seems to want to kill me, I don't want to go back to him. Yes. That's correct." I couldn't help the slight snap in my voice. I was growing tired of being questioned and manipulated.

The Abbott General smiled sharply. "You would return to Lucius, if he didn't wish you dead?"

That was a leading question, if ever I'd heard one.

Simon gave me the faintest of nods. Time to tell the truth. I had the feeling that Father Cho was fairly astute at sorting fact from fiction anyway. "No, Father. No. I would not choose to go back to him."

"Or do what you formerly did?"

"No, Father." I breathed deeply, not wanting to remember what I had done. All those dead faces. All those bodies. Too much death and blood at my hands. I spoke the truth, I realized. I didn't want to go back to that. "No, I would rather not return to the Night World. I do not agree with Lucius' . . . tactics."

Father Cho's gaze sharpened. He steepled his hands, head cocked. "What does that mean?" he asked. "That you do not like what he does or that you want to stop what he does?"

"Both," I said shortly. "I will give the evidence you need against him. I will tell the Fae he sent me to kill a human." Then had to stop as a wave of fear iced my skin. I'd done it now. Taken the step that couldn't be taken back. For a moment the room seemed to shrink around me, caging me in. The carving on the arms of my chair dug into my palms as my grip tightened.

Breathe.

I tried to slow the racing of my heart. The three men stayed silent as I concentrated on drawing oxygen into my lungs.

Finally, "Will you swear to that?" Father Cho asked.

"Is there an oath I can give that you would value?" I asked. "I don't believe in your God, Father."

"What do you believe in?"

Right now I wasn't at all sure. "I offer you my word," I said. "It's up to you if you choose to accept it."

He smiled at me suddenly, the creases at the corners of his eyes deepening. "You are not what I expected," he said.

"You're not the first person to say that to me."

His smile widened. "I expect not. All right, then. I will take you at your word. You are granted Haven here at the Brother House until such time as your testimony to the Fae can be arranged."

"How long will that take?"

"A few days," Simon said. "The council will have to be told of our plans and then they'll liaise with the Speaker for the Veil."

"That's a lot of people," I said. The Speaker for the Veil was supposedly the sole voice of the Fae queen, but in reality he had a retinue of aides and bureaucrats. The human council had twelve members of itself and the human government only spread from there. Too many tongues that could wag. "What if Lucius finds out?"

"We can take steps to prevent that," Simon said.

Like he'd taken steps to keep his work with Atherton secret? But I couldn't bring that up as an objection. "And afterward?"

"I would imagine that you will need protecting until after the negotiations," Father Cho said. "You will stay here."

My heart sank. They were going to keep me locked up—or try to. "What if I don't want to?"

The three of them looked at one another. "Let's not borrow trouble, child," Father Cho said eventually. "The most pressing matter is to get your testimony to the Fae."

The stone walls seemed to press in on me as my stomach churned. I'd made my choice. Now I had to live with it. I made myself relax, taking another deep breath.

The room smelled faintly of incense but mostly of cool air and the three men around me. Those three and many more, I realized. Other fiercely masculine scents hung in the air. Traces of sweat and leather and smoke. It made me want to breathe deeper still. My stomach tightened at the thought. Was that the need talking? I clasped my hands tightly together in my lap, studying them for a moment.

It couldn't be the need. I wouldn't let it be.

"Which rather leaves the question of exactly what you are to do for the next few days," Father Cho said.

I raised my head. I hadn't thought about that. I could help Simon search for Lucius' source, if he would let me, but I couldn't tell the Templars that. "Perhaps I might help Simon at the hospital, Father."

It was the best I could do. We needed them to be willing to let me move freely if I was going to hunt a spy. Otherwise I would be limited to what I could do at night. Limiting my hunt to half the available hours of the day would hardly be helpful.

Father Cho looked to Simon. "Would that be acceptable to Lady Bryony?"

Simon's mouth went flat. "Leave Bryony to me."

He shifted in his chair and his leg brushed mine. Heat flared through me. Hunger for him or something else? I dropped my gaze to my hands again, not wanting my expression to betray me. Were they shaking? Apart from the hunger for pleasure, the need brought with it tremors and cramps and other unpleasant symptoms if it wasn't fed. I thought last night that it had been more than sated. Was I wrong?

Hells, I needed to talk to Atherton again.

As we left Father Cho's office, I stayed silent, thankful to be leaving under my own power and with some degree of freedom. Guy didn't leave us as we walked and we'd gained an additional escort in the form of Liam. I was still all too aware of the scent of healthy males around me. It wasn't quite the burning of the need. Not quite, yet it still unnerved me.

Though not quite as much as what I had just agreed to do. Contemplating that particular folly made the rest of my surroundings fade into the distance somewhat.

"I think we should move Mother and Hannah," Simon said to Guy. "If word of this gets out . . ."

"Yes," Guy agreed. "I'll do that. Saskia should be safe enough at the Guild Academy."

"I've already sent a message to the Master of Iron that there may be trouble. He'll take appropriate action."

That got my attention. Simon's sister was a mage too? Or one in training? A metalmage from the sounds of it. Who was at risk now, because of me. Much like the rest of his family.

Another weight to bear if something went wrong.

I shook my head to chase away the thought, as my nails dug into my palms. I needed something to work off some of the confusion of nerves and fear and anger I was carrying. "Where are we going?"

"I'm headed to the weapons hall to drill the novices," Guy said. "You could come along."

Weapons hall? Where I'd be surrounded by Templars with lots of naked steel in their hands? Not exactly the sort of exercise I'd had in mind. "I really think—"

Guy grinned at me. "Scared, are you? I was hoping you could assist. I'd imagine you've got a few tricks up your sleeve the puppies won't have seen before."

Beating up novices. Perhaps that wouldn't be so bad. In fact, it held a certain appeal, I realized as my stomach suddenly steadied. Training was something familiar. And a smart fighter never passes up an opportunity to study the technique of a potential foe. I hoped I would never have to fight a Templar, but who knew what the Lady might bring? I brushed a strand of hair back off my face. "I'm not scared of baby knights," I said.

"Good," Guy said. "That's settled."

Simon's expression was concerned as he looked from Guy to me. "I think I'll come too, just to make sure no one ends up bleeding to death."

Guy laughed. "Don't worry. I won't hurt her."

I tilted my head at him, hands on my hips. "What makes you think I'm the one in danger?"

The weapons hall was exactly that. A single-storied stone building standing squatly on a substantial portion of the grounds to the rear of the Brother House. Inside, it was one huge rectangle, divided into smaller rectangles only by the changing surface of the floor. One-quarter flat slate tiles, one-quarter packed dirt, one-quarter cobblestones, and the last pale yellow sand.

The walls were lined with long, low wooden benches and hung with row upon row of swords, axes, longbows like Liam had used, crossbows, pikes, and other various metal and wooden instruments of destruction. High windows let in plenty of light.

Which meant that I'd be limited to only my physical abilities. Looking over the twenty or so assembled men, most of them even younger looking than Liam, I didn't think that was necessarily going to be a problem, despite the scowls of disapproval several of them directed at me. Not happy with a female in their hallowed halls?

Guy bellowed at them to line up and then Liam started taking them through a series of moves I was familiar with—stretches designed by the priests of a sect from the Silk Provinces. But I merely watched, trying to get a feel for the men I could be fighting.

The novices wore loose wool breeches and sleeveless tunics in various shades of gray and dirty white. The Templars, apart from their crosses, didn't seem to be overly fond of color. They all had cropped hair and sported identical looks of concentration as they began the drill.

Beside me, Simon and Guy watched too. Guy's expression was finely calculated between intimidation and intent study. I wouldn't want to be the student who fumbled a drill in front of him. But no one made any overt errors at this point. Simon, on the other hand, wore an expression that I couldn't quite interpret.

The novices moved smoothly through the sequence, muscles flexing in unison. Some of them shot hostile glances my way whenever they faced me. I resisted the urge to smile. They were like the young Beasts, full of swagger and ego. And like the young Beasts, they were well trained. To a man, they were tall and strong and moved in the same lithe powerful way as Simon and Guy and Liam. Nerves balled in my stomach. Perhaps this wasn't a good idea after all.

But I wasn't about to act like a weak female and prove their prejudices correct. I channeled the nerves into concentrating even harder on the men, picking out weaknesses. Eventually the sequence came to its conclusion and Guy barked a few more orders. The knights fetched swords from the racks on the walls—no wooden practice weapons here, it seemed—and paired off in neat rows along the length of the hall.

"Do you want to watch or work?" Guy said to me.

"Work."

He nodded toward the racks. "Pick a sword." He turned to Simon. "Do you want to drill with her?"

Simon shook his head. "You know the answer to that."

They exchanged one of their inscrutable looks. Guy shook his head and turned back to me. "You can drill with Liam."

I did as I was told. But I took my time, testing the blades to find one with the correct balance and weight, wondering why Simon had refused as I did so. He knew how to fight; he'd said Guy had trained him. Why deny himself the opportunity to practice? I pushed my puzzlement away as I studied the swords. If I wasn't focused, then I'd come off second best on the practice ground. None of the blades was perfect, given they were sized for men, but I can handle a heavier sword than any human female my size and I found a close enough match without much trouble.

I took my place opposite Liam. We were working on the dirt, which was perfectly fine by me. I'd been trained to fight anywhere. I rarely met resistance. My powers allowed me to use stealth and most of my victims never saw me. But assassinations weren't the only thing I did for Lucius, and, even with my training, Simon's sunlight had given him the advantage when it mattered most. I frowned, remembering, and almost got clobbered by Liam when Guy yelled out the first command.

I ducked just in time and came back to full alert, shaking off embarrassment. Liam's white teeth gleamed at me as he grinned. I set my own teeth. There was no way I was going to let myself be bested in front of all these knights.

Guy started shouting instructions in rapid succession and we moved to his commands. Blocks and thrusts and parries blurred together. Liam was good, but despite his height advantage, my experience let me hold my own. Still, he didn't hold back and I rapidly started sweating.

It felt good to move. To do what I was trained to do. To lose myself in the rhythm of combat and not *think*.

But slowly, even through the dance of strike and counterstrike, through the need to focus on the sharpened steel being swung at my head and the man swinging it, I became aware that part of me wasn't paying attention to the fight. Instead, part of me was tracking the sight of all the male bodies around me, the play of their muscles, the smell of their sweat.

Tracking and wanting it.

Wanting them.

Not just Simon, who stood on the sidelines, as strong and sure as any of them, the light through the windows making his hair glow bright gold. No, this wasn't caused by him.

As soon as I became aware, the need swooped and flared, almost causing me to stumble as a fierce piercing jolt of desire shook through me.

Night-scalded *hell*. I blinked sweat out of my eyes and redoubled my efforts, hoping I could drive the need out through sheer physical exertion. It had worked in the past.

It didn't work so well now.

"Stop!" Guy roared. My sword met Liam's for one final ringing clash that echoed around the hall as everyone else drew apart faster than us. There were murmured comments from the knights as I turned to face Guy, sword still at the ready.

Perhaps they thought I couldn't hear, but my ears caught the muttered "What's she even doing here?" perfectly clearly.

Apparently Guy's hearing was quite acute as well. "*She*," he said with deadly emphasis, "is here to show you puppies how things are done in the real world." He strode across to the wall and selected a short sword.

My heart sank. Fight Guy? While fighting the need? Not quite what I was hoping for.

"Lily, would you care to demonstrate what a real fight looks like?" Guy hefted the sword. I was glad he'd chosen a smaller weapon than his usual blade. I had a chance of getting within reach of him without getting my head taken off.

I looked across at Simon, the reason I was here in the middle of all of this. The one who'd turned my life upside down, and suddenly in place of the need, there was anger. Fury almost. What right did he have to bring all this trouble into my life? "I'll fight Simon," I said coldly.

Beside me, Guy made a half-choked sound of amusement.

Simon's eyebrows shot up. Then he shook his head sharply. "I don't fight for entertainment."

"Scared to fight a girl?"

He stood there, arms crossed. "No. I'm not going to fight you, Lily."

I set my teeth as my anger kicked up another notch. Did he think just because he'd bested me once he could do so any time he chose? I reached for the dagger at my hip, transferring my sword to my left hand. "Well, if you won't fight for entertainment, how about for real?" I said, and launched myself across the floor.

❋

I watched Lily's face as she came toward me at a flat run. She was serious, that much was plain. Something had pushed her too far and right at this moment, I didn't doubt she'd draw my blood if she could.

I didn't want to fight but I was going to have to. A few rounds at least, until she calmed down. I drew my sword, waiting until the last possible moment before raising it to meet her blow and spin away.

Across the sand Guy grinned at me. The bastard was enjoying this. Well, his turn would come. Lily's next attack came lightning fast and for the next few minutes I was occupied with stopping her from succeeding in taking my head off.

She was good. More than good. I already knew that. And, as we fought, I felt the familiar unwanted exhilaration sing through my veins. It felt good to have the sword in my hand, good to swing it.

Too good.

Which was reason enough to shut her down as soon as possible. My opportunity came soon enough. She overreached after a particularly vicious flurry of blows and tipped slightly off balance. I took advantage of her distraction as she tried to recover to duck under her guard, reached out and pressed my hand against her neck, sending a jolt of power down the nerves of her arms to numb them. Her sword and dagger fell to the ground.

"Bastard," she hissed. "That's cheating."

"I said I wouldn't fight you," I replied. "So, your choice. Do you want the use of your arms back?"

She bared her teeth at me but nodded.

I bent to retrieve her weapons, keeping my eyes on her to make sure she didn't decide to try to kick me in the head. "All right. Now, if you want to hit someone, I'm sure Guy will oblige."

"Fine," Lily spat. "A real warrior would be more of a challenge anyway."

I shook my head at her. "We'll talk about this when you've calmed down." I reversed the nerve block, passed her the sword and dagger, and stepped back off the sparring field.

Lily glared at me for a long ten seconds or so, then turned to Guy. "You have any problem fighting me?" she said.

He shook his head, grinning nastily. "None whatsoever. Real-world rules okay by you, shadow?"

"Real-world rules?" she questioned. "What are those?"

"Anything goes," Guy said, and drew his sword.

Five minutes later I was beginning to wonder if I'd made a mistake in reversing the nerve block. Lily didn't seem to have calmed down any. She and Guy were fighting like old-school gladiators.

I kept my hand on my sword, ready to intervene and fighting down my own instinct to join in with an effort of will. I sparred with Guy occasionally to keep my skills in, but we didn't fight full out. I had stepped away from that path a long time ago and didn't want the reminder of just why I'd made my choice.

Lily flipped backward to avoid Guy's sword swinging almost too fast to see at her torso. She landed in a crouch, swept up a handful of sand, flung it at Guy's face, and then drove forward with a flurry of blows that had the watching knights roaring approval and Guy retreating.

But only for a moment. Guy grinned fiercely, feinted, executed a neat spin of his own that finished with a side kick that would've broken her ribs had it connected. Having been the recipient of just such a kick on more than one occasion, I winced reflexively.

But Lily just dodged, her eyes fixed on Guy, sword flashing as she attacked again.

Despite my own dislike of the whole situation, I had to admit I was torn between pleasure at the sheer beauty of her in full flight, braided hair swinging behind her, the sleek lines of her body arcing gracefully, and heart-clutching fear that one of them was going to get seriously hurt.

Steel rang as they fought. Fought dirty. Nothing measured or by the book. They both used elbows and fists, feet, and the terrain as they battled. Exactly the way I'd been taught all those years ago.

I watched, pulse pounding, as Lily ducked another potentially fatal blow, ran full tilt past Guy to leap and grab a shield from the wall and send it spinning back toward him. Guy moved, but not quite fast enough, and the shield caught his sword at precisely the right—or wrong– angle and sent it flying from his hand.

Lily pressed the attack, reversing her sword neatly to

drive the pommel like a hammer toward Guy's head as he recovered from the force of the shield's impact. Her shirt was wet with sweat, turning it transparent in places. She wore something underneath, but it didn't do much to hide the swell of her breasts beneath the thin cotton.

Suddenly I wanted everyone else to disappear, so I could tackle her to the sand and get my hands on her again. Work out the adrenaline and confusion in a way just as primal as the fight going on in front of me.

Guy dove for his sword, but Lily kicked it out of his reach. Then a crazed smile lit her face and she threw her own sword away, switching to kicks and blows.

Her speed and ferociousness—a stomach-jolting reminder of exactly who she was and how she'd gotten that way—as she closed with Guy was breathtaking, but without the sword, Guy had the advantage of height and reach and weight. Within a minute or so, Guy stepped close, ducked her flying punch to his head, caught her, twisted, and sent her sailing through the air to land in a crashing series of rolls in the sand.

"Enough!" The words tore from my throat before I was even aware of opening my mouth. Guy turned and held up his hands with a nod. The novices broke into a round of applause as Lily lifted her head from the sand, body tensed. She registered that Guy wasn't attacking and relaxed before rolling slowly to a seated position. When our gazes connected, she looked surprised to see me, as though she'd forgotten I was there.

Her cheeks were flushed from the fight, but it seemed to me they grew suddenly pinker. Her hand came up to smooth the hair from her face, tongue flicking quickly to moisten those lush lips. She pushed to her feet, the action pressing her breasts forward against her shirt again.

Gods and suns. What was wrong with me that seeing her like this—seeing her display those skills that made her a killer—only made me want her more? Her eyes stayed with mine and the air seemed to crackle between us.

Which wasn't going to do either of us any good while we were stuck in the gods-damned Brother House.

Guy came toward me, brushing sand from his clothes, looking disgustingly cheerful. "She can fight, little brother."

I kept my eyes on Lily. She stared back. "Yes, I know.

Still, I'd appreciate it if you didn't break her. We've spent quite a bit of time healing her the last few days."

Guy laughed, then winced, touching a reddened mark on the side of his face. "As long as you ask her to extend me the same courtesy. Ow," he said meditatively, feeling along his jaw. Then his attention snapped back to his novices. "Right, puppies. That's how it's done. Now, stop lazing about. Liam, second drills, please."

I didn't pay much attention as the knights exchanged their swords for long padded staffs. Instead I crossed to Lily, who stood on the sandy square brushing her clothes clean, much as Guy had done.

My hands itched to help her. "Need some assistance?" I said softly.

Her pupils flared, her eyes clear of their earlier fury, and unless I was imagining it, her cheeks darkened further. But she stepped out of reach.

"No, thank you," she said slowly. She swiped at her sleeves a few more times, then dropped her hands.

Damn. This was almost as awkward as those first few minutes on the roof. She was jittery around me. Nervous as . . . well, as a virgin who'd been deflowered and wasn't sure of her lover's response the morning after. Was that why she'd been so angry earlier?

Not that I could do anything to reassure her right now. Not with this particular audience. "Are you done here?"

She looked past my shoulder, at the sparring knights, a peculiar expression shading her face for a moment. Then she nodded. "Yes. I'm done."

Chapter Sixteen

))

I kept my distance as we walked back to the main building. Adrenaline from the sparring session buzzed through me, but underneath the high, the need sang too. Simon smelled far too good.

My surge of anger had faded, burned away by exertion. Though Simon's reluctance to fight still puzzled me. I sighed, feeling suddenly tired. And in need of clean clothes. I rubbed my forearm where it was scraped from one of my falls. I could feel similar abraded patches on my ribs and left thigh. Leather would have spared me those.

"Let me see that." Simon reached for my arm.

I twitched it away. "It's just a scrape. And why I need more leathers," I said.

He frowned but didn't try again. "Are you planning on picking more fights?"

"Who knows what I'll have to do in the next few weeks?" I said. "Why didn't you want to fight me?" I added.

"I don't believe in violence."

"You fought at Halcyon," I objected. He had fought me at his house too.

"I will fight to defend myself. I don't do it for entertainment."

"Why not?"

"That's a long story."

"Well, we're stuck here together for now, aren't we?"

"Some other time."

"Why not now?"

"I'm not in the mood for remembrances right now, Lily. Particularly not those remembrances. Like you said, we have time." His voice gentled on those last few words, but his eyes were distant blue.

Perhaps we didn't. Neither of us knew what might be coming. I needed to know now. Not just so I knew if he would fight beside me, but because I wanted to know the man.

"Tell me," I said softly. "You're good with a sword. Why won't you fight?" I hesitated, then laid my hand on his arm.

He pulled his hand away as though I'd burned him. "Because I like it too much."

I turned and walked away, moving fast. Gods. I should have kept my mouth shut.

But Lily wasn't the kind of woman who'd let the subject go, and sure enough, I heard her footsteps start behind me after a few seconds.

Gods and fucking suns.

I didn't want this. Not now.

There was a door beside me in the corridor. I grabbed the handle, and was inside, locking the door behind me before I had time to think. Considerate of the Brothers to leave the key. Better still, the room—some sort of office—was empty. I took a few steps, wondering what in hell I was going to do next.

"Simon?" Lily's voice came through the door, soft but definitely annoyed.

"Go away," I said to her. At least the sun was still shining so she couldn't just walk through the wall.

Behind me there was a soft rattle followed by a clink. Before I realized what she was doing, the door opened and Lily stalked through, hairpin in one hand.

"I don't need darkness to pick locks," she said. She closed the door, then leaned firmly against it, blocking the exit.

"I said, go away."

"No." She cocked her head as she shoved the hairpin back into her coiled red braids. "Of course, you could make me but that might be difficult without fighting me."

"Lily—" I said, warningly

"Simon," she said in the same exact tone. The same anger that had flared at me across the weapons hall darkened her eyes again. "I'm not going anywhere. You took me from my world. You asked me to put my life at risk for you. Last night you came to my bed. So now I'm asking you to do something for me. Let me *in*."

I spun away from her, walking toward the window, reaching for the sunlight blindly. The old glass was thick and dusty under my palms. Familiar. Tied up with everything I didn't want to remember.

"Simon?" A hand touched my shoulder, light as a feather, then dropped away. "What happened to you?"

I kept my gaze on the window. Everything was blurred and wavy. No clearer than my mind. "What makes you think anything happened?"

"I have a passing familiarity with pain," she said.

"Damn it, Lily—"

"You told me I couldn't keep running. What makes you think you can?"

She had me there. Gods and fucking suns. I'd wanted her to let me in and she had. If I couldn't do the same, then I'd been wrong all along and I had just been thinking with my cock. I turned to her.

"I was a novice here once," I said slowly.

Her eyes widened. "You were a Templar?" Her forehead creased, then eased. "Oh. That's what Liam meant."

"Liam?"

"I asked him why he was a Templar instead of a healer like the other sunmages. He said sometimes people change paths. He was talking about you."

"Yes. But it's not that simple."

She shook her head. "I would imagine not." She reached for my hand again and tugged me toward the desk, perching against it. "Tell me."

Two simple words. They shouldn't hurt quite so much. But it wasn't the words, not really. It was the memories.

"My powers rose when I was seventeen. Later than some," I said. "Guy had joined the order a few years earlier, when he turned sixteen. He was my brother, my hero back then. I wanted to follow in his footsteps, so I left school, convinced my powers were a sign I was meant to be a holy warrior. I didn't listen when anyone talked about being a healer. I thought I knew why I'd been given my power. For a time, it seemed I was right." I took a deep breath, though the smells of the Brother House didn't make it any easier to fight the memories.

"What happened?" Lily asked.

"Everything was fine for the first year of my novitiate. It's mostly schooling and learning to fight at that age. And learning to channel my power. Easy enough, even though I tried too hard to live up to my brother's reputation. He truly was born to this."

Lily considered this. "He fights very well," she said. "But I think the only difference between you and him is that he is more in practice."

I laughed. She didn't know how close she was to the truth. "Maybe so. But back then I wanted to be better than him. He was my hero but a rival too. Two stupid, arrogant boys, butting heads as much as we got along. He liked bossing me around a bit too well, I thought. At the end of my first year, he swore his final vows. He knew he had a true calling."

"And you?"

"I thought I did, back then. I was good at swordplay even though I'd never done anything real. And I knew I wanted to help people, much like Guy."

"So, what changed?"

Now came the heart of it. My chest ached but I made myself continue talking. "Do you remember the night we met? I told you a little of my family."

"Yes. Guy and your parents and two sisters. Hannah and Saskia?"

"That's right. But I had another sister."

"Had?"

Lily's voice was very soft now. I didn't look at her. "Edwina was two years younger than me. Just sixteen. Just being introduced into society. She was headstrong. They're *all* headstrong."

"Why should the girls be any different from you and Guy?" Lily said.

I snorted and the ache eased for an instant. "You sound like Mother."

"Edwina," Lily prompted.

"She got involved with a fast set. They did the sorts of things you do when you're young and stupid. Went places they weren't supposed to go, mixed with the wrong crowds. The sort of thing most of us scrape through with only the odd hangover or gambling debt or broken heart to show for it. But Edwina—" I stopped, swallowed. "Edwina fell in love with the wrong man. He was a Nightseeker. We didn't realize at first. He hid his proclivities well. But she followed him into that world."

Lily made a small unhappy noise. "Go on."

It took an effort to comply. I'd spent too many years locking these memories away and not letting them escape. But the bonds were frayed now and the images rose, fresh as they ever had been. "It was Mother who realized something was wrong. She caught Edwina in a lie about where she'd been and told her she was not to be allowed out for a month. Edwina seemed to accept it at first, but she ran away two days later.

"Mother sent for Guy and me and we looked for her. It took nearly two weeks to find her. When we did it was obvious she'd drunk from one of the Blood by then. She was locked." I paused, sickened. "She refused to leave with us. The Blood threw us out of the Assembly."

"You left her there?"

"I thought we'd come back for her. That we'd go to the order and they'd help us rescue her."

"But she was locked. It was too late."

My eyes burned suddenly. "Yes. That's exactly what Father Cho said. But I couldn't accept it. I was determined to try. I thought Guy would help me."

"He didn't?"

I shook my head. The edge of the desk bit into my palms. I tried to loosen my grip. "He followed orders. He was young and full of his calling, I know that now. The Templars believe the locked are lost. They also believe in the good of the many, not the one."

"So, what did you do?"

"Me? I was full of my own particular brand of righteousness. I knew that I could save her. That she would listen to us if we could just get her back. I talked some of the other novices and some of Edwina's friends into joining me and we staged a raid on the house where she was kept to try to take her back." I turned, letting myself look at her for the first time.

Her eyes were bright with sympathy. "Don't tell me the rest. Not if you don't want to."

"No, you should know. And I need to tell you." I paused, seeking the right words. "Needless to say, it didn't go well. We got in, got to Edwina, but she wouldn't come with us. Screamed the place down. There were Nightseekers and Trusted guarding the locked. Too many of them. There were only six of us. We fought but we were losing. I'd never fought a real fight before and I was so angry . . . something just took hold of me. I didn't know who I was anymore, I just knew I had to fight them. Kill them. I liked doing it. Gods, Lily. I *liked* it. I went crazy. For a while I was even beating them. But then one of them got through my guard, sliced my side open, and before I realized what I was doing, I called sunlight, called fire.

"What happened next was like a nightmare. The house caught fire. Smoke and fire and screaming, that's all I remember. I still don't know how I got out but I did. But three of the boys who'd come with me didn't."

"And Edwina?"

"Edwina was killed in the panic. Or that's what they told me. Her body was found amongst the others. For all I know, I killed her myself."

"No!" Lily's hand closed over mine. "No. You wouldn't do that, Simon. You wouldn't hurt someone you loved."

"But I did. She died because of me."

Lily looked away for a moment. Then her voice turned fierce. "She died because she chose to do as she did."

"Maybe." I had heard that argument countless times. Nearly enough to make me believe I agreed with it. "Anyway, the three of us made it back to the Brother House in the confusion. Father Cho—well, let's just say I was surprised he didn't kill us himself, he was so furious. I don't know exactly what happened—I was at St. Giles being patched up and then, once I knew Edwina had died, I was . . . lost for some time—but there were no repercussions. Maybe only the locked ones died and the Blood didn't think it worth pursuing. After all, no Blood were harmed."

"Just humans," Lily said, voice cracking. "I'm sorry,

Simon. I can't imagine what it must be like to lose someone like that."

I didn't want her sympathy. It might just break me. "It was a long time ago." I stood, wanting to be gone. "And in some ways it turned out for the best. I gave up the order and joined the healers. It's who I am now. Who I was meant to be."

"But—"

"Story time is over," I said. "I need to be alone. You should go back to your room."

)

It was several hours before I summoned the courage to knock on Simon's door. I spent the time alone in my room, wishing I hadn't pressed him to tell me anything. His pain had filled the air of the room like a living thing. Dousing me with an icy dose of reality. Behind his words were other truths. I knew now that the disgust I'd heard in his voice when he'd spoken of the blood-locked was real. As was his determination to defeat Lucius. The Night World had broken part of his world. He wouldn't stop trying to mend it. His search for a cure was a search for redemption, in a strange sort of way.

And I'd learned one other thing. He could never learn the truth about me. Or anything he'd ever felt for me would disappear faster than a blown candle. And now I cared what he thought. Not just because I wanted his cure or wanted his protection. Because of him.

The thought of him knowing what I was burned like acid in my throat, a painful fear I couldn't swallow away. It even swamped the need, dulling its roar.

When I finally rose from my bed, to wash and change out of the clothes I'd fought in, I knew what I had to do. Get back to Atherton. See if he could think of anything else to try to conquer the need. Anything to keep Simon from knowing.

Simon answered my knock, which eased my fear a little. I thought that he might not be ready to speak to me. Nor was I sure how to convince Simon to take me back. What excuse did I have, after all? Simon wanted to keep the ward and Atherton a secret, so he was hardly going to take me there without a good reason.

Simon sat on his bed, back against the rough stone wall, a book lying facedown on the blanket beside him. He looked up as I entered but made no move toward me. Nor did he indicate that I should join him. I stayed near the door, hesitating.

"Did you want something?" Simon asked.

His voice was polite, his eyes distant. Angry. That much I could decipher. But unlike the males in the Blood Court, keeping his anger tightly leashed. I hoped that Atherton had some alternatives for me to try, because I didn't think Simon would be joining me in bed again anytime soon. "I think I should start looking for the informant," I said, coming straight to the point. The truth seemed safest for now. "I should go back to St. Giles."

"Right now?" He sounded tired and I wondered what he'd been doing in the hours that had passed. Working at St. Giles? Pushing himself hard as usual.

"There's nothing else pressing for me to do, is there? I can't just sit around here while I wait to talk to the Fae. I need to do something. If we can find out whether or not Lucius knows about what you're doing down there, then we may learn something about whatever it is that he's plotting." We might even work out whether it was me or Simon he was after. If it were only me, then that might make any choices I had to make down the line easier.

My words seemed to get his attention. He straightened on the bed, gaze sharpening. "Father Cho would want you to be escorted."

"You could take me, couldn't you?" Surely once we got there and Simon was distracted by his patients, there would be a chance for Atherton and me to talk.

For a moment I thought he would refuse. But then he rose. "All right. We need to tell Bryony anyway. The ward's the best place for that."

Simon took the lead as we headed back to the tunnels. We didn't pass any Templars in the tunnel from the Brother House, and when we passed through the gate, Simon dealt with the possibility of anyone seeing us by pulling a charm from his pocket.

"Can you shadow here?" he asked, twining the leather thong that held the charm through his fingers.

"Yes."

"Good." He nodded once, then disappeared from view.

I blinked. An invisibility charm. That took strong magic, but magic was hardly in short supply around St. Giles.

"Come on," Simon's voice came from thin air.

I shadowed, then followed the soft sound of his footsteps through the tunnels. Once we were through the first of the doors, he disabled the charm. I followed his lead and stepped out of the shadow.

"What are you doing here?" Atherton asked as we greeted him. He stopped whatever it was he was doing with the racks of glass tubes spread before him on his desk.

Simon joined him. "I've sent Bryony a message, asking her to meet us here. She needs to know about Lily's theory. Is everything all right here?"

I hoped Atherton would say something that would make Simon go into the ward itself, but no such luck.

"Everything is normal," Atherton said. His head swiveled toward me. "What's happening outside?"

"So far, so good," Simon said. He reached out and lifted one of the racks, studying the pale liquid in the tubes. I resigned myself to biding my time as they started to talk medical things I didn't understand. My chance would come.

Or maybe not, I thought as the outer door swung open and Bryony joined us.

"My apologies," she said. "I was in a consultation." She looked at Simon, not at me. "What's so important that I had to sneak down here during daylight?"

"Lily has a theory," said Simon. "One you're not going to like."

He filled Bryony in quickly, starting at the very beginning. She stayed silent until he came to the part about someone selling them out to Lucius.

"There is no informant!" She spoke indignantly, ring glinting as she gestured to emphasize her point. "Our staff are trustworthy."

I resisted the desire to roll my eyes. Of course, none of Bryony's perfect Fae would ever do anything untoward. "Can you think of another reason why Lucius would try to kill Simon? Have there been any other attempts on other sunmages?"

Bryony did her own more elegant version of a head toss.

"Who knows why Lucius does anything? There could well be other reasons."

Simon looked like he wanted both of us to grow up. "If there's even a possibility, we can't ignore it," he said. "It puts too much at risk."

"You think she's right? She knows nothing about St. Giles," Bryony said.

"She knows a lot about Lucius, though," Simon shot back.

His defense of me brought a bubble of relief. My stomach eased for the first time in hours. "Obviously it was a mistake to think you would see reason about this," I said as Bryony opened her mouth to argue. "Simon, I'm sure we'll manage without her."

"Why, you—" Bryony broke off, her expression shocked. "We have to go," she said, and whirled toward the door.

Chapter Seventeen

))

Simon and I followed, hastening our steps as Bryony broke into a run.

"What is it?" I asked as we sprinted through the tunnels and up the stairs.

Simon didn't slow. "Someone triggered the alarm wards."

Some sort of emergency? What? The first thing that sprang to mind was an attack. *Lucius.* Lords of hell, he was never going to leave me alone.

Bryony didn't even look to see if we were following as we reached the domed entrance hall of the hospital. A group of healers, both Fae and human, were clustered near the front door. I spotted Harriet and the Fae healer— Chrysanthe, that was it—amongst them. One of the men stepped forward as Bryony came to an elegant stop. Simon and I skidded to a less coordinated halt behind her.

"What's happening?" Bryony demanded.

The man pointed toward the front lawn. "Out there."

The three of us turned in unison, looking out through the glass-paneled doors.

"Gods and fucking suns," Simon muttered.

As curses went, it hardly seemed bad enough. Beyond the doors, beyond the marble tiles that marked the boundaries of the Haven, stood a line of Beasts in hybrid form. Thirty or more of them. Their choice of form was a clever disguise, but that wasn't the problem here. No, the problem was the fact that they each carried a burden in their arms.

A still form of a human.

Too still. The bodies—that seemed the right word—appeared too limp even for blood-locked. I couldn't see any movement at all, though that might be the slightly wavering view through the thickened glass door.

I stepped closer, fury spiking through me, warring with the fear that made my mouth taste like ash.

"Lily, stay back," Simon barked.

"No."

I shook him off, pulled open the door, and strode out onto the marble stairs.

To my surprise, Bryony came with me. And it was she who spoke first, addressing the Beasts.

"What do you want?"

"The soulless one." The growling words came from the tallest of the Beasts, the one who stood at the center of the line. His fur was a dark ominous brown, almost black. A Rousselline if I had to guess, though other packs shared those darker tones.

"She is protected under the laws of Haven," Bryony said firmly. Despite her words, I had the feeling she wished she could just hand me over.

"Then, I must deliver you a message from Lucius."

Bryony's hands tightened in her skirts, but her voice stayed steady. "What is it?"

"He wishes you to know that *he* returns what belongs to others." The Beast gave a snarling laugh, then tossed the body in his arms toward us. It fell with a nasty cracking thud just before the edge of the marble. The sound of bones breaking. It—no, he, now that I could see the face—lay still, limbs slack and unmoving, distorted into awkward angles from the fall.

Definitely dead. Ashes turned to acid as nausea swept through me. I locked my knees reflexively, groping for control. No reaction. I could do this. I was accustomed to witnessing Lucius' atrocities.

Beside me, Bryony made a choking noise and I heard Simon give an order in a harsh tone, but I couldn't make out exactly what he said through the roar of my pulse in my ears.

I stepped forward, but Bryony's hand closed like granite around my wrist. "Stay where you are."

The Beast looked at me and gestured, his hand cutting through the air like the strike of a sword.

The other Beasts, as one, repeated what he had done. A rain of bodies landed on the grassy verge, each dull impact reverberating through me like a thunderclap.

Dead.

All dead.

So *many*.

My fault.

"Lucius reminds you that there are plenty more where these came from," said the Beast. "He will keep returning what is yours until what is his returns to him."

My stomach rolled and I set my teeth so I wouldn't vomit. So many dead. Even the blood-locked didn't deserve this. Death at a whim. Death to prove a point.

Lucius wasn't going to stop, I realized. He would keep coming for me. People would keep dying. Because of me. More families would face loss and pain as Simon's had. Simon himself would be hurt by this, would blame himself.

So much pain. I wasn't worth it.

I had to go back.

I took a step forward, breaking Bryony's grip. Simon reached for me. Caught me, his fingers iron around my arm. "What are you doing?" he said fiercely.

"I have to go back," I said.

"Give us the wraith," the Beast called across the marble.

"Leave this place." Bryony's voice rolled and boomed. Fae magic charged the air, making it crackle.

The Beast stepped back, swept a mocking bow. "I remind you, Lady, that we have violated no laws."

I realized, with a sickening rush, that it was true. They had committed no violence on Haven grounds. And if all the dead were blood-locked, then these deaths were not a crime. The locked were presumed, under the terms of the treaties, to have forfeited their rights of protection. Killing one wasn't murder. More the natural order of things. Though why the humans had ever agreed to such a thing when the treaties were first struck was beyond me. They must have been truly desperate to survive, to stop the war and the killings

As I was now. "I have to go back," I repeated.

"No!" Simon said.

I tried to break his grip but he was too strong. "Let me go."

"No." Before I could respond he picked me up bodily and carried me back into the hospital and into the nearest room. The door crashed shut with a bang as he kicked it closed.

I punched his back. "Put me down."

He did so but he didn't let go of my arm. My wrist ached from the force of his grip.

"Have you lost your mind?" he bellowed.

"No," I yelled back. "I've just come to my senses. This isn't going to work, Simon. Lucius isn't going to stop. He's going to keep coming. Doing worse and worse things."

"Once you testify—"

"That will be too late. More people will be dead."

"People will die if you don't testify." His voice was quieter now though no less forceful.

"Not like this," I said. My throat closed as I saw the bodies again, heard the sickening thuds as they hit the ground.

Simon's mouth twisted. "If you leave, then we won't be able to stop him."

"If I stay, you won't be able to stop him either," I said. "You don't know who those people out there were, but he won't stop with strangers, Simon. He'll come after those you love. Do you want to lose Guy? Or your sisters?"

He turned pale and let go of me then, stepped away, eyes burning. I'd struck home.

"With your testimony—" he started to say.

"No." I shook my head. "No. I can't stay. You and Bryony can talk to the Fae. They'll believe what she tells them."

"It's not the same as you talking to them."

"It will have to be good enough."

He closed his eyes, then opened them. They were dull, no spark of warmth in the blue at all. "You wanted this all along, didn't you?" His voice rasped, roughened by anger. "To go back?"

"No!" The denial was automatic, and I knew it was true now. I didn't want to go. Didn't want to leave him or what he offered. Even if believing in that vision of the world was worse than grasping at straws. "No. I don't want to go. But

I have to." I twisted to look back at the door. Was Bryony still facing down the Beasts? The tang of Fae magic still prickled the air. "It's the only way."

He looked like he didn't believe me, and pain clenched my heart. "Please, Simon, you have to believe me. I have to go. I still might be able to help you. Maybe I can find out who his informant is. I'll do what I can. You can still stop him." Or I could, I realized. Stop him in the way I knew best. Kill him. Though attempting Lucius' life in the middle of the Blood Courts was pretty much suicide, maybe I could bring myself to try.

But I couldn't think of that or whatever might wait for me when I returned. For now, all I could think about was the man before me. The one who'd seen me. The one I was leaving behind to return to the dark. I reached up and pressed a kiss to his mouth, not knowing what else to say. "Thank you."

Then I turned and ran before he could stop me. Ran through the doors, past Bryony and toward the Beasts, who drew their weapons as I approached. I half skidded to a halt and held my hands up. "I'm here," I said. "I'm coming willingly."

One of the Beasts stepped forward, beckoned to me with a long gray finger. The claw curving at its tip gleamed black in the sun. Feeling like I was walking to my execution, I moved forward, into his reach. As he pulled me toward a waiting carriage, I turned. Simon stood on the marble, standing in a shaft of sunlight, face grim, as still as the statue of St. Giles looming above him.

Our eyes met, his searing mine. I turned away, not wanting to see any more when there was no way to make things right between us, not wanting the last memory of him to be that stony gaze. As I stepped into the carriage, surrounded by the hot stink of the Beasts, I remembered what he'd said earlier. He'd been wrong. We hadn't had time at all.

It was Ricco who came for me. I should have expected it. He probably volunteered for the job. Certainly his expression of gloating anticipation was enough to add to the fear that had steadily grown as I'd sat in my locked room for several hours after the Beasts returned me to the warrens. I could have run, of course, could have shadowed and escaped, but I'd made this choice to stop the bloodshed. Defection at this point could only make things worse.

So I sat and waited for sunset and Lucius' summons.

Sat and wondered whether he would simply kill me where I stood when I finally faced him.

If I died, would I have changed anything? Probably not. The lords of hell would have a place for me and I wouldn't protest that I didn't belong there.

But I didn't want to die.

Determined not to give Lucius any cause to find fault with me, I changed out of the clothes Simon had given me at the hospital, putting the soft green cotton away, carefully buried at the bottom of a drawer where nobody could find it. Maybe one day I would let myself look at it again. Maybe one day I would be able to remember without feeling as sick as I did right now.

Or maybe one day I just wouldn't care anymore. Who knew?

I dressed myself, instead, in my version of Court dress. Black trousers, a shirt of black silk that glimmered like stars reflecting off water at midnight, and a black velvet jacket cut away from the waist so I could easily reach my weapons.

I rebraided my hair, twisting each tail tight and jabbing pins in with more force than necessary. I had just secured the last braid into place when the key turned in the lock and Ricco flung the door open.

"Hello, slave," he said. "Lucius wants to see you."

I ignored him and finished my work before turning to face him, my expression held carefully unmoved. "I'm ready."

He shook his head, his grin a slash of malice. "Wouldn't want to be you right now. Boss has been highly unhappy since you went away."

He was trying to scare me. I didn't let him see that I was already scared. Ricco's posturing hardly registered in light of the fact that I was about to face Lucius.

I didn't wait for Ricco to try manhandle me out of the room, simply walked past him and out the door, heading for the hall. The corridors were unusually busy for so early in the night, groups of Trusted scurrying here and there. Making sure their masters were ready for the Court, no doubt. A few of them glanced at me with fear as I passed.

I ignored them. I was too busy trying to stay calm, to move like I didn't care. The warrens smelled like the Blood. Scents of death and pain. All too familiar. All too subtly enticing. Under the fear, the need prowled, alive again as the places and smells I associated with Lucius filled my senses.

The hall was, as I'd expected, full. It wasn't as silent as the last time I'd been summoned here. This time there was a murmuring whisper as I passed through the doors, Ricco at my heels. The ranks of the Blood turned to inspect me as I passed and not all of them looked kindly on me.

Danger.

The sensation of peril crept around me like a fog. Surrounded by predators. What was to stop any one of them leaping out and trying to kill me? Nothing.

Nothing perhaps, except for the man I walked toward.

Lucius sat, half sprawled in his chair as if bored by the proceedings, but the pinpoint focus of his regard as I approached gave lie to his pose of indifference. His face might have been a polite blank mask, but his eyes burned. I didn't know whether fury or another emotion fueled the red threads in the brown depths, but at this point it didn't particularly matter.

I had made my choice.

Now I would live or die by it.

The tension in the room thickened, settling around me like fog. Hate and rage and fear rode the air, brushing my face with chilly fingers and closed around my throat to choke off my breath and dry my mouth.

I told myself it was nothing out of the ordinary, that this was just the usual atmosphere of the Court, but in truth it didn't feel normal. But I didn't know if it was the atmosphere that had changed or whether, having spent time in a place where not everyone lived their days shrouded in fear, I now knew the difference.

Lucius was a study in black and white this evening. More white than black, in fact, as his brocade coat was white, as was his shirt. A dull dead white like fresh bone. Was he planning to decorate the pale expanse of brocade with another color before the evening was out?

His fingers splayed over the arms of his chair, the ruby rings glinting darkly, the only hint of color apart from his eyes.

I stopped at the customary distance from his chair and bowed. "I have returned, my Lord." I'd decided that the only way to play this was to act as if I had been held against my will. Anything else would only be a quick passport to the lower realms.

Lucius stayed silent. The back of my neck prickled as I kept my bent pose, instincts screaming that I was completely exposed.

Behind me, Ricco made a small satisfied noise and shifted. Drawing a weapon perhaps?

The silence stretched and thickened. Then, just as I was readying myself to reach for my dagger, Lucius waved a hand, permission to rise.

"You left us, my shadow."

I straightened slowly. Lucius' face was grim and the red in his eyes had brightened. "I was taken, my Lord. Unwillingly." I fought the urge to step back. This close I could smell him, and his scent brought the need scorching to life. I wanted to run. I wanted to throw myself at his feet.

"Taken by who?"

There was no point lying. He knew very well where I'd been and who had held me. "The sunmage and the Templars, my Lord."

"And how did they hold you so long, my shadow? You who slip through the night unseen."

This part would have to be a lie. "They used the sun, my Lord. I could not shadow to escape at night and by day I was guarded."

"You should have tried to escape."

"I took the first opportunity to return." I willed him to believe me, even as I wondered exactly why I'd been so stupid as to put myself back in his grasp.

"Is that so?"

"Yes, my Lord."

He straightened abruptly, rings sounding dully against the wood of the chair as he tapped his fingers. "You could have escaped days ago. You were in the border boroughs with the sunmage. You could have killed him and left. Instead you killed a Beast."

The words were icy. So cold I could almost feel the room chill around me. For a moment everything seemed to grow dark, as though the candlelit lamps had all guttered at once.

Even the need retreated as fear thickened in my belly. One wrong word and it would all be over. "I did not think it wise to kill him before witnesses, my Lord. I am known to be yours. The humans would use that against you. So I bided my time. I knew you would come for me."

"The Kruegers are unhappy with their loss."

It wasn't as though any of the Beast packs were that well disposed toward me to begin with. "He would have killed me," I said. "He attacked us with no quarter."

I didn't know if that was strictly true or what the Beast might have done had I not reacted so definitely to his assault, but right now I was building the case for me to keep my head. So I would tell the tale my way.

Behind us the Court stood in frozen silence. Anticipation joined the roiling atmosphere, as each of them waited to see what happened here. No doubt most would be trying to guess which way the dice would fall.

Lucius' hands stilled. The lack of movement was more unnerving than the slow tattoo of the rings. "You could have left with the Beasts at the hospital."

"Perhaps. If I'd killed the sunmage. Which again, would have led trouble back to you, my Lord. Not to mention there was a troop of Templars nearby. The Brother House is right beside St. Giles. I did not think we would make it back here. So I chose to let the humans believe I was on their side." I held my breath. In this situation there was no use simply groveling. Lucius had to believe me. Otherwise I would just be marking time until he had me killed.

Lucius tilted his head at me. "So you only had my welfare in mind? How gratifying."

"She lies, my Lord," Ricco said from behind me.

My hand dropped to my dagger but I didn't move. Ricco wouldn't dare to attack me without Lucius' permission. So I needed to watch Lucius. "I am telling the truth, my Lord," I said.

"Do not listen to her," Ricco snarled. "She will betray you, my Lord. I will prove her lie in blood."

Lords of hell. A blood challenge. I hadn't anticipated such a thing. Nor did I think that Ricco had the wit to come up with such a ploy by himself. He would not risk his neck without some promise of high reward. The question being who was pulling his strings—Lucius or some other player. I wished desperately I could turn and see the rest of the Court.

"On your blood, liar," Ricco said with increasing vehemence.

The snarled challenge hung in the air. I stayed where I was. "Fight me," he went on. "You don't deserve to live." He sprang, raising gasps. I moved too, though he was faster, as the Blood always are. His first blow struck my cheek, snapping my head back. I spun away, settling my dagger into my hand. Lucius hadn't moved from his seat; instead, his face was amused as he watched us.

"My Lord?" I gasped, as Ricco attacked again. Another blow connected. I wanted to shadow, but to do so when Lucius had not given me permission to defend myself would be foolhardy.

Lucius smiled at me. "Challenge has been made. One of you will die, shadow," he said. "If you wish to prove you are still mine, then I recommend you ensure that it isn't you."

Kill or be killed. That was clear enough. Disgust clogged my throat. This was the world I had come back to. But at least here, the victims weren't so innocent. I didn't like Ricco but I didn't wish him dead. But I wasn't willing to die to let him prove that he was worthy of Lucius' regard.

I stared at Ricco as he circled me, planning his next move. His expression of hate hadn't changed and his fangs showed as he grinned a feral grin and flexed his muscles. Posturing. Stupid. Had he not heard Lucius? Or did he just think he would win because he was Blood and I was not?

I tightened my grip on the dagger and as Ricco sprang again, I shadowed. The idiot hadn't expected that and he lost his balance, flailing before he recovered to a half crouch, looking around wildly for me. I stepped, twisted, let go of the shadow and let my dagger carve an unerring path across his throat. For a moment he gaped at me, then his brain caught up with the messages of his body and he fell, head going in one direction as the rest of him fell toward me.

Blood sprayed like a fountain from the stump as his heart beat a last few frantic beats, brilliant red arcing across my face and body. As the body hit the floor with a thump, the scent of the blood suddenly filled my nose, rich and red and sweet. Not Lucius' blood, true, but vampire blood just the same.

I clamped my mouth closed. I couldn't afford to taste it. Not now. I didn't know if Ricco's blood would have the same effect on me as Lucius', but I couldn't take that gamble. But the smell . . . blood roared in my ears and my vision fogged. The room seemed silent beyond that pounding heartbeat, the Blood frozen in place, variously staring at Ricco's corpse and me and Lucius. Some of them looked dismayed, some delighted. Ignatius Grey, in particular, was smiling broadly.

Was he the one who'd planted the idea of a challenge in Ricco's head? It seemed his sort of scheme.

"Somebody take that away." Lucius gestured toward Ricco's headless corpse. "Burn it." Trusted appeared from nowhere. Three of them lifted the body and another grasped the head by the long white hair, now striped red. The Trusted gulped once, looked slightly green as blood dripped from the stump of the neck and splattered onto his shoes, then hurried after the other three. Everyone watched them leave in silence.

I could feel the blood sliding slowly down my cheek and wanted desperately to wipe it off but stayed still, keeping my attention on Lucius.

His gaze returned to me. "We appear to have settled that for now, my shadow," he said. He turned his attention to the rest of the Court. "Anyone else?"

Silence.

"Very well." He pushed himself to his feet. I fought the urge to shrink back as he came toward me. "Now, shadow, we have business at Halcyon."

There didn't seem to be any reply I could make. So I merely inclined my head, then followed him from the hall, pausing only to reach out and take a handkerchief from the coat pocket of one of the Blood as we passed.

Thirty dead.

I scrubbed my face, trying to force myself awake, dunking water over my head as though it could wash me clean. No such luck. The day had turned into one long nightmare. I'd helped carry the bodies into the hospital, helped check each of them for any signs of life.

Started the long and tedious process of identifying each of them so that families could be told.

Thirty dead.

The words wouldn't leave my head. Thirty dead. My fault. I was the one who'd taken Lily from Halcyon.

And my fault because, even though she'd walked away, even through the horrors of the day, it was Lily my thoughts kept returning to.

Lily who drove the grief and anger churning my stomach. Lily, and my failed vision of bringing Lucius to his knees. There was nothing left of that hope now, just as there was nothing left of whatever fragile bond Lily and I had been building. Had any part of it had been real? Had she just been biding her time, waiting to get away?

I might never know.

I rubbed my damp hands against my trousers, trying again to remove the feel of cooling flesh. I hated touching the dead. No life. No warmth. They filled me with a chill that even the sun was unable to chase away.

The Blood have that same chill. Lily had lived with it her whole life. Was living with it again, presumably.

Just as I was living with the reality of what I'd done and the not so concealed expressions of blame on the faces of some of my fellow healers. None of the Fae had spoken the words, but they didn't need to. The accusation in their eyes and the too-polite tones as they worked beside me, Chrysanthe and Oleander and Bard and the others, made their feelings clear enough.

No more than I deserved.

Gods. My head ached and my eyes burned. I sank into the chair by my desk and rested my head in my hands, wishing desperately that I could heal myself. Or stun myself senseless. Or do anything even remotely useful.

"Simon?"

I didn't look up. "If you've come to tell me I fucked up, don't bother." I didn't need a lecture from Guy on top of everything else. One of us would end up bruised if he tried. In my current mood, it was likely to be him.

"I came to see if you're all right."

I lifted my head, blinking against the gritty ache in my eyes. "I've spent all day with dead bodies. How do you think I am?"

Guy shrugged. He leaned against the doorframe, looking rumpled and dusty. The Templars had taken on the task of carrying messages to the families we had identified so far. And trying to keep the human boroughs from spilling into violence as word of what had passed at St. Giles spread rapidly.

"Pissed off. Feeling guilty. Quite possibly planning something stupid like trying to get her back."

I shook my head. "No." Not exactly the truth. I had considered going after Lily for a few dark minutes, but I wasn't suicidal. Not quite. "No, I won't be going after her."

His scarred eyebrow lifted. "Really?"

"Yes. She made her choice."

"Good." He brushed some of the dust off his clothes, then crossed the room to sit opposite me, slumping from his normal military bearing. The chains of treaty law must have weighed heavy, just now. I was sure he'd rather be in the Night World boroughs, hunting down Lucius and the Beasts.

"I am still going to talk to the Fae, though."

"Will it do any good?"

"I don't know." I doubted it. The Veiled Queen might take the word of Lucius' shadow as evidence against him, but mine? With no other proof, even if she believed me, she wouldn't act. Still, I had to try.

"I'll tell Father Cho. He'll be able to organize a meeting with the Speaker. Though after this afternoon, I imagine you don't need us to be granted an audience."

Probably not. But going through the Templars might be more discreet. I still had a slim chance of bringing my plan off. So I needed to try not to fuck that up too.

))

There were stares as we walked through Halcyon. Lucius usually drew attention, but tonight the eyes were on me. I had used the handkerchief to clean my face and hands as best I could without water, but blood still stained my hands and stuck to my face, drying into crusty flakes.

At least the smell was less prominent when it dried. But even if I'd gotten the worst of the spatter off my skin, there was still a heavy spray across my clothing. Red does show against black, especially as it dries. The humans in the gathered crowd might not realize exactly what it was, but every Blood and Beast in the place would be all too aware.

I followed Lucius automatically, part of my brain still numbed by what I'd done. Back in the Court just a few hours and already I'd killed. I didn't know if I could do it over and over again. I used to be able to mostly lock it away from my mind, but something was different. I kept seeing the look of shock on Ricco's face and hearing the thump of his head hitting the floor over and over again.

And beyond my disgust was something more disturbing still. The aching fire of the need, called back to life full force by the scent of vampire blood.

What did that make me?

How could I fight it?

One thing was clear through the roil of emotions. If I was to stay here, until I could come up with a way to get away from Lucius and the City and this gods-damned hell-hole, then something needed to be different. Some things had to be on my terms or by the time I got away, I might no longer be anyone I recognized or anyone I wanted to be.

We ascended to the stairs to Lucius' suite. The part of me not sickly numb was all too aware of what had happened the last time he'd brought me here. But tonight, if he tried violence, I would fight back. After all, I had nothing to lose.

The door closed behind us, deadening the sounds of the Assembly, and we were alone. I stayed near to the door, breathing shallowly. Lucius' scent surrounded me, fanning the need to an evermore piercing heat. I didn't know how much longer I would be able to hold it off. How long would it be before I begged Lucius for relief? Despite everything I resolved, would the addiction win?

"Come closer." Lucius stood by his desk, curiously still, white hair gleaming in the gaslight. For a moment, his pose reminded me of Atherton.

And I remembered the other vampire's words as I moved in obedience to Lucius' command. *Something changes in their blood and it can become irresistible if one is not careful.*

The Blood could suffer from their own version of the need. Lucius had only drunk from me once, but maybe once was enough. I did not flatter myself that I was irresistible, but this was to do with blood. I had been drinking from Lucius for nearly fifteen years. Far longer than any blood-locked human could survive. If anyone's blood should be tempting to Lucius, it should be mine. He might hunger for me. Hunger I might just be able to use.

Of course, the stakes of the game would be very high. My life.

But I'd been risking my life in the Court for as long as I could remember. Nothing was different now but me.

I could choose to play or not.

Chapter Eighteen

Lucius moved finally, resting his weight on the edge of the desk. The rubies flashed at me as I kept my gaze on his hands, worried that too many of my thoughts could be read on my face if I met his gaze.

"So, shadow, you have returned to me."

"Yes, my Lord." I had to look at him to reply.

"And you are unhurt?"

I felt my brows lift in surprise. Lucius had never been overly solicitous of my well-being. "Yes, my Lord."

This time it was he who raised an eyebrow. "The Templars did not try to . . . persuade you to anything?"

"They didn't use violence. I think they were hopeful of convincing me to help them without force. I wasn't there long enough for them to change their minds."

"And what do you think it was that they wished to convince you to do, exactly?"

"Your attempt on the sunmage angered them," I said carefully, trying to calculate the line between truth and lie and credibility. "I think they were planning some sort of revenge. They wanted details of the work I do for you."

"What did you tell them?"

"As little as possible. They knew who I was, of course, and I think the Templars would have liked to get more out of me, but the sunmage is a typical healer. Softhearted. He has no stomach for violence." I tried to make my tone dismissive, scornful even. "His brother is far more dangerous from what I saw. He was the one who questioned me." Did that sound plausible? Guy was the Templar, after all.

Lucius' expression was unchanging. I watched him, head and heart aching even as my body burned. I had no way of knowing whether he believed me. No way to know what he would ask or do next.

"But you spent time with the sunmage?"

I tensed. Was he asking or did he know? If he knew, then he did indeed have a spy somewhere in St. Giles. Of course, he could be merely working from information provided by the Beasts who had seen me with Simon. "Yes, they used him at night to hold me. Him and others. They prattled on endlessly about redemption." I risked the lie. Unless Lucius' spy was actually in the Brother House, he would have no way of knowing what had happened there. The thought of a Night World spy infiltrating the Templars seemed far-fetched. Much more likely it was someone in St. Giles. But who?

If I could find that out and somehow get the information to Simon, then I would have done something worthwhile at least. But I would have to tread carefully. My job now was to quell any doubts in Lucius' mind about me. Ricco's death had hopefully done part of the job, but I knew it would take time before Lucius would trust me like he had before.

"I can see why you wanted him dead," I added. "All that piety is irritating."

"Is that so?"

Had I pushed too far with my lies? Well, then I had to brazen it out. "Yes, my Lord. I am sorry I could not kill him for you."

"Would you try again if I sent you?"

My heart stuttered for a moment. Then, "Yes, my Lord." I would try. Though, if it came to that, I would make sure to fail. "Though he is well guarded now. And his brother would look to you were anything to happen."

Did Lucius have the sense to wait for a time, let things settle before he renewed his campaign against Simon? I hoped so. Time would give me breathing space to determine a strategy.

"His guards are not your concern."

I nodded once, feigning assent to this statement. My face

felt stiff, partly because of the dried blood glued to my skin. "I would like to wash, my Lord."

He frowned.

"I do not like the stink of Ricco's blood. It offends me." I hoped to imply that perhaps it was Lucius' blood that I wanted to smell instead.

Lucius smiled. "You did me a service, killing him. He had grown too ambitious."

If I'd been asked to pick amongst the Court, I would have named Ignatius a greater danger than Ricco. He had the brains to go with the ambition. But I wasn't going to offer Lucius political advice. "I am always happy to be of service, my Lord."

"Is that so?" He moved then, fast as always, until he stood mere inches from me. This close, his scent stole my concentration, made the need rage in my brain and through my body. I closed my eyes, trying to fight it.

"Do you hunger, shadow?"

Yes. I bit my lip to stop myself from saying the word. I wanted the blood but . . . only last night Simon had been in my bed. It was too soon. Surely I could resist for one more day? But then, "Yes," I said, unable to stop myself. I kept my eyes closed, I didn't want to see his face. Didn't want to see him gloat.

There was a touch, soft as a spider drifting across my cheek, where I was bruised from Ricco's blow. My skin quivered and revulsion and lust curdled in my stomach.

"I have missed you, my shadow." There was hunger in his voice. Unmistakable hunger. I didn't need to open my eyes to know. He wanted me. Wanted my blood.

Think.

I tried to gather my will, but it was like pushing through fog. No way to gain purchase with the scent of Lucius surrounding me, making my senses sway and reel. "My Lord?" was all I managed to say.

"Look at me."

I opened my eyes, lifted my head, all too aware that doing so bared my throat. I wondered if my heartbeat was as loud to him as it seemed to me.

Lucius was smiling. "So eager?" Another spider-soft touch, this time drifting his fingers across the place in my neck where the pulse beat. "I am glad to see it."

He stepped back then, expression changing rapidly to rigid restraint. "But I have business tonight, my shadow. I must speak with the Beasts."

A reprieve. My knees went loose and I had to lock them to stay standing. With a little space between us, my self-control reasserted itself in a small way and I could think again. What business was so important that he would put off what he so obviously wanted? What was he plotting with the Beasts? Could his spy be a Beast?

Unlikely. I hadn't seen any Beasts working at St. Giles and they didn't have the magic to avoid the wards set around Simon's patients. So, what role were the Beasts playing here? Was Lucius planning another attempt on Simon? The thought turned me to ice.

Lucius seated himself behind his desk, lifting a pile of correspondence from a black lacquered tray. Apparently he was done with me.

"Do you have further need of me?" I asked.

His eyes met mine with what felt like a physical blow. "Tonight, you may occupy yourself downstairs," he said. "Try not to kill any other members of my Court." He lifted the uppermost envelope on the pile and turned it over to view the seal, lifting a nastily sharp-looking dagger from his desk to slit it open.

I bowed slightly, lowering my eyes. As I did so, the next envelope in the stack caught my attention. It glimmered slightly, eerie green-gold. The Fae sealed their messages with wards. Who was sending Lucius sealed letters?

Those Fae who dealt with the Night World tended to meet with Lucius in person and in groups. Nothing committed to paper. Then again, I had never before paid much attention to Lucius' business, so perhaps I was wrong.

Or perhaps this was from the spy. Could they be Fae? It seemed absurd, but the wardlight was there in front of me, proof that a Fae had written, or at least sealed, that envelope. I wanted to grab the letter and vanish but resisted that suicidal impulse. Instead, I straightened, not wanting him to see my attention. There was nothing on the face of the envelope other than Lucius' title and name in elaborate script. The writing struck me as female but offered no other clue.

"Night keep you, then, my Lord," I said.

He nodded. I turned to leave.

"Tomorrow night, my shadow." His voice came just as I reached the door.

My hand stilled on the heavy metal handle. I turned back. "My Lord?"

For a moment his eyes seemed to glow red. "Tomorrow night, we shall deal with these hungers, you and I. You will come to me."

$$\big)\big)$$

Soap stung my eyes as I scrubbed the blood from my face. If only it were so easy to scrub Lucius' last words from my mind. Tomorrow night. That was when I would truly rejoin him. When I would drink his blood to ease the ache in my body and, most likely, he would drink mine unless I had misunderstood him. In truth, I didn't know if I even cared anymore. I felt several lifetimes older than this morning, my mind battered and bruised by everything the passing hours had wrought.

I splashed clean water on my face and wiped my eyes, trying to believe it was only the soap that made them sting. My reflection stared back at me, pale and exhausted, as white as one of the Blood. Very different from the happy face I'd seen when I'd bathed at the Brother House. I didn't even feel like the same person. I didn't know what I felt like.

But I had made my choice. To end the bloodshed and return here to this place that was all I had ever known before Simon had blazed into my life. Surely it couldn't be so hard to be as I had once been? I had survived in this world for a long time. Surely I couldn't have lost the knack for it in a few short days?

My mouth curved grimly. The knack perhaps I still had. But whether I still had the stomach for such a life was less certain.

My fingers twisted the towel into a knot. My life for many. My choice. But had it been the right one? Would Simon survive, would he be able to stop Lucius? Lady, let it be so. I stilled suddenly, remembering the glowing letter. What secrets did it hold? Something that might help the humans? If they succeeded, there might be some slim chance for me to escape from Lucius once more. A greater

chance than any plan I had been able to devise of getting
free of Lucius while he yet lived.

I was stuck here, with Lucius, for now, but perhaps I
could do as I had promised Simon. Do some good. All I
needed was to know what Lucius was up to and what was
in that damn letter.

Everything seemed hushed as I walked back toward Lucius' suite from the bathroom. The noises from the Assembly below seemed distant from the gray of the shadow.

But despite myself and the knowledge that no one could
see me in the shadow, uneasy guilt dogged me. Never before had I tried to use my powers against Lucius. Planning
to defy him and actually doing it—going against a lifetime
of ingrained obedience—seemed to be two different things.
Biting the hand that holds your chains is harder than it ap-
pears.

I gritted my teeth, standing outside the door. Was Lucius
still inside? It must have been a good quarter of an hour
since I'd left him and walked on shaky legs to one of the
upper bathrooms. Had the Beasts joined him in the suite or
were they elsewhere in one of the private dining rooms or
other chambers? Lords of hell, let them be elsewhere. If
anyone was in the room, I could enter undetected, but unless the letter was lying open on the desk, I wouldn't be
able to read it without leaving the shadow. If I had to wait
for Lucius' office to be empty, I might lose my nerve, or my
opportunity if he summoned me.

Before I could decide what to do, the door swung open,
wood passing through me to bang against the wall, and Lucius strode out, pushing the door shut behind him and locking it. I held my breath, tempted to squeeze my eyes shut.
He was so close, my mind shrieked that he would sense me,
even though I knew that was impossible.

But my fears were unwarranted. Lucius merely pock-
eted the key, then smoothed his long jacket before walking
away.

My knees almost buckled in relief. No one else would be
in the room at this hour. Lucius guarded his inner sanctum
well. There would be a few Trusted who were allowed access but not during the height of the night while Lucius was
conducting the business of his Court.

Seizing my chance, I stepped through the door and hur-

ried over to the desk. The pile of correspondence still lay in
the black lacquered tray, the top few envelopes slit open as
I had seen him do earlier. At first glance I couldn't see any
that glowed green gold.

Hells.

I started to let go of the shadow, then paused. Were
there wards around the room? Something to detect me? I
scanned carefully but couldn't sense or see anything to indicate worked magic. Still, I stayed shadowed as I scanned
the desk again, searching for the letter as my heart raced.
Minimizing any time I had to spend solid would be the safest course. As would getting what I had come to do done in
the fastest possible time.

The desk held a bottle of ink and a pristine black quill,
the pile of letters and a large red bound ledger. I studied
the ledger, then frowned. It did not seem to lie entirely flat
against the polished wood. Was there something beneath?

I would have to risk it. I let go of the shadow, senses
straining for any hint of alarm, and lifted the ledger.

Success! I stifled my instinctive whoop of satisfaction.
Beneath the book lay the warded letter. Even better, it too
had been opened, its protective ward broken. I picked it up
and turned it over.

There was no return address, nothing but a blob of dark
green wax, with a curious impression of flowing lines that
could almost be . . . I squinted, trying to decide . . . nothing
like any seal I had ever seen. Nothing to tell me of the writer's identity.

That would be too easy, I supposed. I turned my attention to the letter within the envelope, sliding the single
page of thin paper free gingerly. I couldn't risk a tear or
fold that hadn't been there before, something that might
alert Lucius to the possibility of tampering.

The writing was the same feminine seeming script as the
envelope. The letter was short and, to my dismay, unhelpful.

To my Lord Lucius,
    Things remain unchanged.
    The work progresses but does not bear fruit.
    *Recent developments have unsettled but not
changed the course of his interest.*
    Though there may be a chance owing to current

*turmoils. He will be distracted. I will watch and wait,
but stand ready if your desires have changed.*

E'hai.

There was no signature. Just a scribbled image of what
might be a leaf. The writer had to be Fae, though. The
warded envelope and the Fae proclamation of loyalty near
the leaf were evidence enough of that much. Not that I had
any idea what the leaf might mean. Nor could I be sure
what they were talking about. It could be Simon. The words
could be interpreted that way, certainly. Or it could be any
one of a myriad of people that Lucius was keeping an eye
on.

I refolded the letter after committing the words, and
that curious image, to memory. I rubbed my fingers across
the seal one last time before repositioning the letter under
the ledger.

It wasn't much but it was a beginning. I smiled slightly,
the expression feeling unfamiliar. I would have to hold to
that. For now, all I could do was play my role, stay alive, and
wait for another opportunity.

"Remember, Simon," Father Cho said, in a low voice. "Be
respectful."

I shot him a sideways glance. "Yes, Father." I bit back the
"I'm not an idiot" hovering on my lips. My temper was running short, frustration and lack of sleep combining to do
nothing to improve it. Perhaps his warning was not entirely
unwarranted.

I returned my gaze to the empty table in front of us. Beside me, Bryony shifted on the velvet-padded stool,
smoothing her skirts into a more precise arrangement of
sweeping folds. I wasn't the only one who was nervous, it
seemed.

We had a right to our jitters. We had been waiting in this
chamber for over half an hour, cooling our heels in the
luxurious surroundings while we waited for our audience
to begin. The delay had not improved my mood and I found
it difficult to sit still and wait. But I did, trying not to think
about everything that was riding on the meeting we were
about to have.

Something about the room had rendered us all mostly silent. Father Cho's intermittent snippets of advice were the only conversation we'd had.

After another five minutes or so, just as my temper began to rise again, setting my fingers to drumming against my thigh, the intricately carved wooden doors behind the table swung open and an immaculately white-robed Fae woman stepped through, bowed, and intoned, "The Speaker comes."

We rose to our feet. The Fae woman stayed in her bow as another Fae walked past her into the room. He too wore white, flowing layers that made it seem as though he floated toward us.

His hair was black, or near enough, dark around a young, unlined face. I caught my start of surprise. There had only ever been one Speaker in the history of the City. Like the queen he served, he was hundreds of years old yet looked even younger than Bryony, who was nowhere near that age.

The Speaker's eyes were a startling shade of gray. Like silvered glass or sun shining on water, infinite and unreadable. An unnatural shade that marked him as Fae clear as day. His gaze met mine and I suddenly felt the weight of his age as he studied me silently. A reminder that the Fae were very different from us. My mouth dried. Why would they ever choose to help us?

I set my teeth. I had to try.

Beside me, Bryony swept a curtsy and I bowed, belatedly, not looking at Father Cho, who, no doubt, was thinking I was doing a fair job of being as disrespectful as he had feared.

The Speaker settled himself behind the table and gestured for us to sit. The Fae woman rose and closed the doors, taking up a stance in front of them. Apparently we were not to be disturbed.

"I will hear you, Simon DuCaine," the Speaker said into the silence.

I stood, taking a moment to gather my thoughts and push away any last doubts. "Speaker, I wish to bring before the Veil a petition." Bryony had schooled me in the protocol well enough over the last day. Blunder in that and the Speaker might choose to take offense and dismiss us again without hearing what we had come to say.

"The Veil will hear."

That was the first hurdle cleared. I relaxed slightly, then started to speak, setting out what we had come to tell. The attempt on my life. Lily's involvement. And finally, the crux of the matter. "Speaker, I lay before you a treaty violation. Lord Lucius of the Blood has attacked a human not of the Night World. He has tried to kill me. I wish the Fae to use that which is their right and call him to account."

The Speaker, who had stayed motionless through the few minutes of my speech, his mirrored eyes fixed on me, suddenly turned his gaze to Bryony. "Does this man speak truth?"

Bryony rose to stand besides me. "He speaks the truth as I understand it, as I have heard it from his lips and those of the . . . assassin," she replied. There wasn't more she could say.

A nod acknowledged her and she sank back down onto the stool. I couldn't look at her; I had to keep watching the Speaker.

His gaze came back to me. "But you have no proof other than your word? The assassin is not to hand to recount whose words set her course?"

I shook my head, stomach churning. "No. She was going to speak, but she is no longer within our reach." I tried to keep any emotion out of my voice.

The Speaker looked thoughtful and for a moment, hope surged, but then he straightened and set his hands flat on the table, the rings of his office, one on each hand that blazed all the colors of all the Families, clinking gently. His pose meant he was about to make his decision. I held my breath.

"The Veil has heard," he said in a clear tone. "And we decline."

My stomach dropped like a stone. No? Gods and fucking suns. I'd known this was likely, of course, but actually hearing it was like a kick from Guy's warhorse. For a moment I felt winded, unable to respond. Say something. I needed a counterargument before we lost our chance. "But—"

He shook his head. "I have spoken. We do not act without proof. We cannot keep the treaty by favoring the word of one about the actions of another. Without the word of the assassin herself, we cannot involve ourselves." He withdrew his hands from the table, folding them into his long sleeves.

Bryony's lessons had stuck well. I knew the finality of that gesture. He had spoken. And I had lost.

))

By midafternoon a combination of restless anticipation and outright foreboding drove me out of my room and set me to prowling the warrens. They offered little in the way of diversion. I had no appetite for food and even less for trying to sit still and do something distracting like read. Eventually, I found myself moving upward, firstly out of the warrens and then up through the five stories of the mansion that sat atop them. I didn't frequent these levels often. When I was younger, my lessons had been held on one of the higher floors, but since then I had lived most of my days in the warrens

But revisiting even slightly familiar haunts didn't hold any temptation today. Instead, I kept climbing until finally I found myself in the attic that ran the entire length of the building on the topmost floor.

The vast room was hot and dusty and smelled of disintegrating clothes and old, old wood. These rooms were seldom aired or even used, judging by the layers of dust on the bare floorboards. So at least here I would be undisturbed and unobserved in my prowling. Alone with my thoughts.

Alone with the need and the dread.

The heat pressed around me, closing in as I stood stockstill in the middle of the room. Air. I needed air. I hurried to the nearest window, wrenched it open with a husking rasp of rusted metal, and climbed out onto the roof.

The pressure on my chest eased abruptly as a breeze caught me and I lowered myself to the tiles, dropping my head into my hands until I could catch my breath.

When I raised my head again, I saw that I had chosen a window on the eastern side of the building, so that the sun came from behind me, warm on my back. Before me, the City rolled out and my eyes came to rest, almost automatically, on the distant dome and spire of St. Giles and the cathedral.

Was Simon somewhere over there? Perhaps sitting in the same sun as me? Might he even be up on the roof of the Brother House looking out at the City too? Did he feel as horrible as I did?

I hoped not. I hoped he had written me off, cast me out of his thoughts as I deserved to be.

Yet I couldn't help looking. Remembering.

My head dropped again and, to my horror, tears welled in my eyes, followed by a sob rising in my throat. I tried frantically to beat back the tears, but they refused to be stemmed and I finally let myself curl into a ball and sob.

I couldn't say what I was crying for or even how long the tears lasted, but eventually they eased and I forced myself to sit again as I scrubbed at my face with my sleeve, desperate to wipe the evidence of my lapse of reason from my face.

Foolish to cry. Foolish and useless.

I hadn't cried like that for a long time. Not since those earliest days when Lucius had beat my acceptance of the blood into me. Or perhaps since the night he'd first pointed out my mother to me in a crowd of Fae and I'd seen her carefully turn her head so there was no chance that she would look upon me. The first time I'd truly understood I was nothing to her.

That night I'd cried in my room until I thought I might die from it. But my tears hadn't changed anything. I was still an abomination to my own mother and she still made sure she never saw me the few times she'd come to the Blood Court. Tears were useless. Then and now.

I had made my choice. Tonight I would go to Lucius and that would be that. Once again he would claim me as his shadow and I would allow him to bind me close with his blood. I had to. I couldn't resist much longer. I was beginning to feel the first aches of need too long denied, gripping my stomach and needling my limbs like pinpricks. In a day or so, maybe less, the pains would start in earnest.

Though not this time. This time I was giving in.

And what exactly did that make me?

A clatter of hooves from below caught my attention. A hackney, plain and unadorned, rolled through the mansion gates, the horses wild-eyed and snorting so close to the scent of so many vampires.

Who was visiting here at this time of day? The Blood kept their own carriages, pulled by horses accustomed, or ensorcelled—I had never quite known which—to those they carried. The Trusted used those when they had need of transport. I clambered farther down the tiles, bracing a hand on a handy chimney pot as I peered down into the forecourt.

The hackney drew to a halt but nobody alighted. The back of my neck prickled. It didn't take long for one of the Trusted to appear at the front door and hurry toward the mysterious vehicle. The man wore the stark black livery of Lucius' private staff. Was the visitor expected, then?

I leaned out as far as I dared, not wanting to be seen but wanting a view of the hackney's occupant if I could see. As the Trusted reached the coach, the blind across the window snapped open and a woman leaned her head through. She was veiled so I couldn't see her face, though I thought the hair beneath the dark tulle was light. She extended a lace-gloved hand toward the Trusted. In it, there was a letter. A letter that, to my eyes, gleamed gold and green, exactly like the one I'd read at Halcyon. And beneath the lace of her glove, something caught the light, flashing bright for a moment. A ring. A Fae Family ring perhaps? I squinted but couldn't make out any identifying colors.

Hells.

The Trusted bowed and took the letter and headed back into the house. The woman's head and arm withdrew back into the carriage and the horses set off with a leap.

I stood where I was, trying to follow their path, but too soon, they were lost to sight around a bend and then merged with the other passing traffic. I couldn't tell one hackney from another from a distance.

But I watched anyway, heart beating fast, while my thoughts whirled.

I didn't doubt this was Lucius' mysterious correspondent or that she was Fae. The question was, which Fae? If I kept my eyes peeled, perhaps I could find out. It was a reason to go on at least.

I didn't dare try to find out where the Trusted had taken the letter. Not in daylight anyway. Nor was tonight the time for investigations. Tonight I had larger problems to face. I shivered then, despite the heat of the sun.

Tonight. Both too long to wait and too rapidly approaching. I needed to prepare myself for what was to come. The sun would be setting soon. Time to embrace the dark.

Chapter Nineteen

)

The nearer I got to the room where Lucius slept, the more the butterflies in my stomach bit and gnawed with tiny sharp teeth. The warrens were quiet as the grave, as though Lucius had passed word he was not to be disturbed. I saw none of the Blood, which pleased me. I didn't want to see their expressions.

They would know why I was going to Lucius' room. They would probably assume that we would do more than share Blood. Maybe we would. The need was a near conflagration, singing insistently in my veins, making it hard to remember what I was trying to do. My body wanted release. I didn't know if I'd be able to resist if he demanded more than my blood.

Simon's face flickered to mind, cutting through the fog of lust for a moment. He had taken me to bed, given me pleasure that wasn't driven by blood and power. Part of me wanted to cling desperately to the memory and part of me wanted just as desperately to be rid of it. But it seemed he had lodged himself firmly under my skin. I didn't know how to shake myself free of him, to forget him. Maybe I shouldn't try.

No. I had to. Thinking of Simon while I let Lucius do what he would to me would be a betrayal.

I walked down another deserted corridor, steps slowing. It was very late. Lucius had waited a long time before sending for me. The summer nights are short in the City and I could feel the first warnings of dawn in my blood. But it was still a little way away. Not that it mattered here in the depths of the warrens. Lucius was old enough that he was not forced to sleep through the day. He could entertain himself with me as long as he wished.

I passed a few Trusted here and there, going about their tasks, but no one bothered me. One or two of the men stared at my chest before ducking their heads and looking away.

No wonder they were staring. I'd dressed for the occasion, donning a black shirt with a thin ruffle around the deep neckline, so it looked like my vest had sprouted frills. I'd piled my braids high on my head so that there was no barrier to my throat. I looked like a Nightseeker displaying myself as a Blood feast.

I turned the last corner and was waved past the guard at the iron door that protected Lucius' outer hall. Once inside, I was alone again. Lucius, unlike others of the Court, didn't worry overly much about protecting himself here in his inner sanctum. He'd won his way to power with war and bloody retribution and it had been years now since anyone had made a direct attempt on his life.

One day I might try to change that, but not tonight. Tonight I needed what he was offering.

My steps slowed further as I walked the last few feet, hand curled around my dagger, as my instincts whispered warnings. Back away from the monster's lair. Flee. At the same time, the need urged me forward. I forced myself to let go of the dagger and raised my hand to knock softly on the door.

"You may enter." Lucius' voice was deep, enticing.

I took one last deep breath. Once I crossed the threshold, there would be no turning back. No pretending I was there under any compunction other than the need. It was my choice. My choice to come to him, my choice to let him feed.

To let him touch me.

Lady, forgive me, I thought fleetingly, then pushed open the door.

The room was lit with gaslights on every wall, brighter than I'd expected. The lamps were soft, but their combined light was enough to show everything clearly. I'd never been in this room before. The honor of being invited to Lucius' inner sanctum was one I'd actively avoided. The scent of blood and fear and pleasure rode the air.

The muscles in my back tightened. I was going to become intimately familiar with that smell. With this room. With Lucius. I shivered slightly, my hand drifting down to my dagger before I forced myself to let go.

Lucius stood in the middle of the room, in front of a large bed. It was carved from some heavy wood, so dark a brown to be near enough to black in the gaslight. Black as the coat Lucius wore.

"Night keep you, my Lord." I bowed correctly, then forced myself to move toward him. Each step felt like it took far too long. I couldn't afford to let him see any indecision or reluctance. I was doing this to buy his trust back. Buy time and freedom.

Buy a chance to one day be rid of him.

I tried to blank my mind and let the need carry me but couldn't quite do it. I needed the blood to give me that complete escape from reality. I hoped he would let me have it before he drank.

As I reached Lucius, he smiled, his fangs white and sharp seeming far more prominent than usual. "Shadow," he said softly. "I have been looking forward to this."

"As have I, my Lord." I forced myself to respond in a pleased tone and moved closer still, then stopped, waiting for him to make a move.

He circled me slowly, like a wild dog stalking prey. When we were once again face-to-face, his smile came again. "Very nice, my shadow. I am pleased."

There didn't seem to be an easy response to that. *Just give me the gods-damned blood* probably wouldn't have the seductive effect I was trying to achieve.

"I am glad to see you choosing wisely," Lucius continued. "I think you too will be glad of it over time. I will reward your loyalty. This city will be changing, shadow."

I cast my eyes down, as my thoughts whirled. Changing? What did he mean? Was he planning something? Something more than killing Simon? Something bigger? His tone was smugly certain, carrying something more than his usual arrogance. "I ask for no reward other than to stand by your side, my Lord."

How I managed to get the words out without choking on them, I wasn't entirely sure. But he had to continue to believe me. Then perhaps I could find out what he had planned.

Lucius made a pleased noise. "And so you shall. You by my side and the rest of them beneath my feet. But enough talking. Tonight we have more pressing business, you and I."

His voice had turned silken and low, the sound of it sleeking across my skin and making me shiver.

He pulled me against him, one hand pulling my head back. It seemed his hunger was to be satisfied first after all. I shut my eyes as his mouth dragged along my neck, tongue stroking wetly across my pulse. I breathed deep, desperate to let the need carry me, let the scent of him fan it so that I wouldn't have to think, wouldn't have to be so aware of what I was doing.

It helped a little, the fog of desire driving away the other emotions ricocheting though me. Fear. Regret. Disgust. Until Lucius' fangs cut through my skin with an icy stab of pain and he began to drink. It only hurt for a moment before his venom numbed the wound and there was only the feel of his lips against my neck, the feel of blood being drawn from me and the horribly arousing press of his body against mine.

I focused on that arousal, seeking oblivion. I didn't want to think or know. I just wanted to be taken away. To be anywhere other than in my own body or my own mind.

As it had in Halcyon, the sensation of him feeding seemed to close around me like a cloak, my pulse slowing to beat like his, intimacy twining between us as he held me and fed. For a few moments I was able to ride the darkness behind my eyes and become nothing more than the sensation, but then he withdrew and before I could do anything, pressed his mouth to mine, kissing me.

He tasted of blood and need and darkness. There was nothing clean or warm in his kiss, nothing like the feelings I had felt when Simon had kissed me. This kiss was more like dying, being possessed by something that might never let you go. Something that would keep you in the dark and hurt you to please itself.

It was horrible even as my body screamed for more of his touch.

He broke the kiss. "Lily," he said, pleasure and satisfaction darkening his voice.

The sound of my name on his lips broke the spell. He had never called me by my name. And I suddenly knew that I couldn't stand it if he did.

"Lily," he said again, and pressed to me again, one hand suddenly between my legs, seeking the buttons to my trousers. Simon's face suddenly filled my mind. The look on his face as he had touched me. The pleasure and delight. The kindness.

I couldn't do it, couldn't let Lucius touch me.

Acting on pure instinct, I shadowed, stumbling back from Lucius blindly, raising a hand that had no substance to try to scrub the taste of him from my mouth, eyes blinded by sudden tears.

It took a few seconds to blink back the moisture, to slow the panic screaming through me. Safe. I was safe in the shadow. He couldn't reach me here.

But as the room came back into focus I saw that, instead of an infuriated Blood Lord waiting for me to reappear, there was . . . nothing. Lucius had vanished.

I froze, twisting my head to make certain of what I saw. Illusion? Magic? What in the names of hell was going on? Every sense strained. Even a vampire fading into the darkness has a heartbeat. Breathes.

Nothing. I reached for my dagger. Whatever was going on, I didn't like it. Time to retreat.

I backed toward the door, dagger still in my hand, still listening. I wished desperately that I could call light with a snap of my fingers like Simon. The darkness seemed to press around me even with my night vision.

I had to get away.

Trying desperately to think what might have just happened, I quickened my steps as I passed through the door.

"Hello, my shadow."

I whirled. "You!"

Lucius' smile was cruel. "Were you expecting someone else?"

Viewed from the shadow, he was a creature of pure white and black and gray, none of his favored red to stand out and draw the eye. "How . . ."

"Ah. How am I here with you, shadow?" His smile grew

wider. Crueler. His fangs gleamed at me, white and sharp.
The memory of them pressed to my throat made me shudder. *Run.* I stayed frozen where I was.

"You haven't figured it out, then? The gift you have
given me?" Lucius said. He reached toward me and I
slashed instinctively with my dagger.

Lucius recoiled with a hiss.

My brain, fogged and stretched with adrenaline and
shock and anger, finally realized what was wrong. He could
see me. I could see him. I was shadowed.

The only way he could see me was if he was shadowed
too.

Run.

This time I didn't fight the impulse. I turned and fled,
running as hard and fast as I could.

Lucius laughed. Then I heard his footsteps as he gave
chase.

The sound of his feet echoed around me. Which made
no sense. In the shadow, he should make no noise against
the stones. In the shadow he was nothing that should be
able to make a noise. Yet the echoes came, relentless.
Pounding.

I ran faster, diving through walls and doors in my panic.
Run.

I didn't know how he'd done it.

I just knew I had to get away.

He kept coming. I could feel him behind me, though I
didn't dare turn and look behind me.

No matter what I did, I couldn't lose him as I made my
way through the myriad tunnels of the warren.

"Shadow," I heard Lucius' voice come through the darkness toward me. "Why run? I can always find you now. You
are *mine*, wraith."

My stomach twisted and clenched, the urge to give up
and let him just take me and end everything a nagging
black demon in the back of my head. I could almost smell
him, closing in on me, but maybe that was just the general
stink of the Blood that permeated this place.

I ran, my heart pounding. Another pulse pounded just as
fiercely between my legs, as if Simon had never touched
me, as if the need had never eased at all. It burned bright
and fierce as it had when Lucius had first fed me, ignited to

full force by what had passed between us. It whispered in my brain. Whispered of what he could give me if I stopped.

I fought the urge to press my hands over my ears, block out that insidious whispering. It would do no good.

Run.

Desperate, I turned again, heading for the outer walls. We were still many levels down, below the surface. But I might have an advantage if I could make my way into the dirt outside those walls. Lucius might be confused by the distracting sensation of fighting his way through the earth. It might slow him down.

So I pushed my way through the wall and into the darkness of the earth, clawing my way forward and up. Up to where the sun might be rising if I hadn't completely lost track of time.

It was hard work. Hard and claustrophobic, with the weight of earth pressing against every part of me. I fought upward, throat and eyes and nose blocked and choking like a mole caught in an airless box, scrabbling desperately for air and life.

Below, I heard Lucius choking and sputtering too as he floundered behind me.

Up. Only up.

I pushed harder as the earth started to feel slightly warmer around me. There were roots of plants as well as earth and rock around me now. Nearly there.

I could just see the faintest of lights ahead. The beginnings of dawn filtering through the tiny gaps left by the plants above.

Up. Faster.

I was nearly there when his hand closed around my ankle. I kicked violently, killing the scream that rose in my throat.

How was he touching me in the shadow?

I didn't know whether he should be able to do or not. I'd never met another of my kind, didn't know what happened when two beings interacted here.

Could he win? Pull me back down to him?

I kicked again, desperate. His fingers slipped and I fought my way upward a few more inches. Tantalizing scents of grass and sunshine wafted through the earth, telling me I was close.

So close.

The fingers came again, his nails raking at me, then finding a grip.

"You are mine," he snarled from beneath me.

I kept pushing upward, alternately kicking and clawing to ascend.

My boot slipped off my foot and I made a last desperate lunge upward, breaking through the top layer of dirt with a coughing scream. I was moving fast enough that my whole body came free of the earth before the faint rays of early sun turned me solid again and I fell with a jolting thud to the ground.

There was another snarling cry from below and Lucius' hand broke free of the earth next to me, pale and grasping, the rubies in his rings gleaming like blood turned to glass in the sunlight.

But, unlike with me, the sun didn't just turn him solid. Him, it wanted to burn. There was a sizzling hiss and his skin started to blacken. I heard another screaming snarl and then his hand disappeared back underneath the earth, leaving me lying, panting and horrified, on the grass just beyond the outer walls of the mansion.

I ran without thinking. No keeping to shadows, no hiding. Instead I sought the protection of the sunlight as I ran. Only the light would stop Lucius from reclaiming me.

For now.

I was horribly aware that my respite wouldn't last. The sky was lightening rapidly as the sun climbed. But inevitably, after sunrise, came sunset. Panic made my breath rasp and my heart pound in my ears.

Sunset.

Lucius could move freely in the darkness. He would find me.

So I ran. Not caring who saw me. Ran in heedless terror. Through sheer luck, no one challenged me on that headlong flight back out of Sorrow's Hill. Luck held when I was able to hail an autocab once I hit Brightown, almost dragging the last of the disembarking passengers from the door in my eagerness to be inside.

I didn't know where I was headed until the driver asked where I wanted to go, his expression somewhat scared as though he thought I might spring at him. God knows what I looked like. I managed to say "St. Giles," through chattering teeth. I wrapped my arms around myself, chilled to the bone as the 'cab rattled into life. St. Giles. Simon.

Safety.

For a time. But even the thought of Simon couldn't chase the chill away.

Lucius could shadow.

He had drunk my blood and now he could shadow.

I pulled my feet up on the seat, loath to leave them on the floor of the 'cab, feeling the grasp of his hand around my ankle once more. My bootless foot bled. Somewhere in my flight I had cut it and not even noticed. I still couldn't feel it now. All I could feel was the fear.

By the time I reached the hospital, I was shivering in earnest, barely holding back tears. The sun was bright in the sky when I stepped across the Haven line, but I couldn't feel the warmth. My skin crawled as I wondered if Lucius lurked below, underneath the earth. If he hunted me even now.

I ran across the marble, fleeing for the safety of the hospital and Simon. And as I ran, only one word filled my mind.

I crossed the threshold and burst into the main hall. Simon stood in the middle of the space, talking to one of the healers. At the crash of the doors behind me, he turned and saw me. He froze.

I brought myself to a halt and stood, shaking, before him, seeing the shock burst into his blue eyes. "Sunlight," I managed to say before I fainted dead away.

I felt as though my heart had turned to stone as Lily sank onto the floor at my feet.

"Get me Bryony," I yelled at the nearest orderly. I dropped to my knees, frantically searching her body. Was she hurt?

No blood. I couldn't see any blood, other than from a shallow cut on her foot. Why in hell was her foot bare?

What had happened? Why had she come back? I scooped her into my arms and carried her to the nearest examination room, yelling for blankets and assistance. Her skin was icy, the cold unnatural somehow.

By the time Bryony arrived, I had Lily stripped—though her bare flesh didn't yield any more clues—and wrapped in blankets, where she lay shivering even though she hadn't regained consciousness.

Gods and suns.

She looked pale. Pale even for her. Small, somehow, under the gray blankets. I'd unpinned her hair to check for wounds, but even the mass of red didn't bring any warmth to her skin.

"What happened?" Bryony asked. To her credit she didn't say "What is she doing here?"

"I don't know." Frustration burned my throat. "I can't see any wounds. Nothing's broken. Nothing's bruised. She just ran in here, said 'sunlight,' and collapsed." I heard my voice rise and gritted my teeth. I needed to keep my head. Lily needed my help.

"Let me look at her," Bryony said. "You're too close to this. You'll do her no good." She elbowed past me and knelt leaned over the bed.

She laid a hand on Lily's forehead, slipped the other beneath the blankets to rest over her heart, and stood there, eyes closing slowly as she went into a trance.

Stupid. I forced myself to stillness. I could've done that much. Instead I'd panicked, displaying no more sense than a first-year mage.

But she'd looked so . . . so helpless somehow.

I'd spent days convincing myself I wouldn't see her again. Shutting down my feelings so I could keep walking and talking. The Fae had said no to our petition. That meant that Lucius would continue and that Lily would continue to belong to him.

I'd tried to accept it. I knew only too well what disasters could come from trying to rescue her if she didn't want to be rescued. I didn't want any deaths on my hands. People had paid the price for my actions before and I was done. But now she was back.

Why she was back was yet to be revealed.

Underneath the worry, another thought rose, unwelcome but unavoidable. She might have been sent back.

Or she might not.

Head warred with heart as I stared down at her, feeling sick. How could I trust her?

Bryony's eyes opened and she pulled her hands away from Lily. "Shock," she said briskly. "But I can't sense any major injuries. Her foot is already healing. I'm going to wake her up."

"No!" The protest made no medical sense, but once Lily was awake, then I'd have to deal with her. Work out what she was doing here. Work out if she could be trusted.

"Yes," Bryony retorted in a decisive tone. "We need to know what happened, Simon. If she's in shock, she'll do better awake so we can get fluids and sugar into her, you know that." She stared up at me for a second, waiting for another process. I folded my arms across my chest, set my teeth. Bryony knew what she was doing.

She moved her hands to either side of Lily's head, thumbs resting on the pale skin of her temples, fingers splaying back around her skull. "Wake up."

Lily's eyes opened almost immediately. Then she bolted upright, looking around the room until her gaze found the window.

"The sun will set," she said in a rush. "Simon, we need sunlight."

"It's early," I said, trying to sound soothing even as I studied her face for any clue that she might be acting rather than genuinely terrified. "Sunset isn't for hours."

"You're safe here," Bryony added. "You're back in St. Giles."

Lily gave her a glare that should've burned her to ashes on the spot. Fair enough, when Bryony had done her best to throw her out of St. Giles previously.

"I need to speak to Simon alone."

Bryony looked as though she was going to object, but I cut her off. "Thank you, Bryony, I'll handle things from here." My heart hammered at a thousand miles an hour and I felt the same way I did when my powers ran low. Shaky and drained. But I didn't need the sun. I just needed to know why Lily had returned.

"I won't be far away," Bryony said in a cool tone. She cast one last inscrutable look at me, then swept out the door, her back indignantly straight.

"Sunlight," Lily repeated. She'd pushed herself into the middle of the bed, clutching the blanket around her, shivering. "Can you call sunlight?"

There was a sunlamp on the table under the window. Most of the wards had them, an easy way for the sunmages to provide more light when it was needed for a surgery or other purposes. Without looking I set it alight, moved it closer to Lily so the light hit her skin.

"There." I sat on the edge of the bed, wanting desperately to take her in my arms and hold her until I was convinced that she was really here. Knowing I couldn't afford to let myself be ruled by emotion. "Sunlight." I wasn't ready to ask her why she wanted a sunlamp burning when the sun was high in the sky.

Lily looked around her, as if calculating the reaches of the pool of light shed by the lamp. "Are there more?"

"I can get more." How many I could keep burning when I was this shaken was a different matter. Besides which, I didn't want to leave her alone until I understood the situation. "But it's still daylight."

She latched on to my arm, fingers gripping hard enough to bruise. "That doesn't matter. It's not safe."

I sat. If she was acting, then she could have a stellar career in one of the theater halls if she ever chose to. Or maybe she had just honed her skills through years of surviving the Blood Court. "Lily, this is St. Giles. It's safe."

"No," she repeated, face twisting. "You don't understand."

"What is it? What happened? Did Lucius hurt you?"

"No." This time the word sounded like a sob. "No, he didn't hurt me. But something's happened. I'm sorry, Simon. It's my fault. I let him. He can—"

She broke off, shivering wildly as she hunched into the blankets. I wrapped my arms around her, trying to lend her my warmth. "He what? Tell me."

"He can shadow," she said.

$$\smile$$

Silence. I thought for a moment Simon hadn't heard me. Which might not be such a bad thing. If he hadn't heard me say it, if no one else knew the truth, then maybe it wasn't the truth. Maybe this was all just a bad, bad dream and I'd been asleep here in the hospital all the time.

But the fear sweat on my clothes and the dirt on my hands and the horrible remembered sensation of being

hunted through the shadow told me otherwise. I clung to
Simon. Lucius in the shadow . . . the one place where I'd
always been safe. More than safe . . . invulnerable. And now
he'd found a way in. I'd *given* him the way in.

"How?" Simon said eventually. He untwined my arms
from his neck, pushed me back gently so our eyes met.
"How is that even possible?"

There was the question I'd been dreading. But there was
no possible response but the truth. "It's because of me."

"How?" he repeated.

"Lucius drank my blood," I said, looking down. "The
night you took me from Halcyon, he fed from me. It was
the first time," I added hastily as he sucked in a breath. "My
blood must have done something to him. It's the only thing
I can think of. He fed again, last night, and when I tried
to—" I broke off, not wanting to explain why I'd panicked
and fled. I couldn't tell Simon Lucius had kissed me.

Simon's face paled, making the shadows under his eyes
darken. "Lucius fed from you and now he can shadow?
He's become a wraith?"

"No. Not entirely. He can't go into the sunlight. That's
how I got away." I shuddered at the memory of burning
flesh. "He's still a vampire but he can shadow."

"But how? Why would your blood give him that power?
Lily, you need to tell me the truth. What are you, exactly?
Who fathered you? Are you part Blood?"

He'd drawn away from me, and his face twisted on the
word *Blood*. It was clear he hated the thought. But no turning from the truth now. "I don't know," I admitted. "Lucius
always refused to tell me. He used to tease me with it, the
knowledge. But it has to be something to do with the Blood.
They can draw the darkness. Shadowing is kind of like that.
Maybe it's Fae magic crossed with vampire. But I don't
know. It doesn't matter. What matters is that Lucius can
shadow." Cold swept through me. I had to grit my teeth to
stop them chattering.

I could feel the panic rising again. "He could be anywhere. Simon, I have to get away from here."

"No. We can protect you." His voice sounded distant.
His expression was closed. And his eyes, when he finally
looked at me, were dark and unreadable.

"How? Are you going to guard me every night? Keep

the sunlamps burning? Wear yourself out? Don't you see,
this explains why he wanted me back so badly. He wants
my blood."

"If he can shadow, then why hasn't he used it to come
for you before now?"

I shook my head. "I don't know. Maybe he didn't realize
straightaway. Maybe it took time for him to learn to control
it or for it to come into effect. Maybe he needed the second
dose to see if it would last." Why was he quibbling over the
details? I didn't care why or how Lucius could shadow. All
that mattered was that he *could*.

"It might wear off."

Hells save me from optimists. "And it might not. I need
to—" I stopped. Needed to what? Run? To where? Nowhere was safe. And even if I could think of somewhere to
go, how far would I get with the need—unslaked because
of my flight—dogging me? Lords of hell. What was I going
to do?

"No," he repeated. His hand sliced through the air. "No.
You're not leaving again. It doesn't make any sense, you'd
be no safer anywhere else."

I huddled into the warmth of the blankets around me,
drawing my knees to my chest and hugging them. I still felt
as though my blood had turned to ice. "It's not safe," I repeated. "Not for you, not for me, not for anyone. Not once
it's dark. He could be anywhere." I wanted to pull the blankets over my head and hide, but it wouldn't help. I sucked
in a breath, trying to will the panic away. "Did you move
your family? Are they somewhere they can be protected?"

"Yes. They're safe." He sat back on the bed. "You will be
too. I'll make sure of it."

"You can't tell anyone," I said, with a sudden horrified
thought. "If this gets out . . . that a vampire drinking blood
from a wraith can do this . . ."

I saw the moment he understood. If this became common knowledge, then every power-hungry Blood would
want to take me. And I was fairly certain that the Fae and
the humans would do their best to kill me to stop that happening. His eyes widened.

"We only have one option," I said before he could say
anything.

"Which is."

"We have to kill him." I had to kill him. To save myself.

"No."

His response was automatic.

"Simon, it's the only way." I heard my voice, heard the begging in it. He had to believe me. Had to agree.

"It's a treaty violation." He was back on his feet, starting to pace.

"Who cares about the damned treaty?"

He swept a hand through the air. "The Fae. The humans. All of us."

"Lucius doesn't."

"That doesn't make it right."

"So you'd rather he wins?" Lords of hell, why was he arguing with me? He'd wanted to stop Lucius. Now he knew that there was more reason than ever to do so. I started to drop the blanket, then realized I was naked beneath it. Hells. I clutched the blanket closer and climbed out of the bed, facing him. "He's going to be unstoppable. He can be anywhere. Kill anyone. He could come after you or your family or . . ."

"Or what?"

"Atherton," I said, fear twisting my stomach even tighter. Lucius would want Atherton dead. "What if he goes after your work?"

Simon's prowling ceased abruptly. "I need to strengthen the wards."

"Wards don't stop me," I reminded him. "They might not stop him."

"It's the best we can do. I can't protect Atherton with sunlight. Let's go."

"Go where?"

"Downstairs."

I didn't like the thought of being down in the dark. Lucius could get to the tunnels if he was able to move through the earth for long enough. He wouldn't have to wait for daylight. "Can I stay here?"

"No," Simon said. "You're coming too."

"Why?"

He looked at me. "For one thing, I don't know if I can trust you."

My mouth snapped shut as the words registered. I took a step back, feeling sick.

Stupid. Why had I assumed he'd welcome me back?

I cast around the room and saw my clothes piled on a chair. I pulled them on quickly, tugging my hair into a loose knot. When I was done, Simon was standing by the door.

"Ready?" he said. He looked unhappy, tension riding his shoulders and stiffening his spine.

I nodded, not trusting myself to speak. He didn't want me back. Well, then. Time for another exit. But not until Lucius was dealt with.

We walked in silence through the hospital, me trailing a little behind him, my shock and disappointment churning in my stomach. But as I walked, resentment joined them. I had risked my life for him. I had gone back to Lucius to stop any more of his precious humans being hurt. I had spied on Lucius to try to help him. I had let Lucius touch me. And he didn't *trust* me?

I came to a halt abruptly.

Simon took a few more steps before he realized I had stopped. He turned back, frowning. "What's wrong?" he said impatiently.

My hand tightened around my dagger. "What do you mean you don't trust me?"

His eyes narrowed. "We don't have time for this."

I lifted my chin. "Make time."

"Gods and fucking suns," he muttered. Then he strode forward, grabbed my arm, and virtually dragged me toward the nearest doorway. He flung open the small door, pulling me through behind him before slamming it shut.

It was dark in the tiny room. Dark and airless. I heard his breath rasping and felt my own heartbeat rise in response. He was angry. His spicy scent was spiked with it, but stronger than the anger was the musky kick of desire.

The need flared with a rush that should've lit my skin. My own wanting followed in its wake, scarcely less fierce.

"You tell me why I should trust you," he said, voice stony in the darkness.

"I came back," I said.

"You ran away from Lucius. Lucius, who you returned to." He sounded like he was speaking through gritted teeth. My eyes were adjusting to the lack of light and I could see him a little. He was staring at me, mouth twisted, hands on hips.

"I went back to him for a reason. To stop people dying."

"And now you're back here. With a tale of how he's a monster and you're scared. Some would say it's very convenient for his assassin to return to me with a story that would make me take her in again."

Idiot man. I drew in a breath. "If he'd sent me back to kill you, you'd be lying dead back in the ward," I snapped.

He made a frustrated sound. "Gods, Lily. We're right back where we started."

"Only if you want to let Lucius win," I said. "If you believe what he wants you to think. Can't you believe something else?" Both of us were breathing heavily. I felt like I should have been able to see sparks arcing through the darkness between us.

"Like what?" he said.

I didn't think. I just stepped forward and kissed him, hard. Then shoved him back. "Like that."

"Lily," he said warningly.

"Simon." I echoed his tone exactly. He made another of those frustrated noises and then he moved.

My back hit the wall with a thud and the stone felt icy against my heated skin.

Desire weakened my knees. "Simon—"

"Don't talk." It was a command, his voice smoke and darkness and anger. His body was so close, heat radiating from him, his breath rasping.

"Simon?"

"Don't talk."

He kissed me, devouring me. Heat streaked through me like a lightning bolt. But there was no light here. Just heat and darkness and desperation.

"Can't we light—"

"No." It was a harsh noise, almost a groan. "No. No light. I can't look at you right now. I just need ..." Something tore in the darkness and for a moment I wasn't sure whether it was my shirt or his until the air hit my breasts.

Mine. then.

Well, two could play at that game. I yanked at the linen under my hands, letting my full strength come out to play. The soft fibers parted like tissue under my hands.

Simon's hands were rough on me and I wanted to be rough too. Wanted to work out this desperate sense of hunger and fury and fear that I wouldn't know this again. Wouldn't taste him or touch him or feel him hard against me ever again.

If sheer desire could meld us together, we should have fused to the stone on the spot, but we were still only flesh and bone, however heated.

His mouth left mine as hands tore at clothing and yanked and pulled until there was just flesh to flesh.

The stone was hard at my back but not as hard as the feel of him between my legs. I gripped him tighter, raised one leg to wrap around his hip, gasped as he lifted me and sank home all in one savage movement.

We stayed suspended then, face-to-face in the dark. I could just see him, sketched in shades of gray as his eyes searched my face. A face I knew he couldn't really see in the darkness.

His eyes closed briefly and I bit my lip, feeling him buried deep within me, hot at my center, but still not hot enough to melt the icy core of fear in my chest. What if he really couldn't trust me again?

"Simon," I said again. A lost sound in the dark.

"Don't." He gripped me harder, tight enough to hurt.

But it didn't really, though bruises would mark my skin in the morning. It had gone beyond pain. I just wanted his hands on me, his body in me, his mouth taking me away from what we faced. What I was about to do.

He thrust then, one hard strike that pushed me against the wall, stone biting into me even as I pushed back against him, wanting what he was giving me.

My hand tightened in his hair, pulling. His mouth came back to me and I nipped at his lip, tugging it with my teeth and curling my inner muscles around him until he thrust again, filling me with heat to chase away the darkness.

And again.

And again.

Again.

More.

Now.

Pleasure washed through me, sparks lighting behind my eyes with colored whirls like a pyrotechnic display.

I met his every thrust, trying my best to let him fill me completely.

I don't know how long it took, how long we moved there in the dark, silent except for the sounds of flesh against flesh and gasping breaths. It felt endless.

It felt like no time at all.

And then inevitably, I began to tremble in his arms, coming apart, until all I could do was hold on more tightly as the pleasure took me.

He followed me with a strangled cry that might have been my name or a plea to whatever gods were listening.

We stayed there, foreheads resting together, breathing deeply as we both came back from wherever it was we had gone.

Then, oh so gently, he eased away from me, lowered me, his hands staying only until it seemed that I could stand on my own.

That last touch was enough to break my heart.

But I couldn't speak. Couldn't move at all as he fastened his breeches again and turned and slipped out the door.

Chapter Twenty

Unholy fucking insane.

There were no other words for it.

I didn't look back as I headed for the hidden ward. What in the name of all the gods, had I been thinking?

First I told Lily that I couldn't trust her, and then I—suns, I couldn't even put a name to what we'd done in the dark. Other than it had felt wonderful and terrible at the same time.

I wanted to do it again.

I wanted her to be gone. My life had been simple before. Now it was an unholy mess.

But mess or no mess, I couldn't forget the feel or taste of her. Couldn't shake free of her. Trust or not.

I shoved my way through the inner door and slammed it behind me. Lily might be following—I hadn't dared look and see—but she could find her own way in.

I paused for a moment, sucked in a breath. I was here to make sure Atherton was safe. I let my senses flick toward the wards protecting the rooms. They seemed whole, no indication anyone had breached them.

I relaxed, then swore as I remembered that wraiths don't trigger wards.

Atherton was tending to the patients. He turned at my muttered curses. "Simon? What are you doing here?"

Before I could answer, his attention moved past me and he frowned. "Who's with you?"

Suns. She was here. I didn't turn. I didn't know what I'd do if I saw her just now.

"It's me, Atherton," Lily said. She sounded calm. My gut twisted, doubts rising again. She shouldn't be calm.

Atherton's head snapped back to me. "The wraith is back?"

She came up beside me then and for a moment, I thought I saw something akin to hurt flash across her face. But she stayed silent, standing slim and straight. Her face was pale, only two spots of color burning in each cheek to show she wasn't marble. She'd found a healer tunic somewhere and pulled it over her torn shirt. Her hair lay loose over the green cotton, fiery in the lamplight. I remembered the feel of it against my skin. Remember the taste of those lips that looked swollen from my kisses.

Don't feel. Think.

"Yes," I said. "And she has some bad news. Lucius can shadow."

I'd never actually seen Atherton look completely taken aback before.

"Shadow? How?" He looked toward Lily. "Did—"

"He drank my blood," Lily said. "Apparently there's a reason that wraiths are feared."

Abominations, that's what the Fae called her kind. Maybe they were right after all. Gods and suns. Lucius with the powers of a wraith. But how? It had to be something to do with what she was, that her blood would do this to him. I swung back to Atherton. "Do you know how a wraith is made?"

Atherton shook his head. "No. I never found out. Lucius does and some of the older Blood might."

"Fuck."

"The Fae must know."

The Fae who never lifted a hand to help unless forced to? Those Fae? Gods.

"We have to stop Lucius. If this is true, no one is safe," Atherton continued.

Lily's face grew fierce. "Stop him? We have to kill him."

I cut her off. "No, we—"

"She's right," Atherton interrupted me in turn. It was unlike him. "Nothing else will stay his hand if he can shadow. Lucius is an infection in our race. One that should be cut out before it spreads."

"He wants to rule the City. He told me as much," Lily said.

"When?" I bit out.

She looked at me, not flinching. "When he fed from me."

Her eyes looked guileless, not a hint of guilt or lies. I wanted to believe her. But gods and fucking suns, Lucius had had his mouth on her skin and his hands on her body. Neither of which I could think about because I needed to stay in control.

"Maybe he was lying. Maybe he knew you'd come back." If he hadn't sent her himself. "Maybe he wants to provoke us into doing something foolish. Like breaking the treaty."

Lily glared. "You're already breaking the treaty." She gestured around the room. "By doing this."

"This is trying to help people. This is about saving lives."

"We'll save more lives by killing Lucius. At this point, does breaking the treaty even matter? If you don't do anything, Lucius will break it for you. More than break it. He'll make it as if there never was a treaty."

"If you're telling the truth."

"Why would I lie? Why would I leave him if that's where you think I want to be? There are plenty of other ways of provoking you humans into doing something foolish. You're just angry that he fed from me."

"Of course—" I broke off, biting down on the words. She was right, I was letting my feelings rule my head. I tried again. "If you're telling the truth, then prove it. You said you'd try to find out about his informant. Did you?"

Her glare intensified. "I looked, yes."

"Now you're going to tell me you didn't find anything? Another convenient story."

She slid one hand down to her dagger. Spiked her temper, had I? Well and good.

"As it happens," she said with edged precision, snapping each word off as if she'd like to bite me, "I did find something but I don't know what it meant. Bryony might."

That stopped me. She had found something? My anger subsided a little. Was I being cautious or just a complete bastard? "Bryony?"

"Yes."

"Then we'll go see Bryony," I said. I wanted this over and done with.

Lily looked slightly confused. "I thought you came down here to check the wards."

Gods. She was right. I fumbled in my trouser pocket, reached for the bundle of charms I carried there, fishing out the black metal circles Guy and I had worn at Halcyon. I pressed one of them into Atherton's hand. "Wear this. If anything concerns you, touch it on both sides and I'll know."

"You think Lucius might come here," Atherton said. His hands twined the cord of the charm nervously around his fingers.

"Yes. He might," I said. "I'll be back. Don't worry."

"He's more likely to come for me," Lily offered.

The thought didn't improve my mood any. "Bryony," I said shortly, and ushered her out of the room.

☽

"Tell me," Bryony said after Simon had marched us back to her office.

For once her voice wasn't openly hostile. Though the words were closer to an order than a request. Across the room, Simon's eyes were guarded as he watched me. It was as though he were two men. The one who'd loved me like we were dying in that dark room below and the one who didn't like what he saw standing before him in the clear light of day. I gripped the back of the chair I stood next to, suddenly exhausted.

"Lucius had a letter in his office. Fae sealed. A woman's handwriting. I also saw a woman in a carriage delivering another letter with the same seals to the mansion this afternoon," I said. "She wore a veil but I thought she had light hair." I watched Bryony rather than Simon. Light hair wasn't very helpful. Half the Fae I'd met in the hospital were blond.

Her face clouded. "What color were the seals?" she asked.

"Green and gold." I knew that the different ways various Fae Families worked their magic changed the colors observed by those who could see the traces of it. I didn't know more than that. Hopefully Bryony would.

Her perfect black brows drew together. "That could be any number of Families," she said. "What did the letter say?"

I rubbed my forehead, trying to remember. It seemed a

long time ago. I pictured the letter, the elegant script. "Something about the work not bearing fruit and turmoils but that 'his' interests hadn't changed."

"That's vague."

"That's hardly my fault," I snapped.

"What else? A signature?"

I shook my head, leaning my weight a little harder against the chair as a sudden ache stung my belly. The need. I'd hoped that perhaps that stupid interlude with Simon—for it had been stupid when obviously it had done nothing to ease his doubts about me—would have sated it for a time. No such luck. The Lady had definitely turned her back on me.

"No. It was signed *e'hai*. That means faithful, doesn't it?"

"Close enough. It has connotations of a sworn loyalty." Bryony's eyes were stormy and the chain around her next shimmered with a darkening sheen of purple. "Was that all?"

"There was a drawing. Some sort of leaf."

Her gaze sharpened. "A leaf? Could you draw it?" She reached to one side and drew a piece of paper from a neat stack, nodded toward the inkpot and quill lying on her desk.

I took up the quill, tried to remember the leaf. Five rounded bumps, two each side and one topmost. My hand shook slightly as I tried to trace it. Fatigue? Or the need? As if in answer, my stomach cramped, my fingers clenching with it. I bit down a gasp. Need, then. I gripped the quill tighter and finished the job, hoping Simon and Bryony hadn't noticed.

"What does a leaf mean?" Simon asked.

"I don't know yet," Bryony said. "Maybe nothing." She held out a hand as I put the quill down.

I passed her my drawing. "I'm no artist."

Bryony frowned down at the image. Then she suddenly dropped it as though it were a snake. "*Shal e'tan, mei*," she spat.

Even I knew that one. It meant something like fuck the Veil. Not the sort of thing I expected to hear from Bryony, though.

"What?" Simon asked. I shot him a glance. He looked confused rather than surprised. Either he didn't know that particular curse or he'd heard it before.

"Ring the bell," Bryony said.

"Is—"

"Ring the damned bell, Simon," she snarled.

He did so. In a few moments, Harriet opened the door after two quick knocks.

Bryony's furious expression didn't improve at the sight of her. "Where's Chrysanthe?" she demanded.

Harriet shrugged. "I haven't seen her. I was close when the bell rang, so I came."

"Fetch Chrysanthe."

Harriet didn't argue. She vanished with alacrity.

"Chrysanthe?" Simon asked incredulously. "You think it's Chrysanthe."

Bryony pushed the paper toward him. "That"—she tapped the leaf with a finger—"is a chrysanthemum leaf. Badly drawn but that's what it is. You've seen Chrysanthe's ring. What colors are the stones?"

His face turned thunderous. I fought the urge to shrink backward so as not to get between the two of them. I'd never imagined that my few meager clues would provide the identity of Lucius' informant so quickly.

"Emerald and something yellow," Simon said. "Gods and fucking suns."

"Exactly," Bryony said. "Chrysanthe is the only one of her Family who works in this hospital. And their emblem has several chrysanthemum leaves." She bowed her head suddenly and I saw her throat working.

Simon sank into the nearest chair. "Are you sure?"

"Of course I'm not sure," Bryony said after a pause. "But she's the one who fits."

"But why?" Simon said, shaking his head. "Why would she do such a thing? She's a healer."

Bryony shook her head. "I don't know. But I intend to find out." Her spine was suddenly razor straight again and her necklace blazed.

I took a cautious step backward, finding a seat myself. Another cramp—my back this time—hit and I bit my lip, determined not to show any pain. After what seemed an eternity, there was another rapid knock on the door.

"Come in," Bryony said.

Harriet entered, looking wary. "I couldn't find Chrysanthe," she said. "No one's seen her for a few hours."

Which meant she'd vanished not long after I had returned.

Simon and Bryony seemed to reach the same conclusion. They exchanged a long look.

"Thank you, Harriet," Simon said, in too calm a voice. "You can go. If Chrysanthe returns, please see that Bryony or I are informed."

Harriet looked from him to Bryony; then her gaze darted to me, curiosity flaring briefly on her face. Then she looked back at Simon. "All right." She apparently knew better than to ask any more questions and backed out of the room again.

"Do you know where she lives?" Simon asked Bryony.

"Yes. She has a flat not far from here."

"Someone has to go see if she's there."

Bryony winced. "Yes."

"Do you think she would go home?" I asked. "More likely she's gone to Lucius to tell him where I am. Nothing else has happened to make her think her cover is blown."

"Or else she's just gone out on an errand," Bryony said.

Simon shrugged. "Perhaps. But we can't risk her slipping through our fingers. We need to take her to the Speaker. Lily can tell him her story at the same time." He smiled suddenly, a vicious smile. "He wanted proof. Now we have it again."

"I will send word to the chambers," Bryony said. "But he may not grant us an audience today."

"Tomorrow is soon enough," Simon said. "We can hold Chrysanthe once we have her. And Lily isn't going anywhere." He cocked his head at me. "That's right, isn't it, Lily? You'll still give your testimony."

Unless Lucius came and killed me in the night. Unless I killed him first. I managed to nod, not wanting to rouse any of the anger crackling through him to further heights. Time enough to convince him that I was right, that Lucius needed to die, once he'd calmed down a little. "Of course."

He nodded. "All right. Then the question is who goes to find Chrysanthe."

Bryony rose. "I'll do it. You have no way to make her return. I can." Her face was implacable and I was glad that I was not Chrysanthe with the wrath of the Fae about to fall on me.

"Very well." Simon paused, then frowned. "There's something else I need to—"

I reached out, gripped his arm before he could say any more. "No, let her go," I said urgently. I didn't want him asking Bryony about wraiths. I didn't want him telling her the truth of what wraith blood did to vampires. The Fae hated my kind enough already. I didn't want them deciding that it was easier to eliminate one wraith than Lucius.

Simon scowled at me. "Lily—"

"Enough," Bryony said, looking exasperated. "Whatever it is, Simon, it has to wait. I need to find Chrysanthe."

Simon's scowl deepened but he nodded agreement. Bryony left us alone and he turned to me, blue eyes snapping.

"You can't ask her," I said before he could start talking. "She can't know."

"Know what?"

"About me. About Lucius and the Blood. You were going to ask her about wraiths, weren't you?" I searched his face.

He nodded. "Why shouldn't I ask?"

"She'll tell the Fae. Don't you see? They'll come after me."

He stilled in the chair. "You don't know that."

"I do," I said. "Trust me." My heart pounded. Would he listen? Would he protect me?

Simon pushed to his feet. "Fine. I won't tell her. But we are going to talk to someone."

"Who?" I asked, climbing to my feet, my legs shaky beneath me, whether from reprieve or the need weakening me, I wasn't sure.

"Guy," Simon said curtly.

Simon led the way to the Brother House, walking in silence. *Do you believe me now?* I wanted to ask. *Do you trust me?* But I stayed quiet. I knew very well there was one good reason for him not to trust me. Because I was still lying to him.

We entered the Brother House through the gate in the tunnels but had only gone a few yards farther when we met Guy coming the other way. His face was half blackened, smeared with soot or ash. He reeked of smoke.

"What in hell happened to you?" Simon demanded, reaching to clasp Guy's upper arm.

"When did she get back?" Guy asked almost simultaneously, shrugging off the touch.

The brothers frowned at each other. "This morning," Simon said. "We need to talk."

"Yes," Guy agreed. "I was just coming to find you. There was a fire at Mother's town house."

Lords of hell. Fear clutched my throat. "Was anyone hurt?"

Guy shook his head. "It was closed up. They're calling it a gas leak." His voice made it clear he didn't believe it.

"Lucius," Simon said at last, voice near to a snarl. "Making a point."

"Something like that," Guy said. "I've organized for Mother and Hannah and Saskia to be moved. They'll be guarded."

"It's Lucius we need to talk about," Simon said.

"I gathered that much," Guy said. "We need somewhere private."

He led us back into the Brother House and up two floors to some sort of meeting chamber. Simon warded the room. When he was done, the three of us took up places around a small oak table, Simon next to me and Guy opposite. Simon briefed Guy in curt sentences.

"Son of a hell-sworn bitch," Guy grated when Simon finished. "This is not good. What's the plan?"

"Kill Lucius," I said.

"Good plan." Guy actually smiled. "How?"

Simon shook his head at both of us. "We're not killing anyone. We get Lily to the Speaker, get the Fae to stop him."

"No," I snapped. "We're past that point. Lady's eyes, Simon, he just burned your house down. We need to end him. Some things you have to fight for," I added, and saw him jerk as my shot hit home. I knew he didn't want to fight, didn't want to tap into whatever dark side of himself he feared, but mere resistance wasn't going to win the day any longer. Lucius had changed the game. "And if you won't help me, then I'll do it alone."

Simon shoved back from the table. "No."

"Yes," I retorted. Once upon a time, I had been willing to go along with Simon's plan to see Lucius curbed, but now I didn't need him curbed; I needed him gone. Both to end the threat to me and maybe, just maybe, to free me from the need. Free me before Simon had to know the truth. Killing him was the simplest way to achieve it.

"It's too late for diplomacy, Simon. Lucius wants to kill you and he wants my blood. If you go to the Fae, the reasons for both those things will come out. Lucius will defend himself. Do you want to lose everything you've been working toward? Do you want every Blood lord hunting me? Or the Fae trying to kill me?" I willed him to see sense, to see that it was the only way. His eyes locked with mine and in the blue depths I saw grief and anger and denial.

Asking him to do this might just break him. Break anything he felt for me at least? But in order to live, I realized with a sickening pain that had nothing to do with the need tightening its claws, I had to be willing to pay any price.

Damn Lucius to the seven depths of hell.

"Please, Simon," I said softly. "We don't have a choice."

For a moment I thought he was going to refuse, but then he looked from me to Guy and the lines of his face settled into grim resignation. "All right," he said flatly. "We kill him. You have any ideas as to how?"

Guy tapped the table with his long fingers, red cross rippling on his skin, his eyes ice cold and his face set in the same grim lines as his brother's. "That might take more than my help, little brother. It might take divine intervention."

"Unless you have some of that to hand, I think we should focus on coming up with a plan," I said. "Lucius wants me back. Can't we use that?"

The fingers stopped their tattoo as Guy's brows drew together. "You think he'll come for you?"

I nodded. "Yes. He'll want more blood. It's not like he has another wraith to hand. I think he'll come tonight if he finds out where I am."

"Well, then, there's only one detail we really need to work out."

"And that is?"

"Where best to place the bait." Guy nodded, a satisfied smile lighting his face.

I stared at Guy, tasting bile. I'd known I'd have to face Lucius again, of course, but now it struck home. I would be letting myself be dangled temptingly in front of Lucius' nose. Offering myself up to his vengeance.

Lucius wanted me. He'd come to get me.

All I had to do was put myself in a position where he thought he could do so. Put myself in his reach.

"So we need to decide where we want to meet him," I said slowly, trying to think to chase away the fear. "Then we can let that leak out. Guy, some of your men could do that, couldn't they? Let it slip that I'm back here and ready to testify? Starting now?"

Guy nodded. Simon still hadn't spoken.

"What's wrong, little brother?" Guy asked.

"It's dangerous."

I shrugged, not wanting either of them to see how scared I was. They might do something stupid like try to stop me. "My life is already dangerous." If I wasn't going to run, then nothing could make things worse than they were already.

"Nothing ventured, nothing gained," Guy added. A very Templar sentiment.

Simon finally nodded, though the movement was reluctant. "Then let's make sure we're the ones who gain."

Relief made me light-headed. I drew in a breath. "Good, we're agreed. The question, then, is where and when we try to draw him out."

Simon touched my arm. The need flared like an oil-soaked torch. The heat bit deep and so did the pain. I set my jaw, steeling myself to ignore its shrieking demands. So another question was how I could manage to do whatever it was we planned while coping with the need as well. It would only get worse from here. I'd pushed my tolerance too far. The cramps in my stomach were a steady dull pain now and my head throbbed.

I almost regretted not having time for Lucius to give me the blood. It might have been enough to—

"Lily?" Simon's voice drew me out of the reverie. "Is something wrong?"

"It's nothing." I inched away from him carefully, scared he would sense my pain. "Let's get to work."

)

Our planning was hasty, but thorough. Guy would organize for rumors of my whereabouts to spread. And find a suitable place for me to spend the night. The guest chambers we'd had previously were too small. Too difficult to fight in.

Simon would do the same job of ensuring that word spread at St. Giles, if it hadn't already.

The details came together almost too easily and barely an hour had passed before Guy left, headed to do what needed to be done.

Which left me with nothing to do but wait. I wanted to stay out of sight as much as possible. For some reason the hidden ward, with all its additional protections, felt safer to me than the hospital or the Brother House. It was irrational; I knew but I needed my strength to fight the need. Even in the few hours our planning had taken, the pain had gotten worse. Based on experience, I had somewhere between twelve hours and a day before I was incapacitated.

But who knew if experience applied? This time I was withdrawing from a much larger dose of blood . . . I had no way of knowing if things would move faster or slower.

Lucius had to come tonight. Or the truth would come out.

In the meantime, I needed to be around as few people as possible, and the hidden ward seemed to be the best solution.

Even better if I could convince Simon to leave me down there for a bit. Having him so close was torturous. The need bit and so did the guilt that I hadn't been honest with him. Still, maybe after tonight, if everything went right, there would be nothing to tell.

I almost sighed with relief as we passed through the last of the warded doors and greeted Atherton. I hadn't been able to convince Simon to leave me alone, but at least he'd brought me here. I sank wearily onto a chair near one of the beds and stared at the bare walls, remembering the elegant leafy spaces of Simon's home. Would I ever get to live somewhere with that sense of light and air rather than between stark stone walls designed to cage me in?

Or was this ward one of the last things I was ever going to see?

I drew my feet up on the chair, hugging my knees. Both to try to feel warm and because locking my hands around my knees hid the shakiness of my hands. I gritted my teeth. I needed to hold on. To resist. I had to be able to fight tonight.

Maybe I should ask Atherton for his blood? Though

how I would get rid of Simon in order to achieve that end was beyond me.

As if to mock me, another pain struck, like a knife to my stomach. It rippled through my guts, then slid up my spine to burst through my head like a hammer blow. I sucked in a breath involuntarily, the noise very loud in the quiet room.

Simon broke off his conversation with Atherton and hurried over to me. His eyes narrowed as I lifted my head wearily to meet his gaze, the pain fading rapidly.

"You're trembling." He crouched down and touched my hand.

I dropped my gaze, pretending to watch what he was doing so I wouldn't have to look at him. "Just nerves."

"Is it?" His eyes searched my face as his hand moved to circle my wrist. "Why don't I believe you?"

Hells. Was he using his healer senses on me? I tried to pull my arm free. "You don't seem to want to believe anything I say today," I countered. "If you were me, wouldn't the fact that Lucius could come walking through a wall at any time during the night make you nervous?"

"Your pulse is racing. Your skin is hot. Are you sick?"

"I've never been sick in my life," I said automatically. Then immediately regretted my words. If I wasn't sick, then something else had to be causing the symptoms.

Simon rocked back on his heels. "There's something you're not telling me."

I shook my head. But another pain struck—so close—too close—and I felt myself start to shadow, wanting to flee to the cool gray world where there was no pain. There perhaps I could make it until tonight. I forced myself back with an effort.

Simon was staring at me. "What was that? Tell me the truth, Lily."

I hesitated, breath coming too fast. I couldn't hide this more than another few hours. Not when it was moving so fast. Was it better to tell or be discovered? I knew what Simon think of me, knew how he felt about those who drank blood. But maybe . . . just maybe, he was better than that. Maybe I did matter to him. After all, would he be so angry at me if he didn't care?

He said, hand still twining around my wrist as if he couldn't quite let go, "Tell me. Or I'll find out for myself."

I stared at him, mind racing. A seemingly simple thing, the truth. But it could change everything. Did I want to see him draw away from me? Dealing with his anger now was bad enough. What would complete rejection be like?

What would it be like to go through the rest of my life knowing that he only cared because of a lie? The voice rose unasked in my head and my heart turned over.

I wanted someone to care for me. The real me. All of me. Even if I died tonight.

Only the truth could give me that, despite the risk.

"Is something wrong?" Atherton's voice came from behind me.

I twisted around. His scarred face was hard to read. Had he heard Simon's question? I knew his loyalty was to Simon, not to me. Would he tell if I didn't? That could only make things a thousand times worse.

"That depends on Lily," Simon said.

I turned back to him, studying him, committing his face to memory. Gold and blue concern. Concern for me. The face of someone who cared about me. Store the memory deep. In case I never saw such a thing again.

"It's the blood," I said softly, and heard Atherton suck in a breath behind me.

"Blood? What blood? Did Lucius do something to you?"

I couldn't speak, couldn't think what to say. I just looked at him. And saw the moment when he understood what I meant.

"Vampire blood?" He dropped my wrist as if it were suddenly on fire. "You drink vampire blood." He stared at me, face twisting.

I nodded, dropped my feet to the floor, bracing myself for whatever was coming next. "It wasn't my—"

"No," Simon added, as if he couldn't even hear me speaking. "Not just vampire blood. Lucius' blood. You're locked to him."

"I'm not locked!" I protested, coming to my feet. "It doesn't work that way."

Simon stepped back, shaking his head, one hand held out as if to ward me off. "Doesn't it? Look at you, you're shaking. You're *addicted*." His face worked. "All this time, I've been trying to help you and you're already beyond help. An addict. Just like—" He bit off the words, eyes blazing. "And that means . . . oh, gods and fucking suns." He moved farther away from me. "You and him . . . you . . ."

I hadn't expected it to hurt quite this much, seeing the expression of disgust on his face. Seeing the warmth die. "We didn't have sex," I said, trying to make him understand. "You know that."

"But you—"

"The blood invokes pleasure," Atherton interrupted in a cool voice. "It isn't a choice on the part of the one receiving, Simon. I doubt Lily drank willingly."

I was grateful for the defense though I doubted it would help my cause, given the source. "Exactly. I didn't have a choice, Simon, don't you see?"

"That's what they all say. It wasn't my fault. Gods. How does someone make you drink their blood?"

Anger burned away some of the sick feeling. If he was going to judge me, then he could hells-damned well judge me on the whole truth. I swallowed hard, reached for a calm voice as the memory rose in my head. "The first time he made me drink, he beat me half to death, then forced me to drink. Does that sound like a choice to you?"

Simon's face was stone. "The *first* time. What about the others?"

"It doesn't much matter after the first few times. All of which involved force." After that, I had to admit, despite the humiliation and anger and self-disgust, I had gone willingly enough to Lucius every time I reached the point where the need drove me to it. "After that, it is, as you said, an addiction. One no one escapes. Hell, Simon, you're a Master Healer and you haven't found a cure. Can you blame me for failing in the same quest?"

"All this time, you've been needing his blood?" Simon said as if he hadn't heard me. "*Thinking* about it. About him."

"It doesn't work that way," I said. "The need is quiet for a period of time after you feed."

"But then it starts to burn, doesn't it? That's what Atherton has always told me." He cursed suddenly, low and vicious. "That's why you suddenly threw yourself at me. You just wanted to someone to bed you, to keep it at bay."

"No." But my protest sounded weak even to my own ears.

Simon stared at me, eyes as distant as the sky they resembled.

"No," I repeated. "Not entirely. What we have is outside that."

"How can it be when you're burning up for another man? Burning up for a goddamned insane Blood Lord. Burning for his blood. As you'll always burn."

"I don't want it," I cried, feeling my voice catch and thicken. I would not cry. Not in front of him. Not if he couldn't understand this. "I *need* it. Believe me, there's a difference."

"Is that why you want to kill him? Because he did this to you?"

"Yes. Partly."

"What's the other part?"

I lifted my chin, met his scornful gaze with steel in my own eyes. "Because nobody is safe while he's alive."

"How can I believe that?" He closed his eyes briefly. "How can I believe anything you say? You've been lying to me all this time."

"I didn't lie. I just didn't tell you."

"You lied when you asked me to come to your bed."

My hands curled into fists. Oh to shake sense into him. But I had nothing to defend me except words. Words I knew he wouldn't listen to. Not while he was so angry. Maybe not ever. "It wasn't a lie. I picked you. You were my choice for the first time. Doesn't that mean anything to you? The one and only time it was my choice and I picked you!"

"Picked me to work off your bloodlust like any Night-seeking whore," he snarled.

My mouth worked but no sound came out. There was no response. If that was what he really thought of me, then there was no point to this. I turned and walked away.

Chapter Twenty-one

"You were too hard on her," Atherton said as the door to the outer chamber slammed shut behind Lily.

"Atherton," I managed, between gritted teeth. "Go. Away."

His face went still. Then he turned and left. The door slammed a second time, hard enough to make the oil lamps swing above the beds, sending shadows scurrying around the walls.

Leaving me alone. Alone surrounded by the blood-locked I'd worked so long to try to save.

Those who had fallen prey to the Blood.

As Lily had.

Anger roiled through me.

I wanted to hurt someone. Wanted to unleash the sun and burn the mess of my life to the ground.

Gods. I wanted not to have to think about it. About Lucius touching her, let alone him seeing her in the throes of pleasure.

No. Why should I care what she'd done? She had *lied* to me. Used me. Felt nothing for me. The need killed all human ties, all natural emotion. I knew that. Those in its grip wanted only the pleasure.

But you want her anyway, a vicious little voice in my head mocked.

Truth, I did. Gods and suns take me for a fool.

But I didn't know how it could ever work between us

despite what I had seen break in those gray eyes when I'd called her a whore.

What I'd felt break within me at the sight.

But I did know one thing. I now had no doubt I wanted Lucius dead.

Unable to stop myself, I kicked out at the chair where Lily had sat. It skidded across the room and crashed into a table, knocking a tray of tubes and instruments to the floor, where they shattered.

Not one of the patients around me stirred.

Which left me looking for something else to hurl.

"Feeling any better?" Atherton's voice came from the doorway.

"No."

"She's not the same as a Nightseeker," he said. "She didn't choose."

"I don't care," I ground out.

Atherton tilted his head and started picking his way across the room, surefooted as a cat despite his blindness. "If you say so," he said, patently disbelieving. "Despite this . . . disinterest, you should still help her do what she wants to do." He reached the mess I made, though how he knew where it was escaped me, and bent to right the table.

"Why?" I knew why I wanted Lucius dead. But I was in no mood to bend to anyone else's desires right now.

Atherton straightened. "There is something I've never told you about the blood-locked."

Gods and fucking suns. Was everyone in my life a liar? "What?"

"I have a theory that killing Lucius might break the addiction."

My jaw dropped. "How? And why in hell are you only telling me this now?"

"Because I never thought we would have a chance to try it out," he said calmly. He folded his arms and propped himself against one of the iron-framed beds.

Killing Lucius could be a cure? Fuck. "How sure are you?"

"It's a theory. There must be something magical involved in the link between the Blood and the locked. We haven't found a physical cause in all these years. Lucius is the head of his Court. He has killed all the older ones and destroyed their Courts over the centuries. His blood runs in all the Blood in this City. His magic. It might hold the key."

Or it might not.

And if it didn't? If Lily—if we—somehow went ahead with the plan and survived and succeeded and yet she still needed the blood? If she would still be forced to choose it every time. Could I cope with that?

Feeling my mind go red with rage once more at just the thought of her needing the blood still, even if it was Atherton who fed her, I doubted it.

But despite that, the dark part of me also felt a desperate need to make Lucius suffer. To end him. So I was going to try, and suns take the consequences.

))

When twilight came, Guy escorted me to the chamber he had prepared. The gaslights had been altered to sunlamps, which left me only with candles until I needed the sun.

Until Simon came to my rescue, that is.

If he did come to my rescue.

I lay down on the bed, stomach churning. I hadn't seen Simon since I'd left the ward. I'd returned to the Brother House, found Guy, and asked for a room and to be left alone. Simon hadn't come looking for me. And he had sent Guy to bring me here.

Guy who had assured me that nothing in the plan had changed.

Which I, apparently, was to take on faith.

It seemed that I was to do this without even a good-bye at the last.

So be it. I stared at the ceiling with eyes that burned from held-back tears and willed Lucius to appear. Every so often, I let myself drift toward the shadow to ease the pain but forced myself back. Part of me wanted the pain. Needed it to focus my anger and will on Lucius. An end was called for. His or mine.

When it grew fully dark, I shadowed fully. That way I actually had a chance of seeing Lucius coming.

The hours seemed endless as I fought both my fear and the need. I was near the edge of my limits. I almost welcomed the idea of death.

At least then I wouldn't be scared anymore. Nor would I hurt.

The cathedral bell tolled midnight, then one, then two. Still nothing.

I paced around the room, so I wouldn't sleep

That would be a quick ticket to death.

No, not death. Merely a return to slavery. Lucius didn't want me dead. He wanted my blood. Though I was sure he had ways of keeping me alive that would make me wish I were dead before very long.

Wraiths live long lives. Not near immortal like the Fae but long enough. No doubt it would feel like an eternity of living hell if Lucius got his hands on me again.

I stared out the window, at the darkened grounds of the Brother House, wondering if he was lying in wait somewhere out there, waiting for his moment.

"Thinking of me?"

I whirled as Lucius stepped through the wall.

He was shadowed, as I was. I stepped backward, angling myself toward the door.

"Going to run again, shadow? Go on. You know how I enjoy the hunt."

I wanted to but that wasn't the plan. I steeled myself. "No. No, I'm not running."

"No?" He tilted his head. "Have you seen reason, then? After your . . . departure."

"You took me by surprise," I said, stalling.

"You ran. You ran straight back to the humans." His voice was a low snarl. I was glad that I couldn't see any color in his eyes. No doubt they would burn scarlet.

There was no point lying. "I wasn't thinking."

"So you have changed your mind? You would come back to me? We could stand together."

"With you drinking my blood to give you . . ." I spread my hand, unable to think of a better way to describe his ability than "abomination." "This."

"Yes. This. Isn't it delightful?" His smile was anything but. "Entirely unexpected. But you could have my blood too. You know you want it. I can feel it in you from here. You hunger, shadow."

I did. Hungered more now that I could smell him. It made me dizzy with want, but I fought for control, trying to remember. I was supposed to stall him. Not just stall him but get him to leave the shadow and distract him. Until Simon could come and bring the sunlight.

And I suddenly had a very clear vision of just how I could do that.

I licked my lips, dizzy from more than just the need now. Fear had turned my spine to ice. Lucius would be able to smell it, but that didn't matter. He was used to me being afraid. Better that he believed I still was. "Yes. Yes, my Lord. I hunger."

His mouth curved with vicious satisfaction. "I thought so. So you have seen sense?"

"What would you give me, if I came back to you?"

He took a step toward me, eyes glittering darkly. "Give you? You are mine, shadow. Why should I give you anything?"

I let myself grow a little more solid, drew my dagger. He paused. He had touched me in the shadow. Was he wondering if I could do the same? He knew very well the damage my blade could do.

"You want something from me. We could come to terms. You wish to take this City. I can help you with that too. But I want . . . more freedom. After all, the humans have offered me anything I want." I prayed he would believe me. Coming as he did from the Night World, where nothing is free, surely it was plausible that I would try to drive an advantage from this situation.

"They do not value you as I do, shadow. They cannot give you what you need." He lifted his wrist to his mouth and bit suddenly. The smell of his blood welled around me.

Irresistible.

Almost.

"No, my Lord." I made myself drop my gaze, let the dagger fall to my side, nerves shrieking at me as I gave him an opening.

He moved swiftly. Too swiftly. Suddenly he was beside me. But I realized I couldn't feel any real sense of his body, not like I had felt when he'd chased me through the warrens. He was insubstantial now. Not like me. More like a ghost. So the effects of my blood were fading. Which had to mean he was even more desperate for it.

I schooled my face to stillness. I couldn't smile. Couldn't

let him see anything but what he wanted to see. The blood scent grew stronger and I bit my lip, feeling my grip on my senses loosen. Soon I would have to leave the shadow. I needed some other sensation to fight the need. In my half-solid state, I could dig my nails into my palm but I barely registered the sensation.

"I have missed you, shadow," he said softly. His voice was right beside my ear though I felt no breath. "Did you miss me?"

I nodded slowly, tilting my head ever so slightly so my hair fell back off my neck, baring my throat. Willing him to take the bait. "Yes, my Lord." I let my voice turn longing. "I . . . I have need, my Lord. Do you not . . . hunger . . . too?"

"Yes." It was just a whisper. The sound of a voice calling from beyond the grave.

"Then—" I let my voice drop too. "Please, my Lord."

His hand drifted across my neck. I felt it then, like the brush of a cobweb. "You want me?"

"Yes, my Lord."

He lifted a hand, moved it toward me, but it passed through me. He snarled softly. "We cannot touch here."

"No."

"Then it's the same for you?"

"Yes, my Lord. I always have to leave this place to touch another." I wasn't going to remind him that he'd touched me before in the shadow. That he was weakened. "That's why I could never kill like this."

He seemed to be considering. I looked up at him, made myself part my lips and lick them. "Please. The need . . . it is very bad."

Lady, let him believe me. "Please, my Lord." Did I sound yearning or terrified? I didn't know.

"You'll come back with me?"

"Yes. When you leave, I'll come with you." Hopefully because I'd be carrying a bag full of his ashes.

"Put down your weapons," he said.

Not completely fooled, then. I pulled the dagger and the stilettos from their sheaths, dropped them on the floor.

"Move back against the wall. Kneel. Put your hands behind you back. Then leave the shadow."

In other words, make myself completely vulnerable. Prove I was trustworthy.

It took every effort of will I could muster, but I obeyed. I shook as I knelt there. Hoping like hell the depth of my fear wouldn't give me away. Though Lucius liked fear. It might add to the temptation.

I tried to remember how to breathe as I waited, unable to tell where he was or what he might be doing. Was he going to take the bait?

Or had I just turned myself into the perfect target? I strained with all my senses, but until he chose to leave the shadow I was as blind as Atherton.

He could pick up my dagger and cut my throat with it before I'd have time to react or call for help.

I had to rely on the fact that he needed me. Hope that Atherton had been right about the possibility of a Blood becoming addicted to one person's blood to make him hungry for me. Hope my blood was doubly attractive because of the power it brought.

Pray to whatever gods might listen to one such as me for protection. Pray that Simon wouldn't leave me to my fate. I had a charm in the pocket of my trousers to call him, but I couldn't touch it now.

"My Lord?" I said softly after an endless minute or so. "Do not tease me, please. I . . . cannot wait much longer."

He appeared before me. Holding my dagger in one hand. My teeth clamped down on my instinct to cry out. I needed him, as he was, solid and solidly distracted, before I could summon help. It would take Simon time to light the lamps. Only a few seconds, true, but that was more than enough time for a vampire to react unless he was lost in something.

That something would have to be me.

Lucius drew the blade up closer to my face, trailed its point against my skin. Not quite hard enough to draw blood.

"You left me, shadow," he said softly.

We could be heard now if he spoke too loudly. I hoped that Simon couldn't hear this. What would he think? That I was exactly as he had presumed me to be? A Nightseeking whore about to get what she wanted.

Would he believe the lies?

And if he did, would he still come when I needed him?

"Yes, my Lord."

"Foolish of you."

I nodded. "Yes. Will you forgive me?" I kept my eyes on his face, hoping I looked suitably terrified and penitent. It wasn't hard to summon the emotion. I *was* terrified.

He could kill me here and now and vanish into the night before the humans could react.

"Perhaps." He smiled and I saw his fangs gleam in the moonlight. "If you prove yourself suitably remorseful."

I stared up at him. I had no words to describe my remorse. Remorse that I'd ever been his creature. Remorse that I was in this position. I regretted many things. But I didn't regret what I was trying to do now. To succeed I needed him to believe me.

"I am sorry, my Lord." I took a breath, then leaned into the blade, letting it slice my face.

Letting the blood spill.

I heard his sucked-in breath as the smell of blood suddenly rose between us. Fresh and rich and inviting. At least I hoped it smelled good to him. To me it just smelled like blood. Like the aftermath of every beating I'd ever taken. Every wound I'd ever sustained.

The blood was wet and hot against my cheek, like the tears I couldn't shed. "Aren't you hungry too, my Lord?"

I heard his heart skip out of its calm Blood rhythm. He was hungry. Hungry for *me*.

I leaned my head, turning the cut side of my face up as I stretched out my neck. "Your blood will taste sweeter to me if I know that you have been satisfied first."

He stared down at me. "Ask nicely."

"Please. Please . . . Lucius." His name was bitter on my tongue. "Don't make me wait."

It happened faster than a snake strike. One minute I was kneeling and bleeding; the next he'd lifted me to my feet, pressing me back against the wall and plunged his fangs into my neck.

It hurt.

Hurt like hell.

But I made myself gasp in delight. Made myself relax into him, hold him close. Forced my revulsion and panic away as I tried to listen to his heartbeat and read him.

Not yet.

Not yet. Not now while his muscles were still tensed.

I pulled his head closer to my neck. More. He needed to take more.

But not too much.

My own heartbeat seemed to pound through me as the blood flowed out of me. Too much and I would faint or die or forget what I had to do.

But then I heard it. The same unified rhythm of his heart beating with mine and the softening of his muscles. Just like it had been in Halcyon. I had him. Fully in the grip of my blood.

Mindless.

Careless.

I felt the seductive pull of that doubled beat, the need to yield filling me as his scent surrounded me. I resisted long enough to remember the charm. I let my hand drift down. Found it as I felt my resolve shatter. Touched it gently, the metal warm against my cold skin. I spoke a single word. "Simon."

To my ears it sounded weak and barely audible. But apparently it was enough.

The door flew open and the lamps blazed to life around me, the room suddenly bright as midday.

Lucius stumbled back from me, fangs rending as he retreated. Wetness gushed down my neck. I clapped my hand to the wound. Blood pulsed against my skin. Too much blood.

I couldn't move, everything suddenly swimming before me. But I could watch.

Watch as Lucius swung toward Simon, shrieking against the light.

His hand connected and Simon was forced back, but he didn't falter. He surged forward, wielding a sword as large as Guy's again as Lucius drew a knife from beneath his jacket and attacked desperately, trying to reach the door and get away from the lamps.

I knew how much each blow Lucius landed had to hurt him. I knew exactly how strong the vampire was, how fast, even as his skin started to smoke and blister. A lesser man would be crushed, would flee.

Not Simon.

He stood against him, seeming to blaze almost as brightly as the sun he called.

And then the room went dark. Simon had let go of his power.

"No!" I screamed, I stumbled forward but my legs crumpled beneath me and I hit the floor, head spinning. More blood poured between my fingers.

I watched them, figures of gray and black, limned in moonlight that glinted off blood-damped blades.

"You want her," Simon said in a voice like granite. "Then you have to come through me."

Lucius hissed, fangs bared. "As you wish, sunmage."

They came together in a clash of metal and I screamed at Simon to use the sun. He couldn't beat a vampire. No one could. He would die.

But he didn't.

No, instead, he fought like a man possessed, blade arcing through the darkness, faster almost than I could see, face full of a terrible intent. His blade connected with Lucius' arm and this time it was Lucius who screamed, not me.

Screamed, then attacked, pressing Simon back with a flurry of strikes from the cruel hook of his knife.

I could smell more than Lucius' blood now. Human blood too. He was hurt.

I tried to drag myself upright, terror closing my throat, but the room swam around me.

"Think of me, sunmage," Lucius snarled as he pressed another attack. "Think of my fangs in her neck. Maybe that will keep you warm in hell."

Simon didn't reply. Just raised his sword again. For a moment I thought he looked to me, but maybe that was just a trick of the moonlight. Then he moved again, leaping toward and past Lucius, and then, before Lucius could turn, whirling to strike again.

He found his target.

His sword cut through Lucius with one blow. Lucius froze, then fell.

The room burst into light again and I saw the shocked, frozen expression on Lucius' face before it burst into flame.

The fire was bright white, dazzling, as was the answering burst as his body followed suit.

Burning.

Ashes.

Gone.

Blood still gushed against my hand, running hotly down my neck. The stink of burning flesh filled my nose, and the vision of Simon's face, half blackened but fiercely victorious, cut a path through the blackness as he bent over me. "Simon," I said one last time before letting the dark take me.

Chapter Twenty-two

"Are you going to sit outside this door forever?" Bryony paused by the door to Lily's room, looking down at me with an amused expression.

I shrugged, keeping my eyes on the door.

For nearly a day, her life had hung in the balance. She had lost far too much blood.

Not that I had been able to help her that first day. Bryony had knocked me out so that they could work on me. Once I'd awoken, I'd taken up my station here. But I hadn't been able to cross the threshold. It had been nearly three days.

"She's fully recovered," Bryony said. "You can go inside."

"I thought you'd be more disappointed about that," I managed.

She ignored my gibe. "How long are you going to keep pretending?"

"Pretending what?"

"That you don't care? You may as well give up, Simon. You're in love with her."

"I—"

"You've hardly left this door, except when Guy's threatened you with bodily harm if you don't sleep or when Atherton's wanted you, for three days now. You snap and snarl at everyone who is caring for her. I think everyone would be happier if you would just go in and see her."

I shook my head, ignoring her in turn. "Any word of Chrysanthe?"

Bryony's lips thinned. "No. She has not been seen in Summerdale or the City. I fear she may be dead."

Gods and suns. Another casualty of this mess. And now we might never know if she really was Lucius' spy.

Bryony nodded, as if she could hear what I was thinking. Then her expression brightened. "Oh. I nearly forgot. I had a message from the Speaker this morning."

My gut tightened. There had been turmoil in the City since Lucius had . . . vanished. I'd been waiting for the Fae to step in, to come seeking whoever might be responsible in order to restore order. "Oh?"

"Yes. He said that the Fae would not be pursuing the matter of Lucius' disappearance. He said that no one could offer him any proof of what had happened and therefore he could not act. He expressly mentioned that I should tell you that."

A chill crept down my spine. A message or a warning? I had no way of knowing.

Bryony smiled. "Everything is as it should be." Then her smile grew crooked. She looked like she couldn't quite believe what she was saying, but her eyes were gentle as she leaned down and patted my arm. "You saved this one, *m'hala*. You won. Lucius is dead. You got to kill him. She almost died to trap him so you could do just that. It's time you forgave her for whatever it is you think she did to you."

Then she turned and went into Lily's room.

I leaned my head my head back against the wall. It wasn't so simple as that. I stared into a space a moment longer, then, unable to stay still any longer, heaved myself to my feet and headed for the roof.

My breath was coming hard when I stepped out into the sunlight, but I ignored the physical discomfort. How my body felt didn't matter.

What mattered was the feeling that I carried something dark within myself now, something no amount of sunlight seemed to ease.

I had killed deliberately. Had taken up my sword and fought.

Ended a life.

Had felt the savage triumph of it as I had done so.

Yes, I'd done it to save lives. To revenge Edwina in some convoluted way. I'd thought it would bring me peace. But there was still guilt. That was the hardest part. I'd killed a monster like Lucius and still felt remorse.

I stared out over the gleaming white marble, dazzling in the sunlight. One death had hurt me, making old wounds fresh again. What did Lily feel with so many to carry?

Did they hurt her?

I turned my face to the sun, shut my eyes, asked for light. But there were no answers.

Lily had come from darkness but she had sought the light. I needed to do the same. Learn to live with who I was now.

I shook my head. Bryony had it wrong. It wasn't a question of whether I could forgive Lily; it was a question, as it had been for a long time, of whether I could forgive myself. And whether Lily might offer me that same absolution.

$$\mathcal{D}$$

I looked up as the door to my room opened but slumped back against the pillows when I saw that it was, as it had been almost every time my door had opened for the last four days, just Bryony.

Bringing with her the tantalizing scent of Simon. Whom I hadn't seen since I'd woken up in this room. His absence felt like a hole that I had no idea how to fill. Every now and then I caught a waft of his smell, but the fact that he was near my room yet didn't come inside didn't fill me with hope.

"He's never coming, is he?" I said.

To my surprise, Bryony smiled briefly. She had been coolly professional all the time she'd been treating me, but her manner hadn't really thawed. "Don't give up just yet," she said.

"What's the point?" I muttered. "There's no future in it. I'm not even human." Simon and I were too different. I had to accept it. Make whatever life I could for myself here without including him in my plans.

A strange expression fluttered over Bryony's face.

"What?" I said.

She looked away, the chain around her neck flashing green, red, blue, red before settling back to orange. Then she looked back, nodded once as if she'd made a decision.

"It was brave, what you did," she said. "A good thing."

A compliment from a Fae? "Thank you," I said. "Simon did more than me."

She shook her head. "No. It took courage. To put yourself in that position. Given that no one can really know the truth of what happened, I think you deserve some reward. So I'm going to tell you something."

I froze. "Something?"

"About wraiths," she said. "And how they come to be." Her eyes narrowed for a moment. "But if you tell anyone you found out about this from me . . ."

"I won't," I said hastily, heart pounding. "Tell me. Who was my father?" I held my breath while she settled herself into he chair by my bed, belatedly wondering if I wanted to hear what she was going to say.

"I don't know his name," Bryony said.

She paused and I nodded, despite the disappointment. I hadn't really thought it would be so simple as asking. "Go on."

"I just know the lore and the story. To make one of the Blood, a human must be turned."

I nodded. I knew this part. Knew how a Trusted might be rewarded for their service by being turned. That they are primed via various rites that involve vampire magic. Then fed vampire blood for days, more each day as the Blood who will turn them feeds from them. They replace more and more of their own blood with vampire blood each day, becoming less human day by day until they die and return.

"It's an unpredictable process," Bryony said.

I nodded again. "There are always some who do not return."

"And some react badly to the preparation. Most just go into a type of rapture and drift away. But there are those who do the opposite and become frenzied near the end. "

I swallowed. "Frenzied?"

"Half insane. Dangerous. And full of lust. The lore says that a wraith is made this way. When a human male about to be turned, one on the very brink taken by the frenzy, is bred to a Fae female, then the child is likely to be a wraith."

But that meant I was . . . My mind reeled. The Blood weren't Blood until they died and came back. Until then, no matter how much blood they drank, they were human.

Which meant I was human too. Partly, at least. Something like happiness suddenly rose. "But I don't understand. How does this happen?"

Bryony sighed. "In your case, all I know is that your father escaped the Blood and came across your mother in his frenzy."

My budding joy receded rapidly. "He raped her," I said flatly.

"Yes." Bryony looked grave. "But your mother decided to go ahead and take the risk of carrying you."

"Then gave me up," I said bitterly. Better perhaps that she had acted earlier.

"I'm sure she took no joy in that," Bryony said, with something almost like sympathy on her face. "But our lore is strong and your kind is to be feared. She would have been given no choice."

"Why?" I said, curiosity driving me past caution. Did the Fae know the truth of what my blood could give a vampire? "Why the fear?"

Bryony rose from the chair, shrugging gracefully. "Your powers go against all our beliefs. No race is ever comfortable with that. Our stories tell dark tales of the things your kind have wrought in the past." She looked down at me, her eyes like midnight. "But you have your truth now. Perhaps it will give you something to hold on to."

"There's somewhere I want to take you."

Simon. I whirled from the bag I was packing to stare at him. Another day had passed since Bryony had told me about my father. Another day more of fighting with myself before Bryony had finally pronounced me fit to leave and announced that Guy had found somewhere for me to stay.

I'd given up on Simon coming for me.

But still, I couldn't help the little leap in my chest as I took in the sight of him, dressed in a white shirt and blue jacket that made his eyes seem more like the sky than ever.

"Come in," I said, not knowing what else to say. What had he been doing for so long? Dealing with the aftermath of what we'd done?

Reports told of an uproar in the Night World with Lucius suddenly disappearing. But there'd been no outright violence involving humans and no further attempts to re-

trieve me—by which I surmised that Lucius had not shared
the secret of my blood with anyone—and that seemed
good enough for now.

No one yet knew who would be representing the Blood
at the treaty negotiations. The Blood would have to sort
out their own house. The rest of us would have to see who
was left standing at the end.

Simon, I realized suddenly, hadn't moved since I'd invited him in. "I said, come in."

"I'd rather you came out." He stayed where he was in
the doorway, as though he feared what might happen if he
crossed the threshold. He looked good. Not burned or
scarred. Once again a healthy golden, glowing male, if
somewhat subdued. No smile playing around his mouth, no
teasing sparkle in his eyes. "Bryony says you're cleared to
leave. Will you come with me?"

We left the hospital by one of the rear entrances. Simon
had a small phaeton waiting in the road. He handed me up
and took the reins.

"Is this yours?" I said, looking down at the calm chest-
nut waiting for Simon's instructions.

"Yes. Well, the horse is. The carriage is my family's."

He clicked his tongue. "Let's go, Red." The carriage
pulled away and I leaned back, drinking in the light of the
early-afternoon sun.

I hadn't been outside for . . . well, it seemed a long, long
time. Too long. I hardly remembered what it felt like not to
be surrounded by stone and marble and glass.

I took a deep breath letting fresh air fill my lungs. It
tasted of the City, like smoke and coal and too many people, but that was still better than the hospital or the Brother
House.

Simon didn't speak as we drove away from the hospital,
making our way through the streets of Bellefleurs.

"Where are we going?" I asked at last.

"You'll see."

I gritted my teeth but subsided into silence again. The
bouncing rhythm of the carriage and the hoofbeats were
not exactly relaxing, but somehow semihypnotic. If he
didn't want to talk, then I wasn't going to talk either. The
breeze from our travels moved softly over my skin and

ruffled my hair, loose on my shoulders. I focused on that, on the sense of ease in the sunlight and warm air, so I wouldn't think too hard about what was to come.

About the fact that Simon and I were going to have to talk when we got wherever it was we were going. That I might not enjoy the discussion.

That I might be in for still more pain. I touched the scar on my neck. I could survive pain. I had to remember that.

We traveled for a few more minutes and the streets started to look more familiar. Simon turned down a lane and drew the carriage into the yard of what looked like a small livery stable. A boy appeared to take the horse's head, and Simon climbed down from the carriage. "We'll walk from here."

I clambered down myself, trying not to bite my lip in frustration as I looked around. Where were we? What was he up to?

"This way." Simon gestured back down the lane and set off. I followed him, more confused than ever.

The laneway was narrow, its cobbles edged by the kind of tall stone fences that spoke of houses beyond rather than businesses. The fences were too tall to see over and anyway, I was too focused on Simon's back to look around. Simon didn't look back as he walked. I followed slowly, running my hand along the smooth sun-warmed gray stones of one wall, half drunk on the sense of freedom that filled me with each step. I was out of St. Giles. And with Simon.

Simon came to a halt a little farther up the lane, produced a key from his pocket, and proceeded to open a skinny metal gate in the next wall.

I caught up to him. "Where are we?" I peered through the gate, into a large garden.

"Don't you recognize it?" Simon said, pushing the gate open. "This is my house." His mouth lifted slightly at one corner as he held the gate for me.

"I didn't come in this way," I said as I passed him. I knew the layout of his house and property. But I'd never seen this part of it before. "Why are we coming in back?"

Simon locked the gate behind us. "Just being careful. Plus, there's something I thought you might like in the garden." He set off again and I hurried to catch up to him. The garden was set out with some care in a series of small areas filled with trees and flowers and shrubs. I passed under an archway covered with ivy only to find myself confronted with a large glass and metal structure. A conservatory, I said to myself. That's what it was called. A place to grow things that needed protection.

Simon produced another key, opened the door, and we walked into the conservatory. It was like walking into a patch of forest, warm damp air sweeping over us and carrying the scents of flowers and trees.

Simon picked up a blanket from a shelf near the door, then walked over to a patch of slate tiles set beneath a group of slender trees I didn't recognize. Their small white flowers scented the air with a heavy perfume.

Simon shook the blanket before laying it down. "We should talk." He sank down onto the blanket, draping his arms around his knees, seemingly perfectly at ease.

But I could hear his heart beating just a little too hard. It made me nervous. I lowered myself to the ground, sitting cross-legged, as far away from him as the blanket allowed.

"I agree." To my credit my voice sounded calm. I sat down and lifted my face to the sun shining through the glass ceiling, hoping the warmth might chase away the cold knot in my stomach. "So talk."

Simon swallowed. "How are you?"

"I am well, thank you." I touched my scar. Lucius' fangs had torn free of my throat too fast and too brutally to heal cleanly. I would wear his mark for life. It was a little tender but Bryony assured me it was fully healed.

Did Simon bear scars too?

He blew out a breath, looking nervous. "I meant . . . after Lucius. Do you still feel . . ."

Oh. I sat a little straighter. He meant the need. "What if I told you it was still there?"

He lifted his chin. "I'll admit it, Lily. It's not an easy thing. But . . . but I—" He stopped and I saw something in his eyes that made my heart ease. Not that I was going to let him off the hook so quickly.

"Yes?"

"I'll try to help you deal with it. I've missed you, Lily." His voice had softened. He looked nervous. It was almost endearing.

I schooled my face to severity. "Missed your Nightseeking whore?" I couldn't help it. The memory of his words—of his rejection—still hurt. They needed to be brought into the light before they could be healed.

He winced. "I shouldn't have said that. I'm sorry. I'd get on my knees and apologize but I'm already sitting down." He smiled tentatively at me.

I arched an eyebrow at him, hiding the smile that wanted to answer his. "There's always groveling on your stomach in the dirt."

"I'm sorry," he said, and I could hear the truth in his words. "I'm a stupid, idiotic, jealous, pathetic man who deserves to have you leave and never look back." He looked away for a time, fingers tracing circles over the blanket's soft surface.

I held my breath. I didn't think he had said all he wanted to say.

"When you told me . . . it was too much like Edwina. Too close to home."

"Edwina chose what she did," I said. "Yet you tried to save her. I didn't choose and you condemned me."

"It brought it all back." He held up a hand. "I know it isn't an excuse. I thought I had made peace with losing her. But then you . . . it was like learning all over again that she was lost and there wasn't anything I could do."

Which for him, would be the hardest part of all. Having to admit defeat, admit he couldn't save his own sister.

I shifted a little closer on the blanket, not touching him, not yet. "I'm sorry, Simon."

"No, I'm sorry. I shouldn't have treated you that way. I was angry, but as I said, that's no excuse. I shouldn't have said it and I shouldn't have behaved like such an idiot afterward. I shouldn't have let you go to face him alone like that. If you had died—"

A different sort of nerves gripped my stomach now. "But I didn't die," I said softly. "And neither did you. Besides, I shouldn't have kept it from you."

"No. You were right. I wouldn't have trusted you if I'd known about it from the start. Wouldn't have gotten to know you. But I did." A hint of a smile ghosted over his face. "I do. I know you now. And gods and suns, Lily, when I saw you there, blood running out of you . . . well, if I could kill him all over again, it wouldn't be enough—"

"Simon," I interrupted, unable to let him go on any longer without telling him my latest truth. "I haven't felt the need since Lucius died."

"Oh, thank the gods," he said, then buried his face in his hands. "Fuck. I'm an idiot, ignore me."

I suppressed the laugh that rose in my throat, trying to still sound stern. "You could have asked me before this."

He dropped his hands, lifted his head to meet my gaze squarely. "I—I needed to work this out in my head. Untangle myself. And I've been busy."

"Busy?"

"Some of the locked woke up. When we killed—"

"You killed," I interrupted. I still hadn't entirely come to terms with the fact that it hadn't been me who'd wielded the blade. I'd wanted to kill Lucius. Wanted to do it myself so I could know with my body that it was true. I had dreams about it. Felt the sensation of swinging a sword, of cutting his head off, and woke wanting it to be true.

But it had been Simon who'd killed. Killed to save me even. Had taken up the sword he'd renounced and fought for me. Part of him had enjoyed it. I'd seen that on his face as they'd fought. He'd let the warrior loose. Had chosen to kill with a blade and his strength in the dark rather than let his powers do the work for him. Lady knew what it had done to him. I knew too well how raw a wound dealing death could leave. For him, with his history, it would be harder still. The healer needed time to heal.

"No, we," Simon corrected. "I would never have gotten near him without you. What you did . . ."

I shivered, hand drifting to my throat again. "I don't want to talk about that. Tell me about the locked."

"They woke up. Not all of them."

"Maybe the ones who fed from Blood who are now dead?" I suggested.

He looked startled. "Yes, that's what Atherton thinks. How did you know?"

"We had a few conversations on the subject. Atherton thinks the addiction only survives when there's a bloodline for the addiction to follow."

"Yes, though I have no idea how that works." He shook his head, looking frustrated. A puzzle the healer couldn't solve, then?

I grinned at him. "Who knows why any magic works? But I'm glad Atherton was right." Not just for me. "How are they?"

"The ones who woke up?"

"Yes."

"Confused. Weak. Some are healthier than others. It's too early to tell what the long-term prognosis is."

"Have you told their families?"

"We will. We want to wait, make sure none of them relapse. That would be too cruel."

"Yes." To be given hope, then have it ripped away from you. This time I agreed with his secrecy. "But don't wait too long." I shivered again. "This isn't over, you know."

Simon frowned. "What do you mean?"

"Lucius—if he was out to rule the City as he said— would have more than one plot in motion. He always liked backup plans." A thought suddenly struck me. "Did they ever find Chrysanthe?"

"No. But the fact that she's vanished would seem to point to her being the spy."

"But we don't know what she was doing for him." Hells. "You need to be careful until you're ready to let people know. Someone else might want to take up where Lucius left off."

"You think he was working with someone?"

"I don't know. That's the problem. Much like you don't know how news of your cure is going to be received."

"It's not exactly a cure yet, is it?" Simon said. "The Blood are never going to agree for us to go around killing them to free the locked."

"No, but it's a starting point. You know the part of the bond is magical at least. That must give you some new ideas."

"Yes," Simon admitted.

The sunlight seemed to chill a little. The Blood—those who had wanted what Lucius had wanted, a return to the old ways, would not take news of a cure well. And who knew what ties Lucius' plot might have into the Beasts and the Fae? Or what other plots there might be? But I couldn't think of that now. I made myself smile at him, let his answering smile warm me again. "That should keep you busy."

He nodded, then eased back on his elbows, turning his

face to the sun. "And you? What are you going to do with your time?"

"I don't know," I admitted. Now that I was healed, I needed to do something. I needed money to keep a roof over my head. But apart from fighting, I had few skills to offer.

"Bryony thought you might be good with plants."

I looked at the abundant life around me, green and welcoming. The urge to reach out and touch and stroke the leaves and flowers tingled through my fingertips. "Maybe. Helping things grow has a certain appeal."

"Bryony is good at knowing what will suit people."

"Bryony thinks she's good at many things," I said tartly.

Simon laughed. "You should give her a chance. And yes, before you ask, I've given her the same speech. I think the two of you would get along well."

I shook my head at him. "One of these days I'm going to ask Guy whether he really did drop you on your head. Bryony is as likely to befriend a wraith as, well, as I am to sprout wings and learn to fly." Despite her telling me about my father, I didn't think she would ever be truly friendly toward me.

"You're too pessimistic."

"And you have way too much faith in people." I laughed suddenly. This had the feeling of an argument we might be having for a very long time.

"Regardless of who came up with the idea, you should think about it," Simon said. "I'm sure we can come up with funding for any schooling you might wish to undertake. We owe you a debt, after all."

I looked away, smoothing my hair for a moment while I thought of a suitable response. "I'm not sure I've done anyone that much of a service. More likely I've just stirred up a wasp's nest. Given people even more reason to dislike my kind."

Simon's brows drew together. "Don't say that."

"What?"

"Your kind."

"It matters, what I am."

He shook his head, pushing up from the blanket. "No. It doesn't. Who you are matters, not what you are."

I tilted my head at him, trying not to hope he might

mean what he said. "So it doesn't matter to you? That I'm a wraith? That my kind are feared?"

He shook his head. "I don't care. Show them they're wrong about your kind. I already know all I need to know about you."

I dropped my eyes, suddenly wanting to cry. The truth about my father hovered on the tip of my tongue. I wanted to tell him that I was human too—at least partly—but something held me back. Something that just wanted to bask in the warmth of his acceptance. I would tell him soon enough. Soon enough but not today.

"All you need to do is let people know you," Simon said gently.

I raised my eyes, saw his shining blue as he smiled at me.

"You've given us a chance to change things," Simon said, shifting a little closer. Now we both sat cross-legged, facing each other over a foot or so of blanket. Such a small space but it felt like a chasm as deep as the warrens.

"Of course, what we do with the chance is up to us," Simon continued. "The same applies to the Blood and how they react."

He took a breath and looked at me. The color of his eyes seemed almost too blue. Full of light. I couldn't look away.

"Studying would fill your days at least," he said slowly. His voice had dropped to a low velvet tone.

My stomach fluttered. "That still leaves my nights. . . ."

"I have some ideas about what you can do with those," Simon said softly. He reached for my hand.

"Such as?" I said, letting him take it. His skin was warm and felt even better than the sunlight on my skin.

"This." He leaned in and his mouth met mine.

This time it wasn't a roaring fire that took me at his touch. No, this time it was something richer, truer. Something golden and glowing like the man himself. Like swallowing the warmth that the sun was pouring onto my back and letting it flow through my veins. Happiness. No, something deeper than that.

Love.

"Don't leave me, Lily," he said when his mouth left mine. "I love you. Stay here with me."

I smiled and reached out to touch his face. "It seems I was wrong about something."

"Oh?" His dimples flashed and the sunlight glinted off his hair, turning it to gold. I wondered if I'd ever tire of looking at him in the light.

"What was that?" he asked.

"I needed a white knight after all."

His smile was bright enough to chase away any shadows that might still linger in my heart.

"Consider me at your service, my lady." He leaned in and kissed me hungrily.

I felt the answering hunger rise in me. Not the need. Just simple longing for this man. Full of love and warmth.

We sank back on the blanket, moving slowly. No need to hide anymore. No need for darkness and the cover of night. "I'm in favor of that idea," I said when we finally came up for a breath. Simon was on top of me, shirt undone, hair rumpled. My shirt was a crumpled thing lying around my shoulders. My skin hummed with pleasure everywhere he and the sunshine touched it.

"So am I," he said. "And I can think of some services I can offer right now."

I laughed at him and took his hand. "Show me."

We lay back down in the light and began all over again.

ABOUT THE AUTHOR

M. J. Scott is an unrepentant bookworm. Luckily she grew up in a family that fed her a properly varied diet of books and these days is surrounded by people who are understanding of her story addiction. When not wrestling one of her own stories to the ground, she can generally be found reading someone else's. Her other distractions include yarn, cat butlering, dark chocolate, and fabric. She lives in Melbourne, Australia. Her Web site is http://www.mjscott.net.

THE ULTIMATE IN
SCIENCE FICTION AND FANTASY!

From magical tales of distant worlds to stories of
technological advances beyond the grasp of man, Penguin has
everything you need to stretch your imagination to its limits.

penguin.com/scififantasy

ACE
Get the latest information on favorites like
William Gibson, Ilona Andrews, Jack Campbell,
Ursula K. Le Guin, Sharon Shinn, Charlaine Harris,
Patricia Briggs, and Marjorie M. Liu,
as well as updates on the best new authors.

ROC
Escape with Jim Butcher, Harry Turtledove, Anne Bishop,
S.M. Stirling, Simon R. Green, E.E. Knight, Kat Richardson,
Rachel Caine, and many others—plus news on the
latest and hottest in science fiction and fantasy.

DAW
Patrick Rothfuss, Seanan McGuire, Mercedes Lackey,
Kristen Britain, Tanya Huff, Tad Williams, C.J. Cherryh,
and many more—DAW has something to satisfy the
cravings of any science fiction and fantasy lover.

*Get the best of science fiction and fantasy
at your fingertips!*

R0064